Father's Trouble$

Father's Trouble$

Carter Taylor Seaton

Mid-Atlantic Highlands Publishing

Library of Congress Card Catalog Number: 2003110851

Hard Cover (Ltd Ed) ISBN: 0-9676051-8-0
Trade Paper ISBN: 0-9676051-9-9

First Edition, Second Printing
Printed in Canada

Cover Photo: Huntington, West Virginia, Ninth Street looking south, circa 1918.
Book Design: Mark S. Phillips / Marketing+Design Group

Mid-Atlantic Highlands Publishing

an imprint of Publishers Place, Inc.
945 Fourth Avenue, Suite 200A
Huntington, WV 25701

www.publishersplace.org

A Note on the Type:

The text of this book was set in Stone Serif, designed by
Sumner Stone (1987). Stone was designed
to solve the problem of mixing different styles of type
on the same page and consists of three subfamilies,
Serif, Sans, and Informal, which can be
mixed successfully with each other.

Dedication

For Mother

There are no mistakes, no coincidences.
All events are blessings given to us to learn from.

Elizabeth Kubler-Ross

Acknowledgments

Although this is a work of fiction, I am deeply indebted to those who helped uncover the historical facts that are the bare bones of the imagined story. Without the willing assistance of John Massie, former West Virginia State Penitentiary Archivist; Debra Basham, West Virginia State Archives research librarian; family members Elizabeth Bain, Catherine M. Skaggs, Marjorie Eaton, Buzz Frantz, DorothyAnn Stinson, Jimmy Seaton and Kris Hillen; Skip and Judy Deegans; Bill Bunch, Bob Withers; L.D. Egnor and his former staff; the Cabell-Huntington Library Reference Department and the books of Doris Miller, Col. George W. Wallace and Jack Feller this story could not have been created.

For instilling the love of reading in me at an early age, I thank my aunts, Nancy and Elinore Taylor. I also thank my lucky stars I was blessed, both in public school and at Marshall University, to encounter excellent and caring teachers who had the patience to teach me proper grammar, composition and research skills.

I owe a debt of gratitude as well to my earliest readers, Elinore and Nancy Taylor, Lennie Michelson, Francesca Ellis, Mary Ann Ladd and to Allison Christie, without whose encouragement the book might never have come to fruition.

Thanks to Dr. John Patrick Grace for his tireless and insightful editing and his leap of faith. And to my beloved husband, Richard Cobb, I offer my everlasting appreciation for his encouragement, vision, honesty and patience.

One

The weekend Maggie Malone stunned her parents with the announcement that she was leaving her "perfect" husband of twenty years, she learned her mother could go her one better. She had a secret which she had been keeping for almost fifty years.

August was not a good time to leave her job as marketing director for the mall. Nonetheless, Maggie had taken a week off from work to drive to Florida to deliver her bombshell. August is not the ideal time to visit the west coast of Florida either, so she was approaching Longboat Key, dreading both the humidity and her parents' reaction to the news. By all accounts, they had a perfect marriage. She was about to announce the end of hers. Over the years, it seemed to Maggie that each time she had reached the conclusion all marriage certificates should come with a sunset clause, she would see her parents — devoted to each other for nearly fifty years — and try again. But finally, she and Andrew had separated, then Maggie had filed for divorce and rented an apartment.

As she drove, Maggie thought about the last time she had given her parents news of this magnitude. It still bothered her. When she was much too young, she had shocked them with the news that she was going to be an unwed mother. This blow to their plans for Maggie's future sparked a range of emotions — from rage at the boy, to predictable disappointment and, finally, unspeakable sadness. Maggie thought, looking back, that they had reacted pretty well, considering.

She had heard, though never actually known, of girls in her situation who were simply kicked out of the house. The worst blow was her mother's pronouncement that Maggie "had broken her daddy's heart." After that, Maggie never felt she measured up in their eyes. They recovered from the shock, offered to get her an abortion, which she refused, and then arranged for her to get married at sixteen. They also supported the predictable divorce which followed a year later, but Maggie worried about what they would say this time. Would they be shocked again? Angry? Or only sadder and more disappointed?

To make matters worse, Maggie was raised by parents who never fought. Not only had she never seen them fight, they both said they never did. Her mother prided herself on being the only one of her siblings to still have the original spouse. Among Maggie's aunts, ex-husbands were called "out-laws." And in her daddy's family divorce just didn't happen. You made a marriage work. Now she had failed at two attempts while their relationship perked right along. However, in her own mind, this divorce was necessary for her emotional survival. *Will they see it that way?* Guilt and doubt gnawed at the edges of her hard-won decision. Maggie dreaded facing them.

Since her parents' retirement, each time Maggie had driven from West Virginia to Florida to visit them, she timed her arrival to coincide with the sunset. She did it again this trip. Timed it perfectly — just in time to marvel at the spectacular blaze of red, orange and gold over the Gulf of Mexico. The approach to Anna Maria Island from Bradenton is due west. This particular day she drove straight into a fireball that seemed to touch the highway. As the sun descended, it set the eastern sky aglow as well. Reaching the final causeway, Maggie turned off the air-conditioning and rolled down the windows to smell the salt air. *I don't know how they do it, but I'd swear the air on the Gulf Coast is lighter than anywhere else in Florida.* The breeze felt like it contained Downy Fabric Softener, but with a fishy odor. Turning onto Bradenton Beach, Maggie abruptly pulled over, hoping to see the so-called "green flash" that allegedly occurs when the sun finally drops into the water; but it didn't happen. Disappointed, she pulled out and drove slowly down Gulf of Mexico Drive to Longboat Key.

When Maggie pulled into the driveway, the lanai door opened

and both parents were at the car before the engine stopped. They hugged, linked arms and went inside; the luggage was left for later. Chuck and Sara Landers' house was set exquisitely on a narrow finger of land with water on three sides. Just beyond the sand flats, where dozens of egrets and roseate spoonbills came to feed each day, was an unobstructed view of Sarasota Bay. In the spacious great room, the blue drapes on the floor to ceiling window-walls were open. The after-glow seemed to have followed Maggie, for the view was suffused with pink. Out in the bayou the shimmering water slapped at the sea-wall. Maggie never tired of this vista. Gazing toward the bay, she silently thanked the builder for his vision.

Two Scotches later Maggie had broken the news. She knew she wouldn't relax until it was off her chest, but it took the two drinks to wash the words out of her throat. Her parents were surprised — but not shocked. Maggie learned they had seen signals which she and Andrew weren't even aware they had been emitting. Maggie had worried for nothing. Once again, her father was supportive and characteristically defensive of "his little girl." His anger was directed at Andrew rather than at Maggie. Her mother, also characteristically, did not ask many questions; but later, Maggie knew she would. Through the years, her parents had used what she referred to as a "two-one punch." She'd tell them something as a couple (two); not much would be said, but her mother (one) would come back later for more, or to reiterate her disapproval. Maggie knew it was coming.

The following morning the wilting humidity temporarily had gone into remission. Maggie lay in bed, relishing the lack of any schedule. *It has been such a long time since I could do this.* She lay motionless, reflecting upon the previous night's conversation. *Mother and Daddy said so little about the divorce. I guess it's not such a tragedy after all. Perhaps I was only projecting my own feelings of failure. All that worry for nothing. Maybe their opinion of me has never been as harsh as my own.* It should have been a very liberating realization, but Maggie couldn't help feeling there was more to be said on the issue. Still uneasy, she sighed, stretched and got out of bed.

When she ambled into the living room, her parents were seated, as usual, at opposite ends of the dining room table with the *Sarasota*

Herald Tribune scattered between them. Maggie smiled at this familiar scene and seated herself between them, ready for more questions about the divorce.

"Good morning," she said brightly.

Instead of "good morning," her father said, more to his wife than to Maggie, "Well, we could go get some bait and fish off the sea wall."

Maggie felt as if she had arrived late to a play and missed the opening lines. Obviously, a conversation was in progress and her day was being planned without her help. Inwardly Maggie groaned; this was typical of her visits with them. Her parents tried to plan each day to the hilt; she would rather do nothing. Instead of interrupting, she picked up a section of the paper and idly gazed over the top at the sporadic splashes of the jumping-jack mullet in the bayou. Sooner or later, she knew they would notice her.

"No, Chuck, you can't go fishing," her mother snapped. "The last time the kids were down here, they tangled the lines on all the rods." She sounded as if she were still angry about that.

"I'll bet I can fix them," said her father. Maggie chuckled behind the paper, knowing that it would take all day, at best. She'd heard this routine a dozen times. He could make a simple project into one of grand scale. By the time he finished, all the rods would be outfitted with new reels, rehung in the garage and the garage rearranged. But there'd be no time left to fish.

Maggie rose to go fix a bagel and pour coffee. Judging from the conversation, the divorce wasn't on their minds at all. *Worried again for nothing.* In response to the question she had not been asked, Maggie chimed in from the kitchen, "You really don't have to entertain me. I'm perfectly happy to just go to the beach or read by the pool."

As soon as the words were out of her mouth, Maggie wanted to bite her tongue. Her mother hated fishing, so this was a father-daughter "thing." He relished their time alone; but for some reason it made Maggie's mother jealous. It was only one of the things Maggie didn't understand or like about her. Therefore, she and her father didn't go fishing as often as they would have liked. A sweet tempered man, her father took great pains not to hurt his wife's feelings. When Maggie came to visit, he always tried to plan activities that Sara enjoyed as well.

"Well, whatever you want to do is fine with me. I've got to go to the post office and run by the art center anyway," he said, sounding wounded.

From the kitchen Maggie peered at her mother who was only partially successful in stifling a laugh. They both knew he would say this. Chuck Landers went to the Post Office everyday for the island gossip, as well as the mail. The Postmistress looked forward to his daily visit and said it was the highlight of her day.

Sara said, to cover her laughter, "OK, fine. You go to the Post Office and I'll go to the beach with Maggs." Still, neither of them actually had said good morning to Maggie.

Maggie would have been happier to go alone for two reasons: one, the peace and quiet would be a sheer luxury and two, she didn't want to deal with her mother's "one-person punch." Now that Maggie had delivered her well-rehearsed speech, she did not want to beat a dead horse. Ending her marriage had been on her mind for months; now she was tired of the subject of D.I.V.O.R.C.E. Maggie didn't know how to refuse gracefully, however. Thinking she had already hurt her father's feelings, she agreed to the outing.

Ready long before her mother, Maggie poured another cup of coffee and began to read the comics. Halfway through *Peanuts*, Sara appeared carrying a COKE beach towel and *The Crystal Cave*. In this, at least, they were alike. Maggie's idea of an ideal day at the beach was the same; her bag held *The Thorn Birds*. *Maybe we'll just read, not talk,* Maggie thought. *Wishful thinking,* her rational self replied. In truth, they were more alike than Maggie would admit. Many said they looked alike; they had the same almost-black hair, easily tanned dark skin, small breasts and wide hips. Now almost forty, Maggie had developed a prematurely gray streak in the front of her hair. Nearly thirty years older, Sara's gray only now was making insidious forays at her temple and forehead.

As the two women walked down the crushed shell driveway toward the beach, Maggie's mother said, "Tell me about the apartment you've rented." This was her mother's not-so-subtle way of getting to the heart of the matter. *Here it comes — the old "one-two"; I might as well get it over with. She didn't even wait until we got to the beach.*

In silent communication, Maggie linked arms with her mother as they crossed the road. Maggie felt her mother was trying to be supportive in what she thought of as a stressful time and she wanted her to know it was all right to ask questions, even though she would have preferred to discuss something else — anything else! By now Maggie had resigned herself to the inevitable inquisition. *My main source of stress was anticipating their reaction—and that's over. It didn't amount to a hill of beans. I guess it won't hurt to talk about it one more time.*

"Watch out for the sand burrs," Sara cautioned, in her "I'm still the mother" tone, as they reached the sandy stretch between the highway and the Gulf of Mexico.

"I'm OK," Maggie responded. She dropped her arm to pick her way through the baby scrub-pines and sea-oats which hid the pow-dered-sugar beach from the ribbon of traffic, "These shoes have hard rubber soles." The pathway wasn't a public access path to the beach, but one of the few vacant lots on the island. The owners were friends of the Landers who told them to feel free to use it; therefore, the beach behind the lot was very private.

The sky and water were of a single cerulean hue. Only a navy blue line and a miniature ocean liner marked the horizon. Unchar-acteristically, the gulf was calm. Insipid waves nibbled at the edge of the sand, leaving a trace of salty saliva in their wake.

Maggie's mother didn't repeat her question until they had ar-ranged their towels and settled onto the beach with their backs to the sun. As Maggie twisted her arm to apply Coppertone to her back, her mother said brightly, "Tell me about your apartment." She tried to sound as if this were the first time she had asked.

"Well, it's really a cute little place on the southside... a garage apartment with just three rooms and a bath, hardly big enough to whip a cat without getting fur in your teeth, but it's all I need. It's light and airy; they repainted it. It has hardwood floors, plenty of closet space and two large windows in the living room. The down-side is... it doesn't have a shower, but a friend is putting one in for me. I'll have to learn how to do dishes all over again, however; there's no dishwasher, either," Maggie explained.

Sara laughed, "I knew that teaching you to do the dishes would come in handy some day."

"Thanks. I appreciate the lesson." Maggie laughed, too. "I'm only taking the furniture I need — my books, paintings and personal stuff."

Sara broke in abruptly. "You be sure to get my mother's desk, sideboard and all the paintings I gave you."

"I *am* taking her furniture; but, I'm not going to strip the walls, Mother. After all, two of the kids are still there. I want it to continue to look like home. I'll get them eventually — or the kids will." Maggie knew this would be a sticky subject. Her mother always made sure that no one, especially Andrew, got more than she thought they deserved, or had a right to. This was particularly true if she had been the original owner or bearer of the gift. It was if she held the rights to its disposition in perpetuity.

"Well, I just don't want Andrew to think they are his and then give them to some new wife," she huffed. Maggie ignored the suggestion that he would remarry and maneuvered the subject back to the apartment. "I'll need to buy a bed and some new pots and pans. Want to come home with me and help me get settled?" Her help wasn't really necessary, however Maggie hoped the suggestion would make her feel needed. When her mother didn't respond Maggie continued.

"You know, the best thing about the apartment?" she asked.

"No, what."

"The peace and quiet. No more yelling. No more worrying about the reaction my slightest remark will have. No more holding my breath, waiting for the other shoe to fall."

Now her mother was silent; obviously this was the part she wanted to understand — the "why" of their breakup. Maggie continued. "It feels so good, after all these years, to finally have some peace. I hadn't expected it to be so absolute. I actually enjoy coming home, even though I miss having the kids there." Maggie had four children, one by the first marriage and three by Andrew.

"What about the kids? How are they reacting to all of this?"

"Oh, at first, they were shocked. Apparently we had hidden our problems better than I thought. They took it fairly well, however.

After all, they are nearly grown and the boys have been out of the house for two years. I really didn't give them much explanation. I was afraid they'd lose respect for their father. I didn't tell any of my friends why either, and it has been a big shock to them. I hear that lots of them can't understand why I'd leave such a "wonderful marriage." 'After all, she has this big house, lots of land, a pool, horses, etc. Who'd be idiot enough to leave all that?' they're probably saying. Boy, we sure had them fooled."

Mother and daughter talked, for about an hour, their books forgotten in the sand. Sara rarely asked questions except to keep her daughter talking, which she did — about the years of misunderstandings, lack of communication, anger, fights and Andrew's drinking, always his drinking. She explained that she had finally grown too tired to fight. She told her mother she just woke up one day and knew it was time to leave. Maybe it was the coward's way out, she suggested, but it was also a matter of survival. Maggie said she just didn't know how else to cope. She knew if she stayed, Andrew's alcoholism would destroy her as well. As she talked, the pain of leaving her children crept into Maggie's voice. She told her mother she'd chosen to make the move to her own apartment, rather than kick him out, as much for Andrew, as she had for their children. She believed Andrew needed to be needed by them.

"What hurt almost as much as anything was that my church friends, at least I thought they were my friends, never called me — not once. I heard from someone that they were talking about me, for leaving Andrew and the kids. How could they! They didn't have any idea what I had been putting up with all those years. They think he's so sweet and charming. Cooking and cleaning up after all those church suppers! Rather than watching him wash plates in the church's sink, they should have seen him smashing plates in our kitchen."

Suddenly tears, not sunburn, stung Maggie's cheeks. She wiped them away with the back of her hand, leaving fine white grains of sand in their place. Maggie half-expected her mother to hug her in consolation, but she was disappointed. Maggie had bared her soul and her mother had not given her a shred of emotional support. *I should have known she wouldn't.* Suddenly Maggie was embarrassed for crying in her presence. Her mother made absolutely no reference to what her daughter had said, but began to speak in a very serious, hollow voice, as if from a dream.

"Maggs, don't you ever let what people say hurt you," she said fiercely. "Our family has always been proud and held their heads up, no matter what."

"I don't have any reason to be ashamed," Maggie stammered, confused by this admonition. The shock of her mother's vehement tone stopped Maggie's self-pity. She looked at her mother and saw tears in her angry eyes.

"I didn't do anything wrong." Now Maggie thought her mother was angry with her.

"That's my point," Sara said. She stopped abruptly and took a deep breath, as if what she planned to say next would take great strength. "Don't pay any attention to what they say. You know the truth about why you left Andrew. You don't need to tell them. Our family has had to endure the gossip of town folks before — had to hold our heads up while we went about our business. You just keep your own counsel and do the same."

Maggie was thoroughly puzzled. She quickly tried to imagine what her mother was talking about. *What gossip?* Family memories flashed by in fast forward, but no mental picture that Maggie could recall prepared her for what followed. Her mother was angrier than Maggie had seen her since she was a teenager. She wanted to ask a question, but dared not interrupt.

Sara stopped again to compose herself. "You remember what I always told you about your grandfather, my father ...how he died of a broken heart after mother died? Well, what you don't know — what I never told you is this — my father, Richard Lawrence Burgher, died in prison."

During the rest of the week the revelation about her grandfather lay between Maggie and her mother like a dead elephant on the living room floor. Neither mentioned it, for fear of having to deal with it. Maggie was so stunned that her mother and the rest of the family had kept this secret for over forty years that she didn't know *what* to think. Her mind raced with questions, but the memory of her mother's pain-filled eyes as she said "He died in prison," kept Maggie from broaching the subject again.

Sara seemed to be embarrassed that she had made the confession, for she never mentioned it again, either. Maggie concluded, from her mother's behavior, that she wished she'd never said a word. For the next four days, Sara was alternately angry and sullen.

One afternoon, after Maggie and her father had taken the boat into the bay to fish, her mother fussed at them like children because they returned five minutes late for dinner. Maggie spent one evening in her room catching up on office memos and her mother pouted because she wasn't in the living room watching TV with her. Little irritants caused big reprimands, until Maggie decided it was time to go home. There had always been a limit to Maggie's tolerance of her mother. This time, she reached it two days earlier than usual.

Although her mother's behavior irritated Maggie, she felt a deep sadness as well. It was clear to Maggie that the pain of what had happened almost fifty years ago had not faded with time. She felt sorry for her mother, but she also felt somehow cheated. Maggie wondered if the pain Sara still held inside was what had prevented them from having a warm, close relationship. *Perhaps Mother was so preoccupied with holding herself together that she couldn't hold me.*

Maggie was also surprised to find herself angry with her grandfather —a man she didn't even know, had never met. *How could he do whatever he did and cause such pain for his entire family? What kind of monster was he? How can I find out? Clearly, Mother isn't going to talk about him ever again. And if Mother won't, neither will Daddy. He's too loyal to do that. If they've kept it such a deep, dark secret all these years, you can bet I'll get nothing from my aunts or uncles, either.* Frustrated, Maggie tried to put the whole thing out of her mind, but it wouldn't go away.

Over the next two days, as she drove north on I-75, Maggie saw very little of the familiar countryside. Her focus was inward, trying to sort out her relationship with her mother in light of this new piece of history. It seemed to Maggie they had spent most of their lives in a kind of cold war. Sad to admit, she didn't think she liked her mother very much. And sadder still, she thought the feeling was mutual. When the book by Nancy Friday, *My Mother, My Self,* appeared in the bookstores, the mere title scared Maggie to death. *What if I do turn out like her?* She searched her internal mirror constantly for tell-tale signs. She also worried that her children would feel the same about her as she did about her mother. *Where and when did we go wrong? No wonder we didn't get along...I really didn't know her.*

Maggie could recall that they had the usual battles of childhood and puberty over what to wear, when to be home, how she could wear her hair, and whether or not she could wear lipstick or cologne; but she assumed that all her friends fought the same battles of independence with their parents. But, the distance between them was deeper than growing pains. She remembered the shame of wearing home-made clothes, while all of her junior-high school girl-friends could shop freely at the best dress shops. She had resented the not-so-stylish creations and the made-over dance dresses; she had longed for a dress — any dress — with a label. Rather than appreciating her mother's effort, she had resented it. Maggie, of course, never understood that they were poor. Her mother talked often about living through the Depression and "making do." But the Depression was long gone, so Maggie just thought her mother was stingy, that it was her nature. And her mother never explained that her father was trying to build a business. By the time he finally succeeded and struck it rich, Maggie was married.

Partly because of her hand-made clothes, Maggie never felt pretty as a teenager. Furthermore, she was never sure if she had a pretty face. She certainly didn't measure up to the *Seventeen* models; they had boobs. She could remember her mother's admonition against conceit each time she tried to sneak a glance at herself in the mirror over the living room sofa. She couldn't tell her mother she was only checking for some tiny hint of improvement. She never would have understood. Or so Maggie thought. Once she asked her mother, "Am I pretty?" Rather than confirming what Maggie needed to hear, her mother replied with a question of her own. "Wouldn't you rather be smart than pretty?" Maggie had replied, "No, I want to be both." She then proceeded to tell Maggie that she had the kind of "late bloomer" looks that would appear when she was older. "You'll be gorgeous at forty," she said. Maggie didn't want to be gorgeous at forty. Forty was ancient. She wanted to be pretty as a picture — *now*. Therefore, Maggie grew up not knowing whether or not people found her attractive and somehow blamed her mother for that lack of knowledge.

A scene from Maggie's past flashed into her mind. She was sitting on the big square stool in front of her mother's favorite chair. She was crying. A boy had just broken her teenage heart by dropping her to date another girl. Maggie's mother was trying to console her by saying, "You are a smart girl; you can get any boy you want. Just get back out there, pick out someone you think is cute and go after him. You can do it. Just use your head." Maggie did as she was told and shortly she had a new boyfriend. She had used more than her head, however. She had discovered necking. And, at the time, it seemed to Maggie, that her mother approved. After all, didn't she chauffeur them to the drive-in movie and turn the rear-view mirror so she couldn't see what Maggie and her date were doing in the back seat? At the time, Maggie thought her mother was cool. Later, when Maggie became a mother of teenagers herself, she wondered what her mother had been thinking. Now she could see she had taken her mother's innocent advice, and even her silly gesture to allow some teenage privacy, as tacit approval to use sex to become popular. Even though her parents both lectured her on being "a good girl," Maggie took it as part of the standard package of parental advice. She had ignored the verbal warnings for the unspoken messages she had received earlier from her mother. She could see that now.

A few boyfriends later, when her mother exploded at the news of her teenage pregnancy, Maggie recalled that she wanted to say, "What did you expect? You encouraged me." But, of course, she hadn't. After the hurtful announcement that she had broken her father's heart, Maggie somehow felt that it was her mother's fault. *I did what you told me to do and now my daddy won't love me anymore.* Not only was she made to feel the obligatory guilt and shame, it was exacerbated by their offer to get her an abortion. In her confused teenage mind, what she had done was a direct consequence of advice given by her mother, and now she was being told she had done something bad. To Maggie, it was just like the day her mother had washed out Maggie's mouth with soap for cussing out the neighborhood bully who was picking on her best friend. Maggie had thought her mother would be proud of her for standing up for her friend; instead she had been punished, severely.

Of course, Maggie had been told often enough that sex before marriage was wrong. But, she also knew of one girl who, in her shame, went for a back alley abortion and died. Of course, Maggie had refused to have an abortion. The very thought scared her to death. She remembered clearly that she had needed her mother's support. She also recalled that what she got instead was the sense that she had brought great dishonor on the family.

Maggie's cheeks stung with shame when she recalled how her mother had forced her to continue with the role of the Virgin Mary in the church play a week after her announcement about the pre-marital pregnancy. She had begged to be allowed to quit, but her mother was adamant. Maggie always believed her mother did it for spite and as an ironic punishment. Now it struck Maggie that her mother simply could not face the possibility of another public scandal. *No wonder she was so angry. It must have brought back all sorts of horrible memories. She made me do that because she couldn't face having her church friends know what her daughter had done. She couldn't face the gossip, again. What on earth did her father do that was so terrible?*

Suddenly Maggie, overcome by long-held emotions, burst into a flood of tears. She steered the station wagon to the side of the highway to keep from having a wreck. She shook as she cried, her head on the steering wheel. When she was spent, Maggie was exhausted — tired beyond what sleep could cure. The tension of the last few months, the discussions of the past few days and the memories she had relived in the past few hours had taken a tremendous toll. She could feel it. She drove to the nearest exit and left the highway. Maggie found a Holiday Inn, checked in and without carrying her luggage to the room, lay down on the double bed, fully clothed, and slept. The last conscious thought she could remember was about her grandfather: *The sins of the father...are visited unto the generations.*

Two

February 1891

Richard Burgher stood in the doorway and stared at the sparse furnishings of his new bedroom. His uncle had allowed him and his brother David to bring their own beds from the farm, but those were the only familiar items he saw. A small square table between the narrow rope-mattress beds held an oil lamp that Richard bet he would have to clean before it could be used. The small bundle of clothes in his arms grew suddenly heavy as he realized that there was no place to store them. Behind him, his mother spoke and her soft, familiar voice dissolved the lump which had formed in his throat.

"It will be all right, Richard, you'll see. You and David may have one of my small chifforobes for your things. We'll put it in the corner, over there. Now smile; remember, it was very kind of your uncle Will to take us in. We must all be grateful. If he hadn't offered, I don't know what we'd have done when your father died. We certainly couldn't have managed the farm alone." As she talked, she had knelt in front of Richard and was looking straight into his huge brown eyes, trying to make him believe that it would be all right.

But when she mentioned the farm, tears sprang into his eyes, making them look larger than ever. "I could too have run the farm. Me and David, we could've!" Richard cried defiantly. His mother held back her own tears, wiped his, took his meager bundle and put it on one of the beds; she gathered him to her and held him in her arms.

"David and I," she corrected. "Some day, son, we'll go back and you both can work the farm. Someday when you are older. But right now, this is our home. You understand? Your father wouldn't want you to be working the farm without his help. He'd want you to be in school now. And that's how it's going to be."

Before Richard could protest further, David burst into the room. "Richard, come quick. Uncle Will's dog has ten puppies." He stopped when he saw his mother embracing Richard. "What's the matter," he asked?

"Nuthin'," said Richard, embarrassed. His mother quickly dropped her arms and rose. "Let's go! Where are the pups?" said Richard. He was easily distracted from his tears as only a child of nine can be.

Mariah Burgher sat on the bed and watched her children go. With a deep sigh, she thought about the past few months — her husband's sudden death from a burst appendix; the sale of the few farm animals and the move from their sprawling farm in Wyoming County, West Virginia, to the new community of Mt. Hope in Fayette County. *Thank God for Will*, she thought. Other than her brother-in-law, she had no nearby relatives to rely on. Though Mariah hated leaving the farm she and Lawrence had built together the past ten years, she had to admit that she was looking forward to the respite which she imagined living in town would offer. *Surely, taking care of Will's home won't be as hard as working the farm.*

The round-bellied puppies were only five weeks old and still had their eyes closed. As he reached into the box, Richard had difficulty distinguishing one pup from another; the squirming bodies were heaped in a pile for warmth and comfort. Legs, heads and tails seemed disjointed as if no one puppy were whole. He reached for the black one on top because it was the easiest to disentangle. Mewing like a kitten, it snuggled into the crook of his arm. As he held it the crying stopped and the pup fell asleep again. Richard stood on the porch with the small animal safe in his arms, surveying his uncle Will's muddy yard, and the sadness returned in a rush. He couldn't help it; the last animal he'd held was the new calf and he was reminded of the farm. He was used to soaring hills and deep, grassy meadows, the smell of freshly cut hay and distant bird calls. Here it wasn't like that

at all. The small fenced yard was flat, with sparse patches of dull
grass; and the smells and sounds of the neighbors on both sides of
Uncle Will's house suffocated him. He didn't know if he'd ever get
used to it. With a sigh, he put the puppy back with its brothers and
sisters and went into the modest house.

The following week, after they had settled into a household routine, Richard and David were enrolled in the Mt. Hope Elementary
School. Richard hated school; the two rooms were stuffed with children and he longed for the open spaces of the farm. First through
third year students were crammed in one room and the older kids
were in the other. The heavy school door opened onto a narrow hallway that divided the two rooms. At the rear of each room was a big,
black pot-bellied stove that hiccuped periodically, spitting out coal-
soot and smoke with each belch. The furnace certainly did the job;
in fact it did it too well. The classroom was suffocating, as if all their
collective breath had been sucked up the stovepipe and exhaled outside. One stove could have heated both rooms.

Richard and David, who was six, were placed in first year together,
since this was the first time Richard had been exposed to formal education. At nine, he was as big as the third-year students; but because
he couldn't read, the other kids laughed at him and teased him, calling him "dummy" or "stupid." His clothes were clean but worn and
he had no shoes, giving the kids another reason to make fun of him.
And the teacher only made it worse by finding him a pair in the
closet of clothes she kept for indigent students. He hated the kids in
the class and talked only when he had to. He spent his recess periods
and lunch hour with David. He didn't even try to make friends. He
was afraid of being laughed at.

Shortly after they had enrolled, David was absent from school
with a bad case of the croup. At recess Richard was alone in the corner of the school yard absently making an arc in the snow with his
foot. Dressed in a too small hand-me-down jacket from his cousin
and oversized brogans provided by the teacher, he was aware that
three of the third year boys were coming his way. His small arms
stuck out of the ends of the rough woolen sleeves giving him a scare-
crow-like look. He wore no socks; his skinny legs rose out of the huge

brown shoes and were barely covered by the too short pants. His shoes were stuffed with cloths to keep his feet from slipping back and forth as he walked, causing him to shuffle slightly as though his feet were too heavy to pick up properly. His overall appearance was ungainly, like a young crane just growing into his oversized feet and body. He was a perfect target for the jibes of the other children.

Even with his head down, hoping he would be invisible, Richard saw that the small band had crossed the yard and were now nearly upon him. He took in a sharp breath of cold air and looked up to face them.

"Whatcha doin', Dickie-bird?" the big third grader from the front row asked. Richard hated being called Dick; but he was afraid of being disliked even more if he insisted on being called by his given name. Therefore, he had never mentioned it. They had figured out that he hated it anyway, and had made a chant of his name. "Dickie-bird, Dickie-bird, Dickie-bird."

"Nuthin'," he said. He tried to remain casual but knew they were up to something since they never talked to him except to tease.

"Nuthin'? Well, that's cause you don't know nuthin', Dummy. That's why you're doin' nuthin. You cain't even read," jeered the red-headed boy who had laughed at him that morning when he was called on to read aloud in class.

As the boy laughed now, Richard noticed the gap in his front teeth that caused him to lisp. He stifled a retort about the lisp, knowing if he said anything, matters would only get worse. He also guessed if he walked away they would follow him. These three were spoiling for a fight. Not that he was afraid to fight; he'd fought David plenty of times. But he knew his uncle Will would punish him for fighting at school and besides his skin tight jacket restricted his arms and his overstuffed shoes would surely trip him if he had to run. As he mulled over his dilemma the third musketeer chimed in.

"Well, say sumpthin'. Cat got your tongue?"

"Probably so, since he's a Dickie-bird." The third grader repeated the hated nickname.

"Dickie-bird, Dickie-bird. Dummy, dummy Dickie-bird." Now the red head took up the cry.

Richard couldn't contain himself any longer. "I'm not a dummy and I'm not a Dickie-bird, either. I'm Richard and I'm smarter than all of you," he shouted into their faces and turned to walk away.

"I think you are a Dickie-bird and a chicken, too," yelled the third grader, shoving Richard so hard that he tripped over his huge shoes and fell face first into the snow. He scrambled to his feet, but fell again, the laces of his massive shoes entangled. With this fall, his lower teeth grazed his lip and the metallic taste of blood was sharp in his mouth. He lay there stunned, choking back tears of rage. He could hear the gales of laughter from the three. The chant "Dickie-bird, Dickie-bird" rang in his ears and seemed to echo from across the schoolyard. It bounced off the frozen piles of soot-covered snow and hit him again and again. Keeping perfect time with the chant was the rhythmic peal of the school bell and the pounding footsteps of the students as they ran back to class.

Picking himself up to rejoin his class, he was aware that the group was gone and in their place was Mrs. Ferguson, his teacher. "What on earth are you doing playing in the snow? Your clothes are soaked." He started to protest, to explain what had happened to him, but the dam of tears he had been holding back burst and he started to cry. Not wanting her to see him as a baby, he put his frozen, wet hands to his face and quickly wiped his eyes making sooty streaks on his chapped cheeks. Aware that his nose hurt, he reached up to touch it just as a tiny trickle of blood and mucus began to run onto his upper lip. Quickly wiping this evidence away with the back of his hand, he mumbled "I wasn't playing, I tripped."

"Well, come inside; you'll catch your death," she ordered, though in a much kinder tone, marching across the barren yard ahead of Richard. He carefully made his way through the snow, avoiding the icy patches for fear of falling again. Upon reaching the narrow board walk leading into the hallway, he glanced back at his tracks in the snow. *Someday, I'll be big enough to fill those footsteps for real and then I'll show them. I'm going to learn to read and get a job. When I grow up I'm going to be rich. I'll be so rich that nobody will ever dare to laugh at me again.*

Three

May 1907

I t would have been a perfect spring Sunday, but for the way it ended. The May air was warm and caressing with none of the summer stickiness that would come later that year. Anna Miller wished it could be spring year round. The sparkling white faces of the trillium smiled from the hillside across the New River and the sweet scent of the lilies-of-the-valley was thick around the house. As she slipped an apron over her good dress and went to help her mother with the Sunday noon meal, she mentally made plans to curl up in the porch swing this afternoon to finish *Pride and Prejudice*.

For the moment, her mind wasn't on the romantic problems of Jane Austen's Bennett sisters; they were on her own. For well over a year she had been seeing a young man whom she had met at a gathering of the Carleton family. Anna flushed as she recalled the moment she first saw Lawrence Burgher; she had immediately been attracted to the tall, chestnut-haired stranger with a widow's peak.

Unfortunately for Anna, her papa did not feel the same way. That concerned her. When they met, he had thought the young man was aloof and unfriendly. He was not favorably impressed by him, not at all. She loved her father and didn't like to cross him; however, she also loved Lawrence Burgher.

In the cozy kitchen Anna scrubbed and peeled the potatoes at the sink, as the sounds of Papa's violin filled the house. It was his favorite pastime; sometimes he played for hours. The sun flirted with the lace curtains over the sink, periodically filling the large yellow room with a warm diffused light. Anna paused in her work, to watch the sun play hide and seek in the clouds and tried to identify the tune, but could not.

"Such an odd hobby for a mine foreman; most of my friend's fathers play cards or hunt in their spare time." Anna said aloud to her mother who was lifting the large roasting pan from the oven.

"Mama, where did Papa learn to play?"

"I'm not sure, Anna, but I think 'is mother taught 'im. She was a very refined lady, don't you know. 'Er whole family was very well off back in England. You should see the pictures of 'er father standing in front of their fine manor house. 'Ave I never shown them to you? They disowned 'er when she married your grandfather Miller because 'e was a coal miner." Her mother bustled from the sink to the big cook stove with the diced potatoes which she arranged in the sizzling juice around the roast.

"I remember seeing those pictures, but I don't remember any of our relatives. I guess I was too small. The only people I know from England are the Carletons; but they aren't really family."

"No, but they are the only family we 'ave 'ere, since your uncle Thomas decided to go out west. I must say, I always thought that was fine thanks to Jack Carleton for bringing 'im to America. 'E should've stayed 'ere with family instead of traipsing off by 'imself." As she talked she puffed up in indignation like a ruffled hen and began pounding out the dough for biscuits.

"Mama, you can't blame someone for wanting to make their own way. Uncle Thomas just wasn't cut out for working in the mines." Anna fingered a loose strand of her dark hair.

"And you think your papa likes 'hit? Well, 'e doesn't, Missy; 'e runs the mines because it's what 'e knows. And 'e told Jack Carleton 'e would when they came from England. 'Onoring a commitment is very important to your papa. And seeing 'is children have a better life is, too." She punctuated each sentence with a cut in the dough with the biscuit cutter, then placed each flat circle on the baking sheet.

Anna always thought her mother exaggerated her Yorkshire

accent for effect when she was agitated. Elizabeth Jane Miller was normally very soft spoken, a gentle, plump, short woman with a jolly sense of humor; but when she was riled, she was as tough as any man twice her size. Anna knew the conversation had strayed inadvertently onto a touchy subject. She tried steering it back to safer ground.

"Tell me more about our family in England. Who is still there?"

"Oh, mostly cousins and the like. All of my brothers 'ave died, but I still get letters from my sister Jenny. Your papa only 'ad two other brothers besides Thomas and we don't 'ear from them. I guess they thought 'e'd lost 'is mind when 'e came to America. They all worked in the mines, too; but for all I know, they could 'ave been killed there. I'd like to go back someday to see Jenny and 'er family; your papa says 'e'll send me, but it would be very expensive." Her tone softened with nostalgia. Anna breathed a sigh of relief as she went to set the table.

"That would be lovely for you. It must be hard, not ever seeing your sister or the place where you grew up. When I was small I loved to hear you tell the stories about our voyage from England — how your family stood and cried as they waved goodbye to you and Joseph and me. I don't know whether I really remember the trip or just your stories about it, though. In my memory it was a great romantic adventure, going to be with Papa, even if it was sad at the same time. I know they'd love to have you visit."

"Some day, per'aps," said her mother wistfully as she joined Anna. They worked side by side in silence for a time, Anna placing the heavy silver flatware on the damask cloth, her mother centering the delicately flowered Haviland china at each place. Both were lost in their own private reveries; but they worked as a team, unconciously anticipating the motions of the other.

"Anna, while you are 'ome from school, will you be seeing that Burgher fellow?"

Anna was startled by the sudden change of subject and not prepared to answer.

"Why do you ask, Mama?" She stalled, knowing that her father did not approve of Lawrence, but not as sure of her mother's feelings.

"Jack Carleton mentioned him the other day. Said 'e was about to graduate from business school. Your letters didn't mention 'im, so I wondered."

"Well, with both of us away at separate schools, we haven't seen each other for some time, but we did write almost daily. He's a wonderful person and I am very fond of him." She avoided answering the question directly or saying that Lawrence had come to see her several times since Christmas.

"'E's quite handsome, isn't 'e? Sounds as if you are serious about 'im. Your papa won't approve of that, you know."

"I know, Mama, but I don't understand why Papa doesn't like Lawrence. How do you feel about it? Do you like him?"

"Jack says 'is people were farmers down in Wyoming County, but that 'e's smart enough. I've only met 'im a few times. 'E seems very sure of 'imself. I understand 'e still owns all that farm land. Does 'e intend to go back to it? You surely don't want to be a farmer's wife, do you? We aren't sending you to college to 'ave you end up on a farm, you know."

"Mama, you know college was your idea; all I ever wanted was to be a good wife and mother, like you. Besides, Lawrence doesn't plan to be a farmer; he wants to have a business of his own."

"You'd best not talk 'wife and mother' to your papa, Missy. 'E isn't ready to give you up to some dreamer, yet. 'E still thinks of you as 'is little girl, you know. What kind of business does this young man plan to 'ave?"

"He's not sure; he hasn't even graduated yet. But, he has grand plans for the future."

"And I suppose they include you? If that's the case, 'e'd best be getting a regular job and forget about 'igh-faluting dreams of businesses. A man needs to be able to provide for a wife before 'e thinks about taking one on. 'E 'asn't actually asked you to marry him, 'as 'e?"

"Yes, Mama, he has, but please don't tell Papa. He plans to come ask Papa for my hand himself."

"Lawz-a-mercy, Anna, you'd better save your young man the embarrassment. Your papa will never consent. You can try talking to 'im, but don't be surprised at 'is answer. Dinner should be ready in a few minutes; please go call your papa."

"Yes, Mama. Do you think there's time now to talk to him?"

"Well, if you don't take too long. But don't be surprised at 'is answer," she repeated.

Anna tried to identify the music now coming through the closed study door as she walked slowly up the stairs. She thought it was Tchaikovsky, but couldn't pinpoint the piece. She removed her apron and smoothed her dress while she waited hesitantly in the dim hallway for the notes to die away. As the last strains faded, she rapped quickly before he could begin again.

"Come in," said the baritone voice from within. Anna opened the door and stepped inside the small sanctuary that was her father's study. Book shelves lined one wall, but most of the volumes there had gathered more dust than fingerprints. Her father stood in the middle of the room before an ornate wooden music stand; the delicate violin looked oddly correct in his work-hardened hands. Albert Willingham Miller was a spare man, slight of stature and dark of skin. Anna was built more like him than like her mother, a genetic fact for which she often thanked God. Nevertheless, she still worried that she would turn pudgy and square in her old age.

"Papa, dinner is nearly ready."

"Thank you, Anna; I'll come right down."

"Papa, could I ask you something, first?" Her voice quavered nervously as she fidgeted with the ties of the apron on her arm, her dark eyes downcast.

"Of, course, Anna. You can ask me anything," he said, smiling.

She stood there, staring at the pattern in the hooked rug, unsure of how to begin. He placed the violin on the burgundy horsehair chair and turned to her.

"Is something the matter, child?" he said, cupping her face in his hands.

"I...I don't know. Mama says...that is...Oh, Papa, I love Lawrence Burgher with all my heart; but Mama says you don't approve of him and would never consent to our marriage. Is that true?" After a slight pause she added, "Please tell me it's not."

His solicitious tone abruptly changed to one of stern fatherliness. "It most certainly is! He'd best not come around here asking for your hand. I will not have a daughter of mine marrying that young dreamer!"

Tears brimmed in her brown eyes. "Papa, you don't understand. He isn't a dreamer, he has grand plans. He's going to graduate from Broadmoor Business College in June. And I know I shall never love anyone else."

"Nonsense, you are far too young to know much about love. It would never work, you are as unlike as oil and water and besides, you are twice the person he is. He may have a head for business, but he acts as if he's better than most, which he is not. He's just a farmer's son who has big ideas. Broadmoor's not a real college, you know; just what does this *business* education make him fit for, anyway?"

"He wants to have a business of his own, Papa."

"Pshaw, he'll be poor as a church mouse. Can't you understand; I want so much more for you. I did not bring this family here from England to see my favorite daughter marry a starving shopkeeper. I came here to make life better for you, your brother and sister. You don't know how hard I've worked to see you get the education your Mama insisted on. You'll not throw that over for him."

"Papa, college isn't for me. I want to marry Lawrence."

"Absolutely not! You can just put him out of your little head."

"I won't, Papa. Nothing you can do will make me not love him."

"Well, we'll see about that. Your mother has been wanting to go visit her family in England and I've been saving to send her. This is the perfect time and I think you should go with her. Maybe an extended trip will make you forget this silly infatuation."

"It's not an infatuation, Papa." She stamped her foot and instantly regretted it.

"Don't you get impudent and argue with me, Missy!"

"I'm sorry, but please don't make me leave, Papa. What about school? I thought that was so important to you and Mama."

"It is. You can finish when you return."

"No, Papa, please."

"Anna, we will discuss it no further," he said. He used a tone that Anna knew only too well signaled the end of the conversation. She left the room with a muffled cry and ran down the hall to her own room.

"Anna!" called her father, but she did not respond. Once she had shut the door, she recognized the piece — Tchaikovsky's *Romeo and Juliet Suite*. Her tears spilled down her cheeks as she flopped onto her four poster bed. Her small shoulders shook with sobs. She gave way, in the solitude, to the despair she felt at her father's unyielding nature, and, fully dressed, cried herself to sleep.

Monday, May 20, 1907

Dearest Lawrence,

Papa is so hard. I tried to talk to him yesterday, but it only made matters worse. Now he says he's sending me to England with Mama. He hopes I will forget you, but I won't. He insists that he will never consent to our marriage. He thinks your plans of being in business are foolish dreams and says that you should get an honest job.

If he knew the real Lawrence Burgher like I do, he'd not feel this harshly toward you. What can we do to change his opinion? Perhaps we could ask Jack Carleton to talk to him.

The worst part is that we leave in two weeks for England and I see no way out of it. Lawrence, darling, you know that I won't forget you and will write you as often as I can. We will be staying at my Aunt Jenny's for the summer. If you can, please write me at her address — Liverton Mines, Yorkshire, England. I can only hope that you will wait for me, trusting in our love as we have both done for the past year. When I return, we will find a solution together.

Your loving,

grade at the same elementary school he had attended. The school had grown and the belching stove no longer put out a cloud of soot; but the school yard where he had been unmercifully harassed was exactly the same.

One snowy January afternoon, he went to the play yard to call in a few straggling boys from recess, but they had slipped in another door. The yard was vacant, except for the echo of the school bell. With the sound of the bell and the pungent smell of snow-trodden earth, Lawrence's memory momentarily flashed back to his days in this yard. He could hear the taunt — "Dickie-bird, Dickie-bird, Dickie-bird" — as it echoed like a chant across the empty space. Instinctively he licked his lip, as if he could still taste the blood from the day he was shoved face-first into the snow.

Never, never again will I be bullied. Dickie-bird is dead. I am Lawrence. So Anna's father doesn't approve. Well, that's too bad. I'm going to marry her, regardless. And I won't teach third grade forever, either. I'll show him. He pulled his muffler more tightly around his neck and marched back into the building.

Anna returned from England to resume her studies at West Virginia Institute of Technology in Montgomery, although her mind was in Mt. Hope. Just before lights out each night, she wrote to Lawrence proclaiming her love and proposing a new scheme for obtaining her father's consent to marry. And each morning she awoke knowing that the plan, which had sounded plausible the night before, was as futile as the rest. She was miserable. Neither the light-hearted pranks of her room-mate, Rebecca Nelson, nor the encouraging letters from her sister Jenny could bring her out of her despondency.

By the time she returned to Thurmond for the Christmas holidays, Anna was visibly thinner. Her mother was worried and said so to her husband. But Albert Miller was adamant. He would never consent to that marriage.

On the night before Anna was to return to school, she went to her room shortly after supper to pack. The tap on her door was soft at first. Anna didn't hear it until the intensity increased and her mother called, "Anna, I'd like to talk to you."

Anna opened the door. "What is it Mother? Come in. We can talk while I pack."

"No, Missy," her mother said firmly. "I want you to stop and really listen to me." She shut the door behind her.

Dutifully, Anna moved the valise to the floor and sat down on her bed, as her mother took the bedside chair. Elizabeth took Anna's hands and looked her daughter straight in the eyes.

"Anna, I know just 'ow you feel about not being with your beau. I know your father will never change 'is mind, and I won't defy 'im; but I think 'e's 'andled this business badly. I'm not giving my approval, mind you; but *I* can see that forbidding you to marry that young man will not stop you, if that's what you want.

"So, instead of me giving you another lecture, I'm going to tell you a story. Maybe you'll learn something from 'hit. When your father decided to come to America to work in the mines, my family did not want me to follow. Of course, we were already married, so they couldn't forbid 'hit; but they weren't 'appy at all. Naturally, I came on about six months later; but I paid a dear price. Except for your Aunt Jenny, the rest of my immediate family died before I could see them again. And, when your father left England, we 'ad three children — Albert Jr, Joe and you. Albert died with the measles a few months after your father left, but with mail so slow back then; 'e never knew until I arrived with just the two of you. Furthermore, I was pregnant and miscarried right after Albert died. Our little passel of four children was only two by the time we met again in the United States." Elizabeth dropped Anna's hands and dabbed at the tears in her eyes, then handed her handkerchief to Anna who was crying openly.

"Mama, why didn't you ever tell me this? Where is my brother buried?"

"We buried 'im in England. Your aunt Jenny and I went to the cemetery when we were visiting, but I didn't take you because you were so upset already. I'm telling you now for several reasons. The Miller women are strong. We don't wallow in self-pity. We figure out a solution and we get on with 'hit. If you really love Lawrence, you'll find a way to be with 'im. But be sure of your decision; you'll have to live with 'hit forever."

Elizabeth stood, reached out and took Anna in her arms. Anna rested her head on her mother's shoulder for a moment, then straightened.

"Mama, I love you. And I love Papa and don't want to hurt either of you. Thank you for sharing your story; it helped."

Her mother patted Anna's arm and let herself quietly out of the bedroom while Anna resumed her packing. Anna slept fitfully that night, mulling over what her mother had told her.

Montgomery, WV
Monday, April 20, 1908

Dear Jenny,

I'm writing you today for three reasons. I have exciting news; I need a favor, and I want to apologize to you.

First, the exciting news. Lawrence and I are married! Stop! Don't scream. Mother and Father may hear you. It's true. We eloped last weekend, took the train to Lewisburg and got married. Rebecca Nelson, my room-mate, (you remember her, don't you?) and I took the train from Montgomery to meet Lawrence and David in Lewisburg. Lawrence had made arrangements with a Presbyterian minister there and we were married in the oldest church in West Virginia. At least, I think that's what they told us. We spent the night at the wonderful General Lewis Hotel, in a room with a luxurious canopy bed. It was beautiful and the food in the dining room was marvelous. Lawrence apologized for not being able to afford The Greenbrier and promised that one day we would stay there. I believe he'll make good on that promise, too.

Now for the favor — Rebecca and I came back to school on Sunday evening. Lawrence returned to Mt. Hope and David left to finish classes at Broadmoor. I plan to finish out the term before we set up house-keeping and I do not want to tell Mother and Father until then. On Memorial Day weekend, I'll be going home and will tell them then. Would you please plan to stay home that weekend to be my ally? I know you often go to a big picnic in Thurmond for the holiday, but I would so much appreciate it if you would stay home this year. I know Father will have a conniption fit, and Mother will probably go on a crying jag; so I need your moral support. Please say you will!!!

And now, the apology. I'm so sorry I didn't ask you to go with me to be our witness, but I had a good reason. I didn't want to put you in the awkward position of having to lie for me to Mother and Father. So, I reasoned that if you didn't go — you couldn't lie, right? I hope you will forgive me. I know we talked about you being my maid-of-honor when I got married, but it was better this way. Now they'll only be angry at me.

Jenny, you should have seen me when I got off the train. I was a mess! I had offered to hold a baby for a young mother who had a terrible case of motion sickness. She was throwing up and needed help. Well, I took the poor thing (he was screaming) and he threw up on me! It was all over my lap. My dress was a mess and I smelled like a barnyard. After I got over the shock, we started laughing. What a way to greet your groom to be! Who wants to marry a smelly woman? Rebecca and I tried to clean it, but the damp stain was still there and so was the odor. Lawrence didn't think it was nearly as funny as we did.

I hope you aren't angry. I love you. Please let me know if you'll stay home.

Your loving sister,

Five

July 1908

Little swirls of dust kicked up and coated the freshly polished high button brown boots of the neatly dressed young man approaching town. Quickening his pace to avoid an oncoming buggy, he stepped up onto the wooden sidewalk. The hollow sound reverberated down the length of raised board. A few of Saturday's Fourth of July parade flags still hung like limp Monday wash on the lamp posts. At the end of the block, the red, white and blue bunting over the bank door drooped with the early morning humidity, while the solid sandstone building shimmered in the heat like a mirage.

Lawrence ran his finger inside his damp shirt collar and hoped he didn't look as bedraggled as the leftover decorations. "Not even ten o'clock and it's already as hot as the hinges of Hades," he muttered to no one in particular. He looked down at shoes turned dull by the road dirt. He reached the end of the boardwalk, took his handkerchief from his breast pocket, wiped his face, shined each shoe on the back of the other trouser leg and, satisfied that he looked presentable, strode through the double doors of the National Bank of Thurmond, West Virginia.

As the beveled glass in the doors rattled behind him, Lawrence stood for a moment to let his eyes adjust to the interior lighting, cave-like in contrast to the punishing sun he'd just escaped. The low melody of voices was rhythmically punctuated by the tinny ding of an opening cash drawer, the echo of footsteps on the polished marble floor and the cooling swoosh, swoosh of the large paddle fans suspended on slender brass poles from the ceiling two stories above. He pulled his father's gold watch from his vest pocket. *Good, I'm early. That should make a good impression.*

Walking slowly past the large wooden cage, he stared at the tellers behind brass-barred windows scurrying like eager monkeys to pass papers and cash to their prosperous-looking customers. Lawrence imagined he could smell the crisp bills as his hand crept to his pant's pocket where he fingered his loose change.

Past the cage, an open lobby held several desks; beyond that he could see one or two offices with closed, frosted glass doors. A schoolmarmish, thin woman with a long neck accented by her high collar was seated at the first desk. She looked up as she heard the approaching footsteps.

"May I help you?" she asked in a detached tone of voice.

"Yes, ma'am. I have an appointment with Mr. Webster. My name is Lawrence Burgher." As he spoke, she looked at him appraisingly and his throat suddenly felt parched, as if he had swallowed the hot dust of the street.

"What time is your appointment?" she asked.

"Ten o'clock, but I'm a little early."

"Well, yes, I see that." She glanced over his head at the wall behind him. "So, I'm afraid you'll have to wait. Mr. Webster has someone with him now. You may have a seat over there, against the wall." She indicated a row of straight back wooden chairs lined up like toy soldiers on a shelf.

"Thank you," Lawrence said and walked to take the seat closest to what he assumed was the President's office. From behind the chilly glass he could hear the muffled sound of voices, one much deeper than the other. He imagined another interview in progress. He stared at the floor to avoid the critical eye of the secretary and took a quick mental inventory of his skills.

"Please, dear Lord, let me get this job," he beseeched silently as he carefully lifted his head to take in the grand interior of the new bank. The gleaming white plaster walls above the wainscoting held gilt-framed pictures of President Roosevelt, Governor Dawson and several men whom he presumed to be directors of the bank. As his eye traveled past the lazy fans, he admired the ornate, gilded crown molding joining wall to vaulted ceiling. After a moment, afraid of appearing unfamiliar with his surroundings, Lawrence abruptly ceased his inspection. Without being too obvious, he could see the gold lettering which labeled the frosty office doors. He couldn't read the names without his glasses, but he was too vain to put them on under the scrutiny of the woman at the desk. As he fingered his father's watch fob, he watched the busy tellers with fascination. *If all goes well, one of them could be me.*

While he waited, his mind replayed the events of the past few years. It seemed as if each one was a step on the road to this bustling new town. Who would have thought that after marrying Anna, against her father's adamant objections, they would settle in her hometown. However, if moving back to Thurmond helped to appease her father and mollify the situation, Lawrence had been more than willing. He had to admit that working in Thurmond would be a far cry from teaching in the Mt. Hope elementary school where he had been educated himself. Thurmond was growing by leaps and bounds now that the railroad bridge had made it into a major coal shipping junction. It was an odd town, however, with the railroad tracks running through the middle of the business district where a road should have been. *I suppose that indicates just how critical the railroad is.* And now he was applying for the banking position that Jack Carleton had told him about. Broadmoor had been a good choice of schools; he had made good grades and now felt ready to take on the business world.

After what seemed like an hour Lawrence was startled out of his daydream at the sonorous gong of the lobby clock; it was just now 10 A.M. and, as if on cue, the door to the farthest office opened. Standing in the doorway was a large, portly man with a huge moustache; he looked to Lawrence like President Roosevelt himself. His crisp shirt collar and the knife sharp creases in his dark gray trousers made Lawrence all the more self conscious of his heat-wilted brown suit. The shiny black shoes peeking from below the generous pants matched the sheen of the gold watch chain across an ample belly.

Lawrence started as the secretary spoke to him. "Mr. Webster will see you now."

He rose and strode toward the office, wondering idly where the previous visitor had gone. President Rufus Webster crossed the expanse and met Lawrence halfway. Thrusting out his fleshy, freckled hand, he covered Lawrence's hand with both of his and ushered him into his office.

"Come in, my boy. Glad to meet you. Jacob Maxwell has told me a lot about you." He spoke warmly as Lawrence quickly took in the quiet richness of the office. Glass front bookcases lined the far wall; the large, thick oriental rug muffled the steps of the two men. "Here, have a seat," the President said. He gestured toward the leather wing back chair in front of his desk. Mr. Webster slid into his desk chair and straightened his onyx cuff links. Lawrence thought him surprisingly agile for such a heavy man.

"So, how are Headmaster Maxwell and his family? I haven't seen them in several months."

"He's fine, sir. At least he was when I graduated last year. Of course, I haven't been back to Broadmoor since then and I really don't know his family." Lawrence was beginning to feel more at ease, knowing that Mr. Webster and his former teacher were real friends rather than mere acquaintances.

Webster laughed. His belly moved up and down against the desk edge. "No, I'll bet you haven't. Once you graduate, you rarely go back, right?"

"That's right, sir."

Abruptly the president came to the point of the interview. "Richard, why should I hire you? I know what Maxwell says, but I want you to tell me yourself."

Lawrence felt his throat constrict again at the sudden shift in the conversation and at the name Richard. He wished he had a glass of water, but was afraid to ask. He also wanted the bank president to know that he never went by his first name, but hesitated to mention it at this time. "Sir, as you know, I graduated from the Broadmoor Business College last spring. Before that, I taught school for several years after finishing normal school, and I tried it again after graduation;

but I didn't feel that I was well suited for it. I really want to get into the business world, maybe even go into business for myself someday."

"Then why do you want a position with my bank?"

"I feel that it would be a good place to learn about being in business. Men who are in business for themselves must come to your bank frequently and I would hope to learn from them, as well as from you. My business courses were quite comprehensive, but learning by doing is what my father taught me as a child."

"What business is your father in?"

"None, sir; he was a farmer in Wyoming County. He died when I was young, but he taught me all he could about the farm, even when I was small. I worked right alongside him, but we had to leave the farm when he died. Then I was raised by my mother and my uncle. He was a stone-mason in Mt. Hope."

"You don't have any desire to go back and be a farmer, I guess?"

"No, sir!" Lawrence was a little surprised at his own vehemence. He didn't mean for it to sound so forceful. "That is, I really feel the future is in business, with the growth of the coal industry in West Virginia and all. Farmers will have a tough time of it. I don't want to get left behind. At Broadmoor, there was a banker who spoke to one of our classes and made the profession sound very interesting. And I should think being a teller would give a person lots of opportunities to meet businessmen."

"Well, you certainly seem ambitious, Richard, but unfortunately we don't have any positions open for a teller. I know that is the job for which you came to apply, but we filled it yesterday."

Lawrence was crestfallen but managed to keep a poker face.

"Did you learn bookkeeping at Broadmoor?" Webster continued.

"Yes, sir. We had to take that as one of our regular courses and I did make good marks."

"Well, I know it's not as glamourous and you won't get the chance to meet the public, but our bookkeeper was just promoted to the teller's post, so now we need to fill his position. Are you interested, Richard?"

Lawrence knew better than to hesitate. A job was a job and with a new wife, he certainly didn't want to go back to teaching eight-year-old children.

"Absolutely, sir. I'd be very interested. When would I start?"

"Would next week be too soon? We can have your predecessor show you around. The starting pay won't be much until we see how you do, but if you live up to Maxwell's recommendation, you should get a raise soon."

"That will be fine; thank you, sir. I'll be here next Monday at eight o'clock sharp," said Lawrence, hoping his voice did not betray his disappointment.

"Good. We can get you settled before the bank opens." Webster rose from his chair, came around the desk and again took Lawrence's hand. With his other hand on Lawrence's elbow, he walked him out of the office.

"Thank you again, sir. I really appreciate it. And sir, I'm called Lawrence, not Richard," he said with confidence.

"Lawrence then," the banker laughed. "Well, Lawrence, don't thank me; thank Headmaster Maxwell." He pumped his hand even harder. "Welcome to the banking profession; it's an honorable one, and I know you'll do it proud."

As Lawrence walked back through the bank, he only glanced at the humming teller's cage. With a leaden spirit, he wondered where his office would be. *I'll probably be stuck away somewhere and never meet a soul.* Then he stepped outside into the glare of the morning sun and blinked. *But the previous bookkeeper was promoted to teller, wasn't he? So, there's no reason that I can't be as well. I wonder how long it will take?*

Stepping off the boardwalk into the street, he barely noticed the dust again accumulating on his shoes. The sun had dried out the limp flags, which now snapped smartly in the breeze. An acquaintance heading up the hill in a wagon called to him, "Hello, Lawrence; where are you going? Need a ride?"

"No thanks, Harry, I'll walk," he yelled. "I've just been hired at the bank and I'm going home to tell Anna. It's not that far."

"It's awfully hot for walking, but suit yourself," Harry returned.

Lawrence crossed to the other side of the road. As he turned to wave to Harry, he caught sight of the Bank of Thurmond in the valley behind him. The haziness had vanished and in its place, the golden-brown stone bank seemed to glow in the summer sun.

Six

February 1910

The doors to the National Bank of Thurmond rattled shut for what seemed like the hundredth time that morning. Lawrence should have been glad, for that meant good business. But every time the door opened, a damp, cold draft swept across the black and white marble floor and crept behind the tellers cage like smoke drawn up a chimney, chilling his feet and legs. *What are all these people doing out on such a raw, blustery day. Looks to me like they would wait until the weather improved.* Glancing up, he could see through the front doors that the sky was unleashing the first round of the day's snow showers.

It wasn't quite cold enough for a sustained snow storm, but it was typical of most West Virginia winter days. The dull gray sky dripped with cold drizzle that periodically changed to sleet when the temperature dropped and the piercing wind sent the cold straight to your bones. Beyond the large glass-paned door, Thurmond had the terminally bleak look that makes you believe spring will never come again. Skeletal trees and dirty patches of snow from the last storm dotted the barren hills that surrounded the town. *If this continues, the streets will be a sheet of ice when the sun goes down.*

As the door opened again, Lawrence saw Jack Carleton step inside accompanied by a man he didn't know. Jack took off his gloves, drew the muffler from around his neck and taking off his hat, brushed the snow from it. His companion wore no gloves or muffler and did not remove his hat, a derby. Crossing the floor toward the tellers' windows, their footsteps clicked in cadence, except that the stranger walked as though his legs moved only from the knees. Although Lawrence had several customers in his line, and a teller to his left did not, the pair waited patiently for their turn in his line. This made Lawrence curious. He was sure he had never met the man and wondered who he was. *How does he know Jack Carleton? Why do they want to see me?* He found himself stealing glances at the man, almost ignoring his present customers while they were speaking to him.

Lawrence thought the stranger looked considerably older than himself, but not quite Jack Carleton's contemporary, either. The stranger was a portly man, so thick in the middle that his coat must have been tailored to fit, for it both hugged his narrow shoulders and cleared his ample girth without gaping at the buttons. He was clearly overweight, but not obese. Below the derby hat, his puffy eyes surveyed the bank appraisingly. Clamped between the thin lips in his under-slung jaw, was an unlit cigar. He looked like an out-of-shape bulldog.

In contrast, Jack Carleton looked as if he did daily manual labor, which in fact he had as a young man in Yorkshire, England. A coal miner then, he had come to America in the late 1880s when wages declined in the English mining industry. Now he owned mines all over Fayette County. Every muscle was still hardened to a fine definition, even those in his jaw. Although nearing sixty, he looked as fit as a man in his forties; only his full head of steel gray hair hinted at his actual age.

The pair stepped forward as Lawrence's last customer walked away. Jack Carleton wasted no time on pleasantries. "Lawrence," he said, "I want you to meet a friend of mine — Edward Keeley. He's been in business in Mt. Hope, Oak Hill and here. Now he's moved to Shapely and has some plans you might find interesting. Can you take some time to join us for lunch?"

Keeley had nodded his head in acknowledgement as Jack Carleton spoke his name, but kept silent, letting his friend make the luncheon arrangements. Lawrence pulled his gold watch from its pocket, snapped it open and checked the time: 11:40 A.M.

"I usually take my meal at noon but perhaps I could go early. Since the snow is picking up, business should slack off some. Let me close up my window and tell my supervisor. I'll join you in a moment."

As Lawrence put out the NEXT TELLER PLEASE sign and prepared to leave, Keeley and Carleton stepped out of the line, walked to the front of the lobby and stood looking out the large arched windows as one of Thurmond's daily passenger trains emerged out of the swirling snow.

"How long has Lawrence been with the bank?" Keeley asked.

"About two years," replied Carleton. "He started as the bookkeeper and became a teller about a year later. Very bright fellow. And ambitious, too. He won't be a teller forever, I can tell you. If you don't give him more responsibility, someone else will hire him. There's no opportunity for advancement here, at least not right away, and he's too eager to wait it out."

Before he could continue Lawrence strode across the lobby wrapping his muffler around his neck as he walked. The hem of his dark brown overcoat billowed behind him. He rushed toward the pair and in one action, clapped Jack on the shoulder with his left hand and put out his right to meet Edward Keeley.

"I'm sorry I couldn't properly shake your hand earlier. Those tellers' cages are quite restrictive. It's a real pleasure to meet you, sir," Lawrence said deferentially.

"Nice to meet you as well, Lawrence," said Keeley. He held Lawrence's grip as he continued. "Jack Carleton, here, has been telling me you are eager to advance in the banking business."

"Well, yes sir, I am." Lawrence lowered his voice in reply. "But perhaps we should discuss that over lunch — not here in the lobby." Lawrence was taken off guard by the abrupt greeting and more than a little embarrassed that Keeley would discuss his affairs in such a public place. And now he was further embarrassed that he had corrected a stranger.

"Well, then, let's go," Keeley laughed heartily at Lawrence's obvious discomfiture. The trio walked three abreast through the double doors into the whirlwind of white. The gathering snow muffled the usual rattle of footsteps on the wooden sidewalk as the men made their way to the Hotel Thurmond. Its second-floor dining room boasted the best meal in town and Jack Carleton knew it. Keeley was obviously a man who enjoyed his food and Carleton knew that, too. As for Lawrence, he was delighted to have the opportunity to eat there. His normal noon meals were Anna's carefully stretched leftovers from the previous evening's meal. Rarely did he eat out and then, only a quick sandwich at the Mankin Drug Co. lunch counter.

After they were seated, Keeley resumed his interrogation without preamble, despite the presence of the patient waitress by his side. "So you've advanced from bookkeeper to teller in less than two years. Where do you go from here?"

Lawrence was again surprised at Keeley's lack of manners and sense of propriety, but tried not to reveal his feelings again. So far, he was a bit put-off by the man; but he was also extremely curious as to why Jack had arranged this meeting. *What possible interest could Keeley have in me?*

"Well, sir, when Mr. Webster hired me, I admitted to him that my ultimate goal was to be in business for myself. I went into banking hoping to learn of good opportunities to do so. Now I realize that tellers rarely have that chance. We merely wait on the customers; and I'm afraid successful businessmen don't see us as their peers, if they see us at all," Lawrence confessed.

The waitress stood silently between Carleton and Keeley waiting for a break in the conversation. Before Keeley could continue, Jack said, "Let's order and then you can ask Lawrence all the questions you want, Edward."

As they studied the menus, Lawrence noticed the impressive diamond ring that dominated Keeley's stubby right hand. Lawrence had never seen a man wear a pinkie ring, much less one so flashy. The center diamond was surrounded by dozens of smaller ones, giving the appearance of one enormous stone. Each man gave the waitress his order and Carleton instructed her to put it all on his bill. He was clearly enjoying the "matchmaker" role he had created for himself. Her task completed, the waitress retreated. Before Keeley could begin again, Carleton began telling Keeley the story of how he came to know Lawrence.

"You know I met Lawrence through his uncle. He was a stone-mason in Mt. Hope. Finest stone-mason I ever saw work. He could lay a perfectly straight stone wall without a level or a plumb-line. Anyway, the summer just before Lawrence went to Broadmoor, he was tutoring young boys and helping his uncle as well. I could see that his heart just wasn't in it. We had a bit of a chat one day and he told me that he wanted to be a businessman — an entrepreneur. Been single minded in that effort since." Carleton continued to reminisce about the past, about Anna's father and uncle — how they had come from England to work with him. Keeley became visibly bored after a while and interrupted Carleton, as if no break had occurred in his own thought processes or conversation.

"And what line of business interests you?" he asked, looking straight at Lawrence.

"When my father died he left my brother and me some farm land in Wyoming County, but I have no interest in farming. I've been selling some of that land here and there. Saving my money to start a concern I can call my own, but I still haven't decided what yet."

"Have you considered developing the land instead of selling it outright?" Keeley continued.

"Certainly, that would be more lucrative; but I don't have the necessary capital to do so. And I haven't worked long enough to get a loan either."

Annoyed slightly that Keeley had interrupted his story and stolen the floor from him, Carleton interjected, "Come on Keeley, give the boy a chance to breathe. That's enough questioning for now." Turning to Lawrence, he asked after Anna and the baby and then explained why he wanted to introduce him to Keeley. While Jack talked, Lawrence couldn't help glancing at Keeley several times, trying to form an impression of this pugnacious looking man. He certainly didn't look like the successful entrepreneur Carleton was describing; he looked more like a fight promoter.

"Keeley, as I said at the bank, has business interests in several fields — he ran the first general store here in Thurmond, began an insurance agency in Glen Jean, and has owned four or five restaurants. I met him when I came here from England; he had several coal companies in Fayette County and we've known each other for years. I can't think of any man with a more diverse business background. And now he's just bought controlling interest in your bank. I guess that makes him your new boss."

Lawrence nearly choked on his roast beef. "Good heavens, Jack, why didn't you tell me that to begin with?"

Jack Carleton put his hand on Lawrence's arm. "He isn't actually going to run the bank, he just owns it. And that's not why I wanted you to meet him. Edward likes to own things but he usually lets other people run them. That's what I wanted you to hear about." Lawrence wiped his mouth and sat back to listen. He was instantly more impressed with Keeley despite his unpolished manner. *Here is a man who could certainly help me get ahead.*

But it was Keeley who spoke next. "I'm starting a new bank in Shapely and I'd like you to come be my head teller. You must know lots of folks there — your daddy being a farmer in that county and all. It would be sort of like a homecoming."

"Sir, I moved to Mt. Hope as a child and don't know anyone back home except the few people I've met in my real estate transactions."

"Well, no matter. I just thought it might be helpful to you and the bank. You're still hired if you want the job. Have you ever considered banking or real estate development, for that matter, as actual careers. They both offer great opportunities for wealth and position. Much more so than owning a general store, or a restaurant, I can tell you. You know, there's only so much labor one man can do to earn a living. The trick I've discovered — and I'll share it with you — is to control the business so that others earn the money for you. And right now, owning land is like controlling money. With the amount of land you have and my bank's money, that property could be developed into housing sites. Shapely is beginning to boom with the railroad coming in and I feel certain that the town will grow substantially. If you were working for me, I'd see clear to loan you the money you would need. And, who knows, someday I may get tired of running that bank, too; and you'd be there to take over. That is, if you are as bright as Jack Carleton says you are."

Lawrence was stunned. Just an hour ago, he was worrying about how to support his growing family. His first child, a daughter, was a year old and Anna was pregnant again. Now, he was being handed an opportunity he had not dared to dreamed about. It sounded exciting, but Lawrence realized that he knew nothing about this man. *Of course, I have known Jack Carleton for some time and I trust him.*

"Mr. Keeley, I'm quite honored that you would ask me to come work for you. But obviously, this is a lot to think about. I can't make a decision without giving it some serious thought. And I must talk to Anna. Can I have a few days? Perhaps we could meet again to discuss the details of the job, as well as how to go about developing my property." Lawrence tried to think of questions he should ask before making any decisions, but his mind reeled with the mere fact of just moving to Shapely. He didn't want to appear mistrustful of his new boss, either. However, it occurred to him that Keeley could simply transfer him to the new bank. Realistically, his fate was in Keeley's hands, whether he liked it or not.

"Took you by surprise, did I? Well, I guess I did. Certainly, we can meet again. Soon, though, hmm? When I make a move, I do it quickly. I'll be in the bank often for the next few weeks. We'll talk then. I guess no one will object if I call you off the floor. It's my bank, now, isn't it?" Keeley giggled like a little boy who had just won all the marbles in a schoolyard match.

The three men finished their dessert and Lawrence excused himself to return to work. Carleton and Keeley lingered over coffee. As Lawrence walked the short block back to the bank, he was unaware that the snow had again turned into a cold, numbing rain.

Seven

February 1910

During the two years Lawrence and Anna had lived in Thurmond, Lawrence had never been inside the magnificent Dunglen Hotel. He'd seen it every day — you couldn't help seeing it. The hotel dominated the hillside across the New River from Thurmond, but it was actually in the town of Glen Jean. The sprawling three-and-a-half story wooden building, built in 1901, had quickly gained quite a reputation as the business and social hub of the New River coal fields. Surrounded by a double-decker porch on three sides, the Dunglen proudly proclaimed its name in giant letters on the roof. From its vantage point high above the train tracks and dust of the town, it far outshone the Hotel Thurmond.

Lawrence knew that many business deals had been consummated around the big stone fireplace in the Dunglen's lobby and he'd heard that the third floor held a gambling parlor for selected guests. Therefore, when Keeley invited Lawrence to join him for dinner, Lawrence was very excited. All day he had eagerly anticipated both the possibility of formally accepting the new position in Shapely and the prospect of dinner at the Dunglen.

Earlier in the week, Keeley had spoken briefly with Lawrence to outline the terms of his offer. Lawrence would be the head teller with two other men under him. His salary would be $1,300 per year, a raise of $2 weekly. Lawrence had excitedly calculated just how much this would improve their lives. He figured he would be able to buy

Anna the washing machine she had seen in the Sears catalog for $7.15. But when he shared this wonderful news with Anna, she was not at all excited. In fact she was upset. He hadn't expected that reaction from her.

They had discussed the move at length. While she was extremely upset at the thought of leaving Thurmond and her family, Anna had to agree that the new position *was* a step up for Lawrence. And Lawrence had to admit it was a shame to leave, just as Anna's family had finally accepted their marriage. She calmed down when he told her of the possibility of seeing the farm land developed, but she cautioned him against putting all his eggs in one basket. In the end, they concluded that the move couldn't be helped if he was to advance. So it was decided — Lawrence would accept the position Keeley had offered.

As Lawrence hurried across the Dunloup Creek footbridge and picked his way up the damp fieldstone steps to the hotel, he felt confident that he and Anna had made the right decision.

Avoiding the dirty vestiges of snow from the last storm, Lawrence stopped to take stock. He certainly didn't want to meet Keeley with muddy shoes or wet trouser cuffs. Satisfied with himself, he glanced up at the hotel. Nestled snuggly in the arms of the mountain in the early winter dusk, it glowed as if all the energy in the gorge were contained within its walls. He continued up the path with a smile. Stepping onto the wooden porch, Lawrence felt for the first time that he was about to become part of that collective energy.

He stood aside as two men pushed open the Dunglen's beveled-glass front doors. He nodded politely, recognizing them as customers of the Bank of Thurmond. They returned his silent greeting. Lawrence slipped behind them through the still open doors and stopped, waiting for his eyes to adjust to the light. The square front lobby was dominated by a massive, two-hearth central fireplace. Approximately ten feet deep and fifteen feet wide at the hearth, the stone structure tapered to a chimney half that size before it disappeared through the beamed ceiling. Lawrence's attention was captured momentarily by the handiwork of the stone-mason who had artistically arranged the smooth stones in a fanshape at the fireplace arch. A picture of his uncle Will — chisel and mallet in hand — working on a stone wall, flashed through his mind. *I'm sure glad I didn't take up his profession.*

He snapped out of his reverie and looked around the room, searching for Keeley. Before he could single him out among the huddled pairs and small groups of men, Keeley called to him from the far side of the open hearth.

"Lawrence, over here."

Lawrence raised his hand in greeting and made his way through the maze of tables.

"Good evening, Mr. Keeley," Lawrence said. As he reached Keeley he put out his hand. "It's a real pleasure to see you."

Almost simultaneously, Keeley said, "You can drop the 'Mr.' when we're away from the bank, Lawrence. And if we're going to be partners, you'd better get used to calling me Edward."

Lawrence laughed nervously, "I don't know if I can do that, yet, sir; but I'll work on it."

As they took their seats, Lawrence looked around the lobby. "This is quite a bit larger than the Hotel Thurmond, isn't it? No wonder folks come here. Look at that fireplace. The mason who built it must have been very talented." Turning back to Keeley, he asked, "Do you come here often?"

Keeley answered, "It's a good place to do a little business. Folks don't seem to bother you. Everyone is minding their own business, seems like. So I do bring folks here a good bit. It's also a good place to just get away to relax. Have a drink or dinner. Would you like one — a drink, I mean?" The remains of an earlier round sat in front of Keeley. He had waved at a waitress as he asked Lawrence the question.

"I'd like a glass of beer, if you don't mind," Lawrence said hesitantly, ordering the lightest thing he could think of. He didn't want Keeley to think him either a heavy drinker or prude.

Keeley relayed their order to the waitress; she nodded and disappeared down the left corridor. "We'll talk a bit over our drinks and then order dinner," Keeley instructed.

"Fine," said Lawrence, sitting forward like a schoolboy called on by the teacher.

"So, are you joining me at Shapely?" Keeley, as usual, got right to the point.

"Yes, sir, I am. I'd be quite honored to do so. Anna and I have discussed the move and while she dislikes leaving her family, I've convinced her it's a good job. The position you offered appears to have quite a bit more responsibility and the salary is certainly more. It's an exciting opportunity. I appreciate the chance to take on more responsibility and to advance my career. When do you want me there? We'll have to find a house, of course."

"I should think you could plan on starting in Shapely in April. Would that suit you? We'll be open by then. You know we chartered the bank last year and have been operating out of temporary quarters. The new bank building is nearly finished. Until then, you continue here in Thurmond and we'll advertise for your replacement. When we find someone, you can train him. After that's finished, you can move on down to Shapely."

"That should be just fine, Mr. Keeley, uh...Edward. As for the other — the land development — could we talk about that a bit?"

"Well, we don't have to rush into that. Let's get you settled at the bank. Get it running smoothly; then we'll talk about land."

Keeley sounded somewhat dismissive. Lawrence was disappointed, but tried not to let it show. He didn't want to let the matter drop, however. Emboldened, perhaps by the heady atmosphere of the Dunglen, he took a chance and pursued the matter, despite Keeley's rebuff.

"I was telling Anna's father of our conversation last week, but I wasn't sure I had all the details exactly right. He asked me several questions which I couldn't answer." Lawrence hoped he could rekindle Keeley's original enthusiasm. The prospect of developing the land, not the bank position, was what really drew him to Shapely. It had been on his mind since Keeley first mentioned it.

"Well, what I had proposed was this — you own all this land, right? What is there — about four hundred acres?" Lawrence's ploy had worked. He nodded, not wanting to stop Keeley by agreeing aloud. "Fine —you put some of it, as much as necessary, up as collateral and the bank will lend you the capital to develop it. As you sell the developed lots, you pay back the bank. See?"

Lawrence *did* see. He saw an almost sure thing. It hadn't occurred to him that the land itself could be considered collateral. Then he stopped dreaming. "But my brother David and I own the land jointly. How would I handle that?"

Keeley shrugged. "How you do that is your business. Either offer to buy him out as you can or make him a partner, too."

"Are you suggesting that this arrangement would make *us* partners? You and I? I thought you were talking about a straight bank loan." Lawrence had taken notice of Keeley's earlier use of the word "partner" but thought he was just being effusive. Now he realized that it wasn't merely an affectation. *Who maneuvered whom into this discussion?*

"I was originally, but there is another possibility. We actually do become partners. You have the land. I'll put up the money for streets, sewers, what have you. We split the profits fifty-fifty. Or rather, I get fifty percent and you and your brother get fifty percent." He laughed and abruptly added, "I'm hungry. Let's order dinner." He flagged down the waitress, almost dismissing Lawrence. The server appeared immediately, almost as if she had been spying on them.

The dining room was at the end of the long corridor to the left of the lobby. Taking their drinks with them, they followed the waitress, who seated the pair at a table overlooking the New River. Although the river was hidden in the dark, the twinkling lights of the depot on its banks gave the illusion of movement below. Thurmond was alive, even at night.

Keeley studied the menu, recommended several entrees to Lawrence and then took the liberty of ordering for both of them. While Lawrence would normally have taken offense at this presumption, he was absorbed in Keeley's proposal and hardly noticed. Before they could resume the conversation, two men hailed Keeley from across the dining room and he excused himself to go visit them.

Lawrence sat back, mulling over the options Keeley had presented. *If I take out loans with the land as collateral, I risk losing it if the lots don't sell. All the risk will be mine. Of course, I'll be wealthy if they do sell. On the other hand, if Keeley puts up the money, we'll be sharing the risk as well as the profits. And he'll actually get more than I do since I have to share it with David. Maybe I should buy him out. What about Keeley's risk? How will he want to protect himself?*

Keeley returned just as the food appeared. Afraid Keeley would begin a new topic of conversation, Lawrence voiced his concerns. "Assuming my brother agrees to this development idea and you put up the money, how are you protected if the development fails?"

"Young man, it's not going to fail. Don't you see? The railroads are crisscrossing Wyoming County. People are moving there in droves. They have to have houses — low cost ones at that. Your hillside is perfect — close to town and accessible to the railroad. As for me, if things don't go as rapidly as we think they will, I can wait. I'm like a duck on a june-bug when I see a good deal, but I'm also as patient as hell watching it pay off."

Lawrence thought this over as he savored his pan-fried trout. Anna never fixed fish. Her meals had a decidedly English flavor; roast beef with Yorkshire pudding was her specialty when they could afford it. He recalled the advice of one of his Broadmoor teachers. It was corny, but true — *If you don't take a chance, you don't win the ranch.* He decided if he wasn't willing to take a risk, he'd never have the wealth and position he'd yearned for since his "Dickie-bird" days. *I always assumed I'd have to take out loans for whatever business I started. I just never realized that I had the collateral all along. Now is the time to make my move. Probably best not to complicate my relationship with my new boss by becoming business partners. Instead, I'll start small and only develop a few acres first.*

Keeley broke into his contemplation. "Of course, there's a third arrangement that protects me and keeps you from having to pay back any loans."

This almost casual suggestion momentarily hung in the air between them.

"What's that?" Lawrence asked expectantly.

"You sell me half of the land. We would become partners, but that would give you the development money you need. Then we work like hell to sell it all and we'll both make money."

Lawrence wiped his mouth and sat back. "That sounds so simple — much less complicated. But I...I'll have to talk to David and do some figuring. Lots of details to work out, but it does sound like a good arrangement." He could see the potential instantly. Cash in the bank would enable him to enter a world he'd only dreamed of before. He'd have his job as well; he certainly wouldn't be risking his family's livelihood by taking this plunge. He became almost giddy over the prospects for his future.

"Great! Now let's drop the business talk and enjoy ourselves. How about a brandy with your coffee to celebrate? After dessert would you like to go upstairs and play a little poker?"

At the mention of gambling, an immediate vision of his mother's sweet but disapproving face flashed through Lawrence's mind. "Thank you, sir. I'll have the brandy, but I'm not a gambler. I'm afraid my risk-taking extends only to business deals." He laughed, trying to make light of his refusal. He'd have given his right arm to see the gambling parlor, but he just couldn't put his mother's stern admonitions against "profligate gambling" out of his mind.

Keeley laughed heartily. "Very well. Perhaps you'll change your mind after you see how good it feels to win a deal or two." He clapped Lawrence on the shoulder. "I think we'll make a good team. Shapely will surely take notice of us."

After coffee and brandy, the two men shook hands warmly. Keeley made his way up the stairs to join the poker game; Lawrence gazed after him for a moment, wishing he'd been able to dispel the memory of his mother. Then excitement about his future overwhelmed him and he dashed out of the hotel and down the hill to share the news with Anna.

Eight

W hen Maggie's boyfriend, Scott Abbott suggested going to the West Virginia Archives in Charleston to conduct genealogical research, Maggie couldn't imagine what she'd look up. *My family has already traced its roots back to Adam. I won't find anything new up there.* But because she was crazy about him, and he was committed to finding his ancestors, Maggie agreed.

Saturday was crisp and sunny; more suited for a football game than an afternoon in a dark room full of musty records. As they drove, Maggie expressed her dilemma.

"Scott, my family has done this 'trace your roots' stuff to death. They know everyone clear back to England. Mother calls it 'ancestor worship'," she confided.

"You mean, you can trace your whole family, on both sides back to England?"

"No, just my daddy's," Maggie replied. "Mother never talked much about her family's background."

"Why not, didn't she know where they came from?" he asked.

"Oh, she knew all right, but she didn't talk about it," she answered, somewhat evasively.

"Why?" he persisted.

Although Maggie and Scott had been dating only a short time, Maggie felt more comfortable talking to him than she ever had with her ex-husband, Andrew, or anyone else, for that matter. She decided to share her Mother's fifty year-old secret with him.

"I didn't know this until a few years ago, but my mother's father died in prison," Maggie said quietly.

"Damn, baby, what did he do?"

For the rest of the short trip, Maggie told Scott the sketchy details that she knew from childhood about her grandfather, pointing out that apparently those facts either had been sanitized, or edited with a hatchet. What Maggie really had was family myth. And she had begun to seriously question it.

"What I always heard was how rich they were before the Depression and I know that my grandfather died very young. I also know Mother's mama came from England as a small child. But how can such a major fact just be swept under the rug? It's like a family pact to keep the younger generation from finding out about having a horse thief hanging in the family tree. All her brothers and sisters knew it, but none of their children. I asked some of my cousins and they were stunned, too!"

The incredulity Maggie felt about this crept into her voice and she realized she was talking to herself as much as to Scott. These questions had been on Maggie's mind since 1979 when her mother dropped this family bombshell.

"Well, Maggie, that's what you should research," he said simply. He had a great knack for cutting straight to the heart of the matter.

"How do I go about it?" she asked, intrigued.

He took her hand and smiled. "I'll show you when we get there."

The West Virginia Archives was housed in a fine marble edifice at the Capitol Complex along the banks of the Kanawha River. Facing a gold-domed Capitol building, it shared quarters with the State Museum and the Department of Culture and History. The couple entered an area that resembled the reading room of a small town library. It was complete with shelves on one side, long tables in the middle and the bespectacled librarian at the front desk. The sign at the front door forbade pens, rather than talking. Pens leave indelible marks on historical volumes, while a stern look from the librarian could stop most conversations. The windows opposite the stacks seemed designed only to shed an investigative light on the history housed there, for the view was of the bare concrete terrace that surrounded the building.

Maggie and Scott didn't linger here, however, for the real treasure lay beyond. As they walked through, Scott gave her a brief description of the books stored on the shelves. Passing through this sunny room into the microfilm projection room, they were temporarily blinded. Scott acted familiar with the sensation, but Maggie was disoriented, as if she had stepped into a movie theater on a bright summer day. As her eyes adjusted, she could see a half dozen people seated at whirring machines. They were staring into dimly lit screens and turning knobs. It struck her that they all looked like gamblers fixated on slot machines, hoping for a jackpot.

Behind this room, which was silent except for the whine of celluloid winding and unwinding on the spools, was the microfilm storage room. Steel cabinets with wide, shallow drawers lined the room. The labels marked what part of the state's history reposed in each tiny fire-proof tomb: *Cabell County Census, 1890-1900; Fayette County Death Certificates by year; Monroe County Births by year; Monroe County Births & Marriages,* etc. Every statistical addition, subtraction, multiplication or division of the state's residents was recorded on these spools of film.

What a treasure — but where do I begin? She realized that she didn't even know exactly what she wanted to find out, let alone how to begin searching for it. After Scott gave her an explanation of the microfilm protocol, "never return film to the drawers; you might put it in the wrong place," he went straight to work, for *he* had a plan and knew what or who he was trying to find. Maggie browsed the drawer labels for a while, traveling back in the state's history. *How will this help? I don't even know when he was born or died.*

Maggie felt like she was in a maze, not knowing where to turn or what reward was at the end if she found her way there. In her stupor she nearly knocked a blond, chubby woman flat on the floor. The woman was squatting to see the labels on the bottom row when Maggie started up the aisle, but Maggie didn't see her. Maggie walked right into the woman from the left, she toppled to her right; but like a Weeble she didn't fall down. Maggie was mortified and as the woman regained her balance, Maggie leaned down, apologized in a stage whisper and quickly dashed to the far side of the room. Still embarrassed, Maggie tried to act engrossed in the file labels there, hoping no one had seen the incident. To her surprise, she noticed that these drawers held microfilm copies of newspapers from all over the state.

If he was such a prominent man, surely his death would have been a big news story. Suddenly she was intrigued by what an old newspaper article could reveal. All Maggie knew was that he died during "The Great Depression," but not the exact year. *Searching these newspapers could take days.* Returning to *Cabell County Deaths for 1928-1932,* she gathered five spools of history in her arms.

Waiting patiently for a free microfilm reader, Maggie contemplated where this single act might take her. She instinctively knew none of her family would be willing to fill in any details of what she might discover. *After all, they haven't talked about it in fifty years, why would they open up now? Isn't it better, after all, to let sleeping dogs lie? That tack seemed to have held them all in good stead for their entire lives. What happened, besides his death in prison, that drove everyone to a pact of silence? And why would I want to open the doors to the past and find out?*

As Maggie mulled over these questions, the Weeble lady rose from a reader taking her notebook and pencil with her. Edging toward her seat, Maggie again smiled apologetically. She stacked her treasure boxes to one side, then realized she didn't know how to work the machine. Since Maggie usually followed her father's credo, "When all else fails, read the directions," she turned on the machine and put the film on the left spool and threaded it to the right, without asking the attendant if this was correct. The light came on, but no words appeared. She turned the right knob, which caused the film to advance; but still no words were visible. Next she turned the left knob and the film promptly unwound. After several more futile attempts, Maggie gave up and begged help from Scott, who was engrossed in the Kanawha County census records. It seemed so simple to Maggie when Scott did exactly what she had done; the difference was — he did it correctly.

As the film whirred successfully from left to right, positioned properly under the glass plate, pages of death certificates scrolled before Maggie's eyes. She felt a bit overwhelmed to see the final official record of so many people. *And this spool covers only 1928.* Maggie soon found that looking at endless records was hard. The blur of words spinning before her eyes, like a television set with a broken vertical hold, made her dizzy. She slowed down the pace, then realized it would take forever at her new speed. She stopped to take stock.

She knew that her grandfather had died after her mother and daddy were married, so she began again from the end, 1932. About halfway through the rolling names she found it — *Richard Lawrence Burgher. DOD – July 24, 1932, Age – 50 years, 1 month and 10 days old.* Maggie sat staring at the facts, trying to conjure up this person to whom she was related, from whom she had descended; but found she couldn't. It was odd; she thought she should feel something, but her memory bank held so few facts about this person that she could have been staring at the death certificate of a complete stranger rather than at that of her own grandfather. It made Maggie melancholy, however, to see any life cut so short. As she read, one line on the page captured her attention. It read, *Place of Death – Moundsville, WV.* Maggie swallowed hard, for she knew this was the site of the West Virginia State Penitentiary. At last she could match this fact with her mother's new version of the family story. *At least she's not lying about it now.*

Maggie printed the death certificate, took the spools back to the storage room, placing them on top of the cabinets as instructed, and headed toward the newspaper microfilm records. Now she had a date to look for. Quickly, she located *The Huntington Advertiser* for July 1932 and raced back to a film reader. As columns by local legendary, but long-dead journalists melted into recipes, weddings, high school sports and ads for $800 cars, Maggie scrolled through issue after issue. She worked slowly, careful not to miss the correct day. It was like seeing a series of Pathe newsreels in slow motion: the soup lines of the Depression, Roosevelt wins the presidency, WWI servicemen march on Washington, DC, to get bonuses promised them, Amelia Earhart flies solo across the Atlantic, the Lindbergh baby is kidnapped, Jack Sharkey beats Max Schmeling and the NY Giants win the World Series.

saloon, but the wind blew it farther on anyhow. A friend of Mr. Keeley's rushed into her home to save her things and threw them into the street. That proved to be the wrong thing to do as the mounds of clothes quickly caught fire there as well. Poor lady. Fortunately, before Mr. Keeley's bank was consumed, they moved the records and cash to the mine company vault in McDonald. He was distraught, however, for the building was destroyed and will take months to rebuild.

I was sorry to learn from your last letter that you were no longer seeing Robert. He seemed nice enough. Are there any new beaus to tell of? Write soon. Give my love to Mama and Papa. I'll write them next.

Your loving sister,

Nine

August 1910

There were times during Anna's second pregnancy she felt like she'd been sick since the moment of conception. Instead of the merely annoying heartburn she'd had with Eileen, she had suffered with gut-wrenching morning sickness for the first three months. Anna hated throwing up more than anything, but each morning she had faced losing her breakfast as soon as she ate it. Finally, she ate only tea and toast so the ordeal wouldn't last as long.

By her sixth month she was exhausted. At first, she attributed her lethargy to the double energy drain of being pregnant and caring for a toddler; but she knew plenty of women who had done that without complaint. Nevertheless, after the morning sickness stopped, she absolutely had no energy. After even the simplest tasks she had to lie down. She tried to rest only when Eileen was napping, but gradually it became difficult even to get up in the morning. Finally, the doctor had ordered bed rest. She had to give in and ask her mother for help.

Elizabeth Miller had come immediately. When Lawrence met her at the train station the following day, she was carrying what must have been the same valise in which she had brought all her worldly goods from England. Now it looked as if she'd brought them to Shapely. Lawrence sighed. He had agreed that they needed her help, but he wasn't looking forward to the lack of privacy her visit would cause. With only two bedrooms, his mother-in-law would be sleeping on the sofa. Lawrence hated that. *After this baby arrives, I'm going to find a larger house.*

Turning the care of the house and Eileen over to her mother had given Anna the rest she had needed — she seemed to have regained the color in her cheeks over the last few weeks. However, her mother feared that the flush was really due to the intense August heat. Despite Shapely's mountainous setting, that entire month had been sweltering. Anna's bed clothes were wet by 11 A.M. The dampness clung to the curtains and mildew formed in the shoes. Not even the evening breeze off the shady hillside behind the house provided enough relief for a good night's sleep.

On Thursday, after another night of sleeping miserably in her own sweat, Anna awoke around 5 A.M. with a dull ache in her lower back. She would have attributed it to the weeks in bed, but she'd felt this pain before. It was a precursor to labor. *Perhaps it's false labor; it's too soon for the baby.* She slowly rolled her lopsided body from her left side to her right, hoping for a more comfortable position, but not wanting to disturb Lawrence. *Maybe if I just lie still, it will subside.*

An hour later, when the alarm rang, the dull ache was still bothering her. Lawrence turned over to kiss Anna good morning and found her wide awake and watching him, as if she'd been waiting for him to open his eyes.

"You're awake early, love," he said sleepily as he reached to lay his hand on her hip. "Anything wrong?"

"I think I'm in labor, darling." Her face took on a pinched look, as she twisted again trying to ease the back pain.

Lawrence sat up, fully awake. "That can't be. It's much too soon, isn't it?"

"Well, I recognize this back pain. It's like no other except the monthly pains and I certainly am not having them. Anyway, it's not that much early, just a month." She didn't want to alarm him.

"Shall I call your mother?" He sounded concerned, now that he was convinced she knew what she was talking about.

"No, let her sleep a little longer. I'll try to get as comfortable as possible while you get ready for work. Then we can wake her, unless Eileen does it first."

"I'm not going to work if you are in labor, Anna," Lawrence said.

"Of course you are. If it really is labor, we can call you later."

Anna knew Lawrence was not good in situations like this. Sickness and pain made him uncomfortable. In fact, he'd left the house when Eileen was born because he couldn't bear hearing Anna scream. He gave in easily to her suggestion.

"Very well, but you have to promise your mother will call if you need me."

"I promise. I'd like you to be here with me — to hold my hand — at least at first. I know it scares you when I cry, but just knowing you are in the next room gives me comfort."

"I'll come as soon as you call, my love." He bent over the bed, kissed her and went to bathe and dress.

After Lawrence tiptoed out of the room, Anna slept again, fitfully. When a loud clap of thunder startled her out of sleep, she awoke disoriented and crying. She looked around the room, trying to take stock of her surroundings through bleary eyes. The back ache was gone, but in its place, she felt an extraordinary heaviness in her abdomen. Outside, rain washed against the house in waves — first from one direction, then another. The sheets on Anna's bed felt as if the window above it had been left open. And although the rain had broken the oppressive humidity, it was still hot and stuffy in the small, dark room.

She sat up, sobbing, trying to understand why. Frightened, she called out to her mother. Then, easing her body into the pillows while she collected her thoughts, she realized she was in labor. And just as suddenly, she recalled, in every detail, the dream that had frightened her. It was as terrifying as it had been in her childhood. Gratefully, for it broke the grip of the nightmare, she heard her mother calling her name.

"Anna, did you call me?" Elizabeth Miller knocked on Anna's door. "Anna?"

Anna wiped her eyes with the sheet and answered in a small voice, "Yes, Mama. Please come in."

Elizabeth Miller entered the bedroom and rushed to the bedside. Sitting down, she put her hand on Anna's forehead and brushed the hair away from her eyes. Seeing that her daughter had been crying, she said. "Anna, dear, what is 'hit? 'Ave the pains gotten that bad? Lawrence told me you thought you were in labor. I looked in a few hours ago and you were sleeping so I didn't disturb you." Elizabeth's Yorkshire accent peeked through her concern.

"No, Mama. The pain isn't bad at all, but I woke in a start from a bad dream and it frightened me. It's the same dream I used to have as a child. Do you remember? Remember how I used to come jump in your bed? Once I got there I would snuggle down in the familiar smells and warmth. Then I would feel safe and could fall asleep again. I wonder why I had that dream today?"

"Yes, I do remember. But you would never tell us the dream, only that you 'ad one and 'hit scared you." At her mother's touch, Anna stopped crying.

"I never told you because it seemed so real that I was afraid it was a memory instead. The details never changed; I dreamed it over and over. Even as a teenager, it scared me. By then I was too old to jump into your bed, so instead I would sneak into the bathroom, sprinkle your dusting powder onto my pillow and climb back in bed. I would nestle my face into your scent and then I could fall asleep."

"Poor Anna. Tell me the dream now, can you?" She stroked her daughter's arm as Anna repeated the dream in minute detail.

"In my dream I am alone, walking in the dark on a slippery wooden floor which tilts crazily first to one side then another — peering into doors which open into big rooms full of people and I'm looking for something or someone, but I don't know what or who. Outside it is pitch black and the air is full of moisture; I can only see clearly when I look into the brightly lit rooms. Suddenly, I am in a white maze, with turns to the right, then left and then right again. Before me is a steep metal staircase with more corridors below. I climb down the narrow stairs, hoping that what I'm looking for is at the bottom. As I descend, I can hear my leather heels striking the metal treads, causing an echo in the stuffy stairwell. From below, the hot air which smacks me in the face smells like the kitchen garbage after supper, sour and damp.

"I follow the lower corridors, choosing left, right and then left until they open into a wide carpeted room filled with men so tall their heads are in the clouds — giants! They remind me of Andersen's fairy tale giants. Hiding in the corner, all I can see are legs; huge legs wearing dark pants and leather boots. The room is packed tightly with these enormous men. I think that the object of my search is on the other side of this room. I try to squeeze through the crowd but I continually bump into another and another pair of those muscular legs. In front of me a huge hand drops down from the clouds holding a small burning stick; but just as quickly it disappears again into the heavens. From above the filmy sky, the loud voices and gruff laughter sound like thunder. They frighten me and I begin to cry quietly. At first none of the giants seem to notice me, until suddenly one of them leans down from the clouds and speaks to me. I jump at the sound of his booming voice so close to my ear.

"'Oh, ho; what have we here? Where did you come from, sweetheart?' he growls at me and I recoil from his hot, stale breath. When he talks, smoke comes out of his mouth. I panic and turn in the opposite direction to evade this ugly monster, but I run into another pair of thick legs. I am trying to squeeze between them when another arm drops below the cloud line and grabs me. His huge hand wraps completely around my forearm and I'm afraid he will snap it like a twig.

"'Where are you going, little one? Where is your mother?' he says, blowing more smoke.

"In that instant, I realize who I am looking for. 'Mother,' I think, 'I've got to find my mother; she'll save me.' I jerk my arm away, dart between the fat legs of the giant in front of me and wiggling like a snake, I slip through the sea of legs and through the wide opening in the wall. My heart is pounding, but I don't stop until I am through the door.

"Outside in the thick damp air again, I start running but my feet slip on the swaying floor. Nearby in the thick darkness I can hear a child crying and then I hear your voice calling my name. Now I'm flying across the wet floor; my feet barely touch it. I run toward your voice, but I trip and fall into a mass of damp cloth. It smells like you. Then I wake up and I'm always crying."

She was crying again with the retelling of the dream. "Did anything like that ever happen to me? Somehow I have it mixed up in my mind with our trip from England. But, in all your stories, you never mentioned me getting lost on the ship. Did I?"

"Bless your 'eart. In fact, you did. We never talked about 'hit. I 'oped you'd forgotten. But 'hit 'appened almost like your dream. You must 'ave got up to go to the toilet and slipped out without me. You know, they were way down the corridor — not in our cabin. I suppose you got lost coming back and wandered into one of the parlors. I woke up, maybe when you shut the door, and started calling to you in the 'allway. You finally 'eard me — I'd taken Joseph and gone looking for you. 'Hit was storming and we were all soaked by the time we got back to our cabin. You cried in my lap until you went back to sleep. Even Joseph cried; you must 'ave got 'im going."

Elizabeth stroked her daughter's hand. "Poor child. You should 'ave told me about the dream years ago. Per'aps 'hit would 'ave gone away." She wiped Anna's tears with her apron hem.

Anna moved closer to her mother. The scent of lavender reached her before she gained her mother's lap. "Mama, your cologne is so familiar, I'd know your smell anywhere." She snuggled closer and could have slept again, but Eileen began calling from her bedroom down the hall.

"I'll get 'er. Would you like some tea?" Elizabeth asked, lifting Anna's head from her lap.

"That would be lovely, but I'm afraid the bed needs changing, again. Would you do that first?"

Before her mother could get the clean linens from the hall closet, Anna felt the first hard contraction. She let out a yelp, stopping her mother in the doorway.

"What's that, Missy? Real labor?"

"Yes, I'm afraid so. For the past few hours the pains have been very mild, but now I think I'm really going to have this baby." Anna sounded somewhat surprised, as if giving birth were not the natural culmination of a pregnancy.

"Shall I go next door and get Beulah to watch Eileen? That way, I can take care of you."

"That's a good idea. She offered to take care of her when the baby came, but she'll probably be surprised to see you today."

"What about Lawrence? Shall I call 'im? Or the doctor?"

"No, let's not do that yet. Lawrence is probably in a meeting and will just worry if he can't get home. It may be hours yet. We can call Dr. McClelland when the pains get closer together." Anna lay back in the unchanged sheets and smiled as she watched her mother bustle purposefully through the doorway. Anna had always admired her mother's ability to "take charge" of any situation. Today it gave her a real sense of security.

By the time Elizabeth returned thirty minutes later to check on Anna, her pains were five minutes apart and she was sweating. It was high noon. "Mama, the pains are much closer together and hard. They really sped up while you were gone. Perhaps you *should* call Lawrence and Dr. McClelland."

Elizabeth rushed out, made her calls, checked on Eileen and was back before another wave of pain surged through Anna. Elizabeth pulled a chair close to the bed and took Anna's hand.

"Did you reach Lawrence? Is he on the way?" Anna asked.

"No, darling, I wasn't able to find 'im. 'E and Mr. Keeley 'ad left the bank about an 'our ago. I left a message, though. I'm sure 'e didn't expect the baby this soon. Dr. McClelland's office said 'e'd be over in about thirty minutes."

"Talk to me, Mama. Tell me the stories of our trip from England. All I remember for sure is that the ship was taller than any building I'd ever seen. People on board were waving. I thought they were waving at me. I love your stories. I've heard them so many times, that I feel like I do remember; but I want to hear them again."

"All right. You take my 'and and when a pain comes, you squeeze. Cry if you must and I'll talk."

Elizabeth took a deep breath and began. "When you were three and your brother Joseph was five we sailed from England on an ocean liner to join your papa in this country." She spoke in the same simple way, as she had in Anna's childhood. Anna relaxed and listened. "It was a grand ship. We 'ad a cabin with bunk beds, a chair and a table. You and Joseph slept together in the lower bunk, so you wouldn't

some laudanum for the pain and she's resting more comfortably now. But I am concerned a bit, as well. I'd have thought she would be farther along, particularly since it's her second baby. I'll watch her for a while and will call you if anything changes. Meanwhile, could you gather some clean towels and such? You know what I'll need — water and lots of towels."

Elizabeth appeared both relieved to have something to do and grateful that the doctor was now in charge. She sat by the window watching for Lawrence, hoping that he had returned to the bank and received the message she had left. The movement of the air in the hot parlor was almost imperceptible as the overhead fan whirred rhythmically. Elizabeth sat motionless except for the fingers of her right hand, which lay on the arm of the chair. Over and over her fingers moved — pressing one at a time, from pinkie to index — as if she were counting them, making sure she still had them all. It was a nervous tic she had acquired from her mother, whether genetically or by imitation, she didn't know.

The front door opened with a bang. Elizabeth started. She must have napped, for she woke with the confusion of not knowing where she was. Upon seeing Lawrence, however, she was instantly awake.

"Thank goodness you are 'ere. Anna's 'aving a bad time, seems like. Dr. McClelland is in there with 'er. "E gave 'er some laudanum, so she's not in as much pain, but the baby isn't much closer to being born, either."

Lawrence blanched and rushed to the bedroom. He knocked and the doctor responded, "Not now. I'll be out shortly."

Lawrence returned to the parlor, looking somewhat lost. He bent down and began gathering Eileen's toys into his arms. "Where is Eileen?" he asked his mother-in-law.

"She is staying with Beulah until the baby comes," Elizabeth explained. "'Earing her mother scream was scaring her." Elizabeth stared in wonder at Lawrence; she had never seen him tidy up a room. She couldn't know his uncharacteristic behavior was the result of his nervousness.

A few minutes later, when the doctor emerged from Anna's room, he looked agitated. He spoke directly to Lawrence. "Good afternoon,

Mr. Burgher. Your wife is resting more comfortably, now that I've administered laudanum. However, her contractions have also slowed, and I'm not sure why. It may be a long wait. I have to make another house call; but I'll be back in, say, two hours to check on her. If you need me before then, have the operator ring the office. They'll know where to find me. She'll be fine. Just needs one of you to sit with her." As he spoke, he rolled down his sleeves, replaced his cuff-links and put on his jacket. He gathered up his hat and bag, nodded and left.

Lawrence said, "I'll go sit with her for a while. You've been at it quite a spell. Perhaps you should let Beulah know the situation." He disappeared down the hall without waiting for his mother-in-law to reply.

Around 3:30 P.M. Lawrence came back into the parlor; his shirt was damp and his tie askew. He said to Elizabeth, "Can you sit for a while? I'm hungry. Is there anything to eat?

Elizabeth looked shocked. "You can eat at a time like this? If I ate, I would be sick as a dog. Look in the ice-box. I think there may be some chicken."

Anna had told her mother Lawrence rarely, if ever, fixed his own supper, so she waited for him to ask her to get it. He did not disappoint her.

"Would you fix me a plate? Nothing much, just a piece of chicken," he asked, as if it were her place to do so.

"Lawrence Burgher, I couldn't even look at food right now. If you want 'hit, you get 'hit!" She drew herself up to her full height and marched into Anna's room, leaving Lawrence to fend for himself.

During Elizabeth's turn at Anna's bedside, the pain returned. It seemed to be even more intense but Elizabeth rationalized it was because Anna was worn out. An hour crawled by with little or no conversation between mother and daughter — only the unspoken communication of touch passed between them. Elizabeth stroked Anna's hand and Anna gripped her mother's like a vise. However, with each successive pain, Anna's cries grew louder and more sustained. Both women were soaking wet and limp with fatigue. More than once, Elizabeth's lips moved as she prayed, *"Dear Lord, deliver* her. I'd rather be going through this myself than watching my child suffer."

Elizabeth was anxiously waiting for Lawrence to come to spell her, when the doorbell rang. She heard it several times. Thinking he was in the house, she said to herself, *"Where is he? Why doesn't he answer the door?"* Finally she patted Anna's hand reassuringly, laid it on the bed and slipped out of the room to answer it herself. At the door was Dr. McClelland, but Lawrence was nowhere to be found. Elizabeth brought the doctor up to date. "She's in a lot of pain again and the cramps are much closer together."

"I'll go examine her now," he said. taking off his jacket as he walked toward the bedroom.

Elizabeth made a quick round of the small house looking for Lawrence; but he clearly wasn't there. Muttering under her breath, Elizabeth complained to the empty rooms. *"Surely 'e isn't outside in this 'eat. I can't believe 'e would leave. I know 'hit isn't pleasant to 'ear Anna cry, but I'm doing 'hit. The least 'e could do is be 'ere. 'E left when Eileen was born, too. Men can be such babies. 'E probably went to the diner to get something to eat rather than lift a finger 'isself. I 'ope if she ever 'as a real crisis, 'e'll be here to 'elp."*

She was on the porch when she heard the doctor call her. "Mrs. Miller, I need you. Anna is very close to delivering the baby. Bring some fresh water and help me, will you?"

Elizabeth dashed into the house, gathered what the doctor needed and headed for the bedroom. Again she prayed, *"Dear Lord, I surely don't want to do this, but..."* she trailed off as he began to give orders. The next hour was a blur of activity that Elizabeth told Dr. McClelland she hoped she could someday forget, and that Anna would never know what had happened.

Over the steady directions of Dr. McClelland, Elizabeth exhorted Anna to "push" while Anna moaned and cried out for Lawrence and, alternately, for God.

Finally, through the tangle of bloody sheets and bare legs, Elizabeth saw the glint of steel and watched. Her expression twisted with agony as Dr. McClelland inserted the forceps to guide the baby to the outside world. Without a word, he delivered the child. With obvious horror Elizabeth saw that the umbilical cord was wound tightly around its tiny neck. The skin of the baby in the doctor's huge palm was the color of a fresh bruise. Quickly, he laid the limp infant on Anna's still distended belly and cut the cord. He leaned over and blew into its tiny mouth, but the child did not respond. To both doctor and assistant, it was obvious that the baby was dead.

While Dr. McClelland delivered the afterbirth and tended to his unconscious patient, Elizabeth took the small bundle to the dresser, laid it on a towel and through her tears, began to clean the body of Anna's second daughter.

Shapely West Virginia
September 30, 1910

My dear sister Jenny,

It is with a heavy heart that I write you while still recovering from the birth and tragic death of our child. Oh, Jenny; I feel so empty. I pray that you never experience this pain. To carry a child, give birth and awaken with empty arms must be the most desolate feeling a woman could possibly have. I pray daily for strength and understanding of God's will for that child.

But I am recovering my physical strength. Mama is still with us, bustling about after Eileen and me. You know how she loves being in charge. I think Lawrence is worn out with the lack of privacy, but I still need her help. Eileen chatters like a magpie now and we can actually understand her, at least most of the time.

Poor Lawrence was almost inconsolable over the baby. He spent so much energy trying to console me, that he became quite despondent. As if his being here would have made a difference either to the baby or me. I was in so much distress that I don't even recall Mama being there. Mercifully, God takes away those awful memories, or women would never have second babies. I didn't blame him for leaving and I wish he wouldn't blame himself. Mama was angry, but I think she has forgiven him, too. I believe women are simply meant for dealing with the true tragedies of life, while men are not. They are better left to handle business.

Lawrence and Mr. Keeley are hoping to advertise for the sale of lots in the Burgher-Keeley Addition by spring. The bank is doing nicely, as well. Lawrence says deposits have increased and I suppose that is good. The new bank building is grand. It faces the corner of First Street and Wyoming Ave. and has black and white marble floors. The president's office is on the mezzanine overlooking the lobby and is paneled in beautiful walnut. Lawrence says perhaps one day, he'll be the president and that will be his office.

Did you hear of the tragic murder of poor Dr. McClelland? You know he was the doctor who attended me at the birth. He was tending to the wound of the druggist last Sunday when a man who was already inebriated came in demanding a draught of whiskey. The saloons were closed, of course; and he thought he could obtain medicinal alcohol. The druggist refused, as the man had no prescription. The two fought; Dr. McClelland took the side of the druggist and the man pulled out his pistol and shot both of them, right there in the drug store. The entire town went to the doctor's funeral. Now we will have to find another doctor to come to Shapely.

Your loving sister,

Anna

December 16, 1912
Shapely, West Virginia

Rebecca Nelson Knox
Charleston, West Virginia

Dearest Rebecca,

It seems such a long time since we have seen one another, nearly two years. I do feel a part of your life, however, as you are such a dedicated correspondent. I regret that I am not more regular with my replies; but with a new baby and a new house, I seem to have very few free moments in which to write. Therefore, I take pen in hand this afternoon while the children are napping to bring you news from Shapely.

I was delighted to hear about the birth of your son! I know Eugene must be so proud. While both Lawrence and I were very grateful for the safe birth of our daughter in November, I feel certain he had hoped for a boy. Thank goodness this pregnancy and birth were so easy. It was as if God were doing me a favor after the horrible experience I had with our second child.

We have named her Sara Jane — partly after Mama. You know we named the baby who died after Lawrence's mother, which hurt Mama's feelings. But now she has forgiven us and is delighted with her namesake.

When we learned I was with child again, Lawrence found a new house just below his development and we moved in early October. What a lovely home it is! It has a fine front porch which spreads from side to side and overlooks the town. He had a windmill built to pump the well-water to a cistern, so we always have plenty of water. Best of all, it has a very large kitchen and four bedrooms. Each of the girls will have her own room and there is an extra for company. Rebecca, you must come see us and the new house! We had room in the parlor for a proper Christmas tree this year and the house looks really festive.

Lawrence is busier than ever. If he isn't at the bank, he's riding his new sorrel mare around the real estate development. He recently began mining the coal under the land, as well. I'm so proud of him. Folks here in Shapely have such respect for him. He sold one of his lots for the building of the new school house. I am delighted that he has proven my Papa wrong. Remember how upset Papa was when we eloped?

Mr. Keeley finally has quit his lawsuit against the newspapers. Lawrence said he really didn't care a whit about what the papers printed, so long as he was able to open his saloon. Once he obtained the proper licenses, he abandoned his efforts in the libel suit. Mr. Keeley seems willing to engage in any business that will make money. I'm glad Lawrence is keeping to more respectable business pursuits.

With warm wishes for a wonderful holiday season, I remain, your loving friend,

P.S. I trust none of your friends lost relatives in the tragic sinking of the Titanic. We read the lists with dread, but did not have any acquaintances aboard. I read of one family in Huntington, and some in Charleston; but we did not know them.

P.P.S. Have you read the wonderful novel by Edith Wharton? Ethan Frome, it is called. The story is told partly as a flashback and is very sad. The ending is quite a surprise, so I won't spoil it. Please tell me what you think of it.

Bank of Shapely
First Street at Wyoming Ave
Shapely, West Virginia

March 20th, 1913

David D. Burgher
Broadmoor Business College.
Staunton, Va.

My dear David:

As your graduation date rapidly approaches, I
hope you are giving strong consideration to my
offer to come to Shapely and join us as bookkeeper at the bank. With the increasing success
of our real estate ventures, Keeley and I are
becoming hard put to handle the many administra-
tive details of both businesses. We would both
welcome the addition of an employee whose
ability we recognize and in whom we can put our
confidence.

I realize that you have not made a final decision as to the professional direction in which
you wish to go, however the practical experience
you will gain in banking will carry over well to
many other professions, should you choose another in the future.

As I await your response with eagerness,
I remain,

Your brother,

Ten

July 4, 1913

I n Shapely, West Virginia, the Fourth of July not only celebrated the birth of the nation; it also celebrated the town's birth. Actually, no one was really sure of the date of Shapely's founding because the records regarding its true settlement were in conflict. Some said the first settlers named it on June 1 and others said July 1, 1859. Even the name was misspelled on some old documents — Shapely or Shapley — no one was really sure. Therefore, in 1900, the town-fathers chose July 4 as the town's founding date and officially declared the name to be 'Shapely.' Perhaps they thought the town had a pleasing shape; on the map it looked as if it were cradled between two mountains.

By now, thirteen years later, a traditional celebration had been established. The buildings all over town were festooned with red, white and blue bunting and flags were hung in all the shop windows, even the saloon's. The entire town closed. Miners, loggers, farmers and railroad men came from the surrounding camps and farms to Shapely. Everyone, young and old, took part in the celebration near the banks of Piney Creek.

This year, the town folks had an extra reason to celebrate — the toll bridge across Piney Creek had finally been completed. Today, before the parade, was the official grand opening and ribbon cutting ceremony. The Mayor, Mr. Josiah Dunnigan, was to drive his buggy across the new bridge from the residential side of Shapely, stop his while the men of the Methodist church hauled long tables to the church yard for the lemonade stands. Anna, David and the children secured a spot near the front of the crowd with a good view of the bridge. Mr. Keeley was to speak a few words before the ribbon cutting, and Anna didn't want to miss his speech. Although Anna still wasn't sure she really liked Keeley, he *was* Lawrence's partner and she had promised Lawrence a full report. The two partners had become very influential citizens since Lawrence moved to Shapely three years before. The Burgher-Keeley Addition had added over fifty new homes to the town in the past few years and they owned the only bank in town. Therefore, Keeley had been asked to make the celebratory speech, while Lawrence headed the parade.

The band stopped playing at about 11:45 and the crowd grew quiet in anticipation. Standing on the bridge were several men, some of whom Anna did not know. She assumed they were with the bridge construction company. However, she quickly spotted Keeley and several other prominent businessmen; these she pointed out to David. To begin the ceremony, Keeley picked up a large white megaphone and walked to the mouth of the bridge.

"Ladies and Gentlemen," he yelled and his words were repeated, a half-syllable behind, by the echo in the valley. "Ladies and Gentlemen, we are gathered here today to celebrate three things: the birth of our nation, one hundred thirty-seven years ago; the founding of our great city, forty-one years ago; and the opening today of our long-awaited toll-bridge." The crowd roared its approval. He continued his remarks by thanking the designers, the construction company and the citizens for their support of the project. "And now Mayor Dunnigan will cut the ribbon and declare the bridge officially open."

Keeley raised his hand in a signal to the mayor on the other end of the bridge. He whipped his horse and started forward in his buggy. The ribbons streaming from the horse's harness and from the back of the buggy fluttered with the motion. He covered the short distance in a trice, brought up the horse and got out to cut the ribbon. Just as he stepped forward to accept the scissors from Keeley, the band began to play again. The sudden clash of cymbals startled the mayor's horse and it lunged forward, jerking the reins from the man's hand. The horse bolted past the mayor, broke through the still taut ribbons and raced past the startled dignitaries. As the empty buggy clattered off the bridge, mothers grabbed loose children and shouted at their neighbors to jump out of the way. Down Wyoming Street dashed the frightened horse with the driver-less buggy jerking wildly from side to side. Several men took up the chase, shouting in vain at the spooked horse. As the group disappeared, through the cloud of dust, Keeley raised the megaphone again in an attempt to restore order. "Well, folks," he said with a chuckle. "I guess that's one way to cut the ribbons. The Shapely Toll Bridge is officially open. Mr. Mayor, did you feed that horse this morning? I'll bet he's just gone home to eat." The crowd laughed and applauded, now that they could see no one had been hurt during the incident.

The parade which followed went off like clock-work. The band regrouped in front of the picnic area, the Masonic Mounted Equestrian Unit lined up in formation and the children marched in a semblance of parade cadence, waving their flags at the applauding audience.

As they passed Anna, David and the children, Eileen tugged at her mother's skirt. "Mama, why can't I march in the parade?"

"Next year, darling. You must be in school to march. You'll be able to march next year." This satisfied Eileen, who was fast becoming a sweet-tempered, amiable child.

"Then when Sara gets to be six, will she get to march, too?" asked Eileen.

"Yes, she will. You'll both be marching and we'll be so proud of you," Anna beamed.

"I hope the horse doesn't run away that time, too," replied Eileen.

Anna ignored this. Instead she said, "Did you see your father, Eileen? He was on the horse in front. Did you see his fancy hat?"

"I saw him, Mama. He looked beautiful," Eileen smiled up at her mother and clapped.

When Lawrence arrived at the picnic, he reported that the mayor's horse had found its way home; but the buggy had lost a wheel. Keeley joined the Burgher family for supper and entertained them by mimicking the look on Mayor Dunnigan's face when the horse bolted and broke through the ribbons. He was funnier than usual and Anna wondered if he might have started nipping on his flask right after the ceremony. As evening approached, Lawrence and Anna settled themselves on a quilt to watch the fireworks. Eileen tucked herself into her father's crossed legs, while Anna rocked Sara in her arms, crooning to her. The gas lights on Wyoming Street had been lit and with the dusk came the commingled smells of newly mown grass and river dampness. They reminded Anna of Thurmond; despite herself, she felt a twinge of homesickness. She reached out and patted Eileen's arm.

"Mama, will the fireworks be loud?" Eileen asked her, trying to squirm out of her father's lap to sit with Anna. Before she could reply, Lawrence pulled Eileen back down and said, "If they scare you, Eileen, we can go home, but you liked them last year. Don't you remember?"

"No, I don't; but I think I'm scared this year," she said, yielding to the suggestion. Eileen continued to fidget and struggle to get loose. "Mama, I want to sit with you."

"Don't put thoughts in her head, Lawrence. She'll be fine," Anna chided quietly. "Stay there Eileen, I've got Sara in my lap. Sit still and watch. The rockets will be beautiful." Lawrence had little patience with squirming daughters. Anna knew that with little provocation, he would take her home.

Just as the fireworks were about to begin, Keeley shouted above the crowd, "Gentlemen, hold your horses; one runaway today is enough." Several men in the group near him nodded and laughed knowingly as the first volley was fired, accompanied by the ringing of all the town's church bells. Immediately Eileen screamed and covered her ears with her tiny hands. Lawrence leaned down. "It's all right, Eileen, they are way over on the bridge." He covered her hands with his own.

The second round of firecrackers exploded and Eileen began to cry. "Take me home, Father, I'm scared. Please, please, please!"

Lawrence gathered his daughter in his arms, stood up quickly and said to his wife, "It's no use. She'll just spoil it for everyone around us. I'll take her home on Jessy. You and David stay and come home in the buggy."

"No, we'll both leave. Sara is asleep and I don't want the noise to waken her. Leave Jessy for David and we'll all go in the buggy. David, do you mind? Edward is still here; you can join him. Give me a moment to gather up our things, Lawrence and I'll be ready." Anna juggled Sara in one arm as she picked up the picnic basket. David stood, allowing Lawrence to recover the quilt. Eileen continued to cry, her head buried in her Father's shoulder and her hands covering her ears. As they picked their way through the patchwork of families seated on the ground, Eileen stopped crying.

"I'm not scared now, Father. It's not loud anymore." She had lifted her head in the momentary lull between rounds of explosives.

"We're going home anyway, Eileen. Maybe next year, you'll enjoy it," her Father said sternly. Eileen began to wail again; this time the tears were those of unhappiness, not fright.

As David turned back to watch the next display of fireworks, Keeley approached him. "Well, David, not much of a welcome to Shapely, was it? Sorry your family had to leave so suddenly."

"Oh, it's just fine, Mr. Keeley. Actually, I sort of welcome the chance to be alone. I love Lawrence and his family, but I'm not much used to being around children all the time. They are just so...constant, you know?"

"I know. What you need is a good stiff drink. Enough of families, lemonade and fireworks. Why don't we go have a drink and get to know one another."

"Where would we get a drink? It's a holiday and the saloons are closed," David replied.

"True enough. But, I've got the keys to my saloon. I reckon a fellow can drink his own liquor, holiday or no. Don't you?"

The two men left the picnic grounds with the fireworks still exploding from the bridge and headed to the Shapely Saloon on First Street. Lawrence's mare danced uneasily, unfamiliar with the rider on her back, while Keeley sat astride his black stallion with the confidence of a seasoned rider. "It's been a while since I rode a horse; she seems to sense it. At school we did a lot of walking or used a buggy,"

David told Keeley. He was doing his best to keep the skittish horse under control. Within a few blocks Keeley stopped. The two men tied their mounts to the rail and Keeley unlocked the doors to his saloon and graciously waved David inside.

"I don't know if you heard the story about my lawsuit against the newspapers. They wrote derogatory stories about me to keep me from getting a saloon license. I sued them for $75,000; but when I got the license, I dropped the libel suits. Bastards! I'd bet anything one of the owners of the paper wanted to open his own saloon. Anyway, I beat them to the punch. And it's been doing real well, too." As he talked, Keeley had turned on a lamp behind the bar, and was looking through the bottles for the brand he preferred. "What do you drink, David?" he asked.

"I'll take a neat bourbon. Thank you," David responded as he surveyed Keeley's bar. Behind Keeley, the gleaming walnut bar-back held a mirror nearly as large as the wall itself. Ornate carvings surrounded the sides of the mirror. The artist had also fashioned an elaborately carved semi-nude woman leaning over the top edge. David whistled. "She's quite risque for Shapely, West Virginia," he remarked, but Keeley made no reply. Tables seating four each lined the right side of the long, narrow room and bar stools stood at attention below the wooden lady. At the rear, David could see another room and at least one pool table.

"A man after my own heart," laughed Keeley. "Why ruin good spirits with ice or anything else, for that matter?" Keeley came from behind the bar carrying two short glasses and a bottle of Kentucky straight bourbon. "Best in the house," he boasted as he set them on the table. Keeley poured two shots and picked up his glass in a toast. "To David Burgher. May his association with the Bank of Shapely be a long and prosperous one."

"Thank you Mr. Keeley. I look forward to it." He clicked his glass against that of his new boss.

"For God's sake, you've got to drop that 'Mr. Keeley' stuff. You make me think you are addressing my old man. Either call me Edward or Keeley like everyone else does. If we're going to work together, you've got to be less formal. Tell me something about yourself,

David. Of course, I know where you were born and all that from Lawrence, but I want to know you — what you want from life."

"Well, Edward...how's that?" David laughed at the easy change in his appellation for Keeley. "Well, as you know Lawrence and I grew up on the farm. After our father died, we lived with our uncle in Mt. Hope. I had a regular childhood and after normal school, I followed Lawrence to Broadmoor Business School. I could never have gone there if Lawrence hadn't paid my tuition. I worked as a messenger boy for spending money, but Lawrence bought the books and paid all my fees. Before I enrolled, I figured I'd become an accountant; after taking the required classes, that seemed so limiting. I studied all the business courses I could, hoping to run a business someday. I really don't want to own my own concern, but I'd make a hell of a manager for someone else."

Keeley tipped the bottle toward David, asking silently if he wanted another. David nodded.

"A good business manager is hard to find. You should not have any trouble with your career choice, if you ever decide to leave us, that is. And, of course, I want to make sure you don't. I guess Lawrence has told you, I've been in several businesses myself. I didn't have the opportunity to go to college. My old man worked in the steel mills and thought college was for sissies. But I've worked all my life. Worked as a stock boy, a baggage handler, dabbled in the dry goods and hardware business...that's how I got the injury that makes me limp. One day I was up on the ladder putting away a crate of shingles at my store — the stock boy had quit — and it fell from the shelf . Knocked me off the ladder and then hit me in the lower back. Never did a day of manual labor after that. Secret to success — get someone else to do the hard work, you do the managing. I told that to Lawrence when he came to work with me, and he has found it to be good advice."

"What other businesses are you involved in?" David asked in a curious tone.

"Coal mining, lumber, banking, and of course, real estate development." Keeley's diamond ring flashed in the lamp light as he downed his third whiskey. "If my old man could see me now," he mused. "Of course, the old son-of-a-bitch is dead. God rest his black soul. He was bad to drink and gave my mother no end of heartache. Life with him was either black or white. When he'd swear off spirits and stay home, there wasn't a funnier man alive. But when he'd go back to the saloons...some days you took your life in your hands just going to get him."

"I can hardly remember my father. I was only six when he died. I think I remember his funeral, but perhaps I only recall hearing the stories of it. I don't even have a photograph of him," David confided in Keeley. "I'm not sure I remember what he looked like. I guess we were too poor to have portraits made, or maybe they just weren't important to farmers, back then."

Keeley continued as if David hadn't spoken. He seemed lost in his own memories. "I remember the night I nearly beat the shit out of my old man. My sister was sick and my mother sent me out looking for him. It took me two hours. I went to every saloon I had ever found him in. When I finally spotted him, he was drunk and ready to fight. That was what he loved to do, next to drinking. I tried to reason with him, but he turned on me. He accused me of wanting the buggy to go out with my friends. Called me a lazy son-of-a bitch because I wanted to go to college instead of working in the mill like he did. As I reached for his arm, to steer him out the door, he swung at me and busted my lip. I almost lit into him, but I knew if I did I'd probably kill him, so I turned around and took the buggy home myself. I left home the next day. I didn't go back until he died at fifty-six. That was almost twenty years later." Keeley swallowed his drink and laughed. "Seems strange for me to be drinking after what I've been through, doesn't it? I don't do it often, because I'm afraid the acorn doesn't fall too far from the tree. I'd never want to do that to a son of mine. But I swore that I'd never feel that powerless again, and I haven't. I'll do whatever it takes to stay on top."

"I'm surprised you even own a saloon, Edward," David said cautiously as if he had the feeling that Keeley would be sorry tomorrow he had shared this story. But he continued to listen. He had always been fascinated with men like Edward Keeley.

"Shit, I'd open a whore house if it would make money. It's not up to me to keep men sober. What they do is their own business. I never blamed the saloon keepers for my dad's drinking. It was his problem, sure enough. Besides, I'm Irish. And the Irish love their spirits." Keeley laughed heartily.

David glanced at his pocket watch. "I'd better head home. Anna and Lawrence will be worried. The festivities have been over for an hour."

"Are you sure? I know where a poker game is. We could go play a few hands. Do you play?" Keeley stood, but left the bottle and empty glasses on the table.

"I certainly do. I played at school to pass the time when I wasn't studying. But I'd better not tonight. Thanks for the drinks, though," said David as he and Keeley walked toward the door.

"Well, some day we'll go over to Thurmond and I'll take you to the Dunglen Hotel. They've got a hellava poker parlor. I tried to get Lawrence to go one night, but he said his mother had preached for years against gambling. How come you aren't of the same mind?"

Out in the street David replied, "I guess I got over it at school. We didn't play for high stakes, but I was good at it. Enjoyed winning. I think Lawrence would too, if he'd let himself."

"Maybe we'll have to work on that together, hmm, David? I'd like to see him loosen up a bit."

David laughed, but made no comment. "I'll see you on Monday, Edward," the young Broadmoor graduate said to his new employer.

Eleven

January 25, 1916

Despite the cold rain that had washed over southern West Virginia for the past week, the daily Virginian Railroad train from Huntington arrived in Shapely on Tuesday at 2:30 P.M. — right on time. Twenty or so people stepped, one by one, from the two passenger cars, glanced up at the downpour and snapped open their umbrellas. Among them was Edward Keeley. Most of the passengers dashed into the station to retrieve their baggage, but not Keeley. With a sheaf of papers under his left arm and the umbrella in his right hand, he left the platform and picked his way across the Wyoming Avenue boardwalk toward the Bank of Shapely. Trying to avoid the sea of mud the dirt road had become, he resembled a tight-rope walker as his knock-kneed gait caused the umbrella to bob with each step.

The bank had closed for the day, but the two brothers inside had been watching his progress and as Keeley approached the door, it opened and he stepped inside. Lawrence and David greeted Keeley warmly. "Welcome back, Edward," Lawrence said, clapping him on the shoulder. "How did it go? Did they accept our offer?"

"Went like clockwork. It's signed, sealed and delivered," Keeley replied. He patted the thick folder under his arm. "Let's go up to the office and I'll tell you all about it."

Walking gingerly to avoid slipping on the now wet marble floor, the trio crossed the bank lobby and climbed the narrow iron stairs near the vault. The circular stairwell opened into a hallway separating the offices of President Edward Keeley and Vice President Lawrence Burgher. The Bank of Shapely had been cleverly constructed with two offices on the mezzanine level, one and one-half floors above the street and overlooking the bank lobby. From here the officers could watch their employees through the long, paned windows on the inside wall of each office. The use of twenty-inch thick masonry in the walls, floors and ceilings not only made the bank fireproof, according to the builders, but the offices soundproof as well. Therefore, the daily activity on the banking floor could be seen from above, but not heard.

Keeley's office stood in sharp contrast to Lawrence's. Both had walnut paneled walls and leather sofas, but Keeley had eschewed carpets altogether, preferring the sound of heels on wood. The most outstanding feature of the spacious President's office was the handsome white marble fireplace and hearth in the center of the rear wall. Keeley's desk was much larger than the one across the hall and it was hopelessly cluttered. Stacks of papers and file folders were piled high on the desk, on a nearby table and on the floor within an arm's reach of his swivel chair. To the untrained eye, it looked as if nothing was in order, but that belied the truth. Edward Keeley knew exactly what was in each folder and could locate any file in the blink of an eye.

As soon as they entered the room, Keeley added the thick folder of papers to one precarious looking stack on his desk and approached the fireplace to light it. "Let's warm this place up a bit. I'm freezing. Those train cars are colder than a coal miner's ass."

Keeley lit the fire and his cigar. Lawrence and David sat perched on the edge of the leather sofa, like little boys at the library story hour, waiting for him to tell about his trip. Keeley had been in Huntington for the past week working to complete the purchase of controlling stock of the Railroad Bank & Trust Company, one of the oldest banks there. Although this deal was of vital importance to both men, Lawrence had not accompanied Keeley to Huntington. Anna's baby was due any day and Lawrence refused to leave her. He still felt guilty for not being with his wife when they lost their second daughter at birth. This time he was determined to be there. Besides, he knew Keeley could handle the purchase negotiations; he'd done it a dozen or more times in his career. Buying a bank was not a big deal for Keeley, but it was for Lawrence. He saw this as his entrance into a world he'd begun to enjoy in the past five years. He deeply regretted not being able to go with Keeley to close the deal, but he knew his place was with Anna.

As the small room began to warm, the smell of wood smoke mingled with that of Keeley's cigar. He leaned back in his chair, rubbed his hands together and put his feet on the desk, causing several folders to slide dangerously close to the edge. Lawrence winced, but said nothing.

"Lawrence, how's Anna? Did she have that baby? Another girl, hmm? Does that make four?"

"Yes, she did, Edward and she's fine. Thanks for asking. We had a boy on Saturday. It's a good thing I didn't leave; I would never have heard the end of it. But it all went very smoothly. Dr. Barrett is a fine doctor and I finally got my son! We named him Richard Lawrence Burgher, Jr. We'll probably call him R.L. or Lawrence...anything but Richard. I've always hated the way people use the name, Dick, as a nickname for Richard."

"They won't if you insist on Richard. Think about it. I'm so glad she had an easy time and that you were here. Congratulations on your son. You deserve a cigar for that. David, you take one too," Keeley added effusively, holding the humidor toward them.

"Come on, Edward. Tell me about the bank deal. I've been dying to know since you walked in. Can't we get down to it instead of discussing family? Did it go as we planned?"

Keeley took a long draw on his cigar, toying with the younger man. He was still savoring the role of deal maker and having fun drawing out the news at Lawrence's expense. "Lawrence you remind me of the story about the old bull and the young bull. Stop me if you've heard it. There was this old bull standing in the pasture with a much younger bull. They wandered over by the fence and spotted a whole herd of beautiful cows in the lower pasture. The young bull said 'Oh my, look at all those cows. Lets's run down there and fuck a couple of them.' The old bull turned slowly to the young one and replied, 'No, son, let's walk down there and fuck them all.'"

Lawrence and David laughed, but Lawrence took his point. "All right, Keeley, I know I may be overly excited; but hell, it's my first big deal."

"I know that, Lawrence, but don't let your enthusiasm show so much. You'll be able to fuck them all if you just stay calm."

And so Keeley began to relate to the brothers how the purchase had come about. "It was as easy as falling off a log. Those five original incorporators we talked to in the fall were very eager to sell when I got to town. They needed the capital for other business interests. One man plans to start a transfer and storage business, and Mr. Dunfee is working on plans for a very large steel mill. I had to promise them seats on the board of directors for the next five years, with a small annual salary; but even at that, I think we got a real bargain. It's a rock solid bank with real growth potential. Hell, I think old Collis P. Huntington had a hand in starting it and he was an astute businessman if there ever was one."

"Did they agree to our offering price?" Lawrence asked.

"I had to go up just a bit. As you know, the initial capitalization was only $100,000 in 1908, and the value of the stock is considerably higher than that now. We had to pay almost that amount for our fifty-five percent interest; but it gives us control *and* leverage. It's only a few thousand more than we offered initially. You'll see all the details when you sign the papers. I have also identified two more investors who are ready to sell and a few more who may be willing in the next few years. We could own the whole damn thing, Lawrence. That's a license to print money these days, especially if we undertake another stock issue to increase the capitalization. We signed the contracts; all you need to do is affix your signature. David can serve as our witness. Sign them and we'll send the papers back tomorrow. Congratulations, Lawrence; you've just bought your first bank!"

As Keeley reached for the folder, his coat sleeve dislodged the stack of files on the edge of the desk and they slid over, one by one. Papers floated through the air and landed on the floor like the debris of a ticker tape parade. "Damn! I should have straightened this mess up before I left," Keeley snorted. Lawrence and David stooped to the floor to help retrieve the spilled documents, but Keeley cried, "Leave them there. I'll get to it later. If *I* pick them up, I can put them back in the right folder. Besides, serves me right. One of these days, I've got to file this shit." The Burgher brothers snickered to themselves. They had heard this before, but Keeley never changed. His desk would be in disarray the next time they met in his office.

Lawrence returned to the sofa and sat on the arm. He continued as if the accident had not interrupted his train of thought, "Thank you Edward, this *is* wonderful news. I'm so pleased it went well. Give the papers to me; I'll sign right now. When will you go to Huntington?"

"Within six months, I'd say."

"And the bank, here. Have you decided what to do? Will you go back and forth?" Lawrence almost dared not broach this subject. He wanted badly to be made president of the Shapely bank when Keeley left. They had talked around this subject, but Keeley had not made a firm commitment by the time he left. Lawrence knew this was still Keeley's bank.

Keeley responded, "I thought about that as I rode that damn train. Hell, I thought, I don't want to do this all the time. I'm tired of it and Clara's tired of it. She wants me to stay home. Now, you and I know I'm not likely to do that; but trying to run both banks on a day-to-day basis won't work. I didn't do that when I owned the banks in Thurmond and Mt. Hope and they were much closer together than these two. So, I'm resigning as president and promoting you to that position, Lawrence. I'll take your job as vice president and come back for board meetings or as you need me. How's that? Of course, the directors will have to give their approval, but that won't be a problem at all."

Lawrence beamed. He ran his hands through his hair, trying to contain his excitement. David jumped up from the sofa and shook his brother's hand. "Congratulations, Lawrence. This is wonderful news, too. A new son, a new bank and a new title all in one week. What an occasion!" Lawrence smiled at his brother, slapped him on the arm, then reached over the folders on Keeley's desk and shook his hand.

"Edward, I can't begin to express how *very* pleased I am. This is just what I hoped you had in mind. You run the Huntington bank and I'll run this one. We'll make a fortune with both of them."

"Hell, yes! We certainly will. I told you when you came to Shapely that I'd get bored and have you run it someday, didn't I? Didn't believe me then, did you? I think we should mark this momentous occasion with a little celebratory drink." Keeley reached into the bottom left drawer of his desk as David and Lawrence looked quizzically at one another.

Keeley laughed as he pulled a bottle of clear liquor and three glasses from the drawer.

"Just because they closed down my saloon, doesn't mean I can't find spirits. To hell with prohibition. This is top quality bathtub gin from the best bootlegger in the county."

Keeley poured drinks for each of them, handed them over his desk and asked, "Now, Lawrence, how are things in Shapely? Has this rain stopped our construction?"

Five years had passed since Lawrence and Keeley had become partners in the Mountainside Realty Corporation. The deal was a slight variation on the one Keeley proposed when he enticed Lawrence to move to Shapely. Initially, Lawrence had sold only enough land to Keeley to capitalize the cost of clearing the hillside and hiring a surveyor for his development. But when it became obvious to both men that their goals were identical, rather than continuing to compete, they joined forces to develop the Burgher-Keeley Addition on the land Lawrence and David had inherited from their father.

"The rain has shut us down, for at least the rest of the week," Lawrence responded to Keeley's question. "The foreman is a bit afraid of mud slides. Some of those lots are fairly steep, you recall, especially on Miller Street and Burgher Avenue. But we should be able to recover the lost time in the spring. Of the seventy-five lots already surveyed, we will have new houses under construction on eight this year, and ten more lots sold. I read in *The Shapely Chronicle* that our population has increased forty-six percent since 1900. I think half of them must have bought from us." He laughed, boasting a bit for the older man.

"So, is our investment paying off?" Keeley asked without smiling.

Keeley could get to the heart of a business matter in a single question.

David answered for Lawrence, as he was the cashier of the Mountaineer Realty Company, as well as of the bank. "Not yet. In order to finance the new home construction, we have to continue to pledge the land as collateral. Our bank still holds fifty acres of the land. Once all the houses or lots are sold, we'll be fine. Of course, the bank also holds construction loans for some of the houses built by the buyers and Mountaineer still holds the land contract, so we are covered either way. In other words, if the borrower defaults on either loan, we've got his ass and ours is covered. And, truth to tell, we haven't done so bad up to now. With the average price of lots at, say $300-$350, depending on location, and the houses selling like hotcakes — we've done all right. It's just that we still have a lot of undeveloped land and the development costs continue to go up. Cash is just a little tight."

Smoke drifted between Keeley and the Burgher brothers. Keeley waved it away with his hand as he leaned farther back in the chair. He took a sip from his glass and said, "Well, in Huntington the paper is full of the war in Europe. They say that since the Germans sank the Lusitania and all those Americans died, it won't be long before we're into it, too. And if that's true, coal production and prices will skyrocket. The demand has already increased dramatically since 1914. Folks will move here in droves to work at Hardman, Yeats Crossing, Red Bank, Deepwater, Bull Hollow — all over. I'll bet my dead grandmother's teeth the population of Shapely doubles in the next five years. I heard the new boarding house is full of folks looking for a place to live now. We'll be just fine. In two to three more years, that land will have been a *great* investment."

Lawrence stood up and paced in front of the fireplace. Excited at the prospect of wealth beyond his current projections, he unconsciously jingled the coins in his pocket. "I've heard the same thing from the Virginia Railroad folks. They say a few coal camps may be built, but most folks would rather live in town. If we add more lots and continue to build affordable houses, at least the foremen and inspectors could buy them, if not the miners themselves. Wages will

go up too, you know. And if coal thrives, so will all the other businesses. This town will grow by leaps and bounds. In the past year
we've gotten two new hotels, a men's clothing store, and a new grade
school. And Dr. Barrett is building a hospital toward the end of the
year, as well. All this growth could make us wealthy beyond belief."

"And," David added, "the coal we've been taking out from under
the Addition has made us quite a handsome profit even before we
sell the lots. I'm glad you suggested we look into that, Edward.
Lawrence and I think it's a much better use of the land than farming
it. Remember how we used to want to go back to the farm, Lawrence,
when we were little kids? Glad we didn't do that!"

Lawrence didn't join David in the recollections of the past; he
was too excited to reminisce. In the warmth of the cozy office and
the glow of the illicit liquor, Lawrence's mind was on the future. He
had just been made president of the bank in a town that looked to be
on the verge of prosperity. And he had become part owner of a ven-
erated bank in one of the largest cities in the state; to say nothing of
his thriving real estate and coal mining interests. Things were definitely looking up. *When I move into this office, it certainly won't stay
looking like this.*

RAILROAD BANK & TRUST COMPANY

HUNTINGTON, WEST VIRGINIA

EDWARD KEELEY, PRESIDENT
MAYNARD HUTCHISON, CASHIER
JOHN OGLETREE, V. PRES.
J.R. THOMAS, ASST. CASHIER

August 16, 1916

R. Lawrence Burgher,
President, Bank of Shapely
Shapely, W. Va.

Dear Lawrence,

Am pleased to inform you that the directors have
authorized a manager for our real estate department. The addition of this position should
enable our bank to take on many more properties,
thus increasing our net profits in that department by more than half.

The directors also encouraged all stockholders
to use their influence to increase the number of
depositors. At the directors meeting, last, it
was stated that if we could double our deposits,
we could show a much larger net profit. The
additional funds can be used in making real
estate loans, on which we cannot only make a
little better rate, but loans which are absolutely safe, further adding to our profits.

It is my belief that, if these improvements are
made, we will need your assistance in Huntington
within a year. Would you undertake such a move?

Yours very truly,

Edward M. Keeley

Edward M. Keeley

Bank of Shapely

$50,000.00 CAPITALIZATION

R. Lawrence Burgher, PRESIDENT
David L. Burgher, CASHIER
Edward Keeley, VICE PRES.
Guy Tickle, ASST. CASHIER

August 20, 1916
Edward Keeley,
President, Railroad Bank & Trust Co.
Huntington, W. Va.

Dear Edward,

Replying to your letter of August 16, I am
pleased to know that you have taken matters in
hand since your arrival in Huntington. I am
also flattered that you would find my talents of
assistance in this regard and will take your
suggestion under advisement. We can discuss it
further upon your next visit to Shapely.

Also am pleased to inform you that we have now
been successful in discouraging the formation of
another bank here. Our reports of success in
the past five years have apparently fallen on
sympathetic ears.

Until your return, I remain,
Yours very truly,

R. Lawrence Burgher

Shapely, West Virginia

August 4, 1917

My dearest Sister Jenny,

Today I take pen in hand to share news with you about which I
have mixed feelings. Lawrence has agreed to join Mr. Keeley at their
bank in Huntington, which is exciting for him, indeed. It means he
will be responsible for a much larger bank than the one here, but he
will only be the Vice President — not the President, as he is now. That
doesn't seem to bother him, however. He says the opportunities are
much greater in Huntington, because it is a much bigger city, with the
potential to grow even larger.

However, I am loathe to leave our home and all our friends here.
With four small children, it will be hard to find time to make new
acquaintances, although Lawrence has promised he will find me a
new girl to help us. I wish Lovey would agree to go with us but she
won't leave her family. She's been such a help since R.L. was born;
I don't know how I'll get along without her.

I am also anxious about where we will live. Lawrence also
assures me that he will find a suitable home for 'a man of his means,'
as he puts it; and that it will be ready when we arrive. Leaving those
details to him seems strange; but I was pleased with this home after
he bought it, so I suppose I shouldn't worry. My biggest concern is
making the move before school begins. I think Eileen will make the
adjustment when she changes schools; but I'd hate to have her get
settled in third grade at Edison, and then move her to a new school
right away. Lawrence needs to be in Huntington as soon as possible,
so if we don't find a home right away, he may go on ahead of us. He
doesn't want that any more than I do; so I'm sure he will work
diligently to find us a home.

The children are well — completely unconcerned about moving —
and happy. Eileen marched in the Fourth of July parade again this
year; but this time she said her arm didn't get tired from waving the
flag. She thinks that makes her grown-up. Actually, at eight, she is

quite mature and helps me every day with her little brother. The parade was somewhat sad this year with so many young men gone off to war. Lots of mothers and older men wept as the flags passed by. On the other hand, the patriotic fervor of the crowd was stirring to see. Those who weren't crying, cheered until they were hoarse.

The baby is such a joy and is the apple of his father's eye. I'm afraid the girls take a back seat when he toddles into the room. Margaret still calls him 'brubber' and refuses to even try saying R.L. However, I'm sure he will insist on it when he gets old enough.

How is your family? I hope the twins are fully recovered from the measles. Such a terrible thing — both of them at once. How did you ever manage? Do you suppose they were exposed at your Fourth of July picnic?

Mother told me of a terrible slate fall recently in Kilsyth. Thank God it wasn't Papa's mine. Write when you can find a free moment. I do enjoy your "twin" stories so much.

Your loving sister,

Twelve

April 1985

Libba Burgher was everyone's favorite aunt. Not only was she Maggie's favorite and that of all Maggie's cousins, she was a favorite of all Maggie's friends, as well. She was the kind of aunt who bought you a much coveted doll after your mother said no. She was the aunt who piled you and all your teenage girlfriends into her 1948 Studebaker, spent the day at the public pool and taught you all to swim. And she wore a strapless bathing suit when most other women were more modest; in other words, Aunt Libba was cool. Best of all, she was the aunt in whom Maggie and her cousins could confide. When Aunt Margaret caught Maggie at a drive-in with a boy, although she was supposed to be at the football game with her girlfriends, and threatened to tell Maggie's mother, Aunt Libba had talked Margaret out of being a snitch. Aunt Libba had never married and, perhaps, for that reason, took great interest in all her siblings' children, even after they were grown.

Because her family was poor, Aunt Libba could not afford to go to college. Right after high school graduation, when she got a filing job with a regional trucking firm in her home town, Huntington, West Virginia, she considered herself very lucky. After years of on-the-job-training, corporate seminars, and experience, she had advanced to a regional vice president's position. This prestigious post brought her to Atlanta twice a year and she relished the opportunity, for she always treated herself to a stay at the Ritz-Carlton in the trendy

Buckhead section of the city. Naturally, Maggie was excited when Aunt Libba called to say she was coming to Atlanta on business and wanted to have lunch with her.

For a woman who had lived in Atlanta only a few months, Maggie thought she was surprisingly good at finding her way around the sprawling metropolis. She was amazed to find that the traffic didn't daunt her. Of course, she had been there many times to visit, but *living* in Atlanta was a very different matter. She usually drove with her map book handy and always plotted her route before leaving home. Nevertheless, she felt like she had adapted quite well to big city life.

Today, as she drove toward Peachtree Street on West Paces Ferry Road, she admired the well-maintained mansions tucked carefully behind ornately scrolled iron gates. Some were partially hidden by beautifully landscaped stands of azaleas. The huge homes made her think of her grandfather — Aunt Libba's father. "Before Father's troubles," she could remember her mother saying, "we lived in a grand mansion with servants and a chauffeur." *Would their house have been this fine?* This phrase, or some variation of it, had been how the story of Maggie's mother's life always began. Despite the new ending to the family myth, which Maggie had only learned in the past few years, the beginning was still true. *If I'm ever going to find out what kind of person he was, I've got to start somewhere. Maybe Aunt Libba will be willing to break the code of silence; we've always been able to talk about anything. I wonder if I just ask her to tell me about her childhood, will she remember enough to help me understand? Would she even be willing to tell me, if she does remember?*

Maggie avoided the valet parking as she pulled up to the Ritz-Carlton. Her new job as assistant marketing director at Perimeter Mall came with a big jump in pay, but she still had not grown accustomed to Atlanta prices. Her mother's frugal nature had found fertile ground in Maggie, and she often found herself pinching pennies just like Sara. This was one inherited trait of her mother's that Maggie didn't mind. Alighting from her car, Maggie ran her fingers through her silver-streaked, black hair. She had been driving with the windows down, taking in the delicious spring air. *Back home, they're still wearing raincoats*. She glanced at the clear blue sky, said a small prayer of thanks and dashed inside to meet her aunt.

As Maggie approached the front desk, she noticed that several men in the lobby were visually following each step. Maggie had the tall, athletic good looks of both her parents, although she thought of herself as too tall to be feminine. The increasing sheen of silver in her hair had not lessened her youthful appearance in the least. On the contrary, at forty-four she looked as if she regularly paid a beautician dearly for this distinctive look. In the past few years, she had begun to study current fashion almost compulsively, telling herself that her position dictated she dress well, which she did. Now that she was not financially responsible for anyone but herself, clothes were her extravagance. Today, she wore a white linen pants-suit with a hot-pink silk shell which served to highlight both her tan and her dark hair. Maggie stifled a smile. *Mother always said I'd be a knockout at forty. Maybe she was right.* She spoke with the uniformed desk clerk, gave him Aunt Libba's name and waited for her to come to the lobby. At the Ritz, visitors were not given a room number — hotel patrons were summoned to the lobby to receive their guests.

The lobby of the Ritz-Carlton Buckhead was surprisingly small, but luxuriously furnished. The Persian rugs, lush draperies and original oil paintings gave it the overall feeling of quiet opulence and "old money." The hotel wasn't old, of course; it was simply decorated to make "old money" feel at home. Maggie took in the rich cherry walls and crystal chandeliers as she waited for Aunt Libba. *They certainly don't have anything like this in Huntington. I'll bet my grandfather would have loved this.*

Since her visit to the West Virginia Archives last fall, her grandfather had been on Maggie's mind a lot. It was almost insidious. She'd be thinking about something totally unrelated, and he would creep into her mind. Even with all the details of moving and taking a new job crowding her mind, he'd pop up at the most unexpected moments. She went to open a new checking account and wondered what his bank looked like. She had dinner at Pano and Paul's, compliments of her boss, and wondered if he had eaten in such fine restaurants when he traveled on business. When she went running through Buckhead's residential neighborhoods, she would imagine him living in each expensive home. Passing a line of antique cars on the Interstate, she wondered what kind of car he had driven. That these things reminded her of a man she didn't know felt strange to Maggie. *How can I be reminded of someone I never met?* She struggled with this lack of real memory more and more and began to feel as if a piece of her own history were missing. As she stared at the bank of gold elevator doors, she resolved to ask Aunt Libba about "Father's troubles."

At last one of the gold doors opened and Aunt Libba swept out in a sea of well-dressed bodies. Maggie had noticed that everyone in Atlanta seemed to have a kind of pent-up purposeful energy to their movements. Not the frantic pace of New York City, just purposeful. *No lollygagging here. Although if these are out-of-towners, it must be catching.* Libba Burgher was dressed somewhat more casually than many of the Ritz-Carlton's guests. Her aqua knit dress and matching cardigan sweater were tastefully stylish in Huntington, but not quite up to Atlanta's fashion tone. At sixty-something, her figure was beginning to "square." Her waist had disappeared as her upper body slid into her hips with the force of heredity and gravity. It was evident that she was built like most of the other Burgher women — square.

Maggie waved to her aunt and strode toward her. They nearly collided in mid-lobby, hugging as if it had been years rather than months since their last meeting.

"Maggs, it's so good to see you." Holding her at arm's length, Libba continued, "Look at you. Such a fancy linen suit!"

"It goes with the job, Aunt Libba. Thanks! You look great, too. How do you like our weather?"

"I always love coming to Atlanta in April. It's still so iffy at home. Pretty one day, rain the next. You remember."

"Sure do, and I don't miss it one bit!" Maggie was definite on that subject. She was glad to be out of the snow belt and below the Mason-Dixon line.

"Let's have lunch. It's on me. Have you ever eaten here?"

"Not yet. I hear it's a five-star restaurant. I'd love to try it, especially if you're buying. Thanks."

Maggie and Libba hooked arms and strolled, heads together, through the lobby toward the dining room. They seemed to be the only people who were not in a hurry to be somewhere else.

Over lunch, the two women swapped stories — the latest antics of Maggie's cousins, news of friends back home (Aunt Libba kept up with everyone), Maggie's new job, Aunt Libba's plans for retirement in a few years, her golf game, Maggie's kids, her new apartment... Toward the end of the conversation, Libba said. "Maggs, I brought you something from home, but it's in my room. After we finish, come on up, and I'll give it to you."

Maggie could not contain her curiosity until the waitress cleared the table. She asked, "What is it Aunt Libba? I can't imagine."

"If I told you now, it wouldn't be a surprise. Just wait. Patience is a virtue, you know!"

Maggie was as fidgety as a kid anticipating her birthday presents by the time they arrived at Libba's room. Maggie loved surprises and gifts. Libba had always given her really special presents, so her mind was racing with the possibilities. Libba walked over to the desk by the window and picked up a flat brown-paper bag with no markings or ribbons. She handed it to Maggie. "Here, this is for you," Libba said in a somber tone incompatible with gift giving.

Maggie folded back the unsealed top, reached inside and pulled out a large, slightly tattered book. The gray cover was ornately carved and the strap which originally held a clasp on one end was missing. It was an old photograph album. Maggie opened the cover and stared at the faces of her maternal grandparents. She gasped. "Aunt Libba, what is this? A family photo album? I've never seen it before. Where did you...have you had this since you were a child?" As she turned the pages, Maggie was stunned to see so many photographs of her mother's family. She had only seen the two hand-tinted portraits of her grandparents that had been on her mother's mantle as long as she could remember. This was truly a treasure!

Aunt Libba explained to Maggie, "When Eileen died last year,

Jack gave it to me. After Father died we didn't take pictures, so my childhood was basically unrecorded. Since I was the baby, he knew I didn't know about their childhood, so he thought I would like to have it. I've looked at it and taken out a few pictures for myself, but I don't want to live in the past, so I'm giving it to you. Because you seem to be the only one of the grandchildren interested in our parents, I thought you might want it."

"I don't know what to say, Aunt Libba. I'm more than thrilled. It's a treasure that I can't wait to explore. Of course, I want it. Tell me about the pictures. Do you know everyone in them?"

"Well, I remember most of them. Here, sit on the bed and I'll tell you what I can." For the next hour, Maggie and her aunt sat on the bed and looked carefully at each picture. Maggie wished she had a tape recorder as Aunt Libba pointed out her brothers and sisters at various ages, her parents' siblings and her grandparents. She showed Maggie which shots were taken in Shapely, even though she never lived there, and which ones were made in Huntington. Candid photos of her grandparents and their children spilled across the pages. In one stern picture, great-grandmother Miller wore a floor-length dress and necklaces which crisscrossed the bosom. Her attire and her visage made her the spitting image of a Catholic bishop. *So that's where the square bodies came from.* The subjects ranged from Aunt Eileen on the wide front porch of a rambling frame house in Shapely to her uncles astride a pair of burros in the driveway of a very large brick house in Huntington. Her aunt told stories, handed to her from her older siblings, of their life before "Father's troubles." But as with her mother's stories, Aunt Libba's also stopped in 1929.

Here was Maggie's missing history...incomplete as it was. She made the snap decision to ask Aunt Libba for the truth about Father's arrest and death in the Penitentiary. "Aunt Libba, a few years ago, Mother told me the real story of how your father died. I'd always heard that he died at a very early age, but she told me he died in prison. I've never asked her to talk about it again, because she was so upset when she told me. You were probably too little to know what was going on, but can you tell me exactly what happened? Even if you were too little to know it at the time, I know you do now. I'm a grown woman, myself. Don't you think I deserve to know about my own grandfather? Why do you all continue to keep it such a deep dark secret?"

Aunt Libba's face had turned scarlet as Maggie questioned her. When she spoke it was with an indignation Maggie had never seen in her. In a controlled, but audibly shaking voice Aunt Libba replied, "How dare you question why we have kept it a secret? You may be a grown woman, but it's still none of your business. Some things are better left in the past, young lady. Why don't you leave well enough alone? I don't know why your mother told you, in the first place; but I'm not going to help you pry. I can't stop you, but I sure won't help. I just can't. I've spent my whole life trying to forget what happened and I will not dredge it up now!" By this point Aunt Libba was sobbing, her shoulders quivering.

"I gave you the album hoping that would be enough; but maybe I shouldn't have even done that. Maybe you'd better just take it and leave."

Maggie tried to stammer an apology, but Aunt Libba was off the bed and across the room flinging open the door. Maggie gathered up the album, stuffed it back in the paper bag and crossed the room. Aunt Libba stood by the wide open door with tears streaming down her face. "I'm sorry, Aunt Libba," Maggie said, as she tried to hug her.

Aunt Libba did not move. "Me too, Maggs," she managed. Maggie stepped into the hallway and turned to say goodbye, but the door clicked shut in her face.

Thirteen

September 1, 1917

Normally, Saturday was Miss Esther Pennyroyal's day off; but she had just begun a new position as the day house-girl for the vice president of the Railroad Bank & Trust Company, Lawrence Burgher, and she had work to do. Miss Pennyroyal's brother, Roger, was the janitor at Lawrence's bank. It was he who had put in a good word for Esther, through the proper channels, of course, when he heard that Mr. Burgher would be moving to town. As she rode the 9 A.M. streetcar to the house on Eighth Street, she was unaware of the passing scenery or the electricity crackling on the overhead lines. Instead, she was thinking of the events of the last month. It seemed she had never been so busy, or so happy.

When Mr. Burgher came to Huntington in August, he had moved quickly. In rapid succession, he bought the house, purchased new Persian rugs and parlor furniture, hired Miss Pennyroyal, and entrusted her with the keys and the responsibility of getting the home ready for his family. Their possessions had arrived last week. She had spent two long days directing the Myers Transfer & Storage boys in placing the furniture and putting away the books, dishes and linens. She sighed, for she was tired, but knew there was still more to do. She opened her drawstring bag to check once more for the key. Looking satisfied that she had not forgotten it, she settled back to plan the day. With each rhythmic click of the wheels, she recited a chore. *Put away the children's clothes. Wash the dishes. Put them away. Wax the furniture. Mop the porch.*

Alighting from the open-sided trolley car, she stood on the sidewalk for just a moment, looking at the large red brick house. The mullioned windows in the second floor bedroom sparkled, evidence of her hard work. However, she clucked her tongue when she saw one window was missing its set of curtains. *How could I have forgotten those?* Mentally she added this to her list of tasks as she smoothed her skirt, adjusted her bonnet, took the key from her bag and marched up the steps with purpose. It pleased her to be in charge of such a handsome residence.

The skeleton key snapped crisply as the brass lock opened. The small woman pushed forcefully against the heavy glass paneled door, stepped into the front hall and closed the door. Behind her, the glass rattled as she stood admiring the gleam of the oak floors, the new floral wallpaper and the freshly washed light globes in the entrance. The clean smell of floor wax permeated the air. At the back of the hallway, she removed her apron from the hook on the wall, hung her bonnet in its place and went to work. In the quiet of the unoccupied house, Miss Pennyroyal wandered from room to room checking for unfinished details to add to her list. Throughout the first floor she walked softly; she did not want scuff marks to mar the hardwood floors. After all, it had taken her a whole day to shine them to perfection after the movers left.

Lawrence Burgher had purchased a large house, much larger than the one he was leaving in Shapely. To the right of the spacious entrance hall, the parlor held the new horsehair sofa and grand piano he had bought as a surprise for Anna. She had wanted a piano since their marriage and now he could afford one. Their dining room table and sideboard looked just right on the new Persian rug in the room to the left of the hall. Miss Pennyroyal hoped the children's table manners were impeccable; she would have hated to see food spills on that lovely ruby red rug. Despite the increasing heat and the bay windows at the front of the house, both rooms were cool; the deep wrap-around front porch provided a buffer throughout the day.

At the back of the house lay the kitchen, pantry and wash room. Miss Pennyroyal ignored these rooms for now; her list already

included the tasks to be done there. A worsted wool patterned runner muffled her footsteps as she mounted the stairs to the second
floor. So far she had only noted one or two details she had over-
looked. Upstairs the hall ran north and south rather than matching
the east-west pattern of the lower floor plan. The master bedroom
was huge and spanned the front of the house. Within this suite, which
was richly furnished with a dark green floral rug and striped wall
paper, was a private bath and dressing room — a real extravagance to
Miss Pennyroyal's mind. *Who would ever have enough clothes to fill
such a large closet?* It was in this dressing room that she had failed to
hang the curtains.

Across the hall were the three children's rooms. Eileen would have
a room to herself; Sara and Margaret were to share the middle room
and the baby — R.L. — had been given the smallest room. As she
walked through each room, she realized that despite the fact that she
had not yet met the children, she already felt as though she knew
them. She had spent a whole day unpacking their clothes and putting away their toys; now she was eager to match the belongings
with their owners. Her mental check-list complete, Miss Pennyroyal
began her tasks. She had a deadline. The Burghers were to arrive
around 4 P.M. and she wanted to welcome the family before catching the last streetcar home.

Lawrence and his family left Shapely in a Model T Ford, but they
arrived in Huntington in a Packard Twin-Six Touring Car. Lawrence
had placed his order with a dealer in Charleston before leaving
Shapely, planning to surprise Anna by picking it up on the way. He
had told himself it was a present for Anna, to lessen her reluctance to
leave Shapely; but he had to admit he looked forward to driving it to
work each day. The Twin-Six design had been introduced a few years
earlier; but Lawrence had ordered the very newest model. Not only
did he keep his order a secret, he knew he would never tell her the
price, either. She would think $3,850 was far too much to spend on
anything, especially a new car, particularly since the three-year-old

Ford had cost only $550.

By the time the sleek black Packard reached the outskirts of Huntington, it was almost 4 P.M. Anna was worn out from the trip and wanted to get to her new home; but Lawrence seemed to gain renewed strength as they drove through Barboursville on the James River Turnpike.

"How much longer will it take to get there, Lawrence?" Anna asked, as she tried to rock R.L. to sleep in her arms. The toddler had been fussing for the past fifteen minutes making them both hot and sticky.

"Not long, my love. It's only a few more miles to Huntington, but I really want to show you around town before we go to the house. It's a wonderful place. You won't believe the skyscrapers...and the streetcars. Did I tell you about the electric streetcars?" Lawrence winced as the sun hit his eyes. He reached up to lower the sun-screen.

"I believe you did, dear. I'll bet they scare the devil out of the horses! How close is our house to town?" she asked, wiping perspiration from the back of her neck with a handkerchief.

"Oh, a mile or so. The residential section is on the south side of the railroad tracks and the downtown area is on the north. It's lovely. Lots of trees line the streets — which are brick, by the way. This new car will float on them. Did you like my little surprise, Anna?"

"Darling, it's a wonderful automobile; but I think you've lost your mind. It was far too expensive, I'm sure," Anna said in a lowered voice. She never wanted the girls to hear her criticize their father.

"Well, it was more than the Ford; but we can afford it. Besides, I want people here to respect us...to appreciate our position."

"Lawrence, you earn respect by your conduct, not with your car or fancy home; you know that," Anna whispered. Then she turned quickly to the squealing which had begun in the back seat and said, raising her voice several decibels, "Margaret, keep your hands to yourself. Sara isn't even close to you. Eileen, can you please keep those two quiet?" Eileen, at eight years old, had become quite adept at keeping her younger sisters in check.

Lawrence ignored her rebuke, chastising the children instead. "Girls, I want you to sit quietly and stop kicking the back of the seats. What's the matter with you? This is a brand new car. I don't want to see a single scuff mark on it when we get out."

Anna turned back to Lawrence and in a more placating tone asked, "Can't we just go straight to the house and drive around another time? They are all exhausted."

"We have to go through town anyway. It will only take a few minutes. This is so much bigger than Shapely! Shapely is a little town; Huntington is a *city!* There are over 11,000 people here. Our life will be very different here, but I think you'll get used to it." Lawrence smiled and put his hand on Anna's knee. "I want you to be happy, Anna, and to live like you deserve. And I want the children to have all the things I never had." Anna returned the smile and covered his big hand with her own.

Shortly, they crossed a steel bridge spanning the narrow Guyandotte river and entered the small town which lay on the other side. Anna stared out the windscreen. "Lawrence, this isn't Huntington, is it?" she asked incredulously. "I thought you said it was a big city."

"No, love," Lawrence laughed. "This is Guyandotte. Huntington is a little farther down the river. You know, legend has it that Collis P. Huntington originally chose this site as the terminus of his railroad; but the town fathers did something to anger him, so he moved down river to Huntington. I don't know how much truth there is to that story, but it's what folks will tell you."

"Well, I'm certainly glad he did. This is smaller than Shapely."

"Father, are we there yet?" Eileen called from the back. "I'm tired of sitting still and I have to go to the toilet."

"Almost, Eileen. Can't you wait just a bit longer? Look out the windows. I'll show you where I work."

As the Burghers entered Huntington, Lawrence began a narrative description of the sights that would have qualified him as a master tour guide. In one short month, he had learned quite a lot about his adopted home.

"Mr. Huntington hired a man named Rufus Cook who laid out the city's streets in a grid. It's easy to find your way around. The streets run north and south and the avenues run east and west. Our house is on Eighth Street, near Eleventh Avenue.

"Where, Father? Is that our house?" asked Margaret as they passed a large brick home.

"No, Margaret; not yet. Just a bit longer. Look Anna, over there is Marshall College. It's a teacher's college. We'll send the girls here when they get older. Out that road to the south is a brickyard where the bricks in our house were made," Lawrence said pointing out his side of the car at the street in front of the college campus. Anna smiled, but was more impressed with the magnificent beech tree and the towered brick building which stood on a rise in the center of the grounds.

He continued, "And on the river to your right is the landing for the ferry going to Ohio."

"Father, what is 'going to Ohio?'" asked Sara. "Is it like going to heaven?"

Anna replied, "No, darling; it's just another place where people like us live...like West Virginia. You'll learn all about it when you go to school next year."

Eileen giggled and began to tease Sara. "You old silly. What's going to Ohio? Is it like going to heaven?" she repeated in a mocking falsetto voice.

Sara whined, "Mother, make her stop!"

"Enough, Eileen!" Lawrence rarely raised his voice; he didn't have to. The children were generally well behaved, especially in his presence. Teasing was the one infraction he never tolerated. Others, he might let slip on occasion; but not this one. As soon as it started, he put a stop to it. Eileen was silent.

They drove without a word for several blocks past several large stone buildings and many smaller brick or frame shops. It seemed to Anna the farther they drove, the closer together the buildings were placed. Finally Lawrence pulled to the curb at an angle in front of a large, two-story, white limestone building. The structure occupied the entire corner of the block and had an impressive arched entrance framed with hand-hewn granite blocks. He pulled on the parking brake and pointed to the brass plaque just above the cornerstone.

"Railroad Bank & Trust," read Anna. "Oh, Lawrence! What a

magnificent building. It's so much bigger than the bank back home."
She turned to him, leaned over her sleeping son and kissed him on
the cheek. "I'm so proud of you, darling!"

Lawrence seemed transfixed by the brass plaque. "I just hope I
can live up to Keeley's expectations," he confessed quietly. "It's a lot
more responsibility. These people are not uneducated coal miners,
farmers and wood hicks, like I dealt with in Shapely. They're savvy
business men. I hope I can hold my own."

"Lawrence, you'll be just fine. You've been the president of a bank;
that will put you in good stead with all of the men in town. They'll
have to be impressed with you. And once they get to know you,
they'll see how capable you are, too."

Lawrence patted her on the knee again and said to the girls, "Want
to see more of the town, girls? Have you ever seen a streetcar?" He
released the brake and reversed the car as a wagon drawn by a dapple-
gray horse approached from behind. The horse spotted the car, whin-
nied loudly and shied to the right as the car began to move.

"Look out, Father. There's a horse behind us!" Eileen called.

"I see him, Eileen — but thank you for warning me. There are
still a lot of horses here, and the automobile drivers must watch out
for them." Lawrence stopped abruptly while the wagon passed. The
girls watched as an old man struggled to regain control of his horse.
As the wagon passed the Packard, the driver shook his fist angrily at
Lawrence, sending the girls into gales of laughter.

Excited by the near miss with the horse, the girls now leaned on
the doors of the car, watching with eager anticipation for the next
adventure. Eileen was on one side; while Margaret and Sara were on
the other, behind their father. Even the baby stirred and awoke, so
Anna held him to the window to see as well.

Lawrence continued the tour, pointing out the Hotel Frederick
where he had stayed when he came to town in August; the Presbyterian Church they would attend and the Anderson-Newcomb and the
Zenner-Bradshaw department stores where Anna would, no doubt,
shop. As they circled block after block, Lawrence was pleased to notice people staring at the shiny new car. Periodically, he waved, even
though he did not see anyone he actually knew. As he drove, the

girls craned their necks as far out as possible to see the tall buildings. Suddenly Sara cried, "Look, Mama, that train car has a string clear to the sky and lightning is hitting it!"

"No, Sara. That's a streetcar and it's attached to the electric lines that run it. And that's not lightning, but sparks of electricity," explained her father as Anna laughed. "Don't you remember that I told you we had streetcars?"

"What's 'lectrikity?'" she asked.

"Sara, you are far too full of questions," he laughed.

As they turned left on Eighth Street, he pointed out two more sights to Anna. "Over there on your side, is the Cabell County Courthouse; isn't it beautiful? See the clocks? You can hear them chime all over town. And on my side is City Hall. I think the courthouse is much grander, don't you?"

"It is beautiful. Such spacious grounds," Anna agreed.

"We're almost home, girls; keep looking." Lawrence hardly needed to suggest that. He looked back and saw that the children were all leaning out of the car, giving it the appearance of a long black beetle with multiple heads and arms. Lawrence smiled. He enjoyed prolonging their arrival — it was like the finale of a play he had scripted. As he reached their destination, he turned the corner and pulled into the driveway at the side of the house.

"Tu-dumm. We're home!" he announced, and he sounded the Packard's resonant horn.

Hearing the horn, Miss Pennyroyal came out on the porch, her bonnet on and her drawstring purse clutched firmly in her hands. She rushed toward the car, skirt flapping. Before the Burghers could get out of the car, she was at Lawrence's side, waving her hand. In one swift motion, she thrust a key at him, turned and ran for the corner.

"Mr. Burgher, thank goodness you're here. I'm nearly late for the streetcar. Here's the key. I have to run but I'll meet your family in the morning. Welcome to Huntington, Mrs. B."

Fourteen

November 20, 1918

For over a year, Uncle Sam had pointed from a poster in front of the Huntington Post Office, encouraging men to volunteer for the war effort. "I Want You," the appeal went. Despite his daily feeling that Uncle Sam was pointing right at him, Lawrence Burgher had not heeded the entreaty. As vice president of the Railroad Bank & Trust Company, he felt he was essential to the economy of the city. He *knew* he was essential to the economy of his family. Therefore, World War I had been fought and won without his help. Now that the armistice had been signed, Uncle Sam was gone from the post office and Lawrence's nagging guilty conscience was quieted. He could get on with his life.

This particular Wednesday morning, a week before Thanksgiving, as Lawrence dressed for the day, he reflected on all he had to be thankful for this year. Standing in his silk one-piece under-suit, he opened the double doors and surveyed the racks and shelves of clothes on his side of the closet. Lawrence prided himself on two things: efficiency and immaculate dress. His suits were arranged with precision, from the most casual blue and white seersucker to his most formal navy-blue worsted wool. His shoes, glistening on the floor rack below, were held in perfect shape by wooden shoe trees. To the left, his shirts were stacked in full view on two shelves in the middle of the closet. This arrangement allowed him to make his selection quickly.

Today, he fanned past several suits before choosing a dark-gray striped one with a matching vest. He removed it from the rack, brushed the lapels and hung it on the clothes caddy. *What a remarkable year this has been. The war is over; the economy is good; no one in our family has had the flu. Thank you, Lord. The bank is doing very well; Mountaineer Realty is doing extremely well...if Burgher Land Company does as well here...yes, a good year, a really good year.* He moved to the other end of the wall of garments and selected his newest white shirt with his monogram on the cuff. As he unfolded it, he noticed a slight edge of brown on the collar. With a deep frown, he tossed it on the chair. *Why the devil can't Miss Pennyroyal keep from scorching my collars?* He sighed and chose another shirt.

Fully dressed, he studied his reflection in one of the full-length mirrors on the inside of the doors. Straightening the square, gold cuff links, he sucked in his stomach. Satisfied that his trouser creases were sharp and his collar was scorchless and stiff as a board, he ran his hands from his temples to the nape of his neck, smoothing down his full dark hair. He smiled slightly, turned and headed downstairs to breakfast.

The familiar cacophony of morning sounds reached him as he took the first step. From the direction of the kitchen he could hear banging pots, running water, and cabinet doors being opened and closed as Miss Pennyroyal prepared breakfast. Behind him, the children called to each other across the hall. Somewhere in the house the new puppy whined to go out. Over it all floated Anna's calm voice, though he couldn't make out her words.

The day started early in the Burgher household. Miss Pennyroyal bustled through the side door each morning at 6:30 and went straight to work. She was a no-nonsense, Appalachian girl whose work ethic was surpassed only by Lawrence's own. By 7:45 she had made sure Eileen and Sara were properly dressed, washed at least one load of clothes and hung them on the line, prepared breakfast, set the table and served breakfast to the entire family.

Anna always rose before Lawrence, put on her dressing gown, closed their bedroom door and went to wake the children. The older girls could usually be counted on to get ready for school, with the urging of Miss Pennyroyal while Anna tended to Margaret, now four, and to R.L. who was just two and one-half. Anna feared that R.L., as the baby and only boy, was becoming somewhat spoiled. He would have nothing to do with the day-girl, try as Anna might to coax him from his python-like grip around her neck into Miss Pennyroyal's willing arms. Margaret, on the other hand, loved Miss Pennyroyal's jolly humor and couldn't wait until her sisters left for school each day to command all of her attention.

Lawrence entered the dining room, picked up *The Herald-Dispatch* from the sideboard and sat at the head of the table. Miss Pennyroyal greeted him and poured his coffee as he opened the paper and began to read. On weekdays, this ritual never varied. Lawrence had the relative quiet of the carpeted room to himself while the children dressed for school. The long table was set for six. Anna always sat at the opposite end of the long table, with Eileen and Sara on the left and Margaret and R.L. on the right. R.L. sat nearest his mother so she could help him eat, for he still wasn't adept at using a fork.

Shortly, Lawrence heard Margaret bounce down the stairs and run into the kitchen, her skirts flying. She grabbed Miss Pennyroyal around the knees.

"Margaret, let go of my skirts. I can't cook your sisters or you any breakfast if you don't let go. I'll have to cook you, if you don't." Lawrence could hear Margaret laughing at the warning.

"Come here, Margaret. Leave Miss Pennyroyal alone. She'll play with you after Eileen and Sara leave. Doesn't she always?" Anna said, as she entered the dining room with R.L. in her arms. She went to Lawrence's side and kissed him good morning.

"How are you this morning, love?" he said, returning a second kiss. "And how are you 'little buddy'?" The whole family seemed to have picked up Margaret's nickname for her little brother. Anna hoped it wouldn't stick past childhood. Lawrence reached out and took his son from Anna.

"I'm fine — only a little nauseous. I think it's going to be easy this time. I've had worse morning sickness." Anna was just three months pregnant and already the daily vomiting had lessened.

R.L. hugged his father tightly and then began bouncing up and down on his lap. Quickly, Lawrence handed the child back to his mother. "Here, Anna, take R.L.; he's rumpling my suit." Anna frowned slightly but put the toddler in his high chair as Miss Pennyroyal brought him a piece of hard toast to keep him quiet until breakfast was served.

"What is in the paper?" Anna asked. She took her seat and accepted the tea Miss Pennyroyal offered.

"The headline is 'Wilson to Attend Peace Conference.' The article goes on to say he'll be in Europe indefinitely," Lawrence read from behind the front section of the paper. "In another headline, we read that the British losses during the war were over $3 million; think of that — three million dollars!" he commented.

"What about local news? I'm so tired of war news. Thank God it's over."

"Well, yes, it is. But the peace treaties still must be signed. We're not entirely out of it yet." Reading again he intoned, 'Mrs. Buffington, First Lady of the City, Died Last Night'."

"Poor lady. Was it the flu?" asked Anna.

"No, a paralytic stroke. They've delayed her funeral until her grandson can be located. He's serving in the aviation service in Texas. I'll bet that will be quite a funeral — widow of the first mayor and all. We should attend, don't you suppose? Speaking of influenza... they still have a lot of it in East Lynn, in Wayne county. Seven died yesterday in what they called a 'belated outbreak.'"

Lowering the paper slightly to look at Anna, he said, "You see, I was right. Just because they lifted the quarantine doesn't mean we are safe. Remember a few weeks ago, right after they reopened the schools and churches — over one hundred new cases were reported. Now I'll grant you, it's nothing to compare with the two thousand cases before they instituted the quarantine; but in your condition, you need to be especially careful. You aren't going to work at the Red Cross Canteen today, are you? Surely they can manage without you, until all this business is past. I think it's important to give back to our community; but your health comes first."

"I agree, darling. I won't go today, but I did want to go shopping. Zenner-Bradshaw is having a suit sale; I'd like to get one that will camouflage my condition a little better. Perhaps it will do through winter, if I don't get too large."

Lawrence put down his paper and smiled at his wife. "You always look so beautiful when you are carrying our child. I love you."

Before Anna could respond to this compliment, the three girls dashed into the dining room just ahead of Miss Pennyroyal. They kissed their father and took their seats as she began to serve breakfast. It was 7:45 A.M.

In the east end of town, Edward Keeley performed his weekday morning ritual, as well; but his heart wasn't in it. Since his wife, Clara, had died of influenza last month, he had approached each day numbly, trying to block out the loss. Never a dapper dresser, now he often looked as if he wore the first outfit he could put together. He threw open the door of his walnut chifforobe and haphazardly rummaged through the top drawer. He was nearly dressed, but now couldn't find two socks that matched. In frustration, he discarded socks one by one. They flew behind him as if he were a dog looking for a buried bone. Finally coming up with a matching pair, he waded through the sea of multi-colored lisle to reach the bed. He sat down, heavily. Groaning, he bent over his distended stomach and tugged on each sock.

Keeley wore a brown tweed suit, despite the fact that it was a little tight in the waist. Straightening, he noticed threads protruding from his middle, signaling a missing button on the vest; but he didn't bother to change. Crossing the sock sea again, he began to plunder his jewelry case for a stick pin. Digging to the bottom of gold and silver cuff links, rings and dress studs, he finally located one and plunged it into his new silk tie. As he glanced in the mirror, he was overcome with a wave of grief. He suddenly recognized the tie as the one Clara had given him for his birthday a week before she died. He dropped to the bed again and put his head in his hands.

Try as he might, he had not been able to rid himself of the memory of her frantic eyes as she vainly struggled for breath just before dying.

He never imagined that a person so young and healthy could die so suddenly and so horribly. One day, she was fine; then she was gone. Oh, she had complained of a dull headache and said her eyes burned; but he never suspected influenza started that way. Just to be safe, he had called the doctor the next day. But by the time the doctor had diagnosed the disease — by the dark-brownish, purple cast to her face — it was only a matter of days until she died.

He had gone over and over it in his mind. *If I had called the doctor the first day. If I had given her a salt-water purgative or Vicks Vapo-Rub or laxatives or put sulfur by her bed. If I'd just been able to find whiskey. Might she not have lived? The doctor assured me that none of these treatments were proven. Still, he didn't try any of them. How did he know they wouldn't work? And where did she contract it? We tried to stay home as much as possible. Did I bring it from work? She always waited until they flushed the streets to go to the grocer.* Finally he had given up. There was no way to know. Even the doctors didn't know what caused this plague. After weeks of self-flagellation, Edward had accepted fate and given himself over to simple mourning.

Now all he did was work, leaving the care of the house and his two children, Edward Jr. and Effie, to the maid. Clara had often complained that he worked too hard; now it didn't matter. She wasn't there to enjoy his company, anyway. If his new coal company took all his time, who would complain? He rose from the bed, jerked on his jacket and went down the stairs to face the day.

Around 10 A.M. Lawrence crossed the black and white marble lobby of the Railroad Bank & Trust Company with a folder under his arm. Nodding absently to customers in his path, he mounted the wide stairs to the second floor and knocked on Keeley's door.

"Come in," Keeley called from within. Lawrence turned the brass door knob and entered.

"Good morning, Edward. How are you doing today?"

"As well as can be expected, I suppose. Sit down. I've been thinking about something and I want to discuss it with you. So far, the bank seems to be prospering but we certainly aren't the largest bank in town. In order to compete, we need to grow. People respect a large bank. We need to increase our capitalization and our deposits. Do you think the banking commission will allow us to increase the former? And how can we accomplish the latter?"

Lawrence crossed his legs, thought for a moment as he absently opened and closed his pocket watch; then replied. "I don't know, but I can certainly write the commissioner to find out. As for increasing our depositors — perhaps we should entreat all our directors to solicit their acquaintances. And we could insist that each loan we grant carry with it the requirement to open an account with us. That may not greatly increase our cash, but the number of depositors we could claim would improve."

"Well, I daresay most borrowers already open an account, if they didn't have one before requesting the loan; but we could try that. And I wish you would write the commissioner. Will we be declaring a dividend this quarter?"

"Absolutely! It appears we will put another $1,000 in the undivided profit account, as well. This has been a good investment already, Edward. Our loan portfolio is growing nicely and my calculation of earned interest this quarter looks to be up. You know this interest isn't actually paid, but I don't see it as a problem. These loans are good and it's not going to catch anyone's eye. When it is paid, our cash reserve will be up, too. Based on this, we could declare a record three percent dividend for the shareholders. What do you think?"

"I'm leaving that up to you. But I do appreciate a good dividend," Keeley responded.

"You always told me that you had to take a few risks to get ahead, Edward."

"And it appears you have done just that, Lawrence. Bringing you to Huntington was a good move — which brings me to another subject. Since Clara's death, my heart just hasn't been on the bank's business. And, as you know, my new coal company is in the formative stages. I think it needs my full attention. Perhaps, if I concentrate all my energy in that direction, I can get my mind back. I'm not

suggesting I actually leave the bank; but I'd like to throw more responsibility your way. I'll check in regularly, but don't look to me for
daily direction any longer. Fair enough?"

"Fair enough. I'm grateful for your confidence. I've learned a lot
from you and am sure I can handle it. I must say, I'm not surprised at
this decision, though. You never stick with one business for very
long, anyway. What did you tell me once — you didn't like to run
things, just liked to own them? But, I understand your reasoning. I
am truly sorry for your loss. I can't imagine life without my Anna."
Lawrence paused for a moment, staring out the window behind
Keeley, then regained his composure.

"Let me show you something." He opened the folder and placed
it on the leather-bound blotter at the front of Keeley's desk. It was
the only level spot he could find, for Keeley still stacked files on his
desk like building blocks. From inside the folder Lawrence took a
map, unfolded it and smoothed it against the bumpy surface. Dotted
across the real estate map of Huntington were a dozen or so red circles.
Lawrence pointed at the marks.

"These are properties that will be sold by the end of the year for
non-payment of taxes. There may be others, but these were listed
recently. I propose to buy as many of them as I can at the sheriff's
auction and then resell them for a substantial profit. I estimate it will
take about $2,000 to get the ones I want. Some are residences and
others are lots. Of course, I could also hold the best of the houses and
rent them. If I borrow the money from our bank, pledge the properties as security and encourage the potential buyers to obtain their
loan from us, we profit in several ways. What do you think?"

"Sounds like a profitable venture, for you. I think we could do
that, even without the loan committee. Just don't let your real estate
dealings interfere with your banking responsibilities."

"Edward, I suspect I can juggle as many balls as you," he laughed,
somewhat insulted by the warning. Rising to take his leave of Edward Keeley he announced, "Burgher Land Company is about to become a reality."

RAILROAD BANK & TRUST COMPANY

HUNTINGTON, WEST VIRGINIA

EDWARD KEELEY, PRESIDENT
R. LAWRENCE BURGHER, V. PRES. & CASHIER
J.R. THOMAS, ASST. CASHIER

December 10, 1918

Mr. R. L Snodgrass
Commissioner of Banking,
Charleston, W.Va.

Dear Mr. Snodgrass:

We are arranging to increase our capital stock
and make a much larger bank and trust company of
our institution.

I would like to know if it is permissible under
the State laws to increase our stock to
$1,000,000.00. If not, what amount would we be
allowed?

I shall be pleased to receive your reply by
return mail regarding this matter, as we plan to
have a Meeting soon, looking toward increasing
our capital.

Yours truly,

R. Lawrence Burgher
Vice President & Cashier

RLB: nt

West Virginia Banking Commission
Charleston, W.Va.

December 12, 1918

Mr. R. Lawrence Burgher, V. Pres & Cashier
Railroad Bank & Trust Co.
Huntington, W. Va.

Dear Sir:

In reply to your letter of December 10, beg to
say that you are authorized to increase your
capital stock to $1,000,000.00. In fact, you
will find that you have the right to increase
it to whatever amount you deem desirable. The
banking laws state "But nothing in said chapters
shall limit the maximum amount of paid up
capital which a trust company, doing a banking
business, may desire."

           Yours truly,

           Robert L. Snodgrass
           Robert L. Snodgrass
           Commissioner of Banking

RLS: mp

Fifteen

Memorial Day Weekend, 1989

The sudden death of a loved one or a close friend has a way of making the bereaved face the possibility of time running out on him as well. Projects lying dormant, relationships gone sour, friendships ignored since the last reunion — all are revived with a frantic effort to beat the final bell. And, so it was with Maggie Malone in the spring her father died, quite unexpectedly, of a heart attack.

Maggie stayed for two weeks in Florida to help her mother deal with the niggling details of the will, probate, taxes and lawyers. As she returned to her Atlanta apartment and suffered through her own mourning period alone, a sudden realization struck her: her dad had been one of the few people she knew who *might* have been willing to tell her the true story of Sara's father and his "troubles." And now he was gone.

She berated herself for frittering away all the opportunities to talk with him about it, believing he'd be there forever and she would somehow find just the right time and way to broach the subject. She had wasted the ten years since her mother told her Richard Lawrence Burgher had died in prison; and she *really* wasn't any closer to understanding "why" than she was that day on the beach. Yes, she knew more details now, but the "why" continued to nag at her. Since then, her interest had peaked and waned depending on what else was happening in her life. Now she was committed to exposing the nearly sixty-year-old secret, regardless. She vowed not to let anyone else die before she could get the truth, but then quickly realized how helpless she was to joust with fate.

For weeks, she stewed over which of her parents' contemporaries she might ask about it. She didn't want to risk making her mother angry or hurting her by an act she would consider betrayal, especially now; but she had to know. *Could I ask Helen French? She went with Mother and Daddy when they eloped? No, she'd probably tell Mother. They do still talk on the phone from time to time. What about...?* Maggie ran over and over the list of names she'd known as her parents' lifelong friends, but none seemed a likely candidate for a conspiracy of silence.

Then, she recalled her mother's favorite cousin, Annie Bartram. Maggie had seen her note of condolence when her father died and noticed that Annie lived in Savannah. Maggie and her mother had talked then about Annie and how their two lives had taken such different paths, despite their closeness as children. Sara said they had not seen each other in years, but kept in touch through annual Christmas notes. Slightly older than Sara, Annie had been married once but only for a very short time. She was a bit eccentric, according to Sara. This was perfect — the daughter of her grandmother's sister Jenny! Maggie felt sure she would know the real story of her grandfather's life. She decided to take a chance.

She obtained Annie's address from a willing telephone operator with a South Georgia accent as thick as sorghum and wrote to her. In the letter, Maggie explained how she had been given the gem of truth she currently held and begged her not to let her mother or her aunts know Maggie was playing Nancy Drew. Appealing to a rebellious nature in her second cousin hinted at by Sara, Maggie hoped Annie was as unconventional as her mother had said and that she just might not give a good damn what her cousins thought. Maggie's hope was rewarded. Annie had written back almost immediately, promising not to give Maggie away and inviting her to Savannah anytime to glean all she could from Annie's memory.

Since Annie said she didn't have a guest room, Maggie had made a reservation for the Memorial Day weekend at the River Street Inn, a small brick hotel that was once a cotton warehouse. Armed with the family photograph album from Aunt Libba, she drove across the state on Saturday morning and checked into a room with a four-poster bed and a view of the Savannah River. Her plans included sightseeing for the rest of the day — Johnny Mercer's home, the birth-place of Girl Scout founder Juliette Gordon Low, the historic cem-etery where Button Gwinnett was buried, the Waving Girl Statue and, if she had time, perhaps the Tybee Island Lighthouse. Maggie had fallen in love with her adopted state and wanted to experience it all.

She was not meeting Annie until Sunday morning; they were to spend the day together, which Maggie figured was more than enough. Maggie had invented an imaginary "friend" to visit later in the day, in case she and Annie didn't hit it off or Annie developed a sudden case of family loyalty and wouldn't talk. On the other hand, if all went well, Maggie could come back on Memorial Day, since she had the day off.

Sunday morning, Maggie woke with the dawn. One window in her brick-walled hotel room faced due east. Lying in the cocoon-like curtained bed, she saw the sun rise over the Savannah River and cast an orange glow on the fog-dampened cobblestones below on River Street. Contrary to the old saw that ran through her head — "Red skies in the morning, sailors take warning...," — she saw the flaming sun as a good omen. It seemed to Maggie that a true light was about to break on her familial past. As she watched day break, she made a mental list of the questions she wanted to ask Annie. First, she wanted details from a personal point of view — exactly what had happened. Then she wanted to learn why? What sort of person was her grandfa-ther? And her grandmother, too? The list grew too long for memory's safe-keeping. Afraid she would let Annie get sidetracked with other reminiscences triggered by the photo album and forget one of her critical questions, Maggie jumped out of bed and jotted down the list on a hotel note pad. Satisfied she had them all on paper, she dressed and went downstairs to breakfast.

The River Street Inn vertically spanned two street levels. The front lobby was on Bay Street; the coffee shop was one floor below and opened onto River Street. Since it was still early, Maggie ate a lei-surely breakfast and read the paper before making her way down the uneven street to Annie Bartram's. She had strolled down the Riverwalk the day before and spotted *Annie's Antiques and Books* near the Waving Girl Statue, but didn't go in. She headed there again, for Annie lived above her shop. Maggie knew the antique store would be closed today, but Annie had said she'd be watching for her at 9 A.M. Maggie glanced at her watch and quickened her step.

As she walked, Maggie was surprised at the early morning heat and humidity of Savannah. *Atlanta never gets this bad until June or July.* She was perspiring heavily by the time she had covered the four block walk. *I'm glad I decided not to go running this morning.* Approaching the paned windows of Annie's shop, Maggie patted her pocket, checking for her list of questions, again. She didn't see the face watching intently through the dusty glass. Before Maggie could raise her arm to knock, the door opened. The soprano tinkle of the bell on the shop door handle harmonized perfectly with Annie's alto greeting.

"Maggie, you look just like your mother. I'd have known you anywhere. Come in, child, come in."

As Maggie stepped over the stone threshold, she felt she should duck. Although it was probably only slightly shorter than a standard door, the low entrance would have been difficult for a pro basketball player. Once inside, the feeling was exacerbated by the hundreds of items hanging from the ceiling. Maggie could hardly take her eyes off the "stuff" to focus on Annie Bartram. When she did, she too saw a family resemblance. Square — Annie was square! Square like her great-grandmother in the photo album; square like Aunt Libba, and square like she, Maggie, was afraid she would become. Annie's greeting was not, to Maggie's mind, a compliment.

Annie wore loose-fitting, wrinkled linen pants and an over-sized man's shirt. Her gray hair was long and twisted into a thick, snake-like coil, pinned loosely to her head. Slender gold pendants swung from her pierced ears and wisps of hair floated around her square face, softening the edges and feathering them into her scalp. On Annie, the family features were transmuted from those of a reluctant matron to their bohemian best. She had obviously made peace with her body. Annie grabbed Maggie and hugged her, laughing. Her broad smile and husky laugh were captivating. Maggie knew immediately they'd be friends.

Maggie stepped back slightly. "Annie, it's wonderful to meet you. Mother used to talk about you a lot; now I finally get to know you for myself."

"How is your mother? I was so sorry about your daddy. He was a really special person. Everyone in the family just loved him."

Tears sprang to Maggie's eyes. She missed her father terribly. "Mother's so pitiful. I always thought she was the stronger of the two and worried about what daddy would do if she died first. But she can't seem to get a grip. She's lost her anchor. It's tough to watch her flounder. On the other hand, she's so damned independent that she won't let anyone help. I stayed for a few weeks to deal with the will and so forth, but she seemed to resent every suggestion I made; so I finally gave up and went home."

"I'm not surprised. She was devoted to your dad from the day they met. Well, more about that later. Let me show you my place."

As they walked through the crowded aisles of *Annie's Antiques and Books*, Maggie noticed how musty and cool it felt. The hot sea air must have crept in under the door, been cooled by an antique fan and stayed that way for years. It wasn't at all unpleasant, however. Instead, the closeness of the damp air, the cluttered shelves and counters, the sleds and lamps overhead, all gave Maggie a sense of security. It was like wandering through your grandmother's basement. The entire back wall was a book shelf, complete with a rolling library ladder, although time seemed to have permanently cemented some books to the shelves. As Annie pointed out her favorite pieces of English furniture, carnival glass, Tiffany lamps and sterling silver tea sets, Maggie wondered if she ever sold anything.

While Maggie stroked polished wood and fingered age-softened quilts, Annie briefly brought her up-to-date on her life. "I left West Virginia after Mother died, which must have been in about 1952. You know she'd had a stroke years back and I had taken care of her. Never worked all those years, except to do for her. I was nearly forty-five when I left. Always wanted to go south. I took a little money Mother had saved and started driving. Ended up here and went to work selling antiques for this old — I mean — earth-old woman, in this very shop. I loved the old stuff. I guess it reminded me of the things we had when I was growing up — before the Depression, that is. And I grew to love her, too; she was like another mother to me. When she finally died, fifteen years later, she left the shop to me. Sometimes I just hate to sell anything; it's like letting part of her go. Turn here, and we'll go up to my apartment," she directed, as they reached the end of one aisle.

The steps leading to the second floor were as cluttered as the shop, as though Annie started up the steps each day with something in her arms and then, too tired to continue, set it down. Books, candlesticks in need of polish, and quilts, which had seen more wear than care, had to be dodged to reach Annie's living space. At the top, Maggie found herself in Annie's living room, bedroom, dining room and den — all were the same large room. Except for an alcove kitchen and a tiny bathroom in one corner, Annie lived in one room. Maggie was fascinated with both the concept and the room itself. Again, it didn't feel cluttered, although it certainly was; it felt homey. Annie cleared the overstuffed slip-covered sofa and motioned to Maggie to have a seat, while she fixed them each a cup of coffee. While she worked, Maggie retrieved her list of questions and studied it briefly. It occurred to her that a tape recorder would have been a good idea.

Annie returned and handed Maggie a large stoneware mug of chicory flavored coffee. She set her own on the army field trunk, which served as her coffee table, and went to a curtained area on one side of the room. She drew back the floral cloth to reveal shelves of albums. They were packed so tightly on the shelves that moving one caused the others to shift, as well. *This must be like Fibber McGee's closet Mother used to talk about.* Annie found the one she wanted and returned to Maggie's side.

"Mother was a scrapbook maker. Every clipping about anyone in the family she saved and put into those books. All the family would send her stuff. I'll bet there's even one of your wedding in there. What I wanted to show you was this one about your mother and father." *She means grandmother and grandfather.* Maggie saw the same obituary she had found on microfilm five years ago. *Old folks have a way of compressing generations.*

"I've seen that before," Maggie admitted. I found it in the West Virginia Archives. But I've never seen any of these other clippings," she said as she scanned newspaper stories about her grandmother and the Woman's Club, her grandfather and the Elks Club. "Apparently they were very active in Huntington, huh? Tell me about them. What were they like?"

"Oh my, yes. They were *very* involved. Your grandfather was sort of reserved — until you got to know him. He was quite a go-getter...determined to show people he could accomplish something in his life. I think maybe that's what caused his troubles. He joined everything. The Elks, the Kiwanis, the Guyandotte Club. People liked him; he was a very kind man. He helped start a camp for girls and was always trying to make things better in Huntington. Maybe that's because he came from such poor folks."

"What about Anna? You know, I have a hard time thinking about them as my grandparents. Mother said so little about them I don't have a clear picture at all. It's hard to attach feelings to people you never saw or knew. In my mind, I think of them as Anna and Lawrence."

"Well, if you'd known your grandmother, you'd have loved her instantly. She was the most loving person you'd ever meet in your whole life. There was nothing pretentious about her; she was always open and gentle. Always ready to help anyone that needed it. And she was quite a joiner, too. She helped organize the Red Cross Canteen during the war and worked with the Woman's Club on the fly-catching contest the year of the flu epidemic."

"Fly-catching contest?" Maggie hooted. "You are kidding? Why would they want to catch flies?"

"Because they thought they carried disease. So they organized a contest to see who could bring in the most dead flies. You know, she was supposed to be president of the Woman's Club during the time of your grandfather's troubles, but they didn't let her. Isn't that cruel?" Annie said.

"Yes, it is. Tell me about that time. Do you know what happened?"

"Well, not really. I mean, I was about twenty-two and we didn't live in Huntington then; but of course, we heard about it through the family. Details, if I ever knew them, I've forgotten. But I do remember that it was a huge scandal. This is about when your mother decided that she wanted to be a Landers instead of a Burgher. That's maybe why there are so many gaps in all this stuff you want to know. She was very disillusioned about the whole family when your father came along. After he came back from West Point at Christmas, they announced that they had gotten married and she moved out. She just sort of turned her back on the family and devoted herself to him. I guess later, she repented and came back into the fold; but I know it must have hurt the other girls."

This unflattering revelation about Sara made Maggie uneasy, almost as if she needed to apologize for her mother's unsupportive behavior. She changed the subject slightly. "How could Lawrence let something like this happen? Didn't he see what it might do to his family?"

"Oh, I'm sure he didn't think about it. He was devoted to Anna; those two loved each other passionately. Even up in years, they couldn't keep their hands off each other. Imagine fifty being considered up in years. No, I don't think he thought he'd get caught. It's like a lot of people, they take chances. And when you are a little arrogant, which he had a big streak of, he probably figured they'd never catch him. It would be all right...it's not like he was actually stealing; just borrowing. Those dummies, they'd never suspect. Especially after he paid it back. But it didn't work out that way. Yes, he could be arrogant...not to his family, but to others. For him to get where he was...but what a shame to lose your home and everything. The real shame was what the family had to suffer."

"You know, I always wondered what made Aunt Margaret so bitter. And Uncle Buddy, too? Do you think it was the shame? The scandal?"

"Well, sure. Imagine...having everything you ever wanted, your older sisters go to college, have fine clothes and suddenly you have nothing. Your mother too, it was her turn and overnight her family is disgraced and she has nothing. No wonder she wanted to switch families."

Maggie thought about her mother and father. *I know they loved each other, but to marry so quickly. Did she do it to escape? There must have been more to it than that to last almost sixty years.* She said, "What an irony — that a man so devoted to his wife and family would put them in such jeopardy."

"Well, he didn't think of it that way. But it was so disgraceful... your own father, being hauled off to prison."

"Who was Edward Keeley?" asked Maggie, consulting her list. "I read his name in the obituary. It was the only name that wasn't familiar."

"I'm not sure, but I sort of remember his name. There *was* an old man with a long gray beard who used to sit on your grandfather's porch, but I doubt that was him. He took me one time to get penny candy, but I don't know who he was."

Maggie crossed off that question and asked another. "What about the houses they lived in? Were you in most of them?"

"All of them. Eighth Street, Pea Ridge, Staunton Road — all of them. One was grander than the next...until he went to prison. Then the houses got worse and worse. I remember when Buddy burnt down the barn in Pea Ridge...Lawrence was furious. The one on Staunton Road is where they had the burros."

"Oh, yes. The famous burros. I *have* heard those stories. But that's where the story always ends. Just sort of trails off, you know?" Maggie said wistfully. "I have a photograph album that Aunt Libba gave me. Would you like to see it? Maybe you can help me identify some of the people or places."

"I'd love to. Want some more coffee? Oh, my goodness. I should be offering you lunch. It's much later than I realized," Annie exclaimed as she rose from the sofa and headed for the kitchen.

"No, I'll just take more coffee. We can eat after we look at the album. I'll take you out to lunch; my treat for sharing your stories," Maggie suggested.

"We'll see. Show me the album," Annie said, noncommittally.

Maggie opened the album on the field chest and the two women hunched forward to inspect the faded sepia faces and fuzzy backgrounds of pictures dating back to 1908. Annie was even better than Aunt Libba at identifying people and places. It was as though she'd been there when the picture was snapped and, in some cases, she had. She pointed out her face among the Burghers in quite a few candid and posed family groups. When they had finished, and Maggie had covered the photos with post-it notes to remind her of Annie's identification, Maggie asked her final question.

"Annie, why do you think the family kept it such a secret all these years? I feel like I don't really know my mother, because the past she shared is only half of the story...and not the half that truly shaped her. I'll bet my cousins feel exactly the same about their Burgher parent, if you were to ask."

"Well, Maggie. Back then, folks buried family scandals. If you didn't talk about it, *it didn't happen*. At first, I'm sure they were just trying to exist, with the Depression and all. But after that, they just didn't want to bring it up — it was much too painful. After you've successfully ignored the truth, it becomes easier to keep telling the lie, or in this case, the half-truth. I'm sorry for you and your cousins. As a young woman, your mother was such fun...they all were. But this just stunted them, I'm afraid. Maybe that's one reason I decided to sort of light out on my own. I needed to be away from all that sadness."

Maggie closed the album and leaned back. "Annie, I can't thank you enough for all you've told me. It really adds some measure of understanding. And you're just great. I wish we lived closer; I'll bet we'd see each other often. Are you ready for some lunch?"

"Maggie, I think I'll take a rain check. That way you'll be forced to come back. I've got a bad back and it kinda kinks up in the humidity. I'm going to get out my heating pad, stretch out on this sofa and read. I appreciate your offer, though. I have loved getting to know you. If you think of any other questions, please call or write me. Or better yet, come ask in person."

"I will, Annie. Thanks again."

The two women rose to go downstairs. Maggie put the album under her arm and followed Annie back the way they had come. As she stepped into the steamy May heat, Maggie's sunglasses fogged over. She removed them and gave Annie a hug. "Bye, Annie. I'll be back soon."

"Bye, Maggs, I hope so," Annie said, unconciously using the same nickname that everyone else close to her had adopted.

Maggie walked past two shops, turned and waved again to Annie. In the heat-wrinkled air the woman who returned the wave looked just like her mother. The mirage brought tears to Maggie's eyes. She turned and headed back to the River Street Inn. *I'm sure there were more questions I should have asked. I'm still not sure about one thing...if he just meant to borrow that money, did someone pull the rug out from under him? If so, the family should have been angry, not disgraced. But as Paul Harvey is always saying...what about "the rest of the story." I'll bet there's more.*

Sixteen

April 1919

lags snapped smartly in the capricious April breeze as Lawrence walked briskly from the Railroad Bank & Trust building to the Guyandotte Club for lunch. The echo of the metal couplings on the flag lines as they bounced against the hollow flag poles seemed to match his hurried steps. The war was over, but patriotism remained strong. Nearly every business in town still flew the Stars and Stripes, and the Guyandotte Club was no exception. The flag pole at the corner of its property was nearly as tall as the inviting three-story brick building with its pillared front porch.

Huntington's exclusive Guyandotte Club was established just after the turn of the century by a group of convivial bankers, attorneys and merchants. Through the years, the membership regularly ignored men of lesser means and admitted to their ranks only those who had risen to the top professionally. Lawrence Burgher had been invited to join slightly more than a year after coming to Huntington. Now the Club was his regular noon haunt. As he approached it this day he noticed that cars filled the angled parking on the street in front of the Club.

Lawrence took the front steps two at a time. Hitting the porch, his heels echoed like a down beat. He stopped just short of flinging open the screen doors, smoothed his hair, readjusted his tie and shirt cuffs and strode through the double doors with purpose. He was running a bit late for his weekly luncheon with Keeley. Since Edward had begun to devote most of his time to his new coal company, he and Lawrence had established this Friday meeting to catch-up on their mutual interests. The two were still partners in the Hilltop Realty Company in Shapely, although most of the land was fully developed; and they still held the reins of the Bank of Shapely — leaving the day-to-day operation to Harry Mortimer, the new president, and David Burgher, who had remained as cashier.

A few men, whom Lawrence didn't know, were standing in the wide center foyer. They nodded politely as he crossed the carpeted expanse and approached the center dining room entrance. The rich aroma of food caused his mouth to water; suddenly he was ravenous. He scanned the room, but did not see Keeley; he turned to his right and headed toward the card room.

As Lawrence searched this room from its entrance, a still, blue cloud of smoke, hovering just below the ceiling, diffused his view. Floating just below the smoke, snatches of conversation, subdued laughter and the click of poker chips filled the air. The richly paneled card room also served as a dining room for those intent on spending as much time as possible at their card game, for gambling was not allowed in the main dining room. In the center, a waiter was clearing the dishes from a table of eight men. The diners were leaning away from the table in an attitude of resigned patience, but Lawrence knew they were eager to begin their game. Each day during the long lunch hour — 11 A.M. to 2 P.M. — this handful of men, who held "positions" rather than "jobs" in the business community, gathered at the same table in the card room. They arrived at 11 A.M. to play cards, smoke cigars and eat lunch. However, their low-stakes games often lasted long after the luncheon dishes were cleared away and the cocktail hour had begun in earnest.

Scattered at tables of two and four around this group were other men of means who came for the good food, pleasant gossip, business news and an occasional hand or two of poker. Keeley, a club member for the past five years, was among the latter group. It wasn't that he wouldn't have played cards every day, for he loved to gamble; he simply wasn't a part of this long standing octet. He signaled to Lawrence from a table to the left of the gamblers. Lawrence saw the signal and headed toward Keeley, stopping several times to speak to friends as he crossed the room.

Passing the "boys," as the regulars called themselves, he spoke laughingly to one, "Don't let them take your money today, Russell. They've been doing it all week; today it's your turn." The group laughed in return. Lawrence reached Keeley's table and pulled out a chair.

"Sorry Edward; Maynard stopped me on the way out to sign some papers. I don't know why he does that — waits until I'm about to leave, then insists I must sign that minute. Very annoying."

"Don't worry about it. I arrived only a few minutes ago myself. How are you? And how's that new boy? Congratulations. What did you name this one?"

"Thank you Edward, I'm just fine and so is the new baby. We named him Stephen Paul. Anna is recovering well, too. However I don't know what she'd do without Miss Pennyroyal."

Edward changed the subject abruptly. "Do you see that empty table to our right? Young Pete Hawkins and his cronies were sitting there, talking. Then, suddenly — even before ordering — they all jumped up and went out. They've been gone well over thirty minutes. They acted like they'd be back, but the waiters don't know whether or not to clear the table for another party. How do you suppose he came to be invited, anyway? Isn't he a bit too young?"

"Perhaps it was his father's connection," Lawrence said. "Don't they automatically let a son join if the father is a member?"

"I'm not sure, but I suppose that could be. Enough of Pete; how was your week?" Keeley asked.

"Excellent, Edward. The new stock subscriptions are coming in nicely. I think we'll hit our $1,000,000 goal by June 30. Did you go to Shapely this week?" Lawrence queried in return.

"No, but I had a letter from Harry Mortimer. He sent the first quarter financial statements which were very strong. David is a very astute cashier; I hope we can keep him."

"Oh, I don't think you need worry about that. He's happy in Shapely. I received a letter from Mortimer as well. The loan committee approved my loan request. I told you about the two houses near me that I'm buying, didn't I?"

"No, I don't think so. Were they on your 'master plan' map?" Keeley joked.

"No," Lawrence laughed. "I just found out they were available. You know my uncle died about a month ago in Mt. Hope and my mother is now quite alone. Well, nearly alone. She and my uncle Will married after I went away to school, and they had a daughter named Lillian. She's about twenty years younger than I am. I guess that would make her about twenty, now. I really never knew her, though. Now that Will's gone, I want to move Mother into a place of her own here in Huntington. Lillian wants to go to college to become a teacher, and I think Marshall is a good choice. These two houses are side-by-side; I thought I'd put Mother and Lillian in one and rent the other."

"Why didn't you borrow the money from our bank here?"

"I thought it better not to have all my paper in one place. Sometimes it's best to keep your own counsel. Another loan here would have to be approved by our board of directors. I just don't want them to know *all* of my business. I learned that from you. You don't have all your eggs in one basket either, Edward. Do you?"

Keeley chuckled, "Certainly not. I merely wondered if that was your thinking as well. Very smart, Lawrence."

"Besides, there's a large piece of land just south of the city that I looked at last week. I'm thinking of buying it also and I wondered if you might be interested. It's a large tract which could be developed like we did in Shapely. We could finance the development costs, sell the lots and hold the notes ourselves, repaying the bank as we are paid. I've had a good profit from some of the other sheriff's sale property which I bought and resold. I can put that up to buy my half. Interested?"

"I might be. Let's go look at it next week. I need to go to Mt. Hope on coal business, but I'll be back by the middle of the week. Our new mine is really producing. At this rate, we're going to have record sales this year."

Just as the waiter approached to take their order, Lawrence was distracted by boisterous laughter from the front hall. Pete Hawkins,

Eddie Long, "Dummy" Jones and two other young men came through the doorway looking heated and excited. Pete was without his suit jacket. On their way across the card room, the group stopped at the large table of poker players. Pete said to the entire group, "Well, boys. I never thought I'd see the day I couldn't get up a bet against these fellows, but I saw it today." The conversation carried across the room.

One of the men asked, just as Pete knew he would, "What happened, Pete?"

"Well, as you know, the boys and I left a little while ago to settle a bet," answered Pete, launching into a story. Pete was an inveterate gambler as well as the club raconteur; however, he always bet on what he considered a sure thing. He rarely lost. "Just before ordering lunch, we got to talking about how close to town the streetcar barn was. I said it was so close I could run from here at Fourth Avenue and Eleventh Street down to the barn at Eighth Street West. Some of the boys got up the money and we left to prove that I could do it. Dummy took my suit coat and he and the other boys got in his car to follow me. When we got close to the car barn, I motioned to Dummy and he pulled along side of me. I said, 'Get a bet up that I can go to the bus barn at 19th Street West.' So he turned to the boys and said, 'Pete wants to bet that he can go to the bus barn.' They put up their money and I kept on running to the bus barn. We got there and I told Dummy to get up a bet that I could keep on going to Camden Park. You know that's another three miles away. Would you believe that they wouldn't bet me? Of course, I won the money they had put up; but I couldn't get them to bet any more. And, I guess technically I won that bet, too, since they wouldn't bet against me." Pete smiled smugly.

Everyone laughed, including Lawrence and Keeley. "That Pete. He'd bet on almost anything, wouldn't he?" Lawrence mused as he picked up the menu again.

Keeley disagreed. "No, Pete only bets on a sure thing. He knew two things when he left. One is that he *could* run to Camden Park and the other is that he wouldn't have to because they wouldn't take his last bet. The moral of that story is never bluff if you don't have the balls to pull it off. Pete may act the fool, but he's really pretty shrewd for a young fellow. Speaking of gambling...have you got time for a hand or two of poker? Or are you still 'minding your mother?'"

"No, I've managed to put mother's face away from the gambling table. I think I can stay for about another hour and I'd be glad to take your money," Lawrence laughed sounding as confident as Pete Hawkins. The memory of his prudish behavior at the Dunglen Hotel in Thurmond when he and Keeley first became partners flashed through his mind.

Keeley remembered it too, for he chuckled as he said, "You've come a long way from the Dunglen, Lawrence. You have a gambler's soul in you after all." The two men grinned at each other. Then they placed their luncheon order.

Seventeen

January 1921

As Lawrence and Anna boarded the C & O passenger train, the *Fast Flying Virginian*, the evening of January 16, the sky overhead was gray and threatening. Old Man Winter was back and he had a nasty attitude. For most of the month the prevailing weather had been the typical West Virginia cycle of drizzle — rain — sleet — snow — drizzle again; but a new storm in Canada headed their way was expected to hit with a vengeance. Anna and Lawrence were making their second annual escape to Florida and couldn't wait to get away. They didn't plan on returning until winter's back had been broken.

Last year they had toured several resort cities in Florida and found they enjoyed the west coast best — particularly Sarasota. Lawrence was not drawn back to Sarasota by the lure of its well known sport fishing, however. Neither had the promotional booklet touting the pristine, confectioner's sugar sand of the Gulf Beaches caught his eye. Instead, Lawrence planned to combine pleasure, in the form of golf, with business. When Lawrence met Owen Burns the previous February on a Sarasota golf course, the two found they had several mutual interests. Both were bankers — Owen Burns had started Citizens Bank in Sarasota — and both were involved in real estate development. Burns had talked then about his plans for an in-town residential area —— Burns Court, and several subdivisions in the outlying areas of Sarasota. Lawrence had been corresponding all year with the entrepreneur. Now that Burns' developments were under way, Lawrence wanted to see if those plans could be adapted to his own real estate developments in Huntington. In his last letter, Burns had agreed to meet Lawrence whenever the Burghers came back to Sarasota.

Anna, on the other hand, was content to have the time to herself. She wanted nothing more than to relax and read — a pastime she had been forced to curtail severely amid her bustling household of six children, a cook and a day-girl. Anna did not intend to worry one bit; she knew they had left the children in good hands. Last year's trip had shown Miss Pennyroyal to be superb in managing domestic details. And, with the additional help of Millie Eubanks, a huge Negro woman Lawrence had hired as their cook after Stephen was born, Anna could truly relax.

The train trip took two and one-half days. The *Fast Flying Virginian* arrived in Richmond, Virginia in the early morning hours to connect with the Seaboard Air Line Railway's *Fast Mail*. The *Fast Mail* left at noon on Monday and slipped through the south for another day and a half, passing mill towns, cotton fields and Spanish moss-covered live-oaks. As Anna and Lawrence watched the scenery scroll past the train window, the sky changed from ominous gray to winter white to cornflower blue. Finally, the couple stepped off the train into the humidity of Sarasota, Florida. It was Tuesday, January 18, at 6:10 P.M., and the sun was just beginning to set over the Gulf of Mexico.

The faint odor of fish wafted through the train station on Lemon Avenue as a warm breeze off Sarasota Bay signaled their arrival in the former fishing village. Lawrence tugged at his collar while he waited for the porter to load their luggage into the hotel car. "Can you believe it's winter, love? Just doesn't seem possible that two days ago we were freezing, does it?"

Anna replied, "No, darling, it doesn't. It must be seventy degrees and it's nearly dinner time. By the way, I'm starving. I hope we can get a reservation in the hotel dining room."

The driver of the hotel car overheard Anna as he reached to open the car door. He responded, "Ma'am, that will not be a problem. The DeSoto serves dinner until 9 P.M." Anna thanked him as the couple slipped into the rear seat of the long, black Cadillac. The short drive to The DeSoto Hotel hardly gave them time to admire the gently waving palm trees which seemed to welcome them to Florida. As they approached The DeSoto in the fading glow of the sunset, the salmon stucco facade seemed brighter than Anna remembered. The driver jumped out of the car, which he left running at the curb, quickly opened the car door, then scurried to also open the richly carved double doors that marked the hotel's entrance. Before he could do so, two uniformed doormen swung open both doors from within. They bowed as the couple made their entrance.

While Lawrence completed their registration, Anna glanced around the lobby. The terra cotta and turquoise mosaic floor and the huge murals depicting Hernando De Soto's Florida expedition seemed a bit ornate for her taste, but she remembered the comfort of the suite they occupied last year and forgave the decorators for their garish style. She looked forward to a good night's sleep in a comfortable bed. Lawrence walked toward her, smiled and slipped his arm around her waist. They strolled across the lobby toward the stairs and ascended slowly, for they had all the time in the world.

"Let's freshen up before dinner, love. I've made our reservations. Are you glad to be here?"

"I can't think of anywhere else I'd rather be. This is lovely. I'd nearly forgotten how relaxing it is without children. Not that I wish we didn't have them; it's just nice to be alone once in a while...just the two of us...you know?" Anna smiled up at her husband. It was as if they were newlyweds, again.

"Indeed I do. I've been looking forward to this for a long time. I want to teach you to play golf this year. Would you like that?"

"That might be fun. Although I don't want to spoil your fun by having to teach me. Perhaps I should take lessons from a professional and then play with you."

"Well, we'll see," Lawrence said, surreptitiously patting her hip. "Maybe we should turn in early tonight," he said softly. Anna looked around to be sure no one saw them, then grinned. Stopping in front of their suite, she answered in kind, "We'll see, we'll see."

After a week of golf lessons, Anna decided to leave the links to Lawrence and go back to her reading under the canopied hotel porch. While she had never considered herself uncoordinated, the concept of hitting a tiny white ball into a hole seemed to elude her. Furthermore, it seemed a total waste of time. And, if she had wanted to walk, she'd rather have done it on the beach. So she and Lawrence had agreed: He could play golf, every day if he liked, and she would read, shop, or play whist with the other guests at the hotel.

The couple did spend each evening together — sampling the cuisine at one or another of the new restaurants in the area or eating in the beautiful, if ostentatious, hotel dining room. The DeSoto also featured a variety of social activities for their guests which Anna and Lawrence often attended. Musical performances by talented local performers, a whist bridge tournament, weekly dress balls and even a performance by an acrobatic troupe were scheduled during their visit. The cultural elite of Sarasota had created a number of cultural events for the growing population of winter visitors, as well. The Burghers rarely passed an idle evening.

By the second week, Lawrence had grown bored with the daily routine of morning golf, poker at lunch and golf again. He wasn't that adept at either game, for he rarely played them at home, and he was eager to see Owen Burns' developments. Burns had been out of town when they arrived, but Lawrence was sure he would be back by now. On Monday, Lawrence called Citizens Bank and found Burns in his office. The two developers talked and Burns invited Lawrence to accompany him on a tour of his subdivisions the next day. He offered to call for Lawrence at 10 A.M.

The morning was sunny and clear as Lawrence descended to the lobby dressed in his pale blue seersucker suit. While he waited, he lounged in the overstuffed leather chair nearest the doors reading *The Wall Street Journal*. He glanced over the top of the paper each time the hotel doors opened, afraid he would miss Owen's arrival. Within ten minutes, he saw the distinguished looking gentleman enter the hotel and noticed immediately that Burns wore a custom-made linen suit. Lawrence stood quickly and greeted the man effusively. "Owen, it's so good to see you again. You're looking quite fit. It seems everyone in Florida looks fit; perhaps it's the sun."

"Good to see you too, Lawrence. Looks like you've had your share of the sun, too. Been playing golf, have you?"

"Yes, but I've decided I'm really no good at it. I'm too impatient. When I play a game, I want to master it immediately. Golf requires too much time to get it right. I guess business is more my game."

"Often, that requires patience too, my friend," Burns cautioned.

"Ah, yes; but I seem to be a better hand at it than at golf," Lawrence laughed.

"In that case, let's go see my new projects. Are you ready?"

"Absolutely," Lawrence answered. Folding *The Wall Street Journal*, he placed it under his arm and followed Owen past the doormen and into the sunlight. Lawrence shaded his eyes as a shaft of light bounced off the car at the curb and hit him full in the face.

"Here's my car," said Burns. Beside the rear door of a new Packard Single-Six Sedan, a uniformed driver stood ram-rod straight. As they approached, the driver opened the door and the two men got in. The chauffeur walked swiftly around the car, slid into the driver's seat and, without a word, steered the large automobile into the traffic.

Lawrence was impressed with both the car and the fact that Owen Burns had a chauffer, but tried not to show it. "I see you are a Packard man, too. I've had my Twin-Six for several years and I've been thinking of trading it for a new one. How do you like the Single-Six?"

"It seems to be a very good car. My driver says it handles quite well, despite its size."

The two men chatted amicably as the car moved slowly through the narrow streets of Sarasota. As they traveled, Owen pointed out some of Sarasota's newest buildings, road projects and developments to Lawrence, mentioning various developers and visionaries past and present — John Gillespie, current Mayor Arthur Britton Edwards, Harry Higel and most recently, John Ringling — who were making

Sarasota a great city. Naturally, Burns didn't include himself in the list, but Lawrence sensed that he too, was one of Sarasota's shining lights. Of those Burns did name, Lawrence had heard only of John Ringling.

"Tell me more about Ringling." Lawrence asked, "I had no idea he was involved in real estate development. I've always thought of him as just a circus owner."

"Are you kidding? He owns more property on this coast than anyone else, I daresay. He owns St. Armands Key, Bird Key, Coon Key, Wolf Key and two thousand acres on Longboat Key, all over there across Sarasota Bay," Owen answered, gesturing to his right. "He bought St. Armands Key several years ago and planned a shopping center and a community of residential lots. Ringling Isles, he called it. Since there was no bridge, he hired an old paddle-wheeler as a work boat and began building sea walls and dredging the canals. Now he's putting in the sidewalks, streets and buildings. Aside from my own projects, I'm managing his developments on Lido and St. Armands Key. My real estate company will be the sole agent when Ringling Isles is ready to sell. And he's going to build a causeway to connect St. Armands to the mainland. My firm has the contract for that as well."

"Mercy. It sounds like you and Ringling have quite a connection. I had no idea your interests were so extensive. You two are changing the face of the west coast. I'm more impressed with you than with those other fellows you spoke about, " Lawrence said admiringly.

"Well, it's been exciting to be a part of helping this little old fishing village grow up. Here we are, my little development — Burns Court," announced Burns.

As the car pulled to the curb beneath a huge Cuban laurel tree, Lawrence added, " You know, I'd like the opportunity to meet Ringling myself, some day."

"Well, if you have the time, we could take the ferry over to Lido a little later; he's usually over there right after lunch. I need to check on one of the crews anyway; maybe we'll run into him," Burns replied.

The two men alighted from the car and spent the better part of an hour walking the property, stopping periodically to look at the blueprints of Owen Burns' dream community. By the time they returned to the shade of the expansive tree, Lawrence was clearly in awe of the scope of Burns' project. In his own mind, he cast about for a way to replicate the in-town development in Huntington.

"Owen, this is a great project, but I'm damned if I can see a way to do anything similar in Huntington. Our city is already beginning to take shape — close in, that is. There's not a large tract of land available that I know of. Perhaps your subdivision designs are more adaptable. Could we go see them, as well?"

"Certainly, Lawrence," Burns said affably. He seemed to Lawrence quite willing to spend all day touring his properties. Lawrence liked that. He could easily see himself in a similar role — checking on his developments, rather than sitting behind a desk at the bank. The big car moved dilatorily toward the outskirts of the city. Lawrence wondered idly if the driver maintained this snail-like pace on Owen's direction or if the Packard Single-Six was simply more sluggish than his older model. By noon, they had seen three more of Burns' developments. Each was laid out with gently curving streets, circular courts and a central mini-park. Lawrence had never seen such innovative ideas. As the driver retraced their route through the Sarasota streets, Lawrence was daydreaming. *What I wouldn't give to develop just one such area in Huntington. They would be in awe of such a revolutionary design. I wonder if I could....*

Owen spoke again, "...and I thought perhaps we'd eat on the pier, and then go over to Lido."

"I'm sorry, Owen; my mind was back in West Virginia. What did you say?"

Burns laughed, "Planning a new development already? I said, if we have lunch on the pier we might see John. He often eats down there while he waits for the afternoon ferry."

"That would be grand, but I don't want to take up your whole day."

"Nonsense, I'm happy to have you along. And I'm making my normal rounds in the bargain," Burns said graciously.

As the Packard pulled up to the dock area at the foot of Main

Street, Lawrence spotted the best looking car he had ever seen. Most cars were square, like a closed box; but this one had a graceful curve where the back wall met the roof line. *What a beautiful car. Look at those wood-grain wheels. And the spare tires mounted in the fenders. Wow!* Lawrence also noticed that in the open chauffeur's quarters sat an erect driver, his hands on the wheel, as if ready to perform his duties at a moment's notice.

"What kind of car is that?" Lawrence asked Owen.

"Oh, that's John's Pierce-Arrow Landaulet. It's one of his newest toys. The man loves his cars. He must be eating in the fish shack. Let's go see if we can find him."

The pair walked onto the long wooden pier that jutted out from the narrow shoreline of Sarasota Bay. Small fishing boats, tied to the pier on either side, bobbed in an undulating rhythm as the gentle waves rolled landward. The motion gave Lawrence a slightly queasy feeling. Suddenly he wished he had not agreed to take the ferry to Lido with Owen.

Owen drew open the screen door to the shack at the end of the pier and motioned Lawrence inside. Small wooden tables-for-two lined one wall of the small, dingy building and a chest high counter ran the length of the other. At one end of the counter stood a large barrel of shrimp. The sign hung above it read "BAIT ONLY." Lawrence nearly gagged at the thought that someone would mistake these thrashing live creatures for a luncheon selection.

Seated at one of the small tables toward the rear was a rotund man with full jowls and sleepy eyes. Lawrence would not have singled him out among the other men hunched over their meals, but this one was wearing a stiffly starched white shirt and a dark red silk tie. He was smoking a long cigar as he studied the parade of patrons.

"There's John," said Owen pointing toward the man Lawrence had noticed. As the two men walked toward him, John Ringling stood up.

"Owen, am I glad to see you. Have you got a moment to...," Ringling began.

Burns interrupted him. "John, I'd like to introduce you to Lawrence Burgher, a real estate developer from West Virginia."

Lawrence smiled heartily and put out his hand to greet the legendary man. "How do you do, Mr. Ringling," Lawrence said, shaking the large, perfectly-manicured hand of John Ringling.

"Hello," said Ringling offhandedly. He shook hands perfunctorily and quickly removed his hand from Lawrence's grasp. "Owen, I really need to talk to you. Can you go with me out to Lido?" He had turned away from Lawrence and was talking closely to Burns. Lawrence stepped backward and colored slightly as the two conversed in earnest for a moment. He did not want to appear to be eavesdropping but standing alone was awkward, too. He busied himself by looking into the bait barrel.

Within minutes, Owen took a step toward Lawrence, looking apologetic, as John Ringling edged himself past the two men and went out the screen door. As the wooden door banged shut, Owen said, "Lawrence, I am so sorry; John needs me to go with him to solve a problem out on Lido. I'm afraid we'll be out there the rest of the afternoon and you'd be bored stiff. Would you mind terribly if I have Reynard take you back to your hotel? Perhaps we can get together again before you leave."

"Of course. You've been more than gracious with your time already. I appreciate your courtesy and look forward to seeing you again," he responded, somewhat formally. He was chagrined at the snub by Ringling, but didn't want to draw attention to his discomfort. "I have some paperwork I've neglected anyway. This will give me a chance to do it. Thanks again for your hospitality."

Lawrence and Owen shook hands outside the fish shack and Lawrence walked back to the Packard, spoke briefly with the driver and got in the rear. As they pulled away, he could see Burns and Ringling waiting at the end of the pier for the ferry. The two men were laughing together.

Anna looked up as the door to the suite opened. She had come back to the room for a short nap after lunch and was lying on the bed, *The Age of Innocence* in her hand. "Lawrence, honey. You're back.

How was your visit with Mr. Burns?"

"Just grand. We had a wonderful morning touring all of his developments. They're quite unique in design. I'm thinking of adapting a few of his ideas to some of my projects. Did you know that he is a partner of John Ringling's? I met him today," Lawrence said somewhat nonchalantly.

"Met who? John Ringling?" Anna said.

"Oh, yes. Owen introduced us," he began excitedly. "Shook his hand. He has huge hands. He's quite an imposing figure...a big man. We had lunch at a fishing shack on the pier," Lawrence lied.

"Did you really?" Anna remarked.

Lawrence continued, "You wouldn't believe the car he has — a Pierce-Arrow. I've never seen such a beautiful automobile. Do you know that they cost over $7,000? Owen has a new Single-Six Packard; with a driver, too. But Ringling's car is really special. And of course, he has a chauffeur as well. I had no idea that Ringling was such a land developer. He owns more land than anyone else on the west coast of Florida."

"He does?" Anna sounded impressed.

"Yes. We chatted about his projects on St. Armands and Lido Key," Lawrence continued to lie.

He saw no reason to tell Anna about the real nature of their meeting. "He's even going to build a causeway and a bridge to the keys." *After all, Ringling* was *busy. I'm sure that if he hadn't been in such a hurry, we* would *have had a grand conversation and he would have taken to me.*

As he relayed, more accurately, the events of his morning with Owen Burns, a knock sounded at the door. "Yes, what is it?" Lawrence called through the closed door.

"There's a call for you in the lobby, sir," came the muffled response.

"Sorry, love. I'd better go take the call." He laughed. "Perhaps it's John Ringling, calling to say how much he enjoyed meeting me."

When Lawrence picked up the receiver, it wasn't John Ringling at all; it was Edward Keeley.

"Lawrence, sorry to interrupt your holiday, but I just received a very disturbing letter from the banking commissioner. The last report of the bank examiners showed, and I quote 'a number of discrepancies and irregularities which I feel it is my duty to immediately bring to your attention and ask that immediate steps be taken to correct.' Lawrence, what the hell is going on? I don't like the sound of this letter at all. He says we have an excessive amount of overdrafts, more loans and discounts than our deposits can support, and that this matter of reported earnings is irregular and must be corrected."

"Edward, I'm sure it's all a matter of our bookkeeping methods. Calm down, it's not so irregular as he makes it sound."

"Well, it sounds pretty bad to me. I know you've been aggressive in making loans; but hell, Lawrence you've got to abide by the rules. You are smart enough to handle it properly. I don't know how to respond to this letter. He suggests we need to take it to the board of directors immediately. I think you'd better cut short this Florida trip and head back here, now."

"But Edward, we've been here only two weeks."

"I don't give a damn if it's been only two days. Get your ass back up here, Lawrence. I put you in charge of this bank, now come back here and run it."

Before Lawrence could object further, Edward hung up.

Eighteen

February 1921

L awrence returned to Huntington on a bitterly cold, snowy Saturday night and spent Sunday afternoon at the bank pouring over the letter from the banking commissioner and the relevant bank records. By Monday morning, Lawrence was prepared to discuss it with Keeley. He took the letter, the bank's books and his notes up to Keeley's office and knocked on the door.

"Come in," Keeley growled. He sounded to Lawrence like a hibernating bear, furious at being disturbed. Lawrence squared his shoulders and shifted the papers under his arm. He opened the office door and saw Keeley sitting hunched forward on his desk, his elbows on two small piles of file folders. The scowl on his face marked him as a man ready for a fight.

"Good morning, Edward. Before you say anything, let me assure you that these 'irregularities,' as the examiners call them, are nothing. We can fix them up right away."

"Well, I sure as hell hope so. I don't like being called on the carpet by the banking commissioner. And I particularly didn't like having to stall for an answer. Now let's go over these points one by one," Edward said, sounding a bit mollified.

Lawrence breathed deeply. Then he sat down in the leather chair in front of Keeley's desk. He pulled out his notes. "Fine. First the overdrafts. Perhaps $16,969, almost $17,000 *is* an excessive amount. We will be more stringent in the future. I've let a few fellows float but I can stop that. As for the discrepancies in the overdraft account, we will be more careful to see that the ledger amounts balance in the future. I'll instruct Maynard to give me an accurate list of overdrafts each day. You know, one or two of those overdrafts were yours, Edward. I saw, however, that you had paid them right after the examiners were here."

Keeley leaned back in his chair, looking somewhat chagrined but offered no explanation.

Lawrence continued and Keeley did not interrupt him. "As for the loans...if we are to be aggressive in capturing business, $890,000 isn't too large a loan balance to have outstanding. However, I *will* make a concerted effort to reduce this as much as possible. I'll get a list of the outstanding loans, and be sure they are either collected or that they are good loans. Part of the problem, as the examiner pointed out, is the decline in deposits. When Huntington National took over the Day & Night Bank some of our depositors went with the larger bank. That hurt us. And, the loss of depositors has made our loan amounts look lopsided."

Keeley scowled again. "Well, what the hell are we going to do about that? We *were* growing quite nicely...now you tell me we are slipping? I suggest we make an all out pitch for new depositors."

"We can do that, Edward. And we can encourage our board of directors, again, to be aggressive about soliciting their business associates." Lawrence sounded positive about being able to correct the decline.

"What about these doubtful loans the examiner pointed out? Shouldn't we simply charge them off?"

"We can do that, too; but it makes our net worth smaller. And of course, that will affect our dividends."

"Well, look at them carefully. We don't want to be carrying too much questionable paper. What about this business of stocks and bonds? I don't like the idea of you buying stock on margin and then carrying it on our books. The examiner was most specific that this practice should not happen again." A scowl crossed Keeley's face. He banged his fist on the desk, causing the files to slide and Lawrence to jump. "For God's sake, Lawrence, you are smarter than that. You should have known that you couldn't do that."

"Edward, I only planned to use the margin for a short period of time. I had a note due on some of my property and had planned to pay it off when it came in. If I had not bought the stock when I did, the price would have gone up dramatically. I can pay the margin today. And I won't let it happen again."

"Well, see that you don't. One more thing...and I don't quite understand this. The examiner says 'the whole situation relative to earnings....' Let's see...oh, yes, here it is," he said, consulting his copy of the letter. "'...your Bank is attempting to operate against an overhead expense that cannot be paid and allow the Bank to make any money at all.' He says you told him that it would be made up by interest of over $8,000 which we will collect by March 1; but it's being carried on our books now as earnings. What happens if it isn't collected? Will we be able to pay our bills and declare a dividend?"

"Of course, Edward. I was told it's a common practice — the bank has done this for years. Besides, I'm confident the interest will be paid. And if we don't report it as earnings, we won't be able to pay the dividend. I think that would be disastrous, don't you?" Lawrence wanted Keeley to understand his position and to agree on his course of action.

"Well, I suppose it would. But you know, I really don't understand some of these things. I'm just an ol' coal operator, not a banker. Remember, I just own banks; never intended to actually run one. That's your job. Just keep it solid and get these problems solved. I'm calling a meeting of the board of directors at the end of the week and you can explain these items to them. Then I'll respond to Commissioner Snodgrass when we have resolved the irregularities."

"That's fine. I should be able to fix up most of these items by then. They won't happen again."

"Lawrence, they'd better not."

Lawrence rose, gathered his papers and left Keeley's office. Although he was very uncomfortable with Keeley's rebuke, he really was concerned about only one item — paying off the margin. The note was still not paid. He would have to go collect it in person and he hated confrontations. There wasn't any help for it, however. He had told Keeley he could pay it. Now he had to make good on his promise.

KEELEY COAL COMPANY
WEST VIRGINIA SMOKELESS COAL

HUNTINGTON, WEST VIRGINIA
Mines in Wyoming, Fayette and Raleigh Counties
Edward M. Keeley, President

February 14, 1921

Mr. R. L Snodgrass
Commissioner of Banking,
Charleston, W.Va.

Dear Mr. Snodgrass:

I received your letter of January 31, but was
unable to speak to Mr. Burgher about it until
Friday last, as he was out of the city. I want
to thank you for bringing these matters to my
attention as I do not know anything about the
banking business; never claimed to. All these
matters are left up to the cashier. Upon his
return, he read the examiners report and
immediately went to work to fix up several of
the items. Our Board of Directors also met and
went over the matters listed in your letter.
I am pleased to report we have cleaned up each
item listed.

I want to assure you that the Bank will be run
on a different line, or I expect to resign and
get out. I trust when you make your next
report, you will find things in a different
condition. Until then, I remain,

Very truly yours,

Edward M. Keeley

West Virginia Banking Commission
Charleston, W.Va.

January 12, 1922

Mr. Edward M. Keeley, President
Railroad Bank & Trust Co.
Huntington, W. Va.

Dear Sir:

I beg to acknowledge receipt of your letter of
the 10th relative to the affairs of the Railroad
Bank & Trust Company. I have noted all you have
to say.

I was pleased, indeed, to find on my last
examination that there was an improvement in the
affairs of your Bank. You, I take it, understand the situation at your Bank very well, now
that the Directors are meeting regularly and
keeping in closer touch with the Bank's affairs.

I note that very few loans have been made during
this year, and I was indeed heartened that you
have reduced your own line of credit, as well.

I also noted from the minutes that you submitted
that the Directors have arranged for a material
decrease in your expense account, brought about
by reducing your forces and also reducing
officers' salaries. The writer fully appreci-
ates that it is indeed hard to reduce salaries;

at the same time, I feel that the action taken by your Directors is a wise one.

A few matters were noted that require your attention, however. On day of examination, there appeared to be a cash shortage of $256.38. This should be charged off the books immediately. I feel that you still have a few notes and overdrafts to charge off which you, no doubt, will work out from time to time.

While the writer has never seen fit to criticize any of the paper of yourself or any of your business concerns, it would seem to be best that the notes of your concerns be endorsed by yourself, personally. I refer particularly to the notes of the Keeley Timber & Logging Company, which on day of examination, were noted to be not endorsed.

On the whole, I can see that your institution is in a decidedly better shape than at the date of the former examination. I am candid enough to advise you, however, that you have a great deal to accomplish before the affairs of your Bank will be in satisfactory shape.

Please keep this office advised relative to all matters of the Bank. I will ask that the letters in reply be signed by yourself and Mr. Burgher.

Yours very truly,

Robert L. Snodgrass

Robert L. Snodgrass
Commissioner of Banking

RLS: mp

Christmas Letter, 1922

Dear Rebecca,

I can hardly believe that a year has passed since we last corresponded. It does seem a shame that we renew the bond between us only during the holidays; but with both our full houses, I suppose that's understandable.

This year has brought us both sadness and joy. In September my father was killed in a slate-fall in his mine at Kilsyth. As the assistant superintendent, one of his tasks was to check the mine for safety. He had gone in to the #1 mine, there being a report of an unsafe roof, and it collapsed on him. He was brought out but died of his injuries a few days later. I suppose in a way, he was a hero, as his death may have prevented that of many others. Mother was devastated, but has recovered her strength.

All the children are growing and healthy. Eileen is now a teenager (can you believe it?) and is growing up into a fine young woman, I can always count on her to help with the others. Sara at ten remains a tomboy. She hates dresses and will wear pants anytime she can get away with it. Buddy started school this year and thought he was terribly grown up until Margaret began to lord it over him. She thinks she's his boss, since they both go to the same school. Stephen Paul still hangs on my skirt tails at three and a half. I wonder if he'll ever stop being a mama's boy? He'd better, now that our newest baby is here.

Our Elizabeth, born on November 2, is the best baby I've ever had, I do believe. She is already sleeping through the night, never cries and seems content to just watch the world. I hope she remains placid.

We lost the services of our Miss Pennyroyal right after the baby came. She decided that she needed to move back to her family's place to care for her aging mother. Thank goodness Mother had moved to Huntington by then. After my father's death, Lawrence suggested that she move here. We put it to her, and she was agreeable. Lawrence owns two houses near us; one is where his own mother lives. We put Mother in the other one. Now the children have to walk only two blocks to see both grandmothers.

We hired a new day-girl, but she doesn't have the good humor of Miss Pennyroyal. In fact, she seems as scared as a wild rabbit. When I talk to her about things to be done, she wrings her hands as if she's being chastised. I don't know if she'll last. Thank goodness we still have Millie. Her laughter and good cooking make up for the ways of Lila Mae Trumbo.

I hope this holiday season finds you and your family healty and happy. May God bless you in the coming year,

Your old friend,

January 3, 1923

Dearest Sister Jenny,

It was so good to see you and all your family this Christmas. I know the trip back to Thurmond with the twins must have been exhausting, especially with all the presents you had to carry home. Thank you for coming; I believe it made Mother's first holiday without Father easier to bear.

You should see Buddy on his new Flying Scot...already, he can really make it go. And Stephen loves the hobby-horse you gave him. He rides all over the house pretending he's a cowboy.

I enclosed the clipping about the upcoming automobile show because Eileen and Sara are going to perform at the opening. Do you remember my telling you that they have both been studying music with Professor Hyldof from Cincinnati? He comes here weekly and gives lessons in piano and violin. Eileen has become quite proficient on the piano and Sara seems to have a knack for the violin. Did you know that Mother gave Father's violin to her for her 10th birthday? I can only hope she possesses his talent for the instrument.

You won't believe what Lawrence has bought now! A farm! After vowing he would never own one again, he bought 10 acres of farm land about 12 miles east of the city. Of course, we aren't going to move there, thank goodness. He has secured a tenant farmer, but he's out there nearly every day instructing the poor man on how he thinks it should be run. We have cows, goats, pigs, chickens and several horses. I think he really loved that farm he grew up on, but he won't admit it. And, as a businessman, he knows it's no place to make a good living. As a child, he was so poor that he would never want that for his children. But this will give them a place to learn to ride horseback. The farmer says he will teach them. Sara is most excited about that prospect.

We are preparing to go to Sarasota at the end of the month. We plan to stay only two weeks this time, as Lawrence is very busy at the bank. Additionally, he has some new real-estate deal that may need tending before long. I find it difficult to keep up with all he does. Just about the time I think I know what he owns, he sells one piece of property and buys another. I simply sign the papers; it's easier that way.

The children don't want us to go to Florida this year, as they don't like Lila Mae Trumbo as well as they did Miss Pennyroyal. However, I feel confident in leaving them in her hands now, as she has gained confidence in her capabilities and really manages quite well. She's just not as jolly as Miss Pennyroyal. Besides with both grandmothers within walking distance, the children will be well cared for.

Take care and keep warm this winter. I'll drop you a line from Florida. I wish you could go with us some time.

Your loving sister,

Anna

West Virginia Banking Commission
Charleston, W.Va.

March 23, 1923

Mr. R. Lawrence Burgher, Vice Pres. & Cashier
Railroad Bank & Trust Co.
Huntington, West Virginia

Dear Sir:

I have on my desk a report of an examination
made of your Bank by our Mr. Stiller as of the
17th, 18th and 19th, instant.

Several past due notes are listed as doubtful
and slow paper. These need to be charged off.
The report also shows that your Bank is carrying
some demand notes on which several months have
elapsed since interest was paid on them. Interest should be paid at least every six months,
otherwise they will be classed as past due and
bad. A demand note should be what the name
indicates, and if it is going to be carried by
the bank, it should be made a time note and not
a demand note.

The report also shows that your bank is carrying
among your assets a substantial amount of stock
shares of several companies. There is no law to
prevent your bank carrying stocks as a part of
its assets, but this practice has been discour-
aged by this department. Ordinarily stocks in
corporations do not represent a fixed asset. It
is usually an investment and has that feature
attached to it. If the company is successful,
the stock is usually good. If the company is not

successful, the stock may not be of any value. Our suggestion to your Bank is to dispose of the stock as soon as you can.

It seems your Bank received a commission for the sale of some 190 acres of land in Lincoln County and also some extra interest on account of the extension given to the people who had purchased the property and that you at once placed this commission and extra interest on the books of the Bank. This make the balance sheet of your Bank show up in a different light than it should actually show, inasmuch as you have put a large earning on your books which you have not yet earned. There is always a possibility that when the end of the time is up for which the extension has been given that the interest will not be paid and you will have to do the whole thing over again. I concluded, however, to allow this to go by, but hereafter, I am advising that in a question of this kind, I do not think that any interest, commission, etc. should be put on the books of your Bank as an earning until the amount is absolutely actually paid.

In spite of these irregularities and with the increase in deposits of $84,000 over the past year, it seems clear that you and your directors have made every effort to keep your institution in shape. I trust upon our next examination, we will find these matters fixed up and will find the bank on firm footing. I regret, however, that this discovery will fall to another man, as my term of office will soon expire. If I have been of material assistance to you in getting your institution straightened out, I am surely glad.

Yours very truly,

Robert L. Snodgrass

Robert L. Snodgrass
Commissioner of Banking

RLS: mp

May 25, 1923

Dearest Jenny,

Now that we are settled, I take pen in hand to describe our wonderful new home. As you know, Lawrence sold our house in town and bought this one overlooking the river about a month ago. It seems we've been repainting and moving ever since. Although we hired Myers Transfer to actually carry our things, packing all that we had took days. And in the middle of all the confusion, Lila Mae quit. Millie, of course, was busy cooking and was no help. So I had to do it. However, in the midst of packing, Lawrence came home with such good news...he had inquired after Miss Pennyroyal (remember that her brother works at Lawrence's bank?) and learned that her poor mother had died. (Not that her death was good news, but the result is.) He contacted her and she will be returning to work for us. The children are delighted, but they could not be any more excited than I. This new house will require someone with her organizational skills.

Jenny, the house is beautiful. It is a large yellow brick situated on a huge lot just east of the city (but not as far out as the farm) on the Ohio River. It has a covered front porch deep enough for lots of furniture and a swing. The center hall has a massive crystal chandelier and beautiful floors. The former owner kept them in perfect condition; there's hardly a scratch. They must not have had children. The parlor to the right is a bit dark, but large; the dining room on the left has a very large kitchen and pantry behind it. In addition to the front staircase, the house also has a back stairway from the second floor hallway to the kitchen. The library behind the parlor is for Lawrence and I plan to use the sun-porch behind the kitchen for sewing and reading. On the second floor there are five bedrooms and on the third, two more. Finally, each of the girls can have her own room. Buddy and Stephen will share the larger room on the third floor, however; and we will leave the other for guests. (That is a hint!)

The sunporch has windows on three sides, which allows a lovely view of the river. Lawrence had the windows redesigned and now they reach from the floor to nearly eight feet tall. From this room, I can enjoy both the morning sun streaming in the windows on the right and in the evening, the glow of the sunset from the left. I believe it is my favorite room. I plan to fill it with plants and wicker furniture. Out in the yard, just at the edge, the previous owners built a gazebo large enough for two to sit down to eat. There is also a swing for the children, a grape arbor, well tended gardens and a two-car garage. The first time we came out to see the house, before Lawrence had actually purchased it, the children ran all over the place. I think they will enjoy the freedom of such a spacious yard.

You know how Lawrence is always pulling surprises? Well, you won't believe the latest one. Two weeks ago he was in North Carolina on business and when he came back, he had a colored boy with him. Sam, is his name. Lawrence knew the house would require extra help, so he went to an orphanage that he had heard about and found Sam, who is about 18 or 19. He needed work and wanted to leave the orphanage to make his way. Lawrence hired him to be our driver, butler and yard man. Lawrence confided that he was a little frightened the Klan would come aboard the train in Raleigh and attach both him and Sam. They have been very active in the South lately, according to the papers.

Sam is such a skinny boy, I hope the work isn't too much for him. We've never had a man around the house before, only the day-girls or the cook. He's going to live over the garage until he can afford his own place. He's real friendly and the little kids follow him everywhere. I'm afraid they get in his way, but he never complains.

I must go now. Friends from the Womens' Club are to arrive soon to play mah-jongg. I learned to play in Florida and find the game fascinating. Eight of us have formed a regular group which plays once a month. Today it's my turn to host the ladies. Millie has made some wonderful lemon squares and brownies. Write when you have time and do plan to come for a visit now that we have lots of room. Until then, I am,

Your loving sister,

Nineteen

The sun had darted in and out between the low clouds all day. Now it seemed to have run out of energy. The sun was gone and in its place was a soft glow of diffused light, as if the sun were simply resting behind the cloud cover until the morrow. The air had a hint of fall; leaves fluttered in pairs from the huge oak in the side yard. The season had changed overnight. Yesterday, Anna had sent the children to school without sweaters or jackets. Today, they were glad to take them. And now, in the late afternoon, as they played "Going to Town" in the backyard, they pulled the sweaters tightly around their chests.

"Going to Town" was the girls' game and they loved it. The boys only tolerated it. The oldest Burgher girls each wore one of her mother's wide-brimmed summer hats and carried an old handbag over her arm. On Eileen, this costume looked almost appropriate. At fourteen she was really too old to play dress-up, but since she had been told to watch the little kids, she had joined in good-heartedly. Margaret wore a black wool shawl as well. Periodically she made a theatrical gesture of flinging the fringed end over her shoulder as she flounced across the yard. Sara, in an uncharacteristically feminine get-up, teetered precariously in Anna's two-inch heels. As she walked, the heels dug small holes in the yard, forcing Sara to hesitate slightly to pull her foot and the shoe from the soft earth.

Buddy and Stephen were perfect pawns for the girls' game. They were forced to play the role of the "shopping ladies' children" and were dragged by the hand, time after time, from their gazebo "home" to the grape arbor "store." This humiliation was made bearable only by the inclusion of their two new puppies and the fact that they did not have to dress in costume.

Sam was in the driveway in front of the garage washing the Packard, but his attention was clearly divided between the task at hand and the children's game of make-believe. It was evident from the smile on Sam's face that he had quickly come to love the Burgher children. And they loved him in return. Periodically, shouts of "Watch, Sam!" rang out across the yard. In answer, Sam raised the hose and squirted it toward the children, forgetting the soap drying on the car. Careful of his aim, he knew the stream of water wouldn't reach its supposed target.

On the sunporch, Anna sat on the wicker chaise longue, reading Willa Cather's *My Antonia*. One of the tall windows was open so she could hear the children. Despite the lingering warmth from the fickle afternoon sun, the dark green tile floor was cool and the breeze off the river made each voile curtain panel waltz with its partner. The room was filled with ferns and spath plants, which gave the impression that the outside vegetation had grown in right through the windows. At the shouts from outside, Anna looked up. She glanced around the room at the sea of green plants. *Soon this will be the only garden still alive.* In the kitchen Millie hummed and muttered to herself as she prepared dinner. The aroma of roast chicken drifted toward Anna. She sniffed and settled a bit more deeply into the chaise longue, knowing the evening meal was well in hand.

Before Anna had finished her chapter, she was startled by a sudden rush of sounds from outside the house. Amid the noise of childish shouts and yelping pups came the rude blare of an insistent car horn. *Why on earth is Sam honking the car horn? I wish he would stop.* She jumped up from the chaise longue and slammed down her book in irritation, losing her place. Further irritated by this, she jerked open the side door to yell at Sam and saw an unfamiliar car in the driveway. Instead of yelling, she stared, open-mouthed. In the driver's seat of the largest automobile she had ever seen, sat Lawrence. He wore a huge grin on his face and his hands gripped the steering wheel as if he would never let go. Although the car resembled their Packard Twin-Six, it was much larger. The deep burgundy metal gleamed like a huge garnet. A shaft of sunlight bounced off the gold trim of the radiator, blinding Anna for an instant. She went through the side door and stood on the stoop.

Anna watched wordlessly as the children gathered in a row at the edge of the driveway. She saw Sam drop the still flowing hose to run over and open Lawrence's door. It was as if they had each been drawn to the car by an invisible magnet. Just as Sam reached for the door handle, Lawrence got out of the car and shouted to the assembled group, "Well, how do you like it?"

Sam was the first to answer. "What is it, Mistah Burgher? Is it ours? It sure is a dandy."

"It's a 1923 Pierce-Arrow Limousine!" Lawrence announced. He ran his hand protectively over the curved front fender. "Look Sam, it has a chauffeur's quarters and a six-cylinder engine with dual valves and dual ignition. That will give you more power without using the accelerator. And it has a greater hill climbing capacity and greater savings in fuel consumption than the Packard. Plus it has leather seats and wooden-spoke wheels."

Anna said, "You sound just like a car salesman, Lawrence." She had left the stoop to join the group who had closed in around the new car.

Lawrence laughed and got back into the driver's seat. Before he motioned for Sam and Anna to look inside, he wiped a bit of perceived dust off the wooden dash board. "See, when Sam is driving, a partition goes up and we can talk to him through an intercom device." He demonstrated by running the partition up and down, then continued his description. "It has a Waltham clock and an air-friction speedometer. They say it's much more accurate than the other type. Get in." As Lawrence opened the passenger door for Anna, the children swarmed into the back as if by a signal. Before he could protest, five children and two puppies were in his new car.

"Sara, get off the upholstery with your dirty shoes," he yelled sternly. "And get those dogs out of the car, Buddy. The very idea. Do you want to ruin my brand new car before it's even broken in?"

"Father, are we going to keep the Packard, too?" asked Margaret. She smoothed her hand over the soft leather seats. "I hope so. Janie Price's daddy doesn't have two cars *or* a limousine."

"Margaret, what a little showoff you are. I'm embarrassed to ride in either one of them. None of my friends has a driver and I don't want them to think we're rich and stuck-up," Eileen complained from the rear seat.

"Well, we *are* rich. Only rich people have a chauffeur. So there," Margaret yelled. She stuck out her tongue at Eileen.

"Girls! Stop that!" their mother admonished. "You should never say that, Margaret. Your father has done very well, but we don't talk about it outside of the family. And Eileen, you should be proud of him and grateful for the nice things you have. Be thankful, not spiteful. Both of you. You hear me?"

"Mistah Burgher, that's the biggest automobile I ever done seen. I'm not so sure I can drive a limousine," said Sam, leaning in the driver's window. The massive car did tower over Sam, who as an adult was barely five feet, six inches tall.

"Oh, you'll drive it, Sam. I'm going to send you to the Pierce-Arrow Training School in Buffalo, New York. It's right there at the factory. You can go on the train. You'll learn all about the car...how to maintain it, fix it, change the tires and how to drive it. I want you to be well trained. And when you come back, I'll order you a gray chauffeur's outfit and cap to go with it. How's that, Sam?" As he spoke, Lawrence opened the door and stepped out again.

"Laws, Mistah Burgher, that'd be real fine," Sam replied, rising to his full height.

Lawrence patted Sam on the shoulder. "Good, Sam. You'll look splendid driving this car. And won't we look fine, ourselves?" He turned to his family for approval.

"Yes," the little kids yelled in unison.

"Now get out and let Sam put it away. It looks like it could rain this evening. I don't want to get it wet," Lawrence said to the children. "Go on, out now."

The children got out of the car and went back to the edge of the driveway to watch Sam drive the big car into the garage. Lawrence wrapped his arm around Anna's waist as they walked into the house.

"Lawrence, that *is* a beautiful car, but isn't it awfully extravagant?" Anna asked in a low tone.

"Well, It is expensive, but I believe if you want people to regard you as successful, you have to look successful. What better way to look successful than to drive a car like John Ringling's? You know, it's the only one in town. Hmm?" He squeezed her around the waist and grinned.

Twenty

June 10, 1924

Lawrence lay in bed, propped up by the pillows he had pummeled into a soft headrest against the solid carved oak headboard. Only a thick cotton sheet covered his legs and lower torso. The fine coating of perspiration on his chest and arms glistened in the moonlight. His face was turned toward the doorway as he watched for Anna's return, a smile playing about his lips. Through the open window he could hear nothing but the secret communication of the crickets that lived on the river bank. *I wonder if crickets enjoy making love? They must, or there wouldn't be so many.*

Full of the euphoria and sense of well-being which always followed their lovemaking, Lawrence smiled broadly as he saw his wife halt momentarily in the entrance to the bedroom. The dim light behind her cast her figure in near silhouette, but Lawrence could still make out her oval face framed by the tight cap of dark brown hair. Her small breasts drooped only slightly after six children and her hips were only a bit too round. She was an attractive woman, but not beautiful, although her husband did not know that. He thought she was stunning and he still counted himself lucky, after sixteen years, to have married her.

"Come here, love," he called softly.

Wordlessly, she crossed the room and crawled back into their bed. She lay on her right side facing the window and Lawrence, in a well-rehearsed rhythm, spooned his body behind hers and held her tightly, cupping one breast with his left hand. This ritual of tender physical communion did not depend on whether or not they had made love. It was the way they always ended their day.

After a moment, Anna spoke first. "This is my favorite place in the whole world. I feel so secure with you here beside me."

"So do I, love," he answered. A moment later, he said, "Tell me again about Jenny's letter."

"Well, all she said was that Nate had lost his job and they were thinking of moving to Huntington. She didn't say so, but I think she misses Mother, too. And, she would like the twins to grow up near her. Do you think you can help Nate find work here in Huntington?"

"Oh, of course. I've done several favors for some of the boys at the club. Now they owe me one or two. I'll ask around."

"Wouldn't it be wonderful for all our children to grow up together?" Anna could just see them all playing together in her yard.

"Yes, it would," Lawrence agreed. "Can't you picture the twins on the burros?"

"Speaking of those nasty animals...did you know they got out again? Sam and the boys had to take garbage can lids and bang them together to chase them out of Mrs. Tutwiller's tomato patch. She was furious."

Lawrence laughed out loud. "I would love to have seen that. How long were they loose?"

"Long enough. It's not funny. All the neighbors hate those beasts and I can sympathize with them. I wish you'd never bought them."

"Well, you wanted something the boys could ride that wouldn't be too fast. And they certainly fit that description. I didn't actually buy them, you know. I already owned them. When my copper mine closed — there they were. It's about all I got out of that worthless investment. I'll tell Sam to reinforce the fences tomorrow, love. I'm sorry they caused you embarrassment."

"I hope that holds them. If they get loose again, maybe we should put them out on the farm. How was your directors' meeting today?"

Lawrence was silent for a moment, then he said, "Honestly, it could have gone better. We've had another letter from the banking commissioner about our outstanding loans. The directors were more than a little upset and they directed it at me. The examiner listed about ten notes he says appear to be losses and another fifteen he says are doubtful — that is, he doesn't think they will ever be collected. The directors blamed me for making bad loans. The truth is, the loan committee approves all of those, but I'm afraid the examiner is right; they do appear to be losses. But if we charge them off, as the commissioner says we should do, it would create such a loss that we wouldn't be able to pay our mid-year dividend. They don't like that idea any more than Keeley and I do. I'm in a quandary as to what course of action to take."

"Oh Lawrence, I'm sorry. I shouldn't have been complaining about the silly burros when you have real worries. What are you going to do? Have you decided?" She disentangled herself and turned over to face him. The furrow between his eyes looked deeper than ever, but she supposed it was simply the shadow thrown there by the moonlight.

"No. I'm not sure, but I'll think of something. One of those loans — a big one — was to capitalize that damn copper mine. How I got talked into that, I'm not sure; but it sure was a bad deal. Now I've got to pay back the bank. It wouldn't look good to have the vice president's loan declared a loss. Don't worry love, I'll think of something," he repeated.

"I know you will, darling. You always do. Turn over and I'll rub your back. Maybe you can relax and go to sleep."

Lawrence turned on his left side away from Anna, willing himself to sleep. It was true; he hadn't been sleeping well at all. Tension had been growing between him and Keeley. Lawrence thought Keeley was being overly critical, since he had learned some of those tricks from Keeley. And yesterday Lawrence snapped at his secretary for a mistake so small he couldn't remember it now. He was worried going into the directors' meeting about the bank examiner's letter and even more so coming out. *Perhaps I could borrow enough from the bank in Shapely to cover that copper mine loan. That would buy me some time. Then when I sell some of the Huntington property, I can pay off that loan. I'll write to David.*

As Lawrence lay there thinking, his broad shoulder was exposed.

Gently, Anna ran her hand back and forth across the highest point and down his side. Slowly, rhythmically her hand moved — until she felt his body begin to melt into itself and relax. She smiled to herself as if she knew the sedative effect that motion had on him. He began to snore lightly. The ability to put Lawrence to sleep with her touch reminded Anna of when her children were babies. All she had to do was stroke their backs or arms and they would relax and fall asleep. Again, she smiled into the darkness. Knowing that she had such a profound effect on the well-being of those she loved filled her with a sense of satisfaction. It made her love a thing of great value.

Twenty-One

August 1991

As she drove north on I-75 to West Virginia, Maggie wondered how many times she'd made this trip since her move to Georgia six years ago. And she wondered how many times she had intended to use some part of her too short visits to search for more information about her grandfather, Lawrence Burgher. Those intentions had led nowhere in the past, but this time it would be different, she thought smugly. This time she had made prior arrangements to do more research at the West Virginia Archives.

Following her visit in 1989 to Savannah to meet her second cousin, Annie Bartram, Maggie had gotten a bit more organized about her detective work. She had made lots of notes and organized the information she had gathered, meager as it was, into a notebook. As she looked at the slim volume, she realized she still had not found the real source of "Father's troubles," as her mother called them. And since she had run out of eyewitnesses willing to talk, she decided to try a less direct approach. She reasoned that somewhere the bank's records must still exist and that a clue must be hidden in the dusty files. About a year ago, she had written to the West Virginia Banking Commission and discovered that records of all closed banks were stored at the West Virginia Archives. They'd been there all along, but she hadn't known it when she was perusing microfilm with Scott in 1985.

Then, a few months ago, Maggie had called the West Virginia

Archives and spoken with Miss Victoria Whitman. From her voice, Maggie formed an instant mental picture of the librarian — right out of central casting — straight, mousey-brown hair and thick glasses. In a timid voice tinged with a West Virginia twang, Miss Whitman had informed Maggie that the records *were* there, but she'd have to make prior arrangements to access them. She sounded apologetic, as if this was a rule she hated to enforce. So, just before leaving Atlanta for this trip home, Maggie called her again and asked to have the records available on Monday, August 12. Now, perhaps, she would get the rest of the story.

As the odometer on her silver Celica recorded the miles, Maggie's mind flitted back and forth between the details of real life and her obsession with this long-dead grandfather. She did this often. Her driving time was her most productive thinking time. She solved many problems this way. Today, classical music and an interstate highway were perfect triggers for introspection. *Why do I care what happened? Is it just curiosity? What do I hope to gain by learning why he went to prison? Am I trying to clear the family's name? Do I think I can prove it was a mistake after all these years? But what if he was guilty, after all? When I find out, what difference will it make? Do I hope that I'll finally understand my mother? Will I ever be rid of this obsession?*

Pent up curiosity got Maggie out of bed at 5:30 A.M. on Monday and by 9 A.M., when the archives opened, she was waiting by the door. In contrast to the humidity already evident in the late summer morning, the archives were dry and cool. Maggie supposed it was part of the temperature control system. Although she hadn't been there since the day she came with Scott, the room was instantly familiar. She remembered that day vividly. At the desk sat a young woman with straight, mousey-brown collar length hair, thick glasses and a premature dowager's hump. *This has to be Miss Whitman. She's just like I imagined. I wonder if her hump was caused by poring over books all day or by osteoporosis.* Maggie walked up to the desk and asked for Miss Whitman, even though she was sure she was already speaking to her.

"I'm Miss Whitman, may I help you," she said. *Bingo! I'm getting good at this!* As she looked up at Maggie, Miss Whitman pushed her glasses back up on her nose. Her pale skin looked as if she had never been outside during daylight, had spent her whole life in the Archive stacks. She smiled shyly and tucked her hair behind her ears. Maggie sensed that Miss Whitman felt more comfortable with the old books than with the people who came to read them.

"Yes, ma'am. I'm Maggie Malone. I called you last week about the Railroad Bank & Trust records."

"Oh, yes. I remember. Did you want to see all of the records? You'll have to wait until Max comes back on the floor. I'll have to go to the stacks to get them; no one else knows where the records are kept," she said, sounding territorial.

"Well, I *suppose* I want to see everything, although I don't know how much there is. I planned to spend the day, so why don't you just bring it all?" Maggie wasn't really sure what she was getting into, but she knew she didn't want to leave any stone unturned. Imagining dozens of boxes, she swallowed hard and watched Miss Whitman disappear into the dark recesses of the building. As she seated herself at one of the long library tables and got out a legal pad and pencil, Maggie looked around. She was amazed at the number of people who were there so early on a Monday morning. *I wonder what they are looking for? Do you suppose they are all doing genealogy? What else would you find here? Bank records, that's what else!* Maggie laughed at her own faux pas.

Shortly Miss Whitman emerged pushing a metal utility cart, stacked top and bottom with four cardboard storage boxes. She wheeled it to where Maggie was seated.

"These are all the records for the bank you asked about. This ought to keep you busy for awhile. But if you need anything, just ask. I'll be right up front." She smiled as if she had delivered a grand gift to Maggie and walked back to the desk at the front of the room.

For a moment Maggie sat staring at the boxes. Based on Miss Whitman's remarks, four boxes wasn't what she expected, although she didn't know exactly what she did expect. On the one hand it seemed like a lot of material to examine. On the other, it seemed a pitifully small collection of documents. *Is this all there is? Is my grandfather's entire career contained in just these four boxes? Compared to the mountains of records kept now, this doesn't seem to be enough to document what happened to him. I have this many personal files for only one year.*

She stood and opened the lid of the first box. It was stuffed full of file folders. Someone had carefully tagged each folder with a scrap-paper label. It appeared to have been done recently, for the label of each folder was handwritten in red felt marker. She wondered if it might have been Miss Whitman. Maggie excitedly skimmed through the labels. The files were labeled by subject matter. Some files held the bank's leather-bound minute books, some contained transcripts of depositions; but most contained the correspondence between the banking commissioner and various people, primarily her grandfather and the man named Edward Keeley. With one glance at the bank's letterhead, Maggie saw that Keeley had been the president of the Railroad Bank & Trust.

Now that she had her hands on the records, Maggie wasn't sure where to begin. It was like disturbing history. *I've always assumed he was basically a good man who just got caught in the banking industry failure. What if I don't like what I find? Maybe I* should *let sleeping dogs lie? No, the truth is what I need.* She took a deep breath and pulled out one of the correspondence files and began to page through it. The letters were all copies; most were on yellow paper on which the word "COPY" was imprinted diagonally in faint red ink. Where two letters pertained to the same subject or there were multiple pages of a letter, the pages had been pinned together with a straight pin. Only a thin line of rust behind the pins indicated the age of these documents, for the carbons were as clear as the day they were typed. *If this had happened today, these records would not exist. They probably would have been stored somewhere on a computer and the technology to read them would now be obsolete.*

She flipped back to the first letter and began to read. At first the letters were ordinary business correspondence. However, as she continued to turn the pale yellow pages, words like "irregular cash items," "low reserves," "past due paper," and "large overdrafts" began to appear. In addition to the letters, some documents appeared to be the minutes of board meetings containing lists of outstanding loans and mundane motions and resolutions. These, Maggie tried to skim over; but when one bank examiner's report noted "the forged Van Horn notes" she stopped suddenly. Van Horn was her great-aunt Jenny's last name.

Her heart sank. A cold shudder coursed through her body. *Dear God, I don't want to find he was guilty of forgery.* Cautiously she turned to another letter, and then another, as if she were afraid of what the next one would reveal. She read for six hours. She read past hunger, thirst and the vague urge to go to the bathroom. At the end of the day, she realized that she could not fully absorb the story contained in these innocuous looking pages. She knew that she would need to read them more than once to truly understand the details. But one thing was clear...her grandfather's troubles were bigger than she had imagined.

West Virginia Banking Commission
Charleston, W.Va.

August 19, 1924

Maynard Hutchinson, Cashier
Railroad Bank & Trust
Huntington, West Virginia

My dear Sir:

We have on our desk a report of an examination
made of your bank on August 11 and 12 by State
Bank Examiners Thompson and Patterson. We wish
to call your attention to four notes made by
Trustees of Second United Baptist Church,
aggregating $2,568.95, and two notes of the
Miller Steel Company amounting to $1,500.00 on
which you have credited earned interest but not
collected. I am at a loss to know why the
officers of your bank directed unpaid interests
on these notes credited to your interest account
before the makers of the notes paid it to your
bank.

At the last examination, I believe the Commissioner called your attention to the amount at
which you carried your furniture and fixtures
and advised that a proper amount be charged off
at the end of each six months. I see that you
have not done this. In justice to your
institution, we believe you should begin
this at once and look after it regularly.

The attached list of past due notes aggregating

$5,785.25 were listed as being losses to your bank. They should be disposed of. In addition, the following are listed by the examiners as being doubtful of collection:

Nannie & T.J. Cunningham	$700.00
C. T. Kyle	1,110.00
U. S. Block Co.	3,535.00
Swastika Silver & Copper Co.	4,000.00
Same	23,385.00

Further, I see listed twenty irregular cash items, amounting to $1,266.89. These items should be disposed of. They will represent a loss to your institution.

On date of examination, your reserve was considerably below the statute requirements. This should be built up and maintained at a higher level.

Mr. Hutchinson, will you please present this letter to your directors at their next regular meeting and report to this department the action taken on items herein called to your attention.

Very Truly Yours,

Sidney R. McCullough
Commissioner of Banking

SRMc/ab

RAILROAD BANK & TRUST COMPANY

HUNTINGTON, WEST VIRGINIA

EDWARD KEELEY, PRESIDENT
MAYNARD HUTCHINSON, CASHIER
R. LAWRENCE BURGHER, V. PRES.
J.R. THOMAS, ASST. CASHIER

August 26, 1924

Mr. Sidney R. McCullough,
Commissioner of Banking
Charleston, West Virginia

Dear Sir:

We have been presented with your letter of August 19, regarding the last examination of the Railroad Bank & Trust Company.

We are in agreement that the attached list of past due notes aggregating $5,785.25 are a loss and we shall take care of them just as soon as we possibly can.

Regarding the other notes, it is quite possible that a few of them will later show losses. However, we believe the notes of the Swastika Silver and Copper Co. will be collected.

Regarding adding interest of the Second United Baptist Church note and the Miller Steel Company note, only earned interest has been added to these notes.

We note what you have to say regarding our

Furniture and Fixture account and will act
accordingly.

Yours very truly,

R. Lawrence Burgher

R. Lawrence Burgher
Vice President

Attest Directors

Edward M. Keeley

Edward M. Keeley

Thomas J. Noonan

Thomas Noonan

Geo. H. Wright

Geo. H. Wright

E C VanZandt

E.C. VanZandt

West Virginia Banking Commission
Charleston, W.Va.

September 9, 1924

R. Lawrence Burgher, Vice-Pres.
Railroad Bank & Trust Company
Huntington, West Virginia

My dear Sir:

Please permit me to thank you and the other directors for your letter of August 26th in reply to our letter of August 19th relative to an examination made of your bank by Examiners Thompson and Patterson. I feel that your directors want to work with this department and will follow any reasonable suggestion from it.

Therefore, I must again bring to your attention the matter of the Second United Baptist Church and the Miller Steel Company. Your bank added interest to the notes, making the notes larger, or, in other words, carrying them on your books for the amount of the principal and adding the interest to them. Your bank credited your interest account with this amount which was never paid. I am of the opinion, Mr. Burgher, that this is irregular and should not be done. I cannot understand why interest should be credited to your bank when it has not actually been paid. I suggest that you charge back the amount of interest you have added to each note and let your note show on its face the amount of the principal only.

Very Truly Yours,

Sidney R. McCullough
Commissioner of Banking

SRMc/ab

RAILROAD BANK & TRUST COMPANY

HUNTINGTON, WEST VIRGINIA

EDWARD KEELEY, PRESIDENT
MAYNARD HUTCHINSON, CASHIER
R. LAWRENCE BURGHER, V. PRES.
J.R. THOMAS, ASST. CASHIER

September 12, 1924

Mr. Sidney R. McCullough
Commissioner of Banking
Charleston, West Virginia

Dear Sir:

Replying to your letter of September 9, I appreciate, as do all of the directors, what you say regarding the interest on the Second United Baptist Church and the Miller Steel Company.

The interest on these notes is payable to us annually, and the interest attached to them was for the first six months and was earned at the time of its being taken. We have always handled notes of this kind in this manner, feeling that it was entirely correct as long as it was earned interest.

I trust this will explain the matter to your satisfaction.

Yours very truly,

R. Lawrence Burgher
Vice President

Twenty-Two

September 1924

T he telephone on Edward Keeley's desk was ringing as he unlocked the door to his office at the Keeley Coal Company. He
made his way across the room as fast as his hobbled gait would
allow, brushed away some papers which partially obscured the phone
and grabbed the receiver.

"Keeley here," he shouted, breathless and irritated.

Lawrence's voice on the other end was almost as loud. "Edward,
are you busy? I need to see you."

"Well, hell, Lawrence; how can I be busy at this hour? I just walked
through my door. What is it?"

"I've gotten another letter from the banking commissioner about
the earned interest account. We need to discuss how to handle it."

"Damn it, Lawrence! I thought we had satisfied him with that
letter from the directors. All right. Come on over. I don't have any
appointments until 10 A.M."

Later in the day, if a person had asked Lawrence about the
morning's weather, he would have had no recollection of it. He was
deep in thought as he walked the few short blocks to Keeley's office.
Several acquaintances from the Elks Club nodded his way; but he did
not see them. He was too concerned about the contents of the letter
in his pocket. *How on earth are we going to handle this? If we charge
back the interest from this account, we won't be able to pay dividends. We
can't let that happen. What the hell would I live on? Everything is mort-*

gaged or leveraged to the hilt and my salary certainly isn't enough. Over and over he asked himself these questions. No satisfactory answers occurred to him.

He reached Keeley's office building in a sweat. As he waited for the elevator, he wiped his brow with his handkerchief, smoothed his hair and stood, impatiently jingling the coins in his right pants pocket. Finally, the elevator car arrived and, forgetting his manners, he rushed ahead of the two women beside him. On the fifth floor, the elevator stopped and Lawrence bolted into the lobby ahead of the other passengers. He strode swiftly down the narrow corridor, past a dozen frosted glass doors with gilt names arched across them to the large office at the end. He opened the door without knocking.

"Miss Newcomb, is Keeley in there?" Lawrence asked the secretary seated in the anteroom.

He pointed to Keeley's inner office door.

"Yes, sir; he is. I'll tell him you're here," she replied, reaching for the telephone.

"Never mind. I'll just go on in," he said shortly. Lawrence's manners had deserted him completely. He opened the door, rushed in and let it slam behind him. Without preamble, he pulled the letter from his pocket and flung it on the desk. It floated momentarily before settling on the piles of folders and letters. Keeley quickly picked it off the desk, as though one more page would topple the stack.

"Good morning, Lawrence," he said. He scanned the letter and then looked up at his partner. "You sounded agitated on the telephone. You look agitated, as well, I must say. Sit down; calm yourself. We can fix this." Keeley smiled around the unlit cigar clamped between his teeth as if he found Lawrence's attitude somewhat amusing.

"We'd better be able to fix it or you and I are going to lose a whole lot of money. I thought you and I agreed that adding the interest to these notes wouldn't be a problem. Correct me if I'm wrong, but when I first came here, hadn't the bank made this a practice for years?" Lawrence was a bit angry that this policy, condoned by Keeley and the other directors for several years, was now causing *him* a problem.

"Yes, we did. And, yes they had. The difference is — they weren't paying dividends back then based on the added interest. It was held in a reserve account in the event of having to discount it back to the borrower. We changed that, remember?"

"Well, should we change it back?" Lawrence asked, afraid of the answer. He knew what problems that would cause him financially.

"Hell, no! It's too late now. If we reverse the policy now, you and I will have to pay back a substantial amount in dividends, which we probably shouldn't have paid out. Besides, it's really a cash flow problem, isn't it? When the interest is actually paid, the account will be correct. The interest *has* been earned, hasn't it?" Keeley sat up straight in his leather chair and thrust forward his bull-dog jaw.

"Yes, it is earned. We attach it every six months, although it is only payable to us annually."

"Well then, just write them back and explain it that way, again. It may be unusual, but I'm confident it isn't illegal. We definitely don't want to change that policy, Lawrence. As you said, there'd be hell to pay for the two of us." Keeley handed the letter back to Lawrence, leaned back in the chair and lit his badly chewed cigar. "Is everything else all right over there?"

"Yes, the bank is fine. I'll write the letter this afternoon. Thanks for the advice. I just hope this satisfies the commissioner." Lawrence looked relieved as he stood to leave. "Take care, Edward. I'll talk to you later." As he left the office, he closed the door more gently. He smiled warmly when he wished Miss Newcomb a good day.

Closing time came and went, and Lawrence was still at his desk. After his secretary left, he locked the door to his office, took two leather bound ledgers from his desk drawer and opened the first one. It contained a running list of his real estate transactions in Shapely. The entries were lengthy and dated back to 1911. Over the years, most of the property had been developed and subsequently sold, or the lots themselves had been sold. However, as he scanned the list, he saw many transactions which still had outstanding balances. He also realized several of the buyers were behind in their payments. Since his firm, Mountaineer Realty Company, held those land contracts, he made a note to write to the buyers before the loan became delinquent. *I don't need to have notes not being paid. That cash flow is paying some of my payments here. And I certainly don't want to foreclose. I don't need a slew of property...I need cash.*

Next he opened a ledger marked "Huntington Holdings." It too contained a list of property, but it was a different sort of list. This list had three columns following the property address: the first listed the price Lawrence paid for it; the next showed the amount still due; and the third column noted the date the demand note or payment was due. As he studied each entry, he could see that he *had* made progress in his master plan. He had succeeded in buying almost all of the property he had marked in red nearly five years ago. *Six Hundred block of Ninth Street — three parcels. Fourth Avenue and Eleventh Street — two parcels. Washington Avenue — two parcels. Guyandotte — two houses. Ninth Street and Eleventh Avenue — two houses. First Street and Fourth Avenue — two parcels. Forty acres on Fifth Street hill...*the list went on. *Most have been good investments. I've already sold Fourth Avenue, Guyandotte and Washington Avenue. But the problem is, some of these folks don't pay me on time and then I can't meet my obligations. I should have insisted on straight bank loans instead of carrying the paper myself. And I have no income from the two houses on Ninth Street — I've got Anna's mother and mine living there. I certainly can't charge them rent. Maybe I shouldn't have bought the farm in Pea Ridge — it certainly isn't paying its way, yet. And then there's that damn copper mine. I've lost almost $30,000 there and still owe the bank the loan I took out for the stock. I can't let that loan go bad. I pledged the Swastika stock, but now it's worthless. I don't guess the directors would want those mangy burros as collateral.* He allowed himself a sardonic laugh.

After poring over his books for an hour or more, Lawrence was exhausted and hungry. However, his assessment of the situation wasn't as troubling as he had first feared. If he could just get his accounts receivable to pay on time and keep the dividends coming from the bank, he would be able to meet his note payments. He needed to sell one or two more parcels to be comfortable, but he was sure that could be accomplished rather easily. His only real problems were the large note for the land on Fifth Street hill and the notes in Shapely for the Ninth Street houses. Oh, yes...and the copper mine loan. He'd put off far too long writing to David about a new loan from the Bank of Shapely to pay off that note at the Railroad Bank & Trust. He made a note to himself to do that tomorrow. Although he hated revealing his loss to his younger brother, he could see no other way to quickly get $30,000. *When the land on Fifth Street begins to sell, I can pay it back. God, I hope it sells quickly. Right now I'm borrowing from Peter to pay Paul. Next thing you know, I'll be robbing one to pay the other. Hmm, I've seen Keeley kite checks to cover cash flow...but I can't let it come to that where I'm concerned.*

He closed his books, locked his office and walked through the dark bank to the street where Sam was waiting patiently at the wheel of the Pierce-Arrow. Lawrence opened the rear door and got into the warm car.

"Let's go home, Sam," he sighed. "It's been a very long day."

Bank of Shapely

SHAPELY, WEST VIRGINIA

Harry P. Mortimer, PRESIDENT
Guy Tickle, VICE PRESIDENT
David L. Burgher, CASHIER

September 23, 1924

R. Lawrence Burgher, Vice President
Railroad Bank & Trust Company
Huntington, West Virginia

Dear Lawrence:

I am in receipt of your letter regarding a loan
of $40,000 to pay off notes currently held by
the Railroad Bank & Trust Company and pledged in
part by your stock in the Swastika Silver &
Copper Mine Company. I am sorry indeed to learn
that your investment has not paid off as you had
hoped. Perhaps silver mining in Colorado isn't
as lucrative as coal mining in West Virginia.
From now on, I'd suggest sticking with something
you understand.

As for the loan, we can certainly undertake such
a note; however, I would suggest that the Directors will look more favorably on it if some of
the unencumbered land owned by our Mountaineer
Realty Company is pledged as collateral.

Regarding the smaller notes you have with the
bank, we note that they are due and payable at
the end of this year. Do you want me to extend
them?

I trust all is well with your family. I understand that Jenny and Nate have moved to

Huntington. Have you been able to secure a position for Nate? He's a good man, although not very industrious. My best to you all,

Warm regards,

David L. Burgher

West Virginia Banking Commission
Charleston, W.Va.

September 25, 1924

R. Lawrence Burgher, Vice-Pres.
Railroad Bank & Trust Company
Huntington, West Virginia

My dear Sir:

I am in receipt of your reply of the 12th explaining the manner in which you handle the earned but not paid interest on the notes of the Second United Baptist Church and the Miller Steel Company.

I think your bank is entirely wrong in setting up this earned, but not paid, interest as an asset and using it for the purpose of enabling you to pay dividends. I cannot get it where you can in any way from this source have a tangible asset whereby you are able to use it. I know that the earned interest makes these notes worth more money than the face value, but, Mr. Burgher, your interest account or undivided profits are not built up until the interest is actually paid.

I thank you very much for your letter and your explanation is very plain, but I think you are wrong.

Very truly yours,

Sidney R. McCullough
Commissioner of Banking

SRMc/ab

Twenty-Three

December 22, 1924

S nowflakes as big as a fingernail had pelted the car's windscreen for fifteen minutes. Sam watched in fascination as they melted against the warm glass and slid like teardrops before dissolving into a puddle on the hood. To the empty car he mused, "Snow this big can't last for long. It'll snow itself out soon." Periodically he turned on the wiper to clear the screen, hoping to see the train pull into the station. As he waited for Anna and Eileen to arrive from their shopping trip to New York, he dozed. Suddenly he was startled by the whistle of the slow moving train. He grabbed his cap, jumped out of the car and ran to the platform to meet them.

After a few moments of searching the faces of the arriving passengers, he spotted them. Both women — at fifteen, Eileen almost looked like a woman — had their faces buried deep in their fur collars against the winter wind. Eileen carried a fox muff as well. They were handsome women and they carried themselves proudly.

"Missus Burgher, Miss Eileen," Sam called. "Over here."

"Good afternoon, Sam. How are you? I'm so glad to see you. It's really snowing up north. I thought we'd never get home."

"Hi there, Sam," said Eileen, giving him a kiss on the cheek.

"Miss Eileen, don't do that. I told you. Young ladies don't kiss Negro mens. You're too old for that."

Eileen laughed. "Oh, Sam, you old fuddy-duddy. You ought to see the wonderful things we bought. I got some gorgeous dresses.

This is going to be a great Christmas. We brought you a present, too."

"Hush, Eileen. No telling secrets now. Sam, our packages and luggage should be in the station in just a few minutes. Eileen and I'll go get in the car. Could you get a porter to help you?"

"Yes ma'am. I'll be right there. You just go get warm."

Anna and Eileen walked through the station to the car while Sam hailed a porter and went looking for their baggage. Within ten minutes he appeared at the car door with a flat baggage cart piled high with packages. At the bottom of the stack was their leather luggage.

"Laws-a-mercy, Missus Burgher, Mistah Burgher gonna die when he sees what all you bought."

"No, he won't Sam. He told us to enjoy ourselves. Besides, lots of these are Christmas gifts. Put them in the car; I want to get home before dark."

"Yes, ma'am." Sam replied as he filled the middle seat with the packages.

The board room of the Railroad Bank & Trust Company was empty except for the two men at the head of the table. A protracted and difficult board of directors meeting had ended a few minutes earlier. The last report from the bank examiners had revealed substantial irregularities, forcing the officers and directors to spend the entire weekend going over the books. This meeting, with the directors scrutinizing every bank procedure and account, was the culmination of three very intense days for the two partners. Edward Keeley looked across the gleaming conference table at Lawrence Burgher and spoke in a stage whisper, as if the other directors were still in the room and could have heard his normally loud voice.

"Well, Lawrence, we made it through another examination. But $55,000 in bad paper thrown out and declared a loss is quite a blow. If George and Irvan hadn't pledged their stock to cover it, we'd have been in really bad shape. We've got to make it up to them. Thank God we cleaned up all our small past due paper before the examiners got here. And how did you manage to make good on that overdraft?"

"I wrote a check on my Shapely account to cover it."

"Is it good?" Keeley asked warily.

"No," Lawrence admitted. "But it will be before it clears."

"God damn it, Lawrence; that's check kiting. You'd better hope they don't catch you."

"You're a fine one to talk, Edward. I've seen you do it dozens of times."

"I know, but not when the damn bank examiners are in town."

"Oh, don't worry about it. I'll handle it. You just mind your own affairs," Lawrence replied in a huff. He hated being criticized about anything, particularly how he handled the bank business.

Keeley did not respond to the affront. "As for our Furniture and Fixture account," he continued, changing the subject, "I thought we were charging off the depreciation. Didn't the commissioner comment on this before? I didn't say anything in the meeting, because I didn't want to embarrass you, but you should have handled that before they came."

Lawrence explained, "I told Maynard to do it at year's end. I didn't think it would matter *when* we did it. The year-end statement is the important one."

Now Keeley raised his voice. "Well, apparently it *did* matter. The examiners were pissed off that you hadn't done it already."

"Look Edward, why don't you try running this damn bank. I'm just as busy as you are. Sometimes I can't keep up with it all."

"Well, that's what we pay you to do — keep up with it. I told you when you started buying property here not to let your real estate business interfere with the affairs of the bank."

Lawrence fidgeted. He was becoming more and more irritated with Keeley and was trying to maintain his composure. He managed to stifle a snide comment about the meager vice president's salary and ignored the rebuke. Instead, he tried to focus Keeley's attention on something more positive.

"I'm glad the board passed an overall resolution allowing us to take out personal loans. I didn't realize that there wasn't one. You've got some big loans, Edward, and so do I. At least that went well."

"Yes, you're right," Keeley replied. However, he was not distracted that easily. "But what about all those loans on which no interest had ever been collected? Did you authorize those?"

Lawrence stiffened and answered evasively, "Not all of them. The loan committee looked at most of them."

"Most?" Keeley repeated. He was again suspicious of Lawrence's hesitancy.

"Well, let's just say some of the loans are not really loans at all. I approved them but they were only made to cover other notes. That's how we fixed up the small accounts to look as good as we did for the examiners."

"What? Do you mean to tell me they were fake loans? Did you sign them? Because if you did, that's forgery, Lawrence."

"God damn it, Edward. I did it to cover your ass, too. You had a pot full of unpaid loans in there. What did you expect me to do? Let them see that you're bleeding the bank."

"Bleeding it? Who the hell do you think owns the damn thing? It's my bank and don't you forget it."

"Hell if it is. I own almost as much stock as you do. Don't you try to make me your whipping boy. And besides, I'm not doing any-thing you haven't done before. I learned it from you."

"Here — at this bank — my bank — you don't do as I do — you do as I say. And I say quit it! I brought you here to run this goddamn bank and to run it profitably. Now get it back on its feet! Do you hear me?" Keeley was shouting at the top of his lungs.

"Hell yes, I hear you!" Lawrence stood abruptly, reached in his pants pocket and retrieved a heavy ring of keys. "I'll quit it, all right! You run the goddamn bank! You're not going to talk to me that way. You can take these keys and shove them up your ass," he shouted back at Keeley. Lawrence rose and threw the bank keys on the con-ference table, nicking the highly lacquered surface. He turned his back on Keeley and stormed out of the room. He slammed the door behind him, causing the door's glass parts to shake and rattle loudly.

Keeley sat in the silent room still livid with anger, but stunned by Lawrence's actions. *Damned arrogant son-of-a-bitch. Who does he think he's talking to? I'm glad he quit. I can't believe the things he's been doing...*

but shit, now what am I going to do? I can't run this goddamn bank and my company, too. Ah, hell, what was he thinking? I've done some shady things before, but not forgery. Of course, he didn't actually *say he signed them. Maybe he got someone to pledge securities...but he did say they were fictitious loans. Shit! This is one hell of a mess. He's right about my loans though...I couldn't have paid them and he knew it. Maybe I was too hard on him. Who else can I trust to keep us protected? Certainly not Maynard. Hell, he lives at the foot of the cross and would turn in his own grandmother. Oh, shit — the auditors! They're supposed to be here after the first of the year. What the devil am I going to do?*

Keeley sat in the board room a while longer staring at the huge oil painting on the long paneled wall. It was a desolate-looking snow scene of a tiny farm house nestled way up a hollow. A thin wisp of smoke rose from the stone chimney. Keeley shivered and rose heavily to go home. His mind was numb. He gathered his papers together and picked up the set of keys and his overcoat. *Hell, I don't even know which one of these opens Lawrence's office.* He put them in his pocket, walked out of the board room and down the marble steps. The glow from the street lights cast a sickly yellow pall on the bank lobby. Slowly he made his way to the front door and stepped outside. Snow blanketed the street and sidewalk and silenced the air around him. He looked up at the sky and could see nothing but snow.

When Lawrence stormed out of the board room, he went directly to his office, jerked open the desk drawer and took out his leather-bound personal ledgers. He put them under his arm, grabbed his hat and coat and ran down the stairs, leaving his office door standing wide open. Outside the bank, the Pierce-Arrow sat idling at the curb with Sam at the wheel. When he saw Lawrence come through the front door, Sam jumped out to greet him and open the car.

"Evening, Mistah Burgher," he said cheerfully.

"Sam," Lawrence replied shortly. He got in and held the books across his knees. He hoped fervently that Sam would not start a conversation. He needed to think and to calm down.

"Miss Eileen and Missus Burgher got home this afternoon, sir," Sam began, but Lawrence cut him off.

"Sam, do you mind...I've had a long day."

"Sorry, sir. No, sir. I'll be quiet." Sam looked puzzled. Usually Lawrence was quite talkative at the end of the day.

Lawrence rode in a daze, idly watching the snow gather on the street. He glanced in the rear mirror and saw it eddy behind them into little snow clouds before resettling on the brick street. *Who the hell did Edward think he was talking to? I'll be damned if I let that uncouth slob talk to me the way he did. I will not be bullied into being his whipping boy. Let him take the pressure for a while and see how he handles it. Maybe I shouldn't have accused him of bleeding the bank but how can he criticize me for things he's done for years. That ass! To hell with him!...Oh shit. What if he decides to cut me out completely? Forces me to sell my stock. I can't live on my real estate business, yet. What have I done? Small as it is—I need that salary. And I need to be sure the dividends continue. But damn, if I let him get away with his bully tactics now, I'll have to kiss his ass the rest of my life. No sir! I won't do it. I'll go to another bank. A man of my talents should have no trouble getting another position. But what about my loans? I've got to clean up that mess. And the check in Shapely. Oh God. How did I let myself get into such a jam.*

Suddenly Lawrence was nauseated. His ears roared. His head pounded. A cold, clammy wave passed through his body. He began to sweat profusely.

"Sam, can you hurry just a bit? I'm not feeling well."

"Sorry sir, I can't. I'm afraid of the slippery streets. But we'll be there directly."

What will I tell Anna? It's nearly Christmas. I can't ruin Christmas for her or the kids. Oh, God; how will I pay for all the presents? I'll bet she spent a fortune in New York. Maybe I should call Keeley and apologize. But for what? I only did what I had to in order to cover both our asses. No, I'll let him stew a while. He'll call me. But what if he doesn't? I've got to get back to the bank. Hell, I don't even have my keys. How stupid! I shouldn't have thrown them at him.

A new wave of nausea rolled over Lawrence as Sam turned into the driveway. The Pierce-Arrow negotiated the incline easily despite the thick snow. As he opened the door for his boss, Lawrence bolted past Sam into the backyard. Through the wet snow he ran. Just as he reached the gazebo, Lawrence doubled over and vomited.

December 23, 1924

MEMORANDUM

TO: Sidney R. McCullough, Commissioner
IN RE: Railroad Bank & Trust Company

This bank was examined as of December 16th, 1924 by Examiners Thompson, Patterson and Rosenfeld. The result of this examination showed that the bank was in very precarious condition. It was also plainly evident that they were expecting us, due to the fact that their past due paper had been fixed up, over-drafts had been reduced considerably and the Vice President of the Bank had made good his account on a check to Shapely.

There were a number of large items sent out of the bank on the day of the examination which had the earmarks of a kite and estimated at about $75,000. These were drawn on Shapely, Thurmond and Mt. Hope.

After the detail work of the bank was fin-ished, Messrs. Patterson and Rosenfeld left for Shapely to examine the Bank of Shapely, where the officers of this bank are the same as the officers of that bank, with the exception of the Cashier at Shapely, who is the brother of the Vice President at Huntington. The examination of this bank did not show where any large items had been received from the Railroad Bank & Trust Company. This is evidence that the entries were made and the items themselves had never left the bank.

After giving this bank a thorough checking up, the Examiners found that they had been tak-ing credit for dormant accounts, placing them in their earning account and paying them out in the form of dividends, The discount records also showed that there was a large number of notes in

the bank on which the bank had never received
any interest.   After going into these items more
closely, the Examiners became suspicious and
thought that these loans were put in the bank
for the purpose of hiding losses, etc.

Their minute book revealed that there had
never been an authorization for loans to either
officers, directors or employees; that there had
never been any depreciation charged off of their
furniture and fixtures, although the bank is in
leased quarters and their lease is to expire at
the end of 1925.   Their rent is nominal and will
in all probability be increased at the expiration of their present lease.

On Saturday December 20th, the Examiners
called a meeting of the Board of Directors. This
meeting started at 10 o'clock and lasted until
6:30 PM. During this time the general condition
of the bank was discussed with all of the Directors.

Monday morning the Directors and Examiners
met again at 10 o'clock and with the Cashier
went over all of the notes in the bank.   After
going over those notes with the Directors,
losses aggregating $55,324.20 were thrown out as
doubtful and worthless assets. The assets were
trusteed with Messrs. Purcell and Wright. The
Directors gave to the bank their notes in the
proportion of the stock owned, secured by what
the Examiners thought was collateral of some
value.   This meeting closed at 5:30 PM, December
22nd, the entries all having been made on the
books of the bank and the Directors and all
concerned seemed to be well satisfied.

Several conferences have been had with the
individual members of this Board, since, and
plans are now on foot to put auditors in the
bank.

REPORT SUBMITTED BY:

Examiners:

Paul R. Thompson

Paul R. Thompson

Ernest James Patterson (signature)

Ernest James Patterson

Sidney R. Rosenfeld (signature)

Sidney R. Rosenfeld

Twenty-Four

January 5, 1925

For the past two weeks, Lawrence had been at home. The first day, he had kept to his bed, claiming he had a touch of the flu. But on Christmas Eve he got up, announced he was staying home for the holidays, and threw himself into the festive spirit. He had convinced himself he had been justified to quit and that he would be able to find a new position after the first of the year. This self-righteous euphoria lasted about as long as the Christmas turkey. By the weekend his spirits had dropped and he moped around the house like a spoiled child who hadn't gotten everything on his Santa Claus list. The children gave him a wide berth after he snapped at them for laughing as they played a new board game.

Lawrence did not tell Anna he had left the bank until the Monday after Christmas. Originally, he had planned not to tell her at all. Gradually, however, he had come to realize he had to tell her. She was far too intuitive. Several times Lawrence had caught her giving him one of her single raised eyebrow looks. He knew it meant she was aware that something wasn't right but couldn't quite put her finger on it. Finally, he confessed to Anna that he and Keeley had fought over some bank business and that Keeley had insulted him. It was the result, he said, of the tension of the past few weeks created by the bank examiners' visit. He admitted he had quit, but assured Anna everything would be fine — he'd get a better position with another bank. She had been shocked by his announcement, but had said she "understood."

The following week he was miserable. With each successive day, he stayed in bed later and later. He couldn't bring himself to call his business associates to make inquiries about other positions — although he knew he should. He had no idea what Keeley might have told them about Lawrence's absence from the bank. Keeley had not called him — not once — and Lawrence certainly had not called him. He tried to occupy himself with his real estate affairs, but that too, was depressing. He owed taxes — which were past due — and, of course, he couldn't pay them.

With each day his mood turned darker until Anna became very concerned about him. They canceled long-standing plans for a New Year's Eve dance because Lawrence couldn't face even his closest friends. In two short weeks, he had become a prisoner in his own home.

Early that morning, Lawrence heard the telephone ring, but he did not answer it.

"Lawrence, the telephone is for you," called Anna.

"I don't want to talk, Anna. Who is it?"

Anna came into his study before answering. "It's Edward Keeley. Talk to him, Lawrence. You can't go on like this. Maybe he's calling to apologize."

Lawrence frowned. "I doubt it, but I'll talk to him." He rose and went to take the call. Anna followed him and stood listening to her husband's side of the conversation.

"Good morning, Edward," Lawrence said into the receiver.

....."I'm fine, thank you."

....."I'm not sure what we have to talk about, Edward."

....."Very well. I'll meet you. What time?"

....."3 P.M. will be fine. I'll be waiting." Lawrence hung up without saying goodbye.

Anna could hardly wait until he put the receiver on the cradle. "What did he want?" she asked.

"He wants to talk to me. I'm not sure why, but he says it's of the utmost importance to both of us. He's picking me up here at 3 P.M. I'm not sure why I agreed to go, but I did."

At 3 P.M. sharp, Lawrence was standing in the kitchen, his overcoat and hat in his hand, when Keeley's car pulled into the driveway. A cold spasm grabbed Lawrence's stomach as he recalled the argument of their last meeting. *I've got to handle this delicately. I can't let him see that I'm desperate, but I need to get my job back. Of course, I have no idea what he wants, so I'm going to let him do the talking.* The rattling horn of Keeley's Packard shook Lawrence out of his inertia; he put on his hat, opened the side door and went out into the icy wind, still carrying his coat over his arm.

As Lawrence climbed into the warm car, Keeley greeted him. "Good afternoon, Lawrence. It's good to see you. How are you?" It was as if the confrontation had never occurred.

Lawrence looked skeptically at Edward. He hadn't expected pleasantries. "I'm doing well. And you?" he responded, cautiously.

"I'm just great. Did you have a nice holiday?" Keeley continued.

"Yes, we did, as a matter of fact. It was lovely. How about you?" Lawrence remained polite.

"Well, I was very busy; but the children and I had a wonderful Christmas Day."

Having exhausted the small talk, the pair rode in strained silence as Edward headed west through downtown Huntington. Lawrence badly wanted to ask about the bank, but held his tongue. As they passed through Central City and onto the James River Turnpike, he noticed that the hillsides still held patches of snow in the shadows. Most of the evidence of the Christmas storm was gone; but in those spots where the sun did not penetrate, the black, wet tree trunks looked like the first marks of a charcoal sketch on pristine white paper. About two miles from the outskirts of town, Keeley pulled to the side of the road and parked. Lawrence stiffened.

Without a word, Keeley pulled a cigar from his coat pocket, unwrapped it and put it in his mouth. Slowly he rolled it around with his tongue, then bit off the end, opened the window and spit out the small wad of tobacco. Lawrence fidgeted in his seat, worrying that Keeley would light the thing and fill the car with cigar smoke and odor. He was also anxious about what Keeley was preparing to say.

"Well, Lawrence," Keeley began without lighting up. "Tell me how the last two weeks *really* have been for you. I'll be frank with you...mine have been terrible. I can't run that bank day to day; I need to be at the coal company. But, I don't know anyone else I can trust to look after my interests at the bank, either. We had a good arrangement, didn't we? I'll admit we both got a little hot under the collar the other day; but truthfully, we need to work this thing out."

Lawrence could sense this conversation was going his way. His neck muscles relaxed. He sat in silence waiting for Keeley to continue.

"Look, I'm not bleeding the bank...but you were right on one count — I couldn't have paid those notes. But the way you handled it wasn't very smart. You should have come to me with the problem. Together, we could have fixed it up."

"All right...I shouldn't have accused you of that. I know better." Lawrence broke his silence. "But you shouldn't have accused me of forgery. I didn't sign those notes. I got some of my buddies to sign the papers. I gave them a few hundred dollars and told them they'd never have to pay back the notes. The new notes were large enough to cover all the small loans and their 'gift.' I'm making the payments now. Those fellows owed me some favors, so they'll never tell."

"Well, all right. But we could have done a better job of handling it, I think. Look, why don't you come back to the bank. I never told anyone you quit. I let them think you were just taking a holiday. It was a good time to do so and no one was the wiser. The others at the bank thought it strange that they didn't know, but I smoothed that over, too."

Lawrence suddenly sensed he had the upper hand; he pressed his point. "I don't know, Keeley. Seems to me, that you don't trust me to handle things any longer. You sound like *you* want to be in charge and have *me* continue to be your lackey. I deserve more respect."

Keeley bristled. "Hell, Lawrence, you did some stupid things. I'm not sure you *do* deserve that respect; but I *do* trust you to look out for my interests. I know you were only doing what you thought best."

"Keeley, if *you* don't have respect for me, do you think anyone else will? My reputation in this town is important to me."

"Lawrence, I'm not going to ruin your reputation. I'm just telling you how *I* feel; and we'll keep that between us. I'll tell you what, you want respect...fine. Would a raise give you more respect? We can do that. And how about if we get the directors to pass a Vote of Confidence resolution? Would that do it?"

"That's not necessary, Edward. Your trust is enough. If you believe I can do the job, without constant bullying from you, then I'll come back."

"Oh, for God's sake, Lawrence. All right. No more fights. I'll see to it, on one condition. Clean up the mess you made, and do it now! And what about that check in Shapely...did you make it good?"

"I did. I had a sale pending on some property and it came in as I expected it to. I have one more potential sale which could cover those loans, too; but if it doesn't happen, I can still make the payments."

Keeley put out his hand. Lawrence took it and they shook. "It's a deal," Keeley said. "Glad to have you back."

West Virginia Banking Commission
Charleston, W.Va.

February 18, 1925

Mr. R. Lawrence Burgher, Vice-Pres.
Railroad Bank & Trust Co.,
Huntington, West Virginia

My dear Sir:

We have your letter of the 12th enclosing copies
of the minutes of your directors meetings held
since December 22nd, together with statements
and exhibits. I was disappointed that your minutes did not contain the authorization of an
audit to be made under the direction of this
department, which I understood was provided for
by your directors at that time. You are requested to bring this matter up in your meeting
tomorrow and have your board enter in your minutes of that meeting a record of the authorization of such audit. I would ask that you kindly
forward to me a certified copy of the minutes of
tomorrow's meeting, at the earliest possible
time after adjournment.

In looking over the list of notes paid and curtailed since December 22nd, it occurs to me that
you have not been collecting the paper which was
most severely criticized by this department. We
would suggest that you give this matter serious

thought and concentrate a little more on large
lines.

Yours very truly,

Sidney R. McCullough
Commissioner of Banking

SRMc/ab

RAILROAD BANK & TRUST COMPANY

HUNTINGTON, WEST VIRGINIA

EDWARD KEELEY, PRESIDENT
MAYNARD HUTCHINSON, CASHIER
R. LAWRENCE BURGHER, V. PRES.
J.R. THOMAS, ASST. CASHIER

February 20, 1925
Mr. Sidney R. McCullough
Commissioner of Banking
Charleston, West Virginia

Dear Sir:

I have your letter of February 18. I note what you have to say regarding the minutes of December 22nd.

I desire to call your attention to the conversation which was had at this meeting regarding the placing of an order for the audit in the Minutes of this Meeting. I recall very clearly that this matter was discussed at some length, and agreed to by your Mr. Thompson and Mr. Rosenfeld that this should not be entered as a matter of record at that time, but should be a general understanding with the Board regarding same.

In order to confirm my statements regarding the matter, as recalled by me and the Directors, I am having them sign along with me, confirming my action in not including this in the minutes of that Meeting. Trust this will be to your satisfaction.

I am enclosing herewith a copy of the Minutes of our Meeting last evening, February 19th, and desire to further say that the Directors and Discount Board are working hard on all large, undesirable lines of credit, meeting promptly and thoroughly going into the whole affairs of the bank.

Yours very truly,

R. Lawrence Burgher

R. Lawrence Burgher
Vice-President

ATTEST:

Edward M. Keeley

Edward M. Keeley

Thomas J. Noonan

Thomas Noonan

Geo. H. Wright

Geo. H. Wright

E. C. VanZandt

E.C.VanZandt

Twenty-Five

1925

As winter melted into spring, Lawrence Burgher was still struggling to prop up his financial house of cards. The crocuses were in bloom, but Lawrence hadn't noticed them. In his zeal to become a real estate mogul, he had made some investments that had been ill-advised. Huntington wasn't Shapely. The city's real estate market, while a profitable investment for a conservative man, was not providing the quick return on investment Lawrence had expected. There had been a tremendous revival in the housing market, but people were buying lots and building new houses. Lawrence had bought existing homes at foreclosure and was now trying to resell them. But these were not what the buying public wanted.

Night after dreary night he stayed late at the office going over his ledgers. With each review of the entries, he could see the situation worsen. The prosperity he dreamed of seemed to be eluding him. Just when he felt security might be within reach, another lump-sum payment would threaten the whole empire. The problem, as he saw it, was still cash flow. Because he had pledged already-mortgaged property for new loans to buy other parcels, he was in danger of losing the former if he couldn't make the payments on the latter. He now realized his comment to Keeley about his ability to meet these payments had been too optimistic. Until something sold, he knew, he couldn't pay off any of the growing stack of notes. Some properties were valuable; if he could just hold out until they sold, he'd be fine.

But just how long would that be? He had to buy more time.

Finally, in late May, Lawrence reluctantly sold the large parcel of land on Fifth Street, south of the city. Although he felt confident that it would be developed some day, he could hold it no longer. He needed the money now; someone else would reap the reward he had envisioned for himself. He was simply happy to sell it at a small profit. This transaction, however, enabled him to make good on several of his smaller notes, thereby improving both his financial outlook and his ability to sleep.

By the end of June, Lawrence was beginning to feel like the up-coming Fourth of July was his own personal holiday. It was hard to imagine that only six months earlier, he had been out of a job and almost at wit's end. His situation had improved — significantly. Several more real estate deals had been consummated, including a parcel in Guyandotte on which he owed a large balloon payment. He still had several outstanding loans at the Huntington bank and some notes in Shapely. But his debt no longer weighed on him as heavily as before.

As for the bank's affairs, he had returned to work eagerly and made a concerted effort to collect or curtail nearly all the small questionable notes. He had written to the commissioner reassuring him of his desire to cooperate fully in getting the bank on a solid footing. Although the commissioner had wanted to send in the auditors following the December examination, Lawrence had successfully argued for a delay until spring. By then, he believed, he could get matters well in hand. The bank examiners' report in March showed a substantial improvement in the bank's condition. The commissioner had been complimentary of their vigorous efforts to get the bank in better shape, but was still critical of the large lines of credit he and Keeley had used. The directors had been meeting regularly with Lawrence to review any new loans. Given his recently precarious job situation, he felt much more at ease knowing the decisions were not his alone.

Lawrence's immediate concern was the bank's current lease. It would expire in six months and the building's owners had advised him they would double the rent for the next year. Lawrence knew the amount was exorbitant, but the owners were adamant. He and

Keeley refused to buckle under. They were looking for other space.

A new office building, reportedly costing $1,250,000, had recently been completed at the corner of Eleventh Street and Fourth Avenue. At fourteen stories high, the Coal Exchange Building was one of the tallest in the city and one of the finest in the state. Elaborately designed with marble floors and walls on the lobby level, it boasted larger offices on each floor than existed currently in any other building in town. The building, owned by the Coal Exchange Company organized by D.C. Schonthal, A. Solof and H.A. Zeller, was rapidly filling with tenants. Lawrence could see marvelous possibilities for increasing the bank's income while acquiring an impressive home for the bank if they were to buy this new edifice. However, when he approached Keeley with his idea, he was met with outrage.

"Have you lost your mind?" Keeley nearly shouted over his vegetable soup. Lawrence had chosen to bring up the subject of acquiring the building during lunch at the Guyandotte Club. His hope that Keeley would not make a scene was short-lived.

Keeley continued to rant. "Buy the Coal Exchange Building? Where on earth would we get the money to do that? Lawrence, you are having delusions of grandeur!"

"Calm down, Keeley. It's not as far-fetched as it sounds. Look at the potential rental income. Fourteen floors of prime office space! The income would pay the mortgage, I'm sure. The bank needs a new home. You agree with that, correct?"

"Correct." Keeley answered more calmly. "But that's a pretty expensive home, Lawrence. What'd it cost to build...over a million, right?"

"Right. But wouldn't the impression we would make be a boost for the bank's prestige?"

"Perhaps, but I'd have to be firmly convinced it was a good investment. Besides, the banking commissioner would never allow it. I recall a similar situation in Glen Jean — we wanted to buy an office building for the rental income and he was opposed to it."

"That's different. This would be our banking home. It's better to own your quarters than to lease them, seems to me. It's a hell of an asset, Edward."

Keeley paused, his soup spoon in midair, then continued to slurp while Lawrence quietly ate his salad. "Edward, just think, if the bank owned this building, the value of our interest in the bank — controlling interest, I might remind you — would increase dramatically."

"That's assuming we could keep it fully leased and it made money for the bank. You always see the potential gain, but not the potential problems, Lawrence."

"And from whom did I acquire this gambler's spirit, Edward? I was pretty conservative when we first met, remember?"

"Well, you've become addicted, Lawrence." He laughed. "You love the art of the deal. Not that it's a bad trait, just potentially dangerous."

And then, Keeley abruptly changed the subject. It was his way of dismissing the issue. For the rest of the lunch hour, they discussed the so-called "monkey trial" and the conviction of John Scopes for teaching evolution. Lawrence, however, refused to be sidetracked. While he let himself be drawn into this trivial discussion, his mind raced ahead. *How can I make this happen? I'm not going to let him dissuade me this easily.* In his mind's eye, he could see himself ensconced on the fourteenth floor of the Coal Exchange Building. His office looked palatial.

Twenty-Six

October 4, 1925

Anna's forest green peignoir was nearly as lovely as the dress she had chosen to wear this evening. Tonight's dinner guests included two minor stockholders of the bank and their wives. Lawrence intended to buy them out and wanted to impress them. *They won't sell to a banker who doesn't already look prosperous.* She could hear his words as she slipped out of the satin robe and laid it on the bed.

The beaded silk had been ordered from New York weeks ago. Anna had been saving it for a special occasion and tonight was that, certainly. She took the heavy dress from the hanger, slipped it over her head, stepped back, closed the closet door and looked at her reflection in the long oval mirror. As she turned appraisingly, she was pleased to see that the v-shaped design of the beading made her hips look narrower than they actually were, and that the square neckline set off her finely chiseled collar bones to perfection. *Lawrence will surely approve.* She smiled to herself.

From her lacquered jewelry box she produced black beaded earrings which almost matched the dress. She considered a necklace of similar beads as well. She held it against her throat, studying the effect in the dressing table mirror; then she rejected it. Anna was glad she'd had her hair cut today; the new shorter style with its large single spit curl on each cheek set off the heavy earrings perfectly. Her dark hair, which some argued was black, was one of her best features and she prided herself on wearing the latest styles. Applying fire red lipstick, she realized she had removed her rings to bathe, reached for them in their familiar Limoges dish and placed them on her hands. She studied her short, slightly masculine hands for a moment, shook her head ruefully and rose to check on the preparations for dinner.

As she descended the curved staircase, Anna could hear Lawrence in the library giving Eileen, Sara and Margaret instructions for the evening.

"Eileen, after dinner your mother and I will bring the guests into the parlor where Sam will serve the brandy. After he's finished pouring, I'll tell them our daughters will entertain. Eileen, you curtsy and go to the piano with Margaret. Sara, you bring your violin and stand beside the piano to accompany them." Sara rolled her eyes in exasperation.

"Have you practiced?" Lawrence noted the look.

"Yes, Father," they chorused.

"And wear your recital dresses, the ones with the lace collars," called their mother as she reached the foyer.

"Yes, ma'am," they chorused again.

"All right. Go dress, " continued their father. "They will be here at 6 o'clock. Sam will call you when we are about to go into the parlor." As Lawrence crossed the wide foyer to speak with Sam, he met Anna coming back from the kitchen.

"Millie has everything under control. Our guests should arrive in about thirty minutes, dear. Doesn't the table look nice?" she inquired. She was especially eager to please her husband tonight.

"Yes, it looks fine; Millie's cooking smells wonderful and you look beautiful," he said as he kissed her cheek. "The evening can't help but succeed," beamed Lawrence. "And even if they won't admit it, I think the girls like showing off for our little parties, don't you?"

"Yes, dear, I'm sure they do."

In the soft yellow candlelight Lawrence sat at the head of the table surveying his guests as Millie bustled about in her crisply starched apron, alternately serving coffee and removing the empty dinner plates. He thought the evening was going very well; there had been lively inquiries about Lawrence's dream of buying the Coal Exchange Building and he had deftly secured the promise of a formal meeting next week to discuss the stock sale. He cast an approving smile at Anna down the length of damask. Millie's roast and Yorkshire pudding had been perfect; the guests were, he thought, properly impressed with his home and his wife's hospitality. As the maid bumped open the swinging door and backed into the dining room carrying a silver tray laden with warm lemon tarts, Lawrence heard the telephone ring. He ignored it, knowing Sam would answer it and could handle almost any domestic matter. Furthermore, it was Sunday; it wouldn't be a business call.

He leaned again to his left, listening intently to Frank Wainwright. Wainwright, a prosperous looking portly man, was the most successful real estate broker in town; in fact, the two had brokered many deals in the past seven years. The subject wasn't houses, however; it was football. "...and I read in the papers that Red Grange is considering becoming a professional player," Wainwright was saying.

"I don't believe it for a minute; that's only a rumor. But he would certainly get rich quickly if he did," Lawrence laughed. Sam appeared at his elbow, taking Lawrence by surprise.

"Excuse me, Mistah Burgher, but they's a call I thinks you should take."

"What is it, Sam?" Lawrence said shortly. "Can't you handle it?"

"No, suh, Mistah Burgher; it's about Buddy." He grimaced, talking in a stage whisper. "He's done got himself in some trouble and it's the...."

Lawrence interrupted him. "Fine, Sam; I'll get it." He stood abruptly and excused himself from the gaping dinner guests.

In the kitchen, he snatched up the dangling receiver. "This is Lawrence Burgher. What seems to be the problem?"

As Lawrence listened, Sam quietly went to the back hall and reached for his chauffeur's cap on the wooden shelf above the coat rack. Of all the duties he performed for the Burghers, driving the sleek burgundy Pierce-Arrow was his favorite. As Lawrence had promised, he had sent Sam to the Pierce-Arrow Training School and had given Sam a custom tailored suit of rich gray livery as a graduation gift. Whenever he drove the handsome vehicle, Sam wore the cap, if not the full outfit.

Sam heard Mr. Burgher slam down the receiver. "Sam, get the car," he barked as Sam reappeared in the kitchen. "That damn Buddy set fire to the shed out at the farm and a deputy sheriff caught him and took him to the county jail." As Sam rushed out to the garage, Lawrence squared his shoulders, unconciously smoothed back his hair, forced a smile and reentered the dining room.

"Ladies and gentlemen, I'm terribly sorry, but I'll have to ask you to excuse me for a while. My son Buddy has gotten into some mischief and I must go straighten the matter out. You know how boys are. Anna, could I see you in the kitchen for just a moment?"

At his announcement, Anna gasped and dropped her fork. Recovering quickly, she stammered, "Goodness, boys can get into more trouble, can't they?" She rose from her place and hurried after her husband through the swinging door.

"Lawrence, what on earth," she demanded.

"I'm really not sure, dear. That's why I must go. It seems Buddy and his friend James were sneaking a smoke in the shed at the farm and it caught fire."

"Oh my word! Is Buddy all right?"

"Yes, he's fine, but a neighbor thought the fire was threatening his house, so he called the sheriff. I gather they were taken to jail only to teach them a lesson; but in any case, I have to go get him. I'm going to wring his neck for ruining my dinner party!"

"Lawrence, good heavens! Be thankful he wasn't hurt! Or anyone else for that matter." Anna tried to calm her husband as relief flooded her face. "I'll entertain the guests until you return. Don't worry; the girls and I can handle it."

"What would those men think if they knew? My child in jail — the very idea! They'll never go through with the stock sale if this gets out."

"Oh, Lawrence, is that bank all you ever think about? I'm sure these gentlemen's children aren't perfect. They'll get a laugh out of it and take it for a boyish prank. Just go! Sam's got the car warmed by now."

Lawrence was silent on the ride to town and if Sam had questions about the incident, he kept them to himself. Staring out the window, oblivious to the passing scenery, the banker tried to think logically, but his mind tripped over question after question. *Jail, my God, I've never even been in one. Where are they holding Buddy — in a cell with a bunch of criminals? Is he all right? Will I have to post a bond? Will he have an arrest record? If this gets in the papers, how will I ever explain it to my associates? Why couldn't they have just brought him home? I'm going to tan his hide so badly he won't be able to sit down for a week.*

The Pierce-Arrow rolled to a stop beside the austere, gray limestone courthouse. No sign marked the site, but the words COUNTY JAIL, roughly stenciled on the squat, wooden side-door were illuminated by a solitary bulb hanging from the tin porch roof overhead. Wisely, Lawrence didn't ask Sam how he knew the jail's location. Lawrence climbed from the rear seat of the car, as Sam swung open the door. He smoothed his hair, pulled his overcoat collar up against the crisp, fall breeze, mounted the chiseled granite steps and stooped to enter the jail.

"I'm Lawrence Burgher. You are holding my son, Buddy and I've come to take him home," Lawrence announced to the uniformed guard at the desk just inside the door. As he flattened his thick, velvet collar, his eyes adjusted to the dimly lit room.

The guard shuffled through the jumble of papers on the desk and without looking up said, "You'll have to wait to see the sheriff 'fore you can do that."

Glancing around, Lawrence noticed that there were no chairs available for visitors. *Just as well. I'd probably catch something.* He looked at the guard with disdain.

"And just how long will that be? I *was* entertaining guests and would like to get my son and leave." As he spoke Lawrence wrinkled his nose at a sharp, sour smell that put him in mind of wet diapers.

He had noticed it as soon as he entered the jail. He was eager to leave before it permeated his clothing. Then it struck him that he might have to actually go to a cell to claim Buddy.

"That depends on how long it takes Sheriff Landers to get here." The deputy seemed more intent on straightening up the mess on the desk than in straightening out Lawrence's problem.

"May I see my son?" he asked with some hesitation, fearing the answer would prompt a trip into the depths of the jail and closer to the source of the odor which now reminded him of burnt collard greens.

"I'll ask the deputy that brought him in."

While Lawrence waited in the cramped entrance, unconsciously fingering the loose change in his pocket, the lanky deputy unfolded himself from behind the desk, stretched fully and ambled down the hall. His footsteps echoed in Lawrence's ears. The deputy seemed oblivious to the stench.

Soon he returned, a pudgy deputy trotting along behind him. "This here's Deputy Sutton. He's the one what brought in your boy."

Deputy Sutton stuck out his chubby hand, but withdrew it when Lawrence ignored it. "Mr. Burgher, your son is fine. A little scared, but unhurt. We only brought him in because we thought he could use the scare. You know, keep him from pullin' such a stunt again? There aren't any charges, but the sheriff has a rule. He always wants to see the boys. Hopes it'll keep 'em from returnin' with a more serious charge. He's on his way now. By the way, your shed is a total loss, but nothing else is damaged. Your man there said he'd be in contact with you tomorrow."

"Thank you. And my son, where is he?" Lawrence said stiffly.

"He's in a cell," he said, jerking his thumb in the direction from which he had appeared. "Sheriff thinks that's good for them too. I'll take you to him."

Lawrence blanched. He realized he had no choice but to follow the deputy into the heart of the jail. He walked gingerly in the middle of the narrow corridor, hoping his coattails would not brush against the stained, damp walls. As he passed the dismal, confining cells he now recognized the unmistakable, acrid smell of stale urine. It stung his nostrils so harshly that he tried not to breathe. Turning the corner, the jeers and hoots from a slightly larger cell caused him to recoil as he faced the half dozen or so unshaven men packed into the drunk tank. He averted his eyes and tried to look straight ahead down the darkened passageway, but it was impossible. A morbid, horrified fascination had gripped him and he found himself watching the mocking eyes which followed him from behind the bars. Each cramped cell was outfitted with two steel bunk beds, a sink and a toilet; many held two men in a space smaller than Lawrence's bedroom closet. The cell walls were the washed-out green of frozen pond water; the names, initials and dates scratched in the flaking paint told the chronology of each cell.

Lawrence was dumbstruck. *How could a man survive in such a place?* After a seemingly endless parade past more cells of slack-jawed residents, the small band stopped before a cell whose sole inhabitant was a clean-cut boy of about ten.

"Father," Buddy called from inside. He had bounded to his feet from his spot on the bunk at the sight of his father. Then realizing he was probably in trouble with him as well as with the authorities, he sat down again. At the sight of his forlorn son sitting in the middle of the cold iron bed, Lawrence's revulsion for the place rose to a new high. He wanted to get Buddy out of there as quickly as possible.

As the guard pulled the clanking key ring from his belt and methodically searched for the one which fit Buddy's barred door, it occurred to Lawrence that a grown man would have difficulty standing upright in that cell.

"You can come out now, son." The guard beckoned to Buddy. "Your father is here to take you home."

Buddy ran out of the cell and flung his arms around his father. Lawrence patted him on the back, then flinched as the cell door slammed shut behind Buddy. He deliberately held Buddy away from him, his hands on Buddy's shoulders and fixed him in his gaze. "I think we'll have to have a long talk about this, son," he said sternly.

"Yes sir," Buddy replied. He quickly wiped away the tears that had welled up at the sight of his father. He knew his father hated to see him cry.

Both father and son were silent as they retraced their steps toward the front of the jail. From behind the bars, the men stared again at the small group; but the sound of the trio's rhythmic footsteps had replaced the jeers. As they reached the end of the corridor, they saw the reason. Sheriff Landers was standing, arms akimbo, at the far end in full sight of the inmates.

He came toward them, his hand outstretched and spoke warmly to Lawrence. "Mr. Burgher, I'm really sorry about all of this. Had I known it was your son, we would have brought him home instead of to the jail. But my deputies have their orders, you know, and they didn't notify me until he was already here. I understand we took you away from dinner guests, but perhaps it will be a good lesson for young Lawrence. Put the fear of God in him, so to speak."

"Or the fear of jail, at least," added Lawrence. He had known Sheriff Landers for many years. They both looked slightly embarrassed at meeting under such awkward circumstances.

"Thank you for coming down, Sheriff Landers. I know it was an imposition for you to leave your family on a Sunday evening as well."

"Well, I think it is important to have a word with these young boys. I'm just sorry it was yours." He turned to Buddy. "Young man, I trust we won't see you in here again? Not a very pleasant place to spend an evening, is it, son?"

"No sir, you won't ever see me again. I promise!" exclaimed Buddy. He put out his hand; the sheriff took it formally with a wink at Lawrence. "Thank you, sir. I won't cause you or Father any more trouble," said Buddy solemnly.

"Very well, Buddy; let's go. Sam is waiting and I'm sure your mother is anxious for us to come home."

"Thank you again, Sheriff. We're sorry to have troubled you," Lawrence apologized. "It certainly won't happen again."

"Not at all, Mr. Burgher. Just doing my job."

Lawrence took his son's small hand, opened the heavy door and paused to fill his lungs with the clear fall air. Then they walked swiftly down the granite steps to the big car idling smoothly at the curb.

Twenty-Seven

April 1926

Lawrence sat staring out the windows of his temporary office in the Frederick Building, an open telegram in his hands. Watching the rain blow against the glass had lulled him into a sense of tranquility which was quite at odds with the reaction the telegram's contents should have created. He looked back at the words for the fifth time..."**YOUR DELINQUENT NOTE DUE FEBRUARY 15 OF $10,470 MUST BE PAID IMMEDIATELY. STOP. PREVIOUS QUERIES TO COLLECT OR RENEW UNANSWERED. STOP.**" The salutation read "**RAILROAD BANK & TRUST COMPANY BOARD OF DIRECTORS.**" He shook his head. It was simply incomprehensible to Lawrence why they had chosen such a formal means of dealing with his old note. He was incredulous. He continued to stare at the small yellow document. Either he was beyond anger or the enormity of the telegram had not fully registered.

After a moment Lawrence took a long contemptuous look around the cramped office he had been forced to occupy on the hotel's mezzanine. When the bank's former lease had expired, they had moved here for want of a permanent home. Over the past six months, Keeley had refused to discuss further the purchase of the Coal Exchange Building and had dismissed Lawrence's other suggestions for new quarters, as well. Lawrence stared out the window again. Through the overcast sky he could see the outline of the Coal Exchange Building at the end of the next block. The lights on the upper floors seemed to wink at him through the rain splashing on the glass. Then, the anger hit him.

Those bastards! They purposely reviewed those loans at the last board meeting when I was out of town. I wonder who proposed sending this telegram? I'll bet it was Keeley. They've let that debt slide for over a year. Why now? Why clamp down now? Has he heard I'm trying to get control of the bank? Surely Frank Wainwright didn't tell Keeley he agreed to sell me his stock. No, he promised to keep our deal under his hat. Well, all right, Keeley; I can play tough, too.

Lawrence furiously wadded the telegram into a tight ball and stuffed it into his coat pocket. He jerked open his lower left-hand desk drawer and pulled out the checkbook for his account in Shapely. Hurriedly, he wrote a check for the entire $10,470 and ripped it out of the binding. He rose, check in hand, and marched down the broad marble stairs to the temporary bank lobby and paid off the note.

Racing back to his office, he retook the steps two at a time. Once inside the room, he realized he was slightly winded. He sat for a moment facing the window, then he ran his hands nervously through his hair and reached for the telephone. First, he called Frank Wainwright and told him he was ready to buy his stock and had prepared a check for $10,000. Next, he called Louden Kitchen and delivered the same message. His third call was to his brother David.

"David, Lawrence here. I need you to handle something for me." Lawrence was all business. "I've written three checks on Shapely, but I need you to delay sending them out of the bank for collection." Holding the receiver in his left hand, he wrote the two promised checks, each for $10,000, as he talked.

"Lawrence, that's pretty tough to do. Are you sure you know what you are doing?" David asked cautiously.

"Yes, I know it is, but I need you to do it. I don't have time to explain right now. Would you also withdraw $10,000 personally, purchase a cashiers' check elsewhere and send it to me? I'll settle with you later."

"Now, look here, Lawrence. You're my brother and I've helped you out before, but this is asking a lot. I don't feel good about this. You'd better tell me what's going on."

"I'll explain when I come up there next week. Suffice it to say, it's necessary."

"All right. If you insist. You're the officer; I'm just the cashier."

"Thank you, David. I appreciate it. All is well in Shapely, I trust?" Now that the business was concluded, Lawrence took the time to exchange a few pleasantries.

"Yes, everything is just fine," David replied dully.

"Good. I'm glad. Good-bye, David." He hung up the phone and turned to look, once again, at the Coal Exchange Building.

The next day, Lawrence delivered the checks to Wainwright and Kitchen and consummated the stock purchases. He now held controlling interest in the Railroad Bank & Trust Company. He felt he was on the verge of realizing his long-held dreams. In his mind, "Dickie-bird" was finally dead. He was about to bury forever the specter of the little boy lying bloody and wet in the schoolyard. *R. Lawrence Burgher is now a force to be reckoned with.*

That afternoon — typical of April in West Virginia — the rain stopped and the sun reappeared. The air had a freshly washed smell, like clean laundry hanging on the line. Lawrence walked across the street to Keeley's office with a spring in his step, avoiding the lingering puddles in the gutter. As he strolled through the First Huntington National Bank lobby toward the elevators in the adjoining office building, he couldn't help thinking wistfully of the sumptuous Coal Exchange Building. *Our bank would be simply grand in that lobby. Now, even if Keeley is opposed to buying the building, I'm confident the other directors will go along with me. It's hard to disagree with the majority stockholder.* He chuckled to himself, feeling quite smug.

Following Miss Newcomb's announcement that he wanted to see Keeley, Lawrence went into his partner's private office. Keeley wore a look of surprise and irritation, despite the prior warning. This amused Lawrence. Their relationship had remained strained since Lawrence's return to the bank in January. He had a feeling Keeley was sorry he had asked him to come back.

"What brings you here, Lawrence? Tomorrow is Friday. Couldn't it have waited until lunch at the club?" Keeley was not hiding his annoyance well.

"Nice to see you too, Edward. Actually, I thought it better to talk in private."

"About what? More letters from the commissioner?" Keeley asked sarcastically.

Lawrence maintained his composure. "No. About a new home for the bank. We've been in the Frederick for four months and it isn't at all suitable. We've looked all over the city and found nothing that *is* suitable. I think we should discuss the Coal Exchange Building again."

"Lawrence, as far as I'm concerned, we've discussed it for the last time. You still haven't convinced me and I don't think you can." Keeley's voice was growing louder and more impatient.

"Well, perhaps it isn't necessary to convince you, now. Perhaps I'll have enough votes to defeat your objection, if it comes to that." Lawrence put his hand in his coat pocket and reared back in the chair, looking like a cocksure prize fighter ready to deliver a knock-out punch.

"What do you mean?" Keeley was on his feet. "Are you considering making a proposition to the bank board over my objections? Because if you are, you'll lose. You seem to have forgotten that I hold the majority stock in the bank, my friend." As he challenged Lawrence, Keeley leaned over the desk and glowered at him.

"No, Edward. You don't. I do. I just bought enough stock from Frank Wainwright and Louden Kitchen to give me controlling interest. I can defeat you on any vote I choose. And, on this one, I will." Lawrence smiled arrogantly.

Edward was apoplectic. The veins in his neck stood out like taut rope. His face was beet red. He slammed his fist on the desk and screamed at Lawrence. "What in hell have you done to me, you bastard? I thought we were supposed to be partners? You ass! You ungrateful ass! I taught you everything you know. Brought you into banking! Gave you your start! Is this the thanks I get? You goddamn son-of-a-bitch!" He was yelling so loudly that Lawrence thought he could be heard in the next office.

While Keeley ranted Lawrence sat calmly enjoying the moment. When he stopped, Lawrence replied. "Edward, I *am* grateful for everything you've done for me. This isn't personal. It's business. You've got your power base — the coal company, several other banks, the timber company, half of Mountaineer Realty, which, may I remind you, was built on my inheritance — and now I've got mine. Now, would you like to talk about the Coal Exchange Building?"

Over the following week Lawrence's euphoria grew to almost manic proportions. Not only had he gained control of the bank, but Keeley had finally agreed with him that the Coal Exchange Building *would* make a good location for the bank. He was still opposed to the purchase however, and thought they should merely lease space, as they had done in the past. Lawrence, on the other hand, had looked closely at the bank's other holdings and felt there might be a way to trade some of those assets for stock in the Coal Exchange Company. If successful, this action would lessen the mortgage the bank would have to undertake. He had quietly begun to make inquiries of Messers Solof, Schonthal and Zeller to ascertain their interest in selling. If they were willing, he planned to put the proposal to his board of directors. He was certain the board would support him.

Socially, he was on cloud nine as well. Word of his recent stock purchases had circulated among the business community almost overnight. Within days he had been invited to join the Guyan Golf and Country Club, the Elks Club and the Kiwanis Club. He was also asked to serve on two new civic boards — one planned to build a summer camp for young girls and the other wanted to establish a day care center for small children of poor families. He accepted them all. It amazed and gratified Lawrence to see the respect and position that came to a man viewed as wealthy and successful. In actuality, of course, he knew he was no better than he had been two weeks earlier; but the aura of money had given him a new, higher status in Huntington. He loved it. The civic acclaim made all he had done seem worthwhile. Yes, he'd taken a few risks and shortcuts, but didn't everyone?

On Friday, April 9, David called to say he had the three checks. They had been presented and would have to be sent out for collection within the next five days. Holding them any longer was just not possible, he said. Lawrence agreed to send him a check before the end of the day to cover the $30,000. When he hung up the receiver, his euphoria had evaporated. He did not have the money to send David.

When he had written those checks last week, Lawrence had hoped it would not come to this. He had "played the float" hoping some real estate deal would come through — but it hadn't. He sat for a moment contemplating his options. *I can send a check from my account here to stall a bit longer, but it wouldn't be good either; and our collection time is shorter than Shapely's. Or, I could try to borrow the money using my home as collateral. Given the telegram of last week, the directors probably wouldn't approve it and I don't have time to go through that process.* Finally, he decided he had no choice.

He wrote out two deeds of title transfer, placing the Pea Ridge farm and his mother-in-law's home in the name of his brother-in-law, Nate Van Horn. Knowing his own credit limit was exhausted, he prepared loan papers in Nate's name to borrow $40,000 from the Railroad Bank & Trust, using the two properties as collateral. He forged Nate's signature, stamped it "**APPROVED**" and took it to the cashier for processing. He asked for a cashier's check for the full amount and mailed it to David with instructions to deposit it immediately. This would cover the three recent checks and replace the $10,000 withdrawal David had made for him. His final telephone call of the day was to Nate.

"Nate, Lawrence here. I hope I'm not holding you beyond closing, but I wondered if you could meet me at the Elks Club before you go home? It shouldn't take long. Jenny's dinner won't even get cold," Lawrence laughed.

Nate replied that he was leaving shortly and would be happy to meet Lawrence.

"Fine. I'll see you in thirty minutes." Lawrence depressed the telephone cradle, but continued to hold the receiver to his ear and dialed again.

"Anna, sweetheart, I'm going to be late for dinner tonight. Please ask Millie to hold it for me and tell Sam to pick me up at the Elks at 7 P.M. I'm sorry if I've disturbed your plans, but I've got to talk to Nate about something. I'll see you later. Goodbye, love."

Lawrence sat in the growing darkness of the office. When he thought about the fact that he had signed Nate's name, he broke out in a cold sweat. *I don't know what else I could have done. If Nate will take the money without knowing what I've done, I'll be fine. I don't want to have to tell him about transferring the property title. It's not legal until I record it, anyway. And, he won't ask where the $10,000 came from. It's not like he hasn't taken my money before. He's already somewhat beholden to me, and if worse comes to worst, I'll ask him to say he gave me permission to sign his name. After all I've done, he wouldn't dare turn me down. What I need is a drink!*

He closed the office and walked through the twilight to the Elks Club. He entered the bar-room and took a stool at the bar. The Benevolent and Protective Order of Elks, No. 313, had erected this club house in 1909 for the enjoyment of their lodge members. As a new inductee, Lawrence was taking full advantage of its privileges, including clandestine alcoholic beverages — despite Prohibition. He actually enjoyed the camaraderie of its members more than he did that of his associates at the Guyandotte Club. Here he felt more at home, and at the same time, slightly superior to many of the members. Here, perhaps because most of the men had themselves risen from lesser positions to those they currently held, he was admired, respected. On the other hand, he felt the members of the Guyandotte Club, most of whom descended from old money, treated him as if he still didn't measure up.

Lawrence addressed the bartender. "I understand a fellow can get a drink from you, if they play their cards right." He winked at the smiling man.

"That's right, sir. You're one of the new members aren't you?" the bartender asked politely.

"Yes, I'm Lawrence Burgher. I was inducted just a few days ago.

What do you have? Not rotgut liquor or bathtub gin, I hope?"

"No, sir. It's good liquor. Whiskey, gin, rye, whatever you want. We keep it in back and don't advertise the fact, of course. But for members, we can get whatever you want."

"Then I'll have a whiskey, neat. Thank you."

"Certainly, Mr. Burgher."

After Lawrence had had two quick drinks, he felt better. Checking his pocket watch for the time, he reached into his pocket, pulled out a small red package of Sen-Sen. He put a bit of the sweet powder in his mouth and returned to the front porch to wait for his brother-in-law. A few minutes later Lawrence saw Nate ascend the wide steps. He waved to get his attention. Nate returned the wave and walked toward the row of rocking chairs where Lawrence was seated.

"Lawrence, good to see you," Nate called.

As Nate approached, Lawrence stood and clapped him on the shoulder. Lawrence thought Nate Van Horn was the most undistinguished-looking man he'd ever seen. He liked him well enough, but recognized that Nate never had made a good first impression on anyone. He was slight of build with dishwater blond hair, which he parted in the middle. His gray-blue eyes looked like cloudy, glass marbles. Because of his habit of ducking his head when he spoke, one always sensed he knew he would not impress those he met and therefore didn't try.

However, once a person got to know Nate, he was very likable; but his shyness had cost him several jobs over the years. Lawrence had secured him a salesman's position at Minter Homes when he moved to Huntington nearly two years ago; but he'd lost it shortly thereafter. Since then, he had been unemployed for several long stretches at a time and had borrowed money from Lawrence to live on. Currently he was doing menial labor for very low wages. Out of necessity, he and Jenny and the twins were living with Jenny and Anna's mother.

"Nate, I'm glad you could come. Let's go inside." Lawrence said as he opened one of the double doors and ushered Nate inside.

After their eyes adjusted to the light in the hallway, the pair proceeded toward the open club room. Lawrence steered Nate to a small table at the rear of the room. As soon as they were seated, a waiter appeared.

"Good evening gentlemen, what could I get you?" he asked politely.

Lawrence spoke up. "A good stiff drink would be nice, but I guess that's out of the question," he said jokingly. He knew the waiter would never serve liquor to a non-member, even if he was a member's guest.

"I'm afraid so, sir. How about a cup of coffee."

"Coffee, it is. Thank you." He nodded at Nate, assuming coffee suited him as well.

Lawrence did not waste a moment on small talk. He looked straight at Nate and said, "Nate, I've got good news for you. I heard of a good position last week that's perfect for you. City Lumber and Supply Company needs a stock supervisor. Esker Waugh is building houses all over town and could use some help. I told him about you and he wants to talk with you about the job. It's yours if you want it."

Nate ducked his head, then cut his eyes up at Lawrence as a large, engaging smile crossed his face. He shook his head in disbelief.

"Lawrence, you're always looking out for me. I don't know how I'll ever repay you for all you've done since we came to Huntington. All of us in that one house has been very difficult for Jenny and for Grandma Miller. Maybe if I can hold on to this job, I can afford to get our own home some day."

"Sooner than you think, Nate," Lawrence responded. He took a check for $10,000 from his pocket and slid it across the table to Nate. As he stared at it, Nate's smile faded and his jaw dropped. Lawrence continued. "Consider this a gift, Nate. Use it for a down payment on your own home."

Nate looked up at Lawrence with moist eyes. "Lawrence, I can't take your money. This is far too much. Not that I can't use it, but I already owe you a lot. I couldn't accept it as a gift and I could never repay a loan that large."

Lawrence said, "Nate, don't worry about it. Someday I may need your help and I know I'll be able to count on you."

Nate continued to shake his head slowly. The waiter returned and put their coffee before them. Lawrence hoisted his cup, urging Nate to do likewise.

"I've never toasted with a cup of coffee, but there's always a first time, I guess. To your success!" toasted Lawrence.

"To success," echoed Nate, softly.

KEELEY COAL COMPANY
WEST VIRGINIA SMOKELESS COAL

HUNTINGTON, WEST VIRGINIA
Mines in Wyoming, Fayette and Raleigh Counties
Edward M. Keeley, President

May 12, 1926

Mr. Sidney R. McCullough
Commissioner of Banking
Charleston, West Virginia

My dear Mr. McCullough:

There are a few gentlemen coming up to Charleston in the next few days to request a charter for a new Building & Loan Association. While I am not in the company and will not be, I do think our town is in need of a large building and loan. It would be a great thing to relieve the banks of a lot of long-term loan paper that they have in them at the present time.

What I want to ask of you is this: I understand that Mr. Burgher is to be one of the incorporators of this company along with Judge Starr and some other gentlemen here in town. Now as to Judge Starr, he is a high-class man in every respect, and he stands that way in this community. Of course, you know the trouble our bank is in, and I wish you would not say anything about Burgher to these men. I am not asking this of you in order to sidetrack their request, but I do think that if the department would criticize Mr. Burgher, it would spread over this town and it would not only injure him personally, but would also injure our bank. The type of men that will be interested in the building

and loan are not going to let Mr. Burgher run
it, in any case.

I have always been a fellow that even if a man
has done wrong, I like to see him turn over a
new leaf and do better. Remember, I am not
writing you this letter to ask you to do something that is not right. I am writing you this
letter as a friend, explaining this situation
the best that I know how. And if I have made a
mistake I want to apologize, because I do not
want to do nothing that is wrong to any man, or
ask anybody to do anything that is wrong for me.

Yours very truly,

Edward Keeley

dict.
EMK:p

TREASURY DEPARTMENT
NATIONAL BANK EXAMINER
OFFICE OF COMPTROLLER OF THE CURRENCY

July 3, 1926

Mr. Sidney R. McCullough
Commissioner of Banking
Charleston, West Virginia

Dear Mr. McCullough:

You possibly know that R. Lawrence Burgher, President of the Railroad Bank & Trust Company of Huntington, was President of the First National Bank of Shapely, and possibly has other connections. Also that his brother, David Burgher, is Cashier of the Bank of Shapely.

In a recent examination of the First National Bank of Wyoming County, I discovered what appeared to have been two kites in the account of R. Lawrence Burgher, for $10,000 each, occurring in April. They looked like two-way kites with the Bank of Shapely, with possibly other banks being involved. I found a further item of $10,000 drawn on the Bank of Shapely by David Burgher, used at Pineville to purchase a Cashier's Check for R.L. Burgher. The First National Bank of Wyoming County makes its collections on Shapely through the Fifth-Third of Cincinnati and this route requires about a week to get returns.

If the above matters have not already been brought to your attention, and you should desire it, I will be glad to furnish further details as soon as a typewritten field copy of my report is returned to me from Washington.

A rather sketchy knowledge of this territory has led me to believe that the above information might possibly be of service. I am sure you will oblige me by treating it as strictly confidential.

Respectfully yours,

Anthony Preston
National Bank Examiner

Twenty-Eight

May 12, 1926

It was late when Lawrence arrived home. The night was filled with the sound of crickets. Fireflies darted across the yard, each lighting a tiny space as it paused in flight. To enjoy it all, Lawrence stopped on the steps before entering the house. A damp, pungent breeze from the river stirred the willow tree, its long branches sweeping the gazebo. The house was silent, but the yard was alive. A soft yellow glow from an upstairs window let Lawrence know that Anna was still awake. He opened the sidedoor quietly and stepped into the dark pantry. Moving on tiptoe to keep from waking the dogs, he ascended the back stairway and walked the long hall to their bedroom. The yellow glow from their room also spilled into the hallway, forming a bright patch of light on the carpet runner.

As he stood in the doorway, his shadow grew larger than life-size behind him. Anna, already in bed, looked up from her book as the light was broken.

"For heaven's sake, Lawrence, you scared me to death! I didn't hear you come in," she gasped.

"I'm sorry, love. I should have called out, but I didn't want to wake the children."

"Look at the time. Have you been at the directors' meeting all this time? Did you eat dinner?" she asked solicitously.

"No, I mean, yes. Wait a minute. No, I haven't been at the meeting all night. And, yes, I did eat. Actually, I ate at the Elks. I've been there quite a while — celebrating."

As Lawrence walked toward the bed, Anna eyed him suspiciously. He was slightly flushed and just a bit unsteady in his gait. She was sure he had been drinking, although she didn't think he was actually drunk, just tipsy. Even becoming tipsy was so out of character for Lawrence that she smiled, like a mother at a naughty child who is too funny to punish. She wondered just exactly what he'd been celebrating, but didn't ask. She wasn't at all angry, just amused. He caught sight of her smile and grinned like Alice's Cheshire Cat.

"Anna," he cried, "I've just been named president of the bank!"

"You've what? Lawrence, how did this happen? Come tell me all about it." She closed her book, laid it aside and patted the edge of the bed for him to sit down.

"Let me talk while I undress. I'm too keyed up to sit still." He began disrobing. "It all came about so quickly, I can hardly believe it myself. As usual, the meeting began after the bank closed. The minutes were read and we discussed renewing a few loans. All of a sudden, Keeley, who was presiding as usual, handed George a letter and asked that it be read. It was his resignation."

"Good heavens, Lawrence," Anna interrupted. Lawrence walked across the room and Anna called after him, "Didn't he tell you beforehand?"

"Absolutely not," said Lawrence from the closet, as he hung up his suit coat. Stepping out of his trousers, he tottered slightly, but regained his ostrich-like stance. "Since I bought out Frank and Louden Kitchen, Keeley's been very aloof. In fact, he's canceled our regular Friday luncheon several times. But he must have been thinking about resigning for a while. He had even sold most of his bank stock."

"Were the other directors as surprised as you?" Anna asked. Lawrence crossed the room again and took a pair of pajamas from the bureau drawer.

"They certainly were. And they voted to reject his resignation. I did too — even though I knew I might have the job if he resigned. I couldn't very well have voted to accept it, could I?"

"No, that would not have looked good at all. Did you really want him to resign?"

"Well, we *have* had our clashes lately. And, I'll admit — I've always aspired to be the president, some day. Nevertheless, his experience is valuable and we've been through a lot together. But, let me tell you the rest. After plenty of discussion...George tried to reason with him...Thomas simply refused to hear Keeley's side and walked out...George suggested we both resign."

"What?" Anna cried. "I thought you were made president? Lawrence, don't tease me!"

"I'm not teasing. We both resigned; then, we switched places. I was elected president and Keeley was elected vice president. You see, some of the directors were so upset with Keeley's resignation, they refused to consider me for president unless he stayed on as second in charge. Finally, he agreed and we were duly elected."

"How did Keeley take that?"

"Well, I'm not sure, but *I* think it was a good solution. He's still involved and I'm in charge!"

"Oh, darling, I'm so proud of you. It's what you always dreamed of. *President R. Lawrence Burgher!* Has a nice ring to it doesn't it? Now, come on to bed, President Burgher." Anna turned back the covers and patted the bed again.

This time Lawrence accepted her invitation and climbed in beside her. She lay with her head on his shoulder and was asleep within minutes. Lawrence, on the other hand, could not sleep. His head pounded and the room seemed to spin slightly. He felt like he was on a slow moving carousel. Gently, he moved Anna's head to a pillow and rolled over. He stared at a rose on the wallpaper, willing it to stay still. Instead, it seemed to meander, as if the outside breeze were making it nod. Lawrence got up and went to get a headache powder. *Surely it isn't the liquor. I didn't have that much.*

Returning to bed, he lay there thinking about the board meeting. He hadn't told Anna how acrimonious the discussion had been or that he had won the presidency by only a slim majority. *I'll have to settle all my accounts, somehow. Those directors will be watching me like a hawk. And if they ever find out about Nate's loan, I'll be fired. Maybe I ought to talk to him.* He finally fell asleep trying to figure out what to do.

The night was pitch black as Lawrence walked through a deserted city. No street lights burned. No cars passed him. No other person approached or followed, yet he felt he was being followed. He walked close to the buildings. Suddenly, from the dark, a hand reached out to touch him. Although he couldn't see anyone, he felt the weight. He recoiled and moved away from the brick wall he had been hugging. Another hand touched his other arm, illuminating a spot on his coat. He jumped again and walked faster. From every direction, hands reached for him. At each touch, he could see a light but no hand nor human form. It was as though the light and the touch were the only form of matter. The touches became stronger and brighter. A shrill sound began to pierce the air from a distance. It seemed to come closer and grow louder, minute by minute, as invisible hands began to grab at Lawrence. He tried to cover his ears, but the hands wouldn't let him. He thought the shrill noise would deafen him, so he began to run. More hands grabbed at him as he turned the corner. Now he was lost. He ran aimlessly. The sound and the hands followed him, until he ducked into a small cubby-hole in the side of a white building. He crouched down and covered his ears. The sound swirled and whistled outside the hiding place, but did not enter. As he cowered there, he still could see the hands as they tried to reach in to grab him.

Lawrence sat bolt upright in bed. His pajamas were ringing wet and he was freezing. He glanced frantically around the room to assure himself he was safe. Anna slept quietly beside him. He took off his wet bed clothes and dropped them on the floor, then climbed back in the bed and curled his body around Anna's. *Dear God, help me figure out a way out of this mess. Now that I've gotten what I wanted, don't let me lose it. I don't want to hurt anyone, Lord, especially my family. How do I fix this? Help me, God. Please help me.*

TREASURY DEPARTMENT
NATIONAL BANK EXAMINER
OFFICE OF COMPTROLLER OF THE CURRENCY

August 3, 1926
Mr. Sidney R. McCullough
Commissioner of Banking
Charleston, West Virginia

Dear Mr. McCullough:

In connection with our conversation a short time ago, about the transactions of Mr. Burgher, I am writing you the detailed memoranda below.

Sept. 14th, 1925   R.L. Burgher deposited check on Bank of Shapely, West Virginia, for $10M. Against this deposit this bank paid Mr. Burgher's check for $10M on September 17. The item on Shapely which was deposited by Mr. Burgher was sent out for collection through the Fifth-Third National Bank, Cincinnati, Ohio. This is the regular collecting channel for this bank, but it requires about a week to collect such items.

April 1st, 1926   R. L. Burgher deposited another check on Shapely for $10M which was collected in the same manner. This bank paid Burgher's check through the Federal Reserve Bank, the check being mailed on the day the deposit was made. As the latter bank collected the item for the First National Bank of Roanoke, Virginia, it follows that the item was issued by President Burgher some days prior to the date of his deposit to cover it.

April 13th, 1926   David Burgher, Brother of President Burgher and Cashier of the Bank of Shapely, gave this bank a check on his bank for $11,500.00. Of this amount $1500.00 was deposited to President Burgher's account. The remaining $10M was paid this bank for its cashiers check issued to David Burgher. This cashiers check bears the endorsements of the Bank of Shapely, the First National Bank of Roanoke, Virginia and of the Federal Reserve Bank.

I hope this information is helpful to you in your situation with Huntington.

Respectfully yours,

Anthony Preston

Anthony Preston
National Bank Examiner

West Virginia Banking Commission
Charleston, W.Va.

August 8, 1926

Mr. Anthony Preston
National Bank Examiner
Washington, D.C.

My Dear Sir:

This will acknowledge receipt of your letter of
the third, enclosing information concerning two
kites of Ten Thousand ($10,000.00) Dollars,
each, being carried by R. Lawrence Burgher and
David Burgher of Shapely.

I thank you most kindly for this information.
We have experienced some trouble in the past
with a rather large kite of Edward Keeley and
his affiliations and both Mr. Lawrence Burgher
and Mr. David Burgher are closely allied with
him. We will highly appreciate any further
information you can give us at any time concerning these men and their operations and, should
we find national institutions involved in kites
from our examinations, we will advise you
promptly.

You may rest assured that the information given
us will be treated in strict confidence and that

the spirit of cooperation evidenced by your
letter is greatly appreciated.

Yours very truly,

Sidney R. McCullough
Commissioner of Banking

SRMc/ab

Twenty-Nine

August 1926

Over the past few months Lawrence had worked feverishly. His days had been filled with meetings and negotiations with one single purpose — buying the Coal Exchange Building. Almost as soon as he was elected president, Lawrence had made this his top priority. Nothing else mattered. And now, only three months later, he had done it! His proposal to trade property already held by the bank for controlling stock in the Coal Exchange Company had been approved, with some dissent, by the directors. As of the end of July, the Railroad Bank & Trust Company had a magnificent new — and permanent — home.

Although the building was new, Lawrence had added a few special touches to his own office. He had repaneled the walls in cherry, and added an oriental rug with heavy fringes and a long cordovan leather sofa. The redecorated office now felt warm and prosperous. His large desk overpowered the room and its elegant appointments, however, leaving no question about who was in charge here.

As Lawrence sat at his desk, he was grateful that the new building had plenty of fans. The heat and humidity that particular August morning rivaled summer in the deep south. The air was laden with moisture, although it had not rained for days. In actuality, the fans, even at high speed, only moved the dampness around; still, they gave the illusion of cooling the office.

Seated before Lawrence, her stenographer's pad on her plump

lap, was his secretary, Miss Perry. As she waited, pencil poised, Lawrence searched intently for several notes on his desk.

"Ah, yes. Here we are. Miss Perry, this is a memorandum to the board of directors. As it pertains to personnel matters, it is strictly confidential. Do you understand?"

"Oh, yes sir. All you say is always kept right here." She tapped her head. "I would never breathe a word." At this she covered her mouth dramatically. She might have been on stage, acting in a play.

"Very well, let's begin." Lawrence dictated, deliberately.

"Gentlemen: Since being elected as president of the Railroad Bank & Trust Company, it has been apparent to me that the one outstanding need is a substantial reduction in expenses. And to that end, I make the following recommendations:

1. That the position of assistant cashier be declared vacant.

2. That Mr. Priddy, the paying teller, be asked to resign.

3. That Mrs. Nichols, stenographer, be asked to resign.

4. That the compensation paid for janitor's services, be reduced to a figure not to exceed $30 a month.

5. That no expenses be incurred without the approval of the president...."

Lawrence continued to dictate the details of his plan which put all the power of negotiating and renewing loans in his hands. He proposed firing the two employees he considered disloyal to him and to the bank. Finally, he recommended promoting one of two loyal employees, Mr. Tatum or Mrs. Anderson, from the bookkeeping department to head teller and hiring an assistant bookkeeper at a substantially lower salary. The net effect was to save $355 per month — a sum sufficient to pay more than half the annual dividend. He was certain the directors would approve. Any savings, no matter how small the amount, was always welcome. He thought the directors would also consider him a good manager. The hidden effect, more importantly, was that Lawrence would have full control of the bank with *his employees* — ones who could be counted on to keep their mouths shut — in positions where they would raise few questions.

After Lawrence finished dictating, he sent Miss Perry back to the outer office to type the memorandum for his signature. Lawrence rose from the desk and stood facing the window waiting for his first appointment of the day. His stance was like that of a soldier at parade rest, except that one hand was in his pants' pocket absently fingering the change it found there and the other moved in a downward arc as he removed the Lucky Strike from his full, almost feminine lips. Today, Lawrence was feeling like the king of all he surveyed. And from his office on the fourteenth floor of the Coal Exchange building, what he surveyed was formidable. The arched windows looked down upon at least a dozen pieces of property he had bought, or bought and resold, in Huntington over the past seven years. While Lawrence was pleased with all he had accomplished, he realized his "kingdom" was poised on a shaky foundation. Just one misstep, he knew, and it could all come crashing down around his head.

He sighed and turned toward the room at the sound of footsteps, his dark hair and pince-nez glasses almost obscured by the veil of smoke. As Edward Keeley approached the desk, Lawrence extended the coin-jingling hand. "So good to see you, Edward," he said with an almost imperceptible upward tilt of his mouth. But his eyes didn't smile or seem to agree with his words. It was his turn to be aloof.

Keeley returned the handshake and laughed at his partner. "Well, Lawrence, you look the part of a bank president. How does it feel to be in charge?"

"It feels pretty damn good, Edward. You ought to know; you've been in this seat. It's amazing how impressed people are with this title. I've had men come to see me — as if they were suddenly my best friend — that didn't know my name a few months ago."

"Yes, and they all want something, don't they?" Edward said sardonically. Without an invitation, Keeley seated himself in the leather chair in front of Lawrence's desk.

"And you, Edward, do you want something? What brings you here today? I haven't seen much of you since you tried to resign. In fact, isn't this the first time you've been in the new offices?" Lawrence was being almost rude toward Keeley for no particular reason, but he couldn't help treating him as he himself had been treated in the past. Once his sarcasm surfaced, he found it hard to suppress.

"Yes, it is. And I must admit, the bank made a good move. I'm quite impressed with what you've done here. How's business?" Keeley was ignoring Lawrence's jabs.

Lawrence softened slightly after hearing Keeley admit he was wrong. "Frankly, it hasn't improved as much as I had hoped; but we haven't advertised our new home, yet. That should change things. Additionally, I just finished dictating a proposal for the board. It outlines a plan of reorganization which will result in substantial monthly savings. You'll hear it at the meeting. You'll be there, won't you?"

"As of now, I plan to be. Lawrence, I really didn't come here to discuss the bank's business. I need you to handle something for me. In the past, I've covered your ass, right?" Keeley scooted up to the edge of his chair and leaned toward the desk as he spoke.

"Right," Lawrence answered shortly. *He never misses a chance to remind me, does he?*

"Well, I've got a bit of a problem and I need you to cover mine. Seems a few weeks ago I sold a huge order of coal to a fellow in New York and now the Yankee bastard claims it is inferior grade. He wants us to take it back — send a damn train to get it — and I've refused. We argued back and forth. He had already paid for it and I deposited the check. Now he has stopped payment on that check, which leaves me holding the bag. I've paid the payroll and some other bills with that money. When the checks I wrote come in, they'll be refused for non-sufficient funds. I'm in a jam here. Can you cover the checks?" Keeley leaned back in the chair and took a cigar out of its case. He unwrapped it and stuck it in his mouth, but refrained from lighting it. Instead, he chewed on the cigar as he waited for Lawrence's reply.

Lawrence stared at Edward in disbelief. *He's asking me to do almost the same thing he bitched at me for doing a few years ago.* Lawrence couldn't resist making Edward suffer.

"Mercy, Edward. Wouldn't that be illegal? Why don't you just write a check on one of your other accounts to cover the shortfall?"

"Don't give me that sanctimonious bullshit," Edward said through clenched teeth. "If I still had control of this damn bank, I wouldn't even be here. I'd have handled it myself. As it happens, I don't have control right now."

"That's never stopped you before," Lawrence laughed out loud.

"You holier-than-thou S.O.B. Who do you think you are talking to? If it weren't for me, you'd still be tutoring little boys. Besides, I know enough on you to put you behind bars for years. Don't give me any crap — just do it."

"All right, Edward. Calm down, I'm only teasing you." Lawrence said appeasingly. He knew Keeley was right. And he sensed he had overstepped the bounds between them.

"Look," Edward said insistently. "I need more time than the float between banks will provide. Don't we have some dormant accounts we could tap for a while? I can put it back before it's ever noticed."

For a moment Lawrence considered the situation. Keeley's remark had brought him up short. However, he quickly realized it would be a good idea to have Edward Keeley beholden to him, for a change.

"All right, Edward. How much do you think you need? I'll see if we can find it."

Keeley paused briefly. "I think about $10,000...yes, $10,000 would cover me."

"Good heavens, that's a lot, Edward." Lawrence was genuinely surprised at the amount. "That could be a problem." He paused for a long moment before adding, "Just relax. I'll take care of it."

"Good. I should only need it until I sue this bastard and get my money back. Three to six months, at most."

"Very well," Lawrence said as Edward rose to leave. Now Lawrence was willing to be solicitous. "Come see me any time. You still have a position here, you know. Are we still having lunch on Friday?"

"Certainly. I'll see you then." Edward left and Lawrence remained sitting at his desk. After Edward closed the door, Lawrence realized that Keeley had never actually said thank you.

Thirty

October 1926

Friday, October 1

The Honorable Elliott Northcott, United States Prosecuting Attorney, left his office early on most Friday afternoons; but today he made an exception. His 3:30 P.M. appointment was too important to reschedule and even though W. J. Kerr was late, Mr. Northcott waited patiently.

At 3:45, Kerr, a slight, dapper gentleman with a neatly trimmed pencil-line moustache, entered the august Federal Courthouse on Fifth Avenue in Huntington. He located Mr. Northcott's name on the building directory and dashed up the stairs. His heels echoed on the terrazzo as he hurried down the second floor hall toward the prosecuting attorney's office, glancing at his watch as he went. Reaching the correct suite of offices, he knocked twice on the door, then opened it without waiting for a response. When the secretary looked up, he began to apologize. He was nearly breathless from running.

"I'm so sorry. I am W. J. Kerr, the Assistant West Virginia Banking Commissioner, and I have an appointment with Prosecuting Attorney Northcott. I'm running behind and hope he hasn't left for the day."

"Not at all, sir," she replied pleasantly. "He's expecting you. Go right in." She indicated the interior door with Elliott Northcott's name and title stenciled in gold on the glass.

Mr. Kerr composed himself, opened the door and stepped inside. From behind the stack of law books on the desk came the stentorian voice of Elliott Northcott. "That you, Kerr? Come in and make yourself comfortable."

Kerr crossed the room, apologizing as he went. "I'm so sorry to be late, sir. The train was delayed in Mason County because a herd of cows wouldn't move off the tracks. So frustrating. I hope you aren't too upset."

Northcott stood to greet his visitor and laughed. "Not at all. I appreciate the time you took to come down here. Now that I know the difficulty you've had, I appreciate it even more. Have a seat and let me tell you what I propose on this Burgher matter." Mr. Northcott wasted no time in getting to the point.

Kerr settled into the chair. He took a notebook from his leather case as Mr. Northcott picked up a letter and began to talk.

"As you know," said Northcott, "one of the National Bank examiners called my attention to this letter to your Mr. McCullough." He waved the letter at Kerr. "It's dated August 3rd and is in regard to the Burgher — Bank of Shapely — Railroad Bank & Trust matter. After I read this, I wrote Mr. McCullough to ask him to come see me."

"Yes, sir; I know. That's why *I'm* here. When he decided to attend the American Bankers Association convention in Los Angeles, he asked me to come down instead."

"Precisely. And I'm glad you did. Mr. Kerr, I've given this situation serious consideration." Northcott paused for dramatic effect. "We have a real case here. I believe we could take Burgher on under paragraph 5209 of the U.S. Revised Statutes. And, as a matter of fact, I am eager to do so. His actions are flagrantly illegal."

Kerr nodded. "So it would appear. However, to charge him with embezzlement would have such a negative effect on the bank — not to mention the people of Huntington — that we are reluctant to do that. In fact, we believe it would close the bank. Burgher is fairly well respected and, although our main concern is to save the bank, we'd like to avoid his indictment as well."

Northcott exploded. "Well respected? How could that be? Surely folks know what kind of man he is. Frankly, I don't see why you've allowed a man of his character to act as president of one of your state banks."

Kerr bristled at the criticism. "Well, of course, you know it's not necessary for a bank to get our permission to elect any man as president, or any other officer — for that matter. But, in point of fact, his election *was* done without our knowledge. Edward Keeley was president until recently. He resigned suddenly and the board elected Burgher. When we learned of the change, we *did* call a special meeting of the board. We discussed the matter very frankly and told them we would compel him to resign if any more irregularities were found."

This seemed to pacify Northcott, although he continued to press his point. "I still feel we should pursue prosecution. We can't let Burgher get away with this. Look here at paragraph 5209." He shoved an open copy of the revised statutes at Kerr. The appropriate paragraph was marked with an X in red pencil. Northcott recited it almost verbatim, as if Kerr couldn't read it for himself. "It states that any officer who embezzles or willfully misapplies any of the funds of a member bank or who makes a false statement or entry with intent to defraud is guilty as hell of embezzlement. He's done all of that, from what I can tell. We ought to take him on." Northcott sat back in his large leather chair as if he had made a convincing legal argument.

"Yes, sir. I agree. He's done all of that, and more. Did Mr. McCullough tell you about the $70,000 Burgher apparently took out of thin air back in 1924? Or the forged notes we found recently?"

"Of course!" Northcott fairly shouted. "I know about *all* of that. All the more reason to indict the man."

"But here's the crux of our dilemma — the name Burgher forged was that of his brother-in-law. We are certain Burgher could get him to state he had given his permission. If so, we could never prove perjury on the brother-in-law's part, nor coercion on Burgher's. It would be messy and almost impossible to win. We've come to you for help in straightening out Mr. Burgher — without legal action."

The Prosecutor looked perplexed and sounded disappointed. "What did you have in mind? I thought you wanted a legal opinion as to whether or not he could be indicted."

Kerr shook his head. "We wondered if you would call on Burgher and give him a good talking to...tell him his dealings with our department have not been satisfactory. Tell him that if he doesn't straighten up, you *will* indict him. A sort of warning shot, if you know what I mean. That ought to put the fear of God into the man."

Northcott laced his fingers together, propped his elbows on the desk and rested his chin on the finger-bridge. The room grew quiet as he sat thinking. Kerr returned the prosecutor's gaze with equanimity. Finally, Northcott broke the silence.

"I *can* see how devastating a bank closure would be for the city. Burgher's reputation be damned. I'd skin him in a minute; however, I'll do as you ask — for the sake of the bank and its depositors. But, so help me God, if he commits one more irregular act, I'll go after him like a blue-tick hound after a rabbit."

"Thank you Mr. Northcott. Mr. McCullough will be so pleased to hear it. Let us know how your meeting with Burgher turns out."

The two men shook hands and Mr. Kerr left the office. Prosecuting Attorney Northcott again laced his fingers — and stared at the closed door.

Friday, October 8

For the past two days Mr. Kerr and his secretary, Bernice Buffington, had been seen around Huntington making their usual unannounced visits to the city's banks. Today, the couple, who looked like Jack Spratt and his formidable wife, were making their third visit to the Railroad Bank & Trust.

On Kerr's first visit, President Burgher had characterized his bank's state of affairs in glowing terms. However, subsequent conversations at another bank had put that report in a suspicious light, so Kerr had decided to dig deeper. In his search, he had uncovered reports which seriously conflicted with the one given by Burgher. He wanted to confront Burgher with these facts; but he wanted to do it outside of the bank and before impartial witnesses. Therefore, he had asked the bank's auditors to call him if Mr. Burgher came to their offices.

At 8:30 on Friday morning, the call had come from Messers Bloom and Yancey, auditors. Lawrence Burgher was in their offices. Mr. Kerr and Mrs. Buffington had hurried there from the Farr Hotel. Now, Kerr, Buffington, Burgher and Joe Yancey were seated in the auditing firm's conference room. The only papers on the table were stacked neatly in front of Mr. Kerr, who was doing all the talking.

"Mr. Burgher, when I came to see you on Wednesday, you plainly stated the bank was doing extremely well and I was very pleased to hear it. When the Federal Reserve man arrived, you even began discussing the possibility of your bank joining the system. I thought nothing of his visit until I visited another of our banks — which shall remain nameless. There I was told the Federal Reserve man was actually in town trying to ascertain the soundess of some checks on your bank, so I tracked him down and put it to him directly."

As Kerr spoke in a clipped professional manner, Lawrence stared at him. No expression crossed the banker's face.

Kerr continued. "He reluctantly told me the true nature of his visit and that Mr. Stamper of the Fifth-Third National Bank of Cincinnati was in town on the same matter. Mr. Burgher, it appears your bank is not doing well at all. You have grossly misrepresented yourself to me."

Lawrence cleared his throat. "Mr. Kerr, I have nothing to hide from your department. As you heard me say yesterday at the Board meeting, our immediate troubles were caused by the sudden withdrawal of public funds. We are simply requesting a new loan from the Fifth-Third for $25,000. Mr. Stamper was in town on that matter. Once we receive it, we *will be* in fine shape."

"But, Mr. Burgher, normally this loan would have been handled by mail. What you failed to mention was Mr. Stamper came here to obtain additional collateral for that loan because your original collateral was insufficient. In point of fact, a $10,000 check you had sent the Fifth-Third for payment, was not certified, as you had told them. They discovered the company did not have sufficient funds to cover the check and were $10,000-$12,000 overdrawn, as well. Additionally, a Certificate of Deposit, which had not been funded, and a note of Edward Keeley's, which was in the air between the banks, were both listed as collateral. Therefore, the $25,000 note was rejected because your assets were inflated by about $40,000. Most of the items listed as the original collateral were like that — either not good, not acceptable or in transit between banks. That's why both men were here. You have a very bad habit of misstating your financial position, sir."

Lawrence Burgher cleared his throat, again. He removed his glasses from his nose and put them in his breast pocket. "I didn't go into these details with you, because I felt they were an internal matter. I believe I told you everything you needed to know when you asked after the condition of the bank."

Kerr reddened, but his professional tone held. "Mr. Burgher, the internal affairs of your bank *are* my concern. In my book, a half-truth is as bad as a lie. And you sir, are a liar."

At this accusation, Lawrence Burgher jumped out of his seat. "How dare you insult me like that! You impudent little..."

But Mr. Kerr cut him off by continuing in a louder voice. "These notes of my meetings with Mr. Pierce of the Federal Reserve and Mr. Stamper of the Fifth-Third prove what I just laid out." He indicated the papers before him. "In fact, Mr. Stamper told me he took about $75,000 of notes and over two hundred shares of the Coal Exchange Bank Company as additional collateral for that $25,000 loan. Mr. Burgher, contrary to your report on Wednesday, that puts your bank in a very grave situation."

Kerr paused slightly then remarked pointedly, "Mr. Stamper and I reported *all* of this to Director Wright of your board yesterday."

Now Burgher blanched and resumed his seat. He replaced his glasses. His eyes narrowed as he spoke. "Mr. Kerr, you didn't need to do that. Mr. Wright is perfectly aware of the bank's situation," he said defensively.

"I wasn't as interested in telling him of the bank's condition as I was in making sure he knew of your actions. I wanted Mr. Stamper to share what he had learned so Mr. Wright would not think I was making misstatements about you," Kerr replied.

"Mr. Kerr, I'll thank you to keep your opinions to yourself."

Lawrence's anger flashed anew.

"And I'll thank you, Mr. Burgher, to mind your 'Ps' and 'Qs.' Make no more deals that might hurt the good credit of the Railroad Bank & Trust — particularly when it comes to giving bad checks or kiting, as we all know has been done in the past." Kerr rose, gathered his papers and nodded to Mrs. Buffington. She got up and collected her handbag. Throughout the exchange, the auditor, Mr. Yancey, had remained silent. Now he remained seated as well.

Kerr looked down at Burgher and warned him sternly. "Be sure you send us an itemized statement at the close of business each day, starting tomorrow. We intend to keep our eyes on you." Kerr put on his hat and left the office with Mrs. Buffington to return to Charleston.

As they reached the lobby, Mr. Kerr turned to his secretary. "Mrs. Buffington, if the daily statement does not arrive in our mail on Monday morning, come to Huntington and get it."

Monday, October 11

Monday morning dawned crisp and cold. Mrs. Buffington had arrived at her office early, despite her busy weekend. She sighed as she looked over the morning mail and saw that she would be making another trip to Huntington. The statement from the Railroad Bank & Trust Company had not arrived as promised. She answered a few letters, then caught the 11:15 train, as directed. Both of her bosses, Mr. Kerr and Mr. McCullough, were out of town. Confronting Mr. Burgher would be up to her.

As she stepped off the train at the Huntington station, she gathered her brown wool coat around her and retied the belt. Leaning against the wind, she walked toward the First Huntington National Bank. There, she called on the president, Mr. Gohen — the unnamed source of information which Mr. Kerr had quoted on Friday. Mr. Gohen could always be counted on for news from the banking community.

"I appreciate your time, Mr. Gohen, so I won't keep you long. Have you heard of any new developments regarding Mr. Burgher or his bank?"

Mr. Gohen, a handsome man with a patrician nose, waved Mrs. Buffington toward a deep leather chair in his inner office. She, however, remained standing. "No, I haven't heard anything new today, although our board met yesterday and this matter was a topic of much discussion. The board members were of the firm opinion that they, of course, would want to help out in the event of a bank crisis. However, they were also in agreement that they would expect to have proper collateral on any loan they would make. And, they would not be willing to put *any* money in the bank without a definite understanding that it would be put under new management."

"I completely understand their position," said Mrs. Buffington. Her chins undulated as she nodded her head.

Mr. Gohen continued. "I'll keep my eyes and ears open. If anything comes to my attention, I'll inform your office immediately."

"Thank you Mr. Gohen. Mr. Kerr will be glad to hear that."

She turned to leave and Mr. Gohen took her elbow to escort her out. "Speaking of Kerr — he seemed extremely disturbed by all of this last Friday."

"Well, Mr. Kerr is a very conscientious man. I'm sure he feels responsible, because of Commissioner McCullough's absence. When you alerted him to the true situation, he knew there would be more to uncover. He doesn't want to leave any stone unturned, so to speak."

"I'm glad the commissioner will be back soon. I expect Mr. Kerr too is glad. Not that Kerr isn't capable, but I hope McCullough demands certain changes be made at Railroad Bank & Trust. The way they elected Burgher is deplorable. I don't know why McCullough stood for it."

Mrs. Buffington puffed up like a setting hen defending her eggs. She firmly pulled her elbow from his grasp and looked the First Huntington National Bank president straight in the eye. "I'm quite sure neither our department nor any one connected to it can be held responsible for that, Mr. Gohen."

"I didn't mean to infer that you were. I just hope Mr. McCullough insists on some changes over there. Have a pleasant day, Mrs. Buffington," he said soothingly. As they reached the outer door, Mr. Gohen opened it for her. Mrs. Buffington said a cursory goodbye and pulled her coat collar tightly around her neck as she stepped once again out into the wind.

Next, she walked to the offices of Bloom and Yancey, auditors, to find out if they had any new information she should have before visiting Mr. Burgher. Mr. Yancey reported he had found the bank in better shape when he had visited earlier in the day, but was surprised to discover the statement had not been sent as promised. He offered to call Burgher to ask why, but Mrs. Buffington asked him to refrain, as she preferred to go there unannounced. Mr. Yancey offered to accompany her and she accepted.

They arrived just before 3 P.M. and were shown directly into President Burgher's private office. Mrs. Buffington had not been here before and was stunned by the opulent decor. President Burgher greeted her warily.

"Mrs. Buffington, what brings you to Huntington again so soon? I thought we had settled everything on Friday."

"I'm here to get your daily statement, Mr. Burgher. You do recall Mr. Kerr instructing you to send it on Saturday? Well, he told me if it didn't arrive on Monday, I should come get it. It didn't arrive, Mr. Burgher."

"My dear lady, you've made an unnecessary trip. It was mailed on Sunday and should have arrived today. If you had telephoned, you could have saved yourself the trouble of the trip."

"Those weren't my instructions, Mr. Burgher. If Mr. Kerr had been in the office, he might have done so; but I was told to come to Huntington. I am just obeying my orders. However, I *can* call my office to see if it arrived in the afternoon mail. If so, you won't need to prepare an additional statement."

"By all means. Here, use my telephone." He turned the instrument toward her and rose to gaze out the window while she made the call.

In a few moments she hung up the receiver. "Very well, Mr. Burgher. The statement did arrive in the afternoon mail."

Burgher turned toward her and smiled smugly. He arched his eyebrows and raised both open palms toward her in a silent gesture as if to say, *See, you fretted needlessly*.

"You see. I'm sure the delay was because it was posted on Sunday. It didn't go out on Saturday because we all left for the Marshall College football game," Burgher tried to explain.

"Mr. Burgher, I'm sure Mr. Kerr would consider the preparation of this statement far more important than a football game. So should you. If you don't give that duty your utmost attention and see that I receive a statement each day, I'll be visiting you often."

"Mrs. Buffington, I assure you the statement will arrive as promised — at least by the afternoon mail."

"Very well. Good-day to you, sir." Mrs. Buffington turned and marched out of the private sanctuary with Mr. Yancey on her heels. She did not wait for Lawrence Burgher's reply.

West Virginia Banking Commission
Charleston, W.Va.

Huntington, West Va.

October 29th, 1926

Honorable Howard M. Gore
Governor of West Virginia,
Clarksburg, West Va.

My dear Governor:

Have been in Huntington since Wednesday noon
endeavoring to help one of our State Banks out
of a very difficult and embarrassing situation.
The condition tonight is critical but tomorrow
being Saturday, and all banks here closing at
noon, we hope to be able to carry them through
to the first of the week.

Their reserve is entirely exhausted and the
executive head of the institution does not seem
to command the necessary confidence such an
emergency required.

Am advised that an appeal is being made to the
State Treasurer for an additional deposit of
Fifteen Thousand Dollars and if this is granted
it will help materially.

I assure you that my best efforts will be made
to save the institution as I fully realize that
a failure in Huntington would be disastrous.

Sorry to burden you with an additional worry at

this time but am required to keep you advised in such cases.

Yours very respectfully,

Sidney R. McCullough,
Commissioner of Banking

West Virginia Banking Commission
Charleston, W.Va.

November 5, 1926
The Board of Directors,
Railroad Bank & Trust Co.,
Huntington, West Virginia.

Gentlemen:

We devoted five days,from October 27th to November 1st, to an effort to help relieve a very
embarrassing situation, caused by a depletion of
your reserve and the inability of your executive
officers to secure the necessary funds to restore it to the legally required amount.

As you well know, through the cooperation of
several of the members of your board, an arrangement was entered into Saturday, October
30th, and consummated Monday, November 1st,
whereby your bank borrowed $150,000.00 from the
Jackson Building and Loan Association secured by
some $309,200.00 of your bills receivable.

Your particular attention is called to the fact
that your institution is not in a position to
secure any further loans, as you already have
pledged the bulk of your assets to secure the
$309,200.00 borrowed as follows:

        Coal Exchange Building Stock $254,000.00
        Bills Receivable $646,071.50

leaving in your own files notes unpledged

amounting to $211,922.07 and stocks and bonds that would be of little value to you as collateral.

I gravely fear that the relief of the past few days will prove only temporary. You must positively refrain from the making of new loans and bend every effort toward having your present loans regularly curtailed so that you will be in position to pay the six (6) Twenty-five Thousand ($25,000.00) Dollar notes given the Jackson Building and Loan Association, as they severally mature.

You also have a large number of notes that are not at all justified by the balances on your individual ledgers. Your President claims that several large loans made since June 30th are more than offset by deposits of the borrowers. However, you should always guard against this practice of extending individual credit against corporation balances. This will, in most cases, lead to trouble sooner or later as you occasionally will awake to the fact that the balance has been withdrawn, but the note is still in your files.

Additionally, your President carried on your books for at least a month, as a balance due from the Colonial Trust Company of Pittsburgh, an item of $25,000.00, when he knew that you had no such credit. On several occasions, when he was questioned about this matter, he assured us that the credit was standing on the depositors account to take care of a charge-back, when in reality at the time the bank was required to charge the item back, an overdraft of more than $5,000.00 was created.

We are fully convinced that a false statement of the condition of your bank was, therefore, presented to the board at a meeting held on October 8th when the false balance was included as an asset of your bank. Furthermore, the Commissioner is not satisfied with some of the transactions that passed through your books during the week of October 25th and your records do not to his satisfaction verify the explanations given.

You will of course say that the thing to do is to get new deposits. This is not only unwise, but practically impossible, with your bank in its present frozen condition. You certainly are not in a position to take care of any new business.

Our recommendation is that you arrange for the services of a competent banker to manage your institution, one who can live on the salary you will pay and who will devote all of his time to his work. The upbuilding of this bank is a real task, worthy of any man's mettle and requires undivided personal attention. We have no feeling whatever in these matters, but have a duty to the depositors of the bank. It is immaterial to us who your officers are, as long as they are men who are capable and who will put the safety of your depositors' money ahead of anything else.

We again admonish you that the State Banking Department is not satisfied with the condition of your institution and in fairness to all, we must say, that, if we find it necessary to return and a situation similar to the one we have just gone through exists, there will be nothing for us to do but proceed to liquidate the bank.

While it is the duty of this department at all times to protect depositors, it is not our purpose or intention to find fault with or censure the banks unnecessarily, but always our desire to aid and assist them as best we can in the successful operation of their institutions. We hope we have your hearty cooperation. You will please have each director present sign the enclosed acknowledgement form and return the same to this office promptly.

Yours very truly,

Sidney R. McCullough,
Commissioner of Banking

Thirty-One

December 27, 1926

"I'm glad it's over," sighed Anna. She poured a fresh cup of tea for Jenny as she talked. "Usually we leave the decorations up over the new year, but this year, I'm ready to see them go."

The two sisters were alone in the warm kitchen. Millie and Sam could be heard moving about the house removing all the trappings of Christmas. Periodically the scent of pine wafted into the kitchen as Sam carried the still fresh boughs and tree outside for burning.

"What's wrong, Anna," asked Jenny gently. "You have seemed so preoccupied over the holidays — since Thanksgiving, really. We haven't had a chance to talk what with all the rushing around, but I've been worried about you."

Anna glanced into the dining room to be certain Millie was out of ear-shot before answering. "It's Lawrence. I don't want him to know I confided in you; but there's something wrong with him. He's very moody and out-of-sorts with the children; and he won't talk to me. I don't know if it's something serious at work or if he doesn't feel well. I've noticed that he's lost his appetite, too. Even his pants are getting baggy in the seat."

Jenny set the delicate Haviland cup in its saucer. "I noticed at Christmas dinner he hardly touched his plate. He wasn't his usual self, that's for sure. He hasn't told you anything? Have you asked him?"

"Well, I've tried." She looked away from Jenny for a moment, then squared her shoulders as if she had made a hard decision and looked back. "Let's take our tea into the sunroom. We can watch the children playing in the snow while we talk."

The sisters walked into the sunroom and resettled themselves close together on the deep sofa facing the back yard. Through the large windows, they had a clear view of the snowy yard crisscrossed with sled tracks and footprints of various sizes. Heavily-coated children ran back and forth, looking like snowmen come to life. Their clothes were covered with snow and they were indistinguishable from one another except by size or the color of their mittens and hats.

"Look at Libba making snow angels. She'll be soaked when she comes in." laughed Jenny. But Anna did not respond or laugh. Instead she began to talk, quietly.

"Remember during Thanksgiving dinner, when Lawrence made a snide remark to Nate about your new house?" Jenny nodded as Anna continued. "I asked him that night what was bothering him, but he brushed it off as nothing. I soon forgot the incident, but shortly thereafter he seemed to drift into — oh, I don't know — it was like his body was there, but not his mind. He'd answer direct questions but I could tell he wasn't really paying close attention. He ignored the kids, too. And Sam came to me one day to ask what was wrong. When he won't talk to Sam, I *know* something is wrong. He acted like Christmas wasn't happening — never discussed the presents for the children at all. He just said, 'Do whatever you want.' Before, he always wanted to know what I was planning and then he'd come up with his own surprise. But not this year. He didn't do anything — not even for me. Not that I mind. I don't think the little ones noticed that he didn't buy me a gift, but I'm sure Eileen and Sara did."

Jenny laid her hand on Anna's knee. "Maybe it's just the pressure of being the bank president. He's got a lot to deal with now. Nate says he wouldn't have that job on a silver platter."

Anna smiled wanly. "Don't you think he's had time to adjust to that? He's been president since May and has seemed to relish the challenge. No, this is something more than just the pressure of the job. The other night, when I got up to use the toilet, Lawrence wasn't in our bed. I thought he might be downstairs because he hasn't been sleeping well, so I went on to the bathroom. The door was closed. I tried the knob, but it was locked. Then I heard a terrible sob from inside. Jenny, it was Lawrence. He was crying."

Tears glistened in Anna's eyes as she covered Jenny's hand with her own. "I went back to bed and never told him what I heard. He would be so embarrassed if he knew. He's such a proud man, you know."

"Oh, Anna. You've got to talk to him. You two have always shared everything. Whatever it is — you'll handle it. He should know that."

"I know it. That's what worries me the most. What could be so bad that he won't tell me?"

Jenny had no answer. The two sat in silence watching the children. The snow had begun falling again, covering the old tracks.

Thirty-Two

March–April, 1927

Winter's long nights and gloomy days had taken a severe toll on Lawrence Burgher. He dreaded both. Nearly every night he tossed and turned, plagued by terrible nightmares. By dawn he wanted nothing more than to cover his head with the quilt and drift into the lethargic sleep that depression brings. Nevertheless, he rose this bleak March day and went to the office — dreading to read the daily statement prepared for the banking commissioner, but afraid to let it leave the bank without his perusal.

The huge loan to the bank from the Jackson Building and Loan Association weighed heavily on his mind, for he knew this was their last chance to remain solvent and independent. If his bank became insolvent, it was subject to either being closed or taken over by another bank. And he knew any change in the bank's structure would precipitate an in-depth audit — revealing the perils inherent in his personal decisions. He still had large overdrafts and an insurmountable debt. Then there was the frightening matter of the forged note.

The bank had been able to make each of the $25,000 note payments to the Jackson Building and Loan in December, January and February by diligently collecting on their good loans, curtailing others and making no new ones. As Lawrence had characterized the situation in a quick handwritten note to Mr. McCullough, they were "running pretty close, but getting along." However, by March 7, the statement showed the bank's reserve had dropped $4,000 below the statutory limit.

Lawrence had promptly received a note from McCullough instructing him to take immediate steps to correct the situation. But Lawrence was at a loss as to how to do that. The bank had collected all delinquent notes possible. All other notes were current and not due for thirty or sixty days. Only Lawrence's past-due notes and some of Keeley's old debts were not being actively pursued, on Lawrence's orders. He could not repay any of them. This, too, was a fact he wanted to keep hidden. If his business friends knew his bank was pressing them, but letting his own notes slide, they would be incensed.

Three days later, Lawrence stood at his office window watching the sky turn black. It was late afternoon, but the approaching storm made the day as dark as if it were dusk. A single lamp on Lawrence's desk threw a diffused yellow reflection on the glass. As the large raindrops began to hit the window, Lawrence stared at them as if he'd never seen rain before. He watched intently, concentrating on each drop as it approached the window, hit the glass and exploded into dozens of tiny droplets. This phenomenon totally absorbed his mind.

He knew he had a telephone call to make before the day ended, and yet he procrastinated. The bank had not made its $25,000 payment to the Jackson Building and Loan Association on March 1, nor could they now. He knew that making the call *could* precipitate a chain of events that would end his career. He felt out of control. It was like watching a tragic movie for the second time — he knew the ending, but he was powerless to change it.

Finally, he dragged himself back to his desk, picked up the receiver and dialed the banking commission's number. After exchanging rather formal pleasantries with Mr. McCullough, Lawrence delivered the bad news.

"Mr. McCullough, I'm loathe to have to tell you this but we have been unable to meet our March 1 obligation to the Jackson Building and Loan Association. I've delayed in reporting this because I think we will be able to meet part, if not all of it, within a few days." Lawrence spoke as positively as he could.

"Mr. Burgher, as you know, when this loan was arranged, it was with the definite understanding that *all* of these notes would be paid promptly at maturity. The Building and Loan is not supposed to make loans of this nature. In your case we made an exception. You know that," McCullough lectured.

Lawrence reddened but maintained his composure. "Yes, sir; I do. I regret very much that we have not paid it, but our deposits are building up again and we are still collecting some on our notes. We should be able to pay on it, as I said, in a few days."

McCullough replied. "I insist on it. You must arrange to take care of this note without delay! And I expect you to pay those notes maturing on April 1 and May 1 when they come due, as well. Remember what I said last winter...if the situation doesn't improve, we will have no choice but to liquidate the bank."

"I appreciate your interest in this matter, sir. You *know* we are doing the very best we possibly can. I will notify you as soon as we are able to make the payment. Good day, sir," Lawrence answered formally. He preempted any further lecture from the banking commissioner by quickly replacing the receiver on its hook.

After he hung up the telephone, the president of the Railroad Bank & Trust turned his chair toward the window and resumed staring at the rain drops. The face mirrored in the yellow glass was a gaunt shadow of its former self. Glassy eyes stared out of darkly circled sockets. Pince-nez glasses gripped a narrow ridge of bone. A stiff collar stood away from a too-thin neck. But Lawrence did not notice his altered reflection. All he could see was the rain. As he stared, Mr. McCullough's words "...nothing for us to do but to liquidate the bank," scratched through his mind like a broken record.

Abruptly, Lawrence rose, retrieved his coat, hat and umbrella from the brass stand and left the bank. Out on the street, huddled under his large black umbrella, he headed west on Fourth Avenue toward the Elks Club. Halfway down the block, he turned and looked back at the Coal Exchange Building. On the fourteenth floor, the tiny spot of light still shone through the window. He stood transfixed for a moment, oblivious to the rain that swirled around him. *What have I done? I'm probably going to lose it all. Oh, God, how did things get so bad?* He turned on his heel and fairly ran towards the warmth and comfort of the Elks Club bar.

April 12

Along the banks of the Kanawha River in Charleston, West Virginia, shafts of sunlight broke through the morning clouds and bounced off the gold dome of the State Capitol building. Deep inside its thick walls, in the banking commissioner's outer office, sat W. J. Kerr and Bernice Buffington. Commissioner McCullough had just returned from a weeklong trip. During his absence, the assistant commissioner and his secretary had carefully followed the rapid deterioration of the Railroad Bank & Trust's financial condition. They were eager to report all the details to their boss. Mr. Kerr was reviewing his notes when Mr. McCullough opened his door and greeted them.

"Good morning, you two. How are you? Come in, come in," the commissioner said heartily.

"Good morning," the two nearly chorused. Mr. Kerr waved his secretary in first. "Glad to have you back, sir," he said as he passed Mr. McCullough in the open doorway.

"It's good to be back. Thank you. Looks like spring is finally here. I don't know about you, but this winter has seemed tougher than usual."

"Perhaps. Perhaps," Kerr agreed without additional comment. He was eager to get on with his report. "Mr. McCullough, Mrs. Buffington and I have several matters to report to you, but the most pressing is the situation at the Railroad Bank & Trust. While you were gone, I'm afraid things went from bad to worse."

"Oh, really? Just before I left, Mr. Burgher was up here saying there were merger negotiations pending between his bank and another in Huntington. I thought he was fairly confident he could deliver enough stock to close the deal. What happened?"

Mrs. Buffington interjected, "The deal fell through because the Coal Exchange building was already pledged to cover the Jackson Building and Loan Association note. Apparently Burgher hadn't revealed that in the beginning."

"I see; the other bank must have coveted that real estate more than the bank itself," McCullough mused.

"That's the way I saw it," said Kerr. "Then on Friday, we received letters addressing two other serious problems." As he placed one letter on McCullough's desk, he began to summarize its contents.

"This one is from the Federal Reserve. Burgher is disobeying their policy to clear *all* checks directly through Richmond. Instead he's sending them to the branch in Cincinnati which, as you know, delays the clearing process. We believe he's doing it to slow the transfer of funds from his bank. They warned him to stop, but he hasn't," Kerr reported. He looked over at Mrs. Buffington for confirmation, and she gave it.

"And, they directed a similar warning to his cashier, but he's ignored that as well. Obviously, Burgher ordered him to do so," she added.

Kerr placed a second sheet on top of the first. "Secondly, this letter from the Jackson Building and Loan reports that the bank has paid neither the March nor the April notes. The Jackson people are very upset, as you can imagine. The president, Mr. Wetzel, points out that another is due in 20 days or less — on May 1. He says when he repeatedly called Mr. Burgher's attention to this, Burgher kept saying he'd get to it in a few days. Burgher claims he has heavy checks coming in for payment, so he can't meet the notes."

McCullough picked up the top letter and frowned deeply as Mrs. Buffington spoke. "Did you tell Mr. Burgher, when they were up here to discuss the merger, that it would be satisfactory to let the notes go for awhile?" she asked.

McCullough exploded. "Hell no I didn't! Did he say that? Excuse my language, Bernice, but of course I would do no such thing. I've been absolutely adamant with him about strict adherence to the payment schedule. I chastised him just last month when they were late with the March payment. He told me they would pay it in a few days. He's lied again!"

Mrs. Buffington looked over at Mr. Kerr and smiled smugly. McCullough continued to rant.

"That does it! We've tried hard to save this bank, but Burgher seems either unwilling or unable to work with us. I'm tired of his shenanigans! We've simply *got* to make a change. Just think what would happen if all our bank presidents were this irresponsible. Maybe Northcott was right; we should go after him. At any rate, before the end of the week, we are going to go down there and see exactly what's going on. Kerr, I want you to draft a memo outlining all you've told me. Then plan to go to Huntington on Thursday morning. Thank you both for your good work. I appreciate all you've done while I was gone. What else do you have for me?"

Kerr and Mrs. Buffington exchanged smiles as they rearranged their papers to report on other bank matters decidedly less exciting.

April 14, 1927

The evening sky had softened into a soft rose glow by the time Lawrence arrived home in the Pierce-Arrow. On the seat beside him rested a pasteboard box, which he left in the car as he wearily climbed out of the rear seat.

When he entered the house and walked straight to his study, no one raised an eyebrow or spoke to him. This had been his habit since late fall. He closed his door and did not reappear until called for dinner.

Throughout the meal, as usual, he picked at his food. He punctuated periods of morose silence with barked reprimands at the children. Anna tried to maintain a pleasant table atmosphere but it was difficult to ignore her husband's sullen demeanor. She was glad when the meal ended and the children had been excused. She had put up with this since before Thanksgiving and was about at her wit's end. In the past the couple had spent some time after the evening meal talking at the table without the children, but lately Lawrence had excused himself along with them and disappeared back into his study. Tonight was no exception.

Anna sat alone for a while as Millie cleared the table, then she rose and went towards the study, determined to talk to her husband about what was bothering him. The door was closed. Before knocking, Anna put her ear close to the door to be sure she wasn't interrupting a telephone call. She could hear nothing. She knocked and turned the door knob at the same time.

Lawrence, seated in his leather wing-back chair, looked up — as startled as a doe in a headlight. He had a drink in his hand and tears were streaming down his cheeks. Anna's heart lurched. She quickly shut the door and went to him.

"Lawrence, darling, what is it?" she asked as she knelt in front of him.

He shook his head and wiped his face with his bare hand.

Anna fumbled in her pocket for a handkerchief and handed it to him, then laid her hand on his knee. "Darling, you've got to tell me what's wrong. I know it's something bad. You've been a wreck for months. Please tell me," she implored.

Still, he shook his head and stared over her shoulder as the tears continued to flow. Anna did not press her husband again; instead she sat quietly stroking his knee as she would to soothe a crying child. Finally, he wiped his eyes and touched her cheek.

"Anna, I love you. Thank you for letting me cry it out. I can talk now. You're right; I have been a wreck for months, and I'm sorry I couldn't talk to you about it. I just didn't want you to worry — I thought I could fix it. But I couldn't and now it's over." He paused for a moment and Anna thought he might cry again. It broke her heart to see him cry. It had happened only once before, when she lost their second baby in childbirth.

"What darling? What's over?" she asked gently.

"Everything. My career. The bank. Everything."

"I don't understand, Lawrence. What are you saying?" she asked again, but with a growing sense of dread.

"Anna, they closed the bank this afternoon. It won't reopen tomorrow. The banking commissioner came down with three other people. They seized the books, after spending the entire day going over them, locked the doors and sent everyone home."

"Why, Lawrence?" she asked incredulously. "Why?"

"We don't have enough funds in our reserve account." He sighed heavily and explained to Anna the commissioner's efforts over the past few months to reorganize the bank to make it solvent.

"That's why I haven't been sleeping. I've been so consumed with trying to find a way to solve it. But nothing has worked. Finally, it's over."

"What do you mean — over? You keep saying that," she asked, afraid to hear his answer.

"I mean I don't have a job. Anna, they took my keys and escorted me out of the bank. They let me gather my personal belongings from my office — watched while I did it — and then took my keys. They even rode down the elevator with me. As we got off, I saw one of them put the notice on the bank doors. I stopped to read it. It said, '**This bank temporarily closed by order of the state banking department pending efforts to secure funds with which to restore its depleted reserve.**' It was horrible. I was afraid I'd see someone I knew."

"Well, see," said Anna. "It's only temporary. Won't things be back to normal when they have the funds?" She still didn't fully comprehend the finality of what had happened at the bank.

"I'm afraid not, love. Even if they *can* reorganize, which I doubt, they won't let *me* run the bank. They say they've lost confidence in my abilities. Someone else will be the president of the Railroad Bank & Trust." He smiled pitifully. "I'm so sorry, Anna. All I ever wanted was for you and the children to have a good life. I wish I could have told you sooner. I know you've been worried sick. I could see it in your eyes. I just thought somehow, some way, it would work out and I wouldn't have to burden you with my troubles."

She sat in stunned silence for a moment; then she responded. "It's all right, Lawrence. I understand, now. I'm so glad you finally told me. I thought you were ill. We'll get through this somehow. It's not the end of the world. We'll all be fine."

"Things won't be the same for a while. With the bank closed and me out of a job — we won't have as much money. Maybe a lot less; I don't know yet." Lawrence reached down and stroked his wife's hair. She laid her head on his knee and they sat together in silence.

A few moments later, Lawrence said, "Would you mind if I went on up to bed? I'm exhausted."

"Of course not, sweetheart. I'll be up shortly. You go on to bed," Anna agreed.

Lawrence rose and gently pulled Anna to her feet. He kissed her gently, murmured, "I love you," and went to bed.

With tears in her eyes, Anna watched him mount the stairs. After he disappeared, she went to the dark kitchen and fixed herself a cup of tea. Upstairs she could hear the children getting ready for bed. Miss Pennyroyal called to Libba to brush her teeth. Anna sat in the kitchen over her tea cup until the house was still. Carrying her cup and saucer, she wandered throughout the house as she mulled over what Lawrence had told her. Finally, after midnight she climbed the stairs herself. She expected to see Lawrence tossing and turning in their bed. But when she reached the landing, she heard his deep breathing. For the first time in weeks, he was sleeping like a baby. She sighed, wondering if she could do the same.

Thirty-Three

1992

Each time Maggie came back to Huntington, she couldn't help but notice how little it had changed. This both comforted and disturbed her. The energy in Atlanta was palpable; it energized her. There she had grown used to living with the rapid pace of change. Apartment complexes seemed to sprout overnight like mushrooms and roads were often rerouted between the morning and evening rush hours. So it was reassuring to see that her home town was still as she remembered it. Cars bumped over residential brick streets as always; the 1920s brick homes stood no less stolidly on the avenues of Huntington's southside like matching Monopoly houses, and the gold-domed courthouse still dominated a full city block downtown.

Yet, she also suspected that attitudes here had not changed, either. That was the disturbing part. It was the reason she had left. It was *still* a small town with a provincial approach to progress. *If it was good enough for my daddy, it's good enough for me* —she'd heard that line all her life. What Huntington needed, some wag once told her, was a rash of high-class funerals. But Maggie believed that even that wouldn't change things; the attitudes of her grandfather's generation had been passed down to her generation, along with the property and businesses held by the same families for ages.

In the year since Maggie had discovered the banking records at the West Virginia Archives, she had read her copies over and over. It boggled her mind to think that her grandfather was a criminal — she just couldn't accept it. She knew that before she could, she had to know *his* side of the story. In those voluminous records, she had found no legal documents, nothing to indicate exactly what had sent him to the penitentiary. Yes, she'd seen the banking commissioner's accusations of gross irregularities; but no record of a trial. The day she was last there, she had asked Miss Whitman, of the archives staff, why those documents were missing. She was told they would be at the local courthouse. Now, on another humid August day, she was back in West Virginia to look for those legal records.

It was just after 9 A.M. when Maggie arrived at the Cabell County Courthouse; but its familiar clock, which looked in four directions from the center tower, said five o'clock. *That's fitting — even the official time has stopped.* As she climbed the marble steps, whose centers had been beveled into smooth craters over time, she recalled coming here with her father. He had worked in the County Clerk's office when Maggie was a child. Back then, the building held a reverent fascination for the nine-year-old. That same feeling came over her again as she opened the heavy wooden doors and stepped into the cool marble halls. She felt she should make all her requests in a church whisper.

Unsure where to begin, Maggie headed toward familiar territory, foolishly thinking someone in the clerk's office would remember her father and might remember her. Although the offices looked virtually unchanged, the people were strangers; she didn't see a soul who looked even vaguely familiar. Maggie waited patiently for a big-busted female clerk to finish helping a very young couple with their marriage license application, then asked where to find records of a trial held in the 1920s. She was told only real estate, birth, death and marriage records were here. Trial records were in the Circuit Clerk's office. In a flash, it occurred to Maggie that some clue to how he lost his real estate holdings might be here, in this office. She then asked the matronly looking woman where the real estate records were and how to research them. The woman, whose overly-teased coiffure complimented her bust, pointed to an open room just beyond her counter as she gave Maggie some hurried instructions, then turned to another teen-age couple who were holding hands.

Armed with a legal pad and an expectant air, Maggie walked toward the records room. *I know he did own a lot of property, maybe I can
find out exactly how he lost it.* The large room was clearly designed
specifically for research. Row after row of chest high cabinets separated by wide aisles lined the room. The narrow shelves of each cabinet were fitted with large metal rollers to facilitate the movement of
the heavy ledgers. They reminded Maggie of the rollers that carried a
casket into a mausoleum vault. Each cabinet also had a slanted top,
like that of a church pulpit, on which to rest the ledgers while taking
notes.

Following the big-haired woman's instructions, Maggie went to a
set of similar roller-shelves built into one wall. Here were the indices
of parties to a real estate transaction, arranged roughly by decade
from 1808-1925. She pulled out the heavy canvas-bound book marked
Grantees: 1910-1920 A–M, in India ink on the spine and carried it to
one of the slant-top cabinets. She carefully turned through the yellowed ledger pages; each entry was beautifully recorded in perfect
Palmer-method script. It was as if her elementary school teachers
had written them as an example of handwriting perfection. Although
the ink had faded to sepia, the familiar name — R. Lawrence Burgher
— wasn't hard to find. In fact, it was repeated several times.

Maggie's heart quickened; she read the entries and jotted down
the notations indicating the dates of the transactions and the number of the deed book in which it was recorded. The first was in 1918,
the year he moved to town. She was beginning to understand the
system: these entries were for purchases only. Grantee books listed
the property by the name of the buyer; grantor books, by the seller.
*So, these properties were bought when he first came to Huntington. No
wonder there are only a few; he must have done most of his buying after
1920.* Maggie went back to the file and pulled out the next decade.
She turned to the Bs and was stunned to see the number of times his
named was recorded. *Gracious, he owned far more property than I ever
imagined.* Again, she noted the deed book numbers and pages. After
an hour or more, she had made copies of all the deeds to property
purchased by her grandfather, at least all that she could find. The last
was recorded in 1927. *I'll read them later to identify where the properties*

are located; but now, I want to look at the Grantor index.

Maggie cleared the decks and started again with the Grantor book for the period, 1920-1930. Again, the handwriting was impeccable. And again, the list of properties naming R. Lawrence Burgher, this time as seller, was long. Curious, she read some of the names of those to whom the property had been sold. Many she recognized as names of her parents' friends — although these purchasers would have been *their* parents. They were surnames which still evoked the aura of prominence in Huntington. *Well, well, look who bought his house on the southside.* It was fascinating reading. As the morning became mid-day, she noticed an odd entry. One of the transfers was made to the Pierce-Arrow Finance Corporation. The sale appeared to have been the result of a Chancery Court order. *Pierce-Arrow? Could this be the same company from which he bought his car? Why would they be buying his property? And why is the court ordering the sale?* Then it struck her. *If he was sued in chancery court and all his property was taken to satisfy his debtors, perhaps Pierce-Arrow instituted the suit. Maybe he hadn't paid for it, either! Such irony! His downfall caused by the symbol of his wealth!*

Quickly, Maggie made copies of the deeds indicated by that index and reshelved everything. She dashed to the Circuit Clerk's office, stopping only at a vending machine for a Coke and nabs. Just as she entered the office, the Judge of the Circuit Court, L.D. Egnor, was returning from lunch. Maggie had known him for years and was glad to see a familiar face.

"Well, Maggie Malone, what are you doing here? I thought you were living in Atlanta," said Judge Egnor.

"L.D., how are you?" Maggie greeted him. "I still live there, but I'm home for a visit. I was just on my way to your office."

"What on earth for? I hope it's nothing official." He laughed.

"No, I'm doing some research on a case in chancery court in the 1920s and I was told the records would be here, in your office."

"Hoo boy, I'll bet no one has touched those files in forty years, but we've got 'em. Right down there in the basement. Let me get one of the girls to help you. Good to see you, and good luck with your research."

Maggie found she was relieved L.D. had not asked her for details.

She was still reluctant to share the story of her "black-sheep grandfather." *I can sure see why Mother was so secretive. I'm not sure I want folks to know about my grandfather's troubles, either.*

The pleasant woman L.D. recruited seemed delighted to leave her daily chores to play detective. Ms. Steward, a thin woman in stiletto heels, showed Maggie a file cabinet of index books as she explained that court cases were listed alphabetically by the defendant's name. Each book covered twenty years. Maggie removed the index for 1910-1930. Without much difficulty, she found Lawrence Burgher's name. When she told Ms. Stewart which file drawer she would need, the clerk echoed L.D.'s remarks, "Goodness, that's way down in the basement. Those records probably haven't been touched in well over twenty years." She told Maggie to wait while she looked for the file box. Maggie could hear her high heels clicking on the metal steps to the basement.

In a few minutes Ms. Stewart reappeared. "All right," she announced as if she'd found a prize. "I've found the file. I put the box on the table downstairs. You may go down and look to see what is there. If you like, you may make copies and then return the documents to the file drawer and leave it on the table."

Cautiously Maggie went down the unfamiliar stairs to a dimly lit, musty basement. The walls were covered with tall metal file cabinets, higher than her head. Cabinets were also lined up throughout the room like library shelves. Just at the foot of the steps, however, was an open area which held nothing but a small metal table and a folding chair. Overhead hung a bare light bulb. In the center of the table was an upright file box, the type in which magazines are often stored. It stood in a small circle of light, like a trophy on display.

Maggie walked around the table to face the box. The angled sides of the metal box revealed the wrapped file folders standing on their bottom edge. They seemed crusty with age. Each brown folder had the name of the case defendant on the outside. The name R. Lawrence Burgher jumped off the cover of the largest binder in the box. Maggie stared at it. The binder was easily four inches thick. She took a deep breath and reached for the file, then hesitated. It was as though she was preparing emotionally for what she would find. She stalled, rifling through the other files instead. But they were records of other cases. Finally, she sat on the wobbly chair, pulled the thick file from its metal casket and put it in her lap. She felt like she was about to exhume her grandfather. She was having second thoughts. *I've gone this far, I might as well know the truth. It's what I've wanted for so long, why am I hesitant now?* No answer came to her. Carefully, she removed the files from the binder.

As she unfolded the dust-covered documents, Maggie feared the brittle pages would break. With difficulty she untied a piece of rotting string that held some smaller binders together. In the heavy manila folder she found a formal complaint of the <u>Pierce-Arrow Finance Corporation et al vs. R. Lawrence Burgher</u>, some pieces of evidence — mostly bank books — and depositions from various witnesses or defendants. Now she eagerly pulled the depositions toward her.

As Maggie scanned the pages of the thickest folder, she discovered with some disappointment, they were only the records of the bankruptcy hearings. *So, he was sued by the Pierce-Arrow Finance Corporation. I guessed correctly.* Dozens of other plaintiffs were also listed, indicating that once he was sued by one creditor, others joined the lawsuit as well. *It looks as if he was forced into poverty! He didn't lose it in the crash at all.* Despite feeling there was more to find, Maggie was eager to read every word of the documents she now held. *If this is just the chancery trial, where are the records of the criminal trial?* Maggie laid the thick records on the table and unwrapped a slightly smaller folder.

Inside, one thin folded sheaf caught Maggie's eye. On the outside was the typed label :

IN THE
COMMON PLEAS COURT OF
CABELL COUNTY, WEST VIRGINIA
FEBRUARY TERM, 1928
THE STATE OF WEST VIRGINIA
VS
R LAWRENCE BURGHER
INDICTMENT FOR A FELONY
A TRUE BILL

Maggie caught her breath. *Oh my God. Here it is. The actual indict-ment.* Her hands shook as she unfolded it and read in stilted legal language the complaint against her grandfather. Tears gathered at the edges of her eyes. She continued reading through blurred vision. *I can't believe this upsets me. I knew I'd find it sooner or later, but I never thought it would affect me this way.* She wiped away tears with dusty hands and carefully refolded the document. Although she wanted to study the records at length, she wanted to do it in private. This was no place to mourn for her family. In a few minutes she had regained her composure. She carried the entire file upstairs and began making copies of everything. It took two copy machines going full-tilt for well over an hour. She copied everything that looked pertinent, closed up the file and put it back to rest in the musty archives.

Thirty-Four

1927-1928

1927

Predictably, public reaction to the closing of the Railroad Bank & Trust was swift. Depositors who could not gain access to their money on Friday were shocked and furious. Despite the newspaper quote by W. J. Kerr, Assistant Banking Commissioner, who had been placed in charge of the bank's affairs, that "the bank would reopen as soon as they were able to realize sufficient funds from outstanding loans," depositors were not mollified. Mr. Kerr was beseiged with telephone calls and was hard pressed to accomplish his daily work.

News of the bank's closure reached Shapely's citizens by Monday. Because Lawrence Burgher and Edward Keeley were also involved in the Bank of Shapely, a "run" on that bank ensued. Panicky depositors demanded immediate return of their money, depleting its reserves in a day and a half. At noon on April 20, the Bank of Shapely was also closed by the banking commissioner. Shortly thereafter, some desperate depositors were reported to be free trading on their deposits in the bank. One party, betting that the bank would never reopen, offered to give his $1,000 check on the bank for an item not worth more than $200 or $300.

Within a week, Commissioner McCullough was deluged with letters from business associates of the two former bank executives, offering to act as receivers of both banks, should such a need arise. Wires from the Federal Reserve Bank in Richmond notified the Department that checks on Railroad Bank & Trust and the Bank of Shapely were being refused payment for lack of funds. The checks had been written by Lawrence a few days prior to the closing of the Railroad Bank & Trust. Other bank stockholders were tainted by the failure as well; rumors flew that all had huge debts, though this was not the case.

The bank closure sounded the death knell on Keeley and Lawrence's friendship, as well; although in reality, it had been terminally wounded in 1926 by Lawrence's coup. In an exigent move to hold on to some of his funds, Keeley asked one of his coal company customers to stop payment on their check to Keeley that had been deposited at the Railroad Bank the day before the bank closed and to issue a duplicate which Keeley could deposit elsewhere. The ploy failed, however when the customer first asked Commissioner McCullough about the propriety of the requested action. He was told Keeley knew it was illegal and the customer refused. Keeley was irate and said so in a letter to the commissioner. He also wrote, demanding Mr. Kerr stop using Railroad Bank & Trust letterhead in conducting the bank's affairs because it still showed Keeley's name on the masthead as president. He said that "advertising, as it does, that I was president at the time of the Bank's closing is hurtful to my reputation." The whole affair was clearly a falling out among thieves.

For sixty days the stockholders and directors of the closed bank— except for Lawrence Burgher, whose forced resignation from the board had been accepted — met often and late trying to reorganize — to no avail. Despite the collection of $35,000 more in loan payments, there were still insufficient reserves to operate. The group desperately sought to avert receivership, casting about to several banks, hoping for a sale. But in late June, the last bank they approached turned them down.

In early June, the Chamber of Commerce's Board of Directors, realizing the effect a bank failure would have on the community and on the depositors, who would get only a fraction of their assets if it closed permanently, embarked upon an unprecedented action. They formed a committee to examine the affairs of the bank to determine if a new bank could be formed. Within a week they showed a plan to the bank's board and to Mr. McCullough. The plan provided for the creation of two new institutions: a new sound bank to take over the Railroad Bank & Trust and a new holding company to take over the Coal Exchange Building. With mixed emotions, the board accepted the plan.

With this vote and the approval of the banking commissioner, the Chamber of Commerce mounted a huge public subscription campaign in late summer to sell stock in the new bank. Its success made banking news. In twenty days, two thousand units of stock were sold, raising over $350,000. It was reported in *Money and Commerce*, a national banking magazine, that never before had a chamber undertaken such a task. It was, stated the article, "the greatest piece of financial reconstruction ever done."

Meanwhile, Lawrence Burgher was waging his own campaign. He had the good grace to quietly resign from the Board of Directors of the two civic organizations on which he had served since gaining control of the bank. And he made himself conspicuously absent from the Elks Club, the Guyandotte Club and the Guyan Golf and Country Club. But he had not disappeared altogether. Curiously, once the weight of the bank's affairs had been lifted from his shoulders and he had shared the situation with his wife, Lawrence seemed energized. Instead of cowering in bed, as he had done in the past, he rose each day with a sense of urgency. He couldn't worry about the bank any longer. He had real estate business to attend to.

In quick succession, he sold two pieces of commercial property in Guyandotte and placed an advertisement to sell his block of properties on Ninth Street. With the proceeds from the Guyandotte sale, Lawrence arranged, through a friend, to buy a large home on nearly ten acres in the Pea Ridge area, near his old farm east of the city. He titled the home in the name of his half sister, Lillian Burgher. His plan for disposal of the Ninth Street properties was thwarted, however, before he could accomplish the sale. The banking commissioner, upon learning of Lawrence's recent deals and plans for this large sale, became convinced that something must be done to conserve any assets Lawrence might have that could help satisfy his enormous debt to the bank. The commissioner went to court and was granted a writ of *les pendens* enjoining Lawrence from disposing of any property because it was material to a legal matter.

Life continued pretty much as usual for the rest of the Burgher family. In fact, as Anna confided in Jenny, it was better. Lawrence was his old self again. Of course, he was mortified by the almost daily newspaper stories about the affairs of the bank, as was Anna. But she believed it was simply a business matter — her husband had done nothing wrong — the bank had just failed. However, Anna *did* notice that no one — not a single soul — called to offer support to either of them. Similarly, at church it seemed to Anna that the Sunday School class grew quiet when she entered the room. In the hallway, when she passed by, ladies averted their eyes. She mentioned her suspicions to Jenny, who told her it was only her imagination.

The new Coal Exchange Bank opened in early December to much fanfare. Depositors' funds had been saved by the chamber's efforts. However, the former stockholders of the Railroad Bank & Trust did not fare as well. They lost their total investment in the failed bank and could not afford to try again with the new. As this became painfully obvious, they became increasingly insistent that something be done about prosecuting those in charge of the failure. Assistant Commissioner Kerr also had heard this demand daily from the bank's depositors. The sentiment was growing beyond the circle of stockholders and depositors, as well. During the stock sales campaign, Chamber of Commerce solicitors were repeatedly asked why those in charge of the bank were not being prosecuted.

Now that the new bank had opened, Mr. McCullough turned his attention to this pressing matter. He wrote to the Cabell County Prosecuting Attorney, Mr. Jacob Veeley, explaining his delay in presenting the facts his department had gathered against Burgher and Keeley saying, "It has been our policy to ask for indictments in only such cases as we were quite sure of our ground and which we felt could be successfully prosecuted. In the Huntington case, the only ground we have found for criminal prosecution appears to be the large overdraft standing on the individual account of Lawrence Burgher,

President of the bank. This overdraft at the time of suspension amounted to $274.77 but was subsequently increased by the charging of uncollected checks and cash items to $8,047.47, the amount at which it now stands. At the beginning of business on April 14, the last day the bank was open, the overdraft was $3,224.77, and during that day two deposits and one check were entered on the account. One deposit of $200 appears to be regular, and the check for $50 was for cash. The other deposit of $2,800 consisted of a check for that amount drawn by Burgher on the Bank of Shapely, located at Shapely, West Virginia, in which he had insufficient funds on deposit. This check was protested at Shapely on April 18, returned through the same channel and was charged back to the Railroad Bank & Trust Company, and by them to the Burgher account on April 23, 1927.

If this is an indictable offense in your opinion, we will, with your approval, arrange to appear before your next grand jury and present the facts."

Upon receipt of this letter, Mr. Veeley responded immediately. He asked Mr. McCullough to come to Huntington on January 17 for a conference to try to establish grounds for a felony indictment which he could present to the February session of the Grand Jury. Mr. McCullough put the date on his calendar and instructed Mr. Kerr and Mrs. Buffington to do the same.

February 1928

The Grand Jury for the Common Pleas Court, Cabell County, met on February 6, 1928, and returned a true bill against R. Lawrence Burgher, for embezzlement of $2800, a felony. The following morning, when the indictment was ordered and returned to Prosecutor Veeley, he went to Sheriff Lucas Landers' office and swore out a warrant for Mr. Burgher's arrest. By noon, Deputy Sutton was on his way to Burgher's home to bring him in.

When the doorbell rang, Anna waited for a moment to see if

Millie would answer it; when she didn't, Anna went herself. A blustery wind whipped around her legs as she pulled the heavy door toward her. Standing on the porch with a piece of paper in his hand was a sheriff's deputy. Anna thought perhaps he was looking for directions.

"Yes, may I help you?" she asked the man.

The deputy removed his hat. "Yes, ma'am. I'm Deputy Sheriff Will Sutton. I'm sorry to bother you, but is Lawrence Burgher here?" he asked, almost sweetly.

"Why yes, he is. I'll get him for you. Would you like to come in? It's awfully cold out there."

"No, Ma'am. I'll just wait here. Thank you, though."

Anna closed the door and turned to see Elizabeth, standing in the hallway. "Who is that man, Mama? He has a gun."

"Hush, Libba. Go upstairs and play. He wants to see your father."

Anna walked swiftly into Lawrence's study and closed the door. "Lawrence, there's a sheriff's deputy on the porch. He wants to see you."

The color drained out of Lawrence's face. He suddenly looked as pale as a corpse. "What does he want, did he say?" he stammered.

"No, darling. He just wants to see you. What's wrong, Lawrence? You look awful."

He rose and rushed past her without an answer. His foot-steps echoed through the quiet house as he strode across the wide foyer. Anna heard the brass knocker rattle as he jerked open the door. She left Lawrence's study and stood at the edge of the hall within earshot of the conversation at the front door. Libba, who had not obeyed her mother, ran across the hall and stood beside her. As the cold wind reached the pair, Libba moved behind her mother's protective skirt.

"I'm Lawrence Burgher. You wanted to see me?" Lawrence spoke to the deputy, recognizing him as the same man he'd had to deal with when Buddy was at the county jail for burning down the barn. He gave no sign of recognition, however.

"Mr. Burgher, I'm Deputy Will Sutton from Sheriff Lander's office. I have a warrant for your arrest." The deputy, who had replaced his hat, showed the warrant to Lawrence.

Lawrence stared at it, but avoided taking it. He protested in a stage whisper, "Arrest? Are you crazy? Arrest warrant for what?"

The deputy was polite but firm. "You can read it in the warrant, sir. But I'm afraid you'll have to come with me." He handed the warrant to Lawrence. He unfolded it and read it without comment.

In the hallway, Anna gave a small strangled cry and covered her mouth before something louder could escape. Libba looked up when she heard it, her eyes wide and terrified. "What's wrong, Mama?"

"Nothing, Libba. It's all right. Shh," she said. But she stooped and wrapped her arms tightly around her daughter and continued listening.

"Come where?" Lawrence asked, although he knew the answer.

"To jail," Deputy Sutton replied shortly.

At this response, Anna, torn between wanting to protect her child and needing to support her husband, grabbed up the five-year-old and nearly ran to stand beside Lawrence. As she reached his side, Lawrence turned toward her slowly, like in a trance. His eyes were red rimmed and suddenly lined with weariness. He took her hands in his.

"Anna, I have to go with Deputy Sutton. Please call my attorney, Francis Patrick, and ask him to meet me at the jail. I'm not sure when I'll be back, but Francis should be able to handle this quickly."

"Lawrence, what is it? Why are they taking you to jail? What is the charge?"

"Embezzlement. They claim I embezzled money from the bank. Don't worry. We'll straighten it out. It's all a big mistake. But, I have to go with him. Don't worry, love," he said reassuringly. His eyes, however, reassured her not at all. He kissed Anna and then kissed Libba on the cheek.

"Take your overcoat, darling," said Anna. It was the only thing she could think of to say. Lawrence walked to the back hall, retrieved his coat, kissed Anna again and went out the front door without another word. The brass knocker banged again. To Anna it seemed much louder than before.

Libba placed her hands on either side of her mother's face and turned it so Anna had to look straight into her daughter's eyes. "Mama, what's a 'bezzleman? Where did Father go?"

Tears sprang to Anna's eyes. She was without a satisfactory white lie for her child. Wearily, Anna put her down on the floor and crouched to her level. "It's nothing for you to worry about, Libba. Father will be home soon. He just had to go downtown to straighten out some trouble with the bank. Now go upstairs, like a good girl, and play."

This time Libba obeyed and marched up the stairs. Anna stood at the foot, gripping the newel post, and watched her for a moment. *Dear God, what is happening to us? What will I tell the other children? Please Lord, be with Lawrence.* Then she turned and went to find the attorney's telephone number.

Thirty-Five

February 7, 1928

After talking with Mr. Patrick, Anna was somewhat relieved. The attorney had assured her he would be at the jail when Lawrence arrived. He told her Lawrence would be released and be home for dinner. Now all she had to worry about, for the moment, was what to tell the children when they came home from school. She sat at Lawrence's desk trying to sort it all out — and trying not to cry. She told herself she had to be strong for the children, but she was not feeling strong at all. *I know Libba will be full of stories about the man with the gun who took her Father away. I don't know what to say, but I've got to tell them something. Maybe I should call Jenny. But, what if it turns out to be nothing? Lawrence won't want Jenny and Nate to know. They will know, however, if I tell the children. Well, I can't worry about whether or not Lawrence will be upset. I need my sister, now!* Her hands trembled as she picked up the receiver to call Jenny.

"Jenny, are you busy? Can you come over here right away?" she asked without preamble.

"What is it? Is someone hurt?" Her sister responded with questions of her own. Anna's tone had alarmed her.

"No, no one is hurt." She paused briefly. "Jenny, Lawrence has been taken to jail," she said. Her voice quavered. At the word "jail" she began to cry and could go no further.

"Anna, calm down. Tell me what's going on," Jenny insisted. But Anna could not respond. All Jenny could hear was the wail of her sister's keening.

"I'll be right there, Anna. Just sit tight."

Less than ten minutes later, Anna heard the side door slam and Jenny call, "Anna, where are you?"

Anna answered, "In here, in Lawrence's study." Almost before she completed her sentence, Jenny appeared in the doorway, still wearing her coat. Anna noticed she was still wearing an apron, as well. Jenny closed the study door behind her and went to embrace her sister. She expected to have to comfort Anna, but Anna was no longer crying. Her eyes were red and puffy, but they were dry. Between their conversation and Jenny's arrival, Anna had composed herself. Now she was pale and stone-faced as a statue.

"All right, tell me what happened," Jenny said.

"There's really not much to tell. It all happened so quickly." Anna related the incident to Jenny as if she were telling her about a bad dream.

"Did Libba hear the conversation, too?" Jenny interrupted.

"Yes, but I'm sure she didn't understand. Lawrence came back in the house and told me he had to go with the deputy to jail. He asked me to call his lawyer and then he left. I had to remind him to take his coat."

"What did they say he did, Anna?" Jenny asked.

"Embezzled money from the bank," Anna said incredulously. "It's ridiculous. Obviously they are wrong. He said it was a mistake."

"Oh, it *has* to be a mistake. Maybe someone who lost money when the bank closed is trying to hurt him," suggested Jenny.

"Do you suppose old Mrs. Tutwiller saw him leave in the deputy's car? If she did, it will be all over town by dinnertime. Oh, Jenny! Promise you won't tell a soul — other than Nate, of course — I don't want this family dragged through the mud. It's already been hard enough with the bank closing."

"I won't Anna; and I'll tell Nate not to say a word outside of the family, too," Jenny promised.

"The children will be home in thirty minutes, Jenny. What do I tell them? And Sam? He'll want to know where Lawrence went without him. Since Libba saw the whole thing, I can't just act like it didn't happen. And what if he doesn't come home? What will they think then? You know, he hasn't been anywhere in weeks — not since they stopped him from selling any more property. He's hardly gone out at all."

"Well, until he *does* come home, you really don't know anything; so I'd tell them the facts. Tell them he was arrested and went to the sheriff's office with the deputy. But I'd be *sure* to say their father's troubles *won't* affect them. He'll work it out and everything will be fine. I'd assure them it was a mistake; maybe mention the idea of someone trying to hurt him because the bank closed," Jenny advised.

"I guess you are right. I have to keep them from worrying. Thanks, Jenny. That's what I'll say." Anna smiled slightly. "I hope I sound convincing, because I'm scared to death. Lawrence looked so frightened that it frightened me. I hope they don't put him in one of those awful jail cells. It made him half sick just to go after Buddy when he burned down the barn, remember?"

"Oh, Anna, a man as prominent as Lawrence? They wouldn't do that, surely." Jenny took Anna's hands and patted them. At Jenny's comforting touch, Anna began to cry again.

"I hope you are right, Jenny. I sure do hope so."

As the Cabell County jail loomed in front of the deputy's car, Lawrence remembered with horror his last visit. The water green walls and the smell of stale urine would forever be etched into his memory. *Dear Lord, please don't let them put me in that cell with the other men.* Sutton opened the door to the jail and motioned for Lawrence to go inside.

"Turn right, Mister Burgher. We're going to the J.P.'s office. Squire Hutchinson will handle it."

"You mean, I don't have to go to jail?" he asked hopefully. His prayers had been answered.

"Probably not. Least wise, not today. You gotta have a bond hearing first. Then, who knows. But, your lawyer should be able to post your bond," Deputy Sutton offered.

The deputy and his prisoner wound awkwardly through a narrow complex corridor. Lawrence had gone ahead of the deputy and had to keep looking back to see if he was heading in the right direction. Finally, the passageway opened onto a wide ante-room flanked by three doors — one on each wall. The names of the Justices of the Peace were stenciled in black on the glass doors. Wooden benches lined the walls. Scruffy men of all ages — and two women, whom Lawrence thought looked like prostitutes — sat huddled in the corners of each bench, as if trying to avoid direct contact with each other. Some stared dejectedly at the concrete floor; others looked up at men in business suits — no doubt lawyers — whose animated conversations echoed around the room. Lawrence looked frantically from face to face, searching for his lawyer, Francis Patrick. He spotted him standing alone in one corner, his left leg bent and his foot propped on the wall. When Patrick saw Lawrence, he waved and ambled over to him. The lawyer never seemed to be in a hurry to go anywhere.

Although Francis Patrick was of average height, he was easy to pick out in a crowd. Red hair inherited from his Irish father had been softened by the stronger genes of his Germanic mother to the color of cream of tomato soup, with lots of cream. His pale white skin had a pinkish tinge, like the inside of a kitten's ear, giving him a perpetually embarrassed look. Because his pale eyelashes and brows made it look as if his eyes were without definition, all his facial features seemed centered around his nose and mouth. And, because his top lip didn't quite cover his teeth, he looked somewhat slow-witted. His rumpled suit, his run-over-at-the-sides shoes and his disheveled shirt bolstered this impression. But to take Francis Patrick for a fool was a mistake — and a mistake made only once. He had a mind like a steel trap. He never forgot a thing, had a photographic memory and, it was said, could out-argue the devil himself. He had been Lawrence Burgher's lawyer for the past five years.

"Francis, thank God you're here. This is preposterous. Get me out of here. I'm not a criminal," Lawrence blurted out.

Calmly, Patrick said, "Let me see the warrant, Lawrence." He studied it for a few minutes and then turned to his client. "Here's the situation: This, today, is merely an appearance before the J.P. Squire Hutchinson will either set your bond or release you on your own recognizance — your good name. Then he'll set a date for the arraignment where you will be formally charged. We'll go in there and get this over with in short order. Then we've got some talking to do."

Three hours later, most of which was spent waiting, Lawrence had been released without having to post bond. During the hearing, he had let Francis do all the talking except when asked his name and address. As they stepped from the confines of the musty jail into the cold fresh air, Lawrence breathed deeply.

"God, I'm glad to be out of there," he said.

"Well, you're not out of the woods yet, my friend. This is just the beginning. I didn't want to discuss your situation in front of all those other people, but we need to talk. Get in my car. I'll take you home."

As Lawrence settled into the front seat, Patrick said, "Lawrence, embezzlement is a felony. You could go to prison. You'd better explain to me what's been going on."

"It's all a mistake. I just wrote a check on my account in Shapely to cover one I'd written in Huntington — just a transfer of funds, if you will — but I didn't get a deposit to Shapely in time and the check was refused," Lawrence lied.

"Come on, Lawrence, you know how those things work. You're a banker for God's sake. Don't bullshit me. If I'm going to defend you, I've got to hear it all, no matter how ugly it may sound, understand? Did you have the money for the deposit or *were* you kiting checks? I know, I know — everyone does it. Lawrence, check kiting doesn't *sound* like embezzlement, but it is!" Patrick lectured.

"Francis, I would never steal money from the bank or from any man, for that matter; but I didn't know what else to do. I planned to make the accounts good as soon as I could; but when they closed the bank, they found out what I'd been doing." Lawrence twisted in his seat toward his lawyer, rubbed his eyes, and ran his hands through his hair. He was preparing to confess.

"Lawrence, I've been your attorney for five years. I've handled a lot of real estate deals for you and I've even sued folks for you. But I never thought I'd be defending you on a felony charge. Just what *have* you been doing that I didn't know about?" Patrick was more than curious; he was afraid he himself had been involved unwittingly in some criminal actions.

Lawrence caught his tone and rushed to reassure him. "It's nothing *you've* been handling. Don't worry. This all had to do with the bank." He sighed, knowing it would take a great effort to say what had to be said. "From time to time, in putting together some of my real estate deals, I had to borrow from the bank. But those deals didn't always make the kind of money I'd hoped. When I couldn't pay the notes on time, I'd borrow again to cover the old notes. Remember when Keeley and I had the falling out back in 1924? Part of that argument was about my loans. The situation improved temporarily, but I guess buying up the stock to force Keeley out was the straw that broke the camel's back. Since then I've paid what I could, but it wasn't enough. When the bank started having financial difficulties, they began pressuring me. I was always behind. I used an old trick Keeley taught me — playing the float. He'd done it for years; we both had. I never thought of it as embezzlement. We always had the money by the time the second check cleared, but this time I got caught. The irony is that I've successfully kited much larger amounts before, and no one ever noticed. This was small potatoes, comparatively."

"Small potatoes or large potatoes, it's still illegal, Lawrence," Patrick said shortly. He showed no sympathy for his client's situation. "Is there anything else they could turn up?"

"No," Lawrence lied again. *I've got to fix that note of Nate's, somehow. If they find that, I'm sunk. Bouncing checks is one thing; forgery is another.* "Can you get me out of this?" he asked his lawyer.

"I don't know. I'll have to study all the facts. You will plead not guilty at the arraignment, however. After they set a trial date it could take a while. Do you have any money to live on?"

"Francis, I'm mortgaged and leveraged to the hilt. Anna has no idea. I just couldn't let her know how desperate I was. I always thought something would work out. I had some money put back when the bank closed, but I've used it. I thought perhaps I could live on my real estate sales, but the banking commissioner stopped me from making any more deals. I'm broke. What on earth will I do?"

"First of all, don't tell Anna all you've told me. Tell her just what the charges are. Explain that you just didn't get a check to Shapely in time. But you're going to have to tell her that you don't have any money. I imagine your creditors will make that pretty clear, sooner or later. Then you're going to have to get a job...a real job that involves a paycheck. And you're going to have to do it quickly, before you lose everything."

Lawrence was silent for a moment. Suddenly, the enormity of what was happening washed over him. He began to cry. Great sobs, his shoulders heaving. Patrick pretended not to hear him; he'd had clients cry before. Finally, Lawrence stopped and pulled himself together. He looked up to discover they were in his driveway. Without a word, he opened the door and got out of the car.

As Lawrence turned to shut the door, Patrick spoke to him. "I'll call you tomorrow. We'll begin to go over your defense. Get some sleep, my friend."

Lawrence nodded and walked slowly toward the house. He let himself in as quietly as possible, but Anna, who was in the sunroom, heard him and called his name.

"Lawrence, is that you? I'm in the sunroom."

"Yes, love. I'm back," he replied dejectedly. As he appeared in the doorway, Anna was stunned to see how tired he looked. He crossed the room, kissed her on top of the head and sat beside her on the chaise longue.

"Are you all right, Lawrence? You look very tired. Tell me what happened," she asked anxiously as she took his hands in hers.

"First, you tell me about the children. Do they know where I've been?" he asked warily.

Anna carefully told him of her conversation with the children. She intentionally omitted Buddy's and Margaret's reactions, however. At twelve and fourteen respectively, they were furious and mortified that what had happened would cause them ridicule. Sara, too, had been worried about what her friends would think until Anna told her to just tell them it was a mistake and to go about her business. There was no reasoning with Buddy and Margaret, however.

They were unforgiving. Anna did not wish to cause Lawrence additional concern, so she edited her story on this point. Instead, she emphasized the little ones' fascination with the part about the gun.

Lawrence listened to Anna's story but she could tell he was only half there. When she stopped, he made no comment. He merely sat quietly, his hands in hers, as if he wasn't even aware of where he was.

"Lawrence, did you hear me?" Anna asked quietly. "Did you hear me say the children are fine?"

"Yes, love. I heard you. Anna, I have to tell you what *could* happen. This charge, embezzlement, is serious. It could take a while to straighten it out, and there will probably be a trial. It's all a mistake, of course; I just didn't get a deposit to Shapely to cover some checks I wrote. This started back before I bought out Keeley. I borrowed a lot of money and haven't been able to pay it all back. The details aren't important, but what I have to tell you is." He paused, searching for how to tell her. Anna saw the pain in his eyes. She laid one hand on the side of his face.

"What is it darling? Whatever it is — we'll get through it. We've gotten through other things, we'll get through this." She tried to sound prepared for the worst, although the thoughts of a trial had her shaking inside.

"Anna, we're broke. I don't have any money — not even enough to meet our household expenses. We're going to have to let Sam and Millie go and cut back drastically — at least until I can find a job."

"Good grief, Lawrence. I thought it was something horrible. We've been poor before; we can be poor again. It's not like you were dying."

"But Anna, who will hire me? In this town? Especially after this appears in the papers."

It was a question Anna couldn't answer. She hadn't considered *that* ramification. The couple talked for a while longer as Millie began to prepare dinner. Finally, Anna rose to Millie's call to dinner, but Lawrence remained seated.

"I really don't feel like eating tonight. Would you mind if I just went up to bed?" he asked his wife.

"No, of course not. I'll make your excuses to the children," she replied.

"Thank you, love." Lawrence rose heavily and went toward the kitchen. He turned and smiled ruefully at Anna.

"I just can't face them tonight," he said. He did not look back at her as he climbed the rear stairway to their room.

Thirty-Six

1928

F acing his children should have been the least of Lawrence's
worries. While Francis Patrick was planning his defense of the
embezzlement charge against Lawrence, a lawsuit was brewing
with consequences which could prove equally disastrous. Last fall,
when the court enjoined Lawrence from selling any property, he had
been forced to begin using his cash reserves. When they were depleted, his creditors began filing suit against him in small claims
court. Lawrence had told Anna they were broke; but he had not told
her about the lawsuits. He had been sued by the banks which held
his various mortgages and notes, by dozens of individuals with whom
he had had business dealings, by the automobile dealer from whom
he had bought his Pierce-Arrow and by the grocer. In all cases, a
judgment was rendered against him. When news of the felony indictment became public, these creditors, sensing their judgments
would never be paid, rushed to chancery court to ask that their claims
against Lawrence's assets be upheld. In March, a joint Bill of Complaint by the Pierce-Arrow Finance Corporation and three dozen other
creditors was filed against R. Lawrence Burgher, *et al*. If successful,
the lawsuit would force him into bankruptcy.

Once again, the Sheriff's deputy made a visit to the Burghers' big
yellow house east of town. And once again, Anna opened the door.
This time, however, Lawrence was not at home and Anna was served
with the Bill of Complaint. The deputy was quick to point out that it

was legal for him to do so, as she too, was a party to the lawsuit. Anna's hands shook as she took the tri-fold sheaf of onion-skin paper and closed the door. She walked somewhat unsteadily toward Lawrence's study, leafing through the legal document, but it was too much for her to comprehend at first glance.

She dropped heavily to the big swivel chair at Lawrence's desk and read the complaint more carefully. Although she didn't quite understand the legal language, she clearly comprehended its meaning. She could see plainly they had been sued for amounts ranging from $205 to $65,000. She caught her breath upon seeing the amounts. *Oh, my gracious! This can't be right. There must be some mistake. We can't owe all this money.* She quickly folded the papers and put them in a drawer, as if they would be less threatening out of her sight. She had no idea what to do. *Normally*, Lawrence would have dealt with this when he came home. But nothing in Anna's life had been normal of late, certainly not since the deputy's first visit a month ago.

First of all, they had to let Sam go. Everyone, including Sam and Lawrence, cried that day. It was like losing a member of the family. Lawrence *did* find Sam a new driving position with friends and afterward Sam stopped by to see the family regularly. The little children still cried each time he left.

Next, Lawrence sold the Pierce-Arrow, which hurt him almost as much as firing Sam. Compared to the outrageous price Lawrence had paid for it, the new owner got a real bargain; but, as Lawrence told Anna, "beggars can't be choosers."

Although Anna still had the services of their wonderful cook Millie, she was no longer cooking. The current day-girl previously had done all the cleaning; but she was dismissed as well. This left Millie to take over those duties while trying to teach Anna to cook for herself. Anna hadn't cooked since she was a young housewife in Shapely. What skills she had in the kitchen were very rusty. The Burghers' stomachs suffered during Anna's relearning process.

Worst of all, Lawrence wasn't even living at home now. He was working in Baltimore selling houses for his old friend, Frank "Bullmoose" Wainwright, who had moved there after Lawrence bought out the real estate developer's stock in the bank. Now Wainwright was building row houses and couldn't keep up with the demand. When Lawrence found himself in dire straits, he had written "Bullmoose" and had been hired on the spot. Lawrence had been gone for three weeks, leaving Anna to cope with the upheaval at home.

She had been slowly adjusting, but this new development unnerved her. She was frantic. *What am I going to do? Should I call Lawrence right now? He'll be at work; I can't bother him there. I'll wait until he gets home tonight, then I'll call him. Perhaps I should call Francis Patrick, though. No, what if Lawrence doesn't want him to know it. Well, that's silly, Anna; he'll have to know. Oh dear, now I'm talking to myself.* With that she jumped up, called Libba from upstairs and went to Jenny's.

Jenny was surprised to see Anna get out of the car and rush toward the house. Since Lawrence had gone to Baltimore, Anna had rarely visited. She was too busy holding herself and her household together. Jenny was at the door before Anna reached the porch.

"Anna, what brings you here this morning? Would you like some tea? And how about you, little Miss Libba, want some hot-water tea?"

"Oh Jenny, I've got to talk to you. I don't know what to do." Anna's voice was quavering. Jenny could see her sister was about to fall apart, so she quickly sent Libba to the playroom with the promise of cookies and tea.

"Here, Anna. Have some tea and tell me what's wrong." She pulled out a chair at the kitchen table and set the tea pot in front of her sister.

"Jenny, the deputy sheriff came back. This time I had to take the papers. Now, we are being sued. We owe...*everyone*, it appears. There was a great long list of names — you'd recognize some of them — then there were banks, businesses, even the grocer...and the amounts are staggering. What's going to become of us, Jenny? Lawrence isn't here. I can't call him until tonight. I thought I should call his lawyer, but I wasn't sure. I've never had to deal with business matters before.

I just don't know what to do."

Jenny did not answer her directly. Instead she said, "Anna, do you remember the story of how Mama came to this country?"

Anna was confused, but replied, "Yes, she told it to me when I was in labor with Mariah. I vaguely remembered sailing somewhere as a child; but I always thought it was just a dream. Why?"

"Remember all she went through...her husband was miles across the ocean, her son died after his father left and she had a miscarriage; but she sailed anyway — with two small children, you and Joe. Remember? Well, that's the stuff the Miller women are made of. You'll find a way to handle this. You handled Mariah's death, didn't you? You'll handle this as well. And I'll be right here to help you, too." She reached over and squeezed Anna's hand.

Anna took a deep breath and smiled at Jenny. "You're right. I'll call Lawrence tonight and he can deal with the legal problems. I *will* handle the consequences, whatever they are. I just became a little frantic when the deputy reappeared. But I won't kid you, Jenny; it's been rough since he left. The fear of what else may happen scares me the most. You know we let Sam and the day-girl go. It was terrible, especially for the children. Sam was like a big brother to the little ones. I'm doing the cooking now and the children complain at every meal. They miss Millie's touch in the kitchen."

"If that's their biggest complaint, I can't feel too bad for them," Jenny laughed.

"No, it's not," Anna said frowning. "The little ones just don't understand what's happening. They miss their father. Libba cries herself to sleep at night. The boys try to act tough, but I know it bothers them. They seem to fight with each other more often. And Buddy's been in trouble at school. His teacher told me he pushed another child on the playground. His grades are slipping, too."

"What about the older girls? Are they completely aware of what has happened?"

"Oh, indeed they are. Of course, right after the deputy came the first time, I told them about the charges, that it was a mistake, that their father just didn't get a deposit to the bank on time. Just like you suggested. Then, we, or rather *I* had a long talk with them just before their father left. I explained money would be tight because the courts wouldn't let him sell any property. They know he went to Baltimore because he couldn't find work here."

"How did they handle it?" Jenny asked.

"Eileen understood, of course. Like the rest of us, she's embarrassed; but she's more concerned about me. She has been staying at home a lot more than usual. Sara and Margaret are more concerned about the effect on themselves. Sara is afraid her friends will talk about her and Margaret is just plain angry that she can't have the new dress she wants. She is particularly upset the Pierce-Arrow and Sam are gone. She loved riding in that car."

"Poor Anna. What did you say to them?"

"I said — over and over — 'your father's troubles are nothing for you to worry about or be ashamed of. People *may* talk, that's just the way they are. But you are to hold your head up and ignore them.' I said 'this family will get through it — together!' I also told them it is a family matter — *anything* they hear at home, stays there. They are *never* to talk about their father's troubles outside of the house!"

"See Anna, you already knew how to cope with this! Did that make them feel better?"

"I think so. Of course, Eileen's new friends at Marshall College are from out of town and won't know about it. It's Sara and Margaret — and Buddy, for that matter — I worry about. I want to protect them, all of them. I just hope I can. I *am* scared. Who knows how this will end."

"You'll be fine, Anna. You'll *all* be fine," Jenny reassured her.

But they were not fine. More lawsuits followed; it was as if the legal floodgates had been opened by the felony indictment. Lawrence, his brother David and Edward Keeley were also indicted in Wyoming County on embezzlement charges stemming from evidence found when the banking commissioner closed the Bank of Shapely. Lawrence was sued personally by Shapely creditors who lost money in the bank's failure. They sued to gain title to houses they had purchased in the Burgher-Keeley subdivision. When Lawrence offered these lots and houses for sale, he had allowed the purchasers to pay in monthly installments; but he had never drawn up written agreements.

Therefore, they still appeared to be Lawrence's assets, which the courts were planning to seize.

On a bright June day, the Cabell County Circuit Court decision was rendered. After much deliberation and ordering of lien priorities, the court seized and ordered sold all of Lawrence and Anna Burgher's real estate property. Lawrence had returned to Huntington for the hearings, but did not actually appear in court. His lawyer, Francis Patrick, represented him with strict instructions to call him at home as soon as the judgment was rendered.

When the telephone rang in Lawrence's study, the couple jumped. Anna's hands were cold and clammy as her fingers reflexively drummed on the chair arm. She knew what to expect if the decision went against them. Lawrence grabbed the receiver and said hello through tight lips. Anna watched her husband for a moment. As she saw his face crumple in despair, she turned away and willed her own face to remain fixed into a smile of support. Lawrence hung up without saying goodbye, put his face in his hands and began to cry.

"Lawrence, tell me. Please. How bad is it?" Anna pleaded.

Lawrence looked up. His expression was that of a bewildered child. It nearly broke his wife's heart, but she remained tearless. He wiped his eyes but the tears quickly reappeared.

"Anna, my love; it's as bad as can be. They've taken it all — every piece of real estate we own — all the Ninth Street office buildings, the lots in the east end, the new house in Pea Ridge, this one and even your mother's home. They didn't believe Lillian could have bought the Pea Ridge house on her teacher's salary. They *still* think I bought it to hide my assets. It will all be sold by the court." He began to sob.

"Anna, I am *so* sorry. I never meant for any of this to happen. You have to believe me. All I ever wanted was for you and the children to have a good life. Now I've lost it all. And all I can say is, 'I'm sorry!'"

"Hush, Lawrence. I believe you. I know you are a good man. We'll survive. I told you that before. You've got a job now; we can live on your salary. Hush now; don't cry, darling. Please!" It took great strength for Anna to keep from joining her husband's sobs, but she knew she must. She knew she had to be strong — now and in the months to come. Anna rose from her chair, walked around the desk and stood in front of her husband to embrace him. As he put his arms around her and nestled his tear-streaked face between her breasts, she stroked his head until he fell silent.

The Burghers' property was sold at auction on the steps of the courthouse the following month. Lawrence had returned to work in Baltimore immediately after the bankruptcy hearing, leaving Anna alone to deal with the family's tearful move. It was one of the hardest things either of them had ever had to do.

Nate had helped her find a clean, two-story, frame house which she could afford on Lawrence's meager salary. The rented house was wedged in between two others just like it. All three were across the alley from a grocery store. The distance between each of the eight houses on the block was no wider than a car. The new home had only four bedrooms, forcing each child to share one with a sibling. Sara and Margaret took one room; Buddy and Stephen slept in another. Anna gave Eileen a room she could almost call her own. It came with the understanding Eileen would share it with Libba when Lawrence was home. Anna also put a small bed for Libba in her room. She hoped it wouldn't be long until she again shared it with her husband; but for now, she was glad for the small child's company.

The first floor of the house would have been adequate for most families, but it was much smaller than Anna expected. Her beautiful furniture, which Lawrence and their lawyer had jealously protected from the sheriff's sale, was packed into the rooms as if it were on display in a furniture store. Her favorite mahogany side-board overwhelmed the dining room, where the matching table sat. With all its leaves removed, the table looked diminished by the move. The living room held, in an odd seasonal juxtaposition, both the velvet couch from the old living room and the bright floral chintz chaise longue from Anna's sunroom. Assorted arm chairs occupied the corners of nearly every room; they rarely matched the prevailing decor.

Adjusting to life in town was hard. Each morning Anna was awakened by the cacophony in the alley below. Long before daylight, apparently intent on making rounds as quickly as possible, impatient produce men, ice haulers and meat vendors pounded on the grocer's back door or yelled at him as if it were high noon. Anna awoke with a headache more often than not. She hated the Southside neighborhood and longed for the quiet house on the riverbank. The children were not allowed to play in the back yard. Broken bottles and rotting food scraps from the grocer's garbage often landed there, so Anna forbade them to go out back except to carry their trash to the alley. Now that Millie also had been let go, Anna assigned the children housework chores for the first time in their lives. It had been a long time since Anna had done housework, and she was twenty years older, as well. The children complained bitterly, but she needed their help. It was a miserable summer for everyone.

In September, the younger Burgher children entered new schools. They adjusted well enough, except for Buddy who, it seemed to Anna, had developed a chip on his shoulder. Several times, she was called to the school because of his fighting. Over the fall and winter, she shared none of this in her letters to Lawrence. He had enough to worry about.

October 12, 1928

My dearest Anna,

How I miss you and the children! What a lonely life forced bachelorhood can be! I go to work each day, which occupies my mind; but at night I do nothing but think of you. I wish I were home.

Anna, how can you ever forgive me for what you've had to bear? I know this is not the life you expected to be living. It certainly is not what I wanted for you, either. Perhaps your Papa was right after all — perhaps you should never have married me.

My love, I'm working harder than I have since leaving the farm. Bullmoose has me overseeing the construction crews one day and selling his row houses the next. I must say, I prefer the latter. Tramping around in the mud is no fun. I fear I've ruined several pairs of my good shoes already. I've enclosed a photograph of our latest project. See if you can spot my name on the big FOR SALE sign.

Although I have no time for seeing all the city has to offer, I find Baltimore to be an exciting place. It's growing by leaps and bounds, even with the national downturn in real estate. Perhaps it is because of its proximity to Washington, DC. Would you ever consider moving here? After the trial, of course. You no doubt know it was postponed until December 5. Francis Patrick successfully argued for a delay to allow me to earn some money to make restitution of the overdraft and to give him more time to prepare. If that date is firm, perhaps I'll be home for the holidays.

How are you and the children faring in the new house? I know it must be crowded what with trying to squeeze in all our furniture. Has Eileen been helping with the housework? How are the little ones adjusting to a new school? Are they making new friends? If they have any difficulty, I'm sure Lillian would help out. You remember she teaches there, don't you? Even though she's not really close to our family, the fact that she's my half sister should count for something. I'm sure she would look after them, if necessary.

How is the weather? Are the leaves turning? I hate to miss fall in West Virginia...it is always so beautiful. Remember how lovely it was in Shapely each year? The hills surrounding the town were always so vivid. It is very cold here. I fear I'm in for a long winter. Give the children hugs and kisses for me, and keep lots for your own sweet self.

Your loving husband,

P.S. Enclosed is a check. I know it isn't much, but it is all I can spare this week.

Thirty-Seven

1929

T he embezzlement trial date, originally set for October 1928 was postponed to December 5, and then again until spring. That date also came and went without a trial. Finally, Lawrence received a letter from Francis Patrick. His trial date, which had been moved twice by the defense and once by the state, was finally set. Francis tried one more delay to give Lawrence additional time for earning the restitution funds, but the judge was not at all sympathetic this time. He said matters had dragged on long enough. It had been more than a year since Lawrence's indictment. The state was eager to try the case.

Wednesday, July 3, 1929

On the second floor of the courthouse, the midday sun streamed through the open windows of the Common Pleas Courtroom, although it probably wouldn't last. It was one of those summer days when the weather couldn't make up its mind. First it had rained, then the sun had returned causing steam to rise from the sidewalks. Now, following another brief shower, the sun was out again. Two paddle-fans suspended from the high ceilings labored to stir the leaden air. Even the long-dead, imperious judges staring down from the somber oil paintings looked hot.

At the front of the large room, the padded chair behind the judge's bench and the hard wooden ones in the jury box were empty. A few men with books and fat files in their arms milled around in the open space before the bench. Spectators, prospective jurors and potential witnesses trickled into the benches in the gallery, like churchgoers, only noisier.

By the time Anna and her three daughters slipped through the heavy courtroom doors, the place was bustling with activity. Holding hands, they snaked through the crowd to the row near the front where Jenny and Nate were already seated. They settled themselves, with Anna next to her sister, then instinctively grasped hands again, each with the woman beside her — Jenny, Anna, Eileen, Sara and Margaret. The four Burgher women stared straight ahead as stage-whispered voices buzzed around them in instant recognition. Sara's face flamed as she heard one dowdy matron say, "My, don't they look high and mighty for the family of a crook?" Sara prayed her mother had not heard the remark.

But Anna was not listening; she was searching for Lawrence in the sea of faces up front. He had arrived only last night from Baltimore and had left the house very early this morning to meet with his lawyer. Finally, Anna saw her husband walk through a small door in the rear of the courtroom behind the shuffling attorney. Lawrence was head and shoulders taller than Francis Patrick and carried himself proudly. Anna smiled in his direction. He did not see her, however, as he made his way to the defense table. The bustling continued in front of the railing; it was like the constant movement of ants. Men scrambled from one side of the room to the other, then back again as if they had forgotten why they crossed it to begin with.

Suddenly a loud crack of thunder split the air, startling the audience. In the moment of quiet which followed, the bailiff hollered, "All rise. Common Pleas Court of Cabell County, West Virginia is now in session. Judge Fenton Calley presiding."

As Judge Calley stepped onto the raised dais, the sound of the sudden cloudburst was muffled by the collective movement of the audience. Once the Judge had taken his seat, the bailiff yelled again. "You may be seated."

Fenton Calley was known as a "no-nonsense" judge, although at first glance his looks belied that label. A deeply receding hairline, squaring jaw and obvious paunch gave him the soft appearance of a kindly grandfather with a welcoming lap. Outside the courtroom, this was probably accurate; but in *his* bailiwick — *his* courtroom — his steel blue eyes were hard as marbles. Rumor had it Judge Calley believed he could tell a criminal merely by the distance between his eyes — those with eyes too close together were immediately suspect. Today, as he surveyed his courtroom, he seemed to be searching for that tell-tale sign in the faces of those gathered before the bar.

At the defense table Lawrence sat ramrod straight flanked by two other men. One was Francis Patrick, the other was co-counsel, E. Flavius Marshall, a new lawyer in Patrick's small firm who looked as sharp as Patrick looked dull. The contrast was remarkable and often served to fool opposing attorneys who didn't know Patrick's reputation. The prosecutor, Jacob Veeley, and several assistants sat at the opposite table. Veeley was a bombastic lawyer who loved the sound of his own baritone voice. Larger than any other lawyer in town, he behaved as if his mere size and booming voice should win his cases. Veeley used condescension and sarcasm as his primary tools of argument. He reminded Lawrence of the school yard bullies.

The courtroom noise subsided to a low hum as Fenton Calley stared at the assembly from the bench. With two short raps of his gavel, the hum ceased altogether.

Judge Calley intoned, "We are here today to hear the case of the State of West Virginia vs. Richard Lawrence Burgher on Felony Indictment No. 33. Gentlemen, are you ready to begin?" He nodded toward Prosecutor Veeley and then toward Francis Patrick. They both returned the gesture. Patrick rose and ambled forward.

"Your honor, we object to the charges in the indictment on the grounds they are insufficient in law and ask the court to quash the same." He spoke as if he were asking a good friend for a favor.

Although this was a standard legal motion, which Patrick didn't really expect to be granted, Anna gripped Eileen's hand tightly as she listened expectantly to the lawyer's arguments. Her wildest hopes were dashed, however, when Judge Calley denied Patrick's motion. When the attorney objected to the decision, Judge Calley took note of it, but moved on. Anna's grip relaxed in disappointment. Her face fell and she sagged slightly in her seat. Jenny looked anxiously at her sister.

"Very well, Mr. Patrick. Are you ready for trial?" asked Judge Calley.

"Yes, your Honor, we are," he responded.

"Mr. Veeley; is the state ready?"

"Oh, yes, sir. We are!" boomed Jacob Veeley.

Judge Calley addressed Lawrence. "Will the defendant please rise?" Lawrence and his team stood in unison. "Mr. Burgher, you are charged with the embezzlement of $2,800 from the Railroad Bank & Trust Company, a felony. How do you wish to plead?"

Lawrence answered in a steady voice. "Not guilty, your Honor. I am not guilty."

At the sound of Lawrence's voice, Anna closed her eyes. She could hardly bear to see him standing there. Her grip on Eileen's hand tightened again. Glancing anxiously at her mother, Eileen noticed a tiny line of perspiration had formed above her mother's lip.

"Very well. Mr. Burgher, you may be seated. Gentlemen, select your jury. Mr. Veeley, begin," Judge Calley instructed.

Shortly after Prosecutor Veeley began to question the first man from the jury pool, the rainstorm subsided and sunlight again poured into the room. With it came flies. They began to buzz the damp faces and necks of members of the crowd. Five people in the row to the Burghers' right began fanning themselves, as if controlled by an unseen puppeteer. The afternoon wore on as the questioning of jurors continued. It was slow and tedious. Margaret, who had recently turned fifteen, soon found the proceedings boring and began to survey the audience. First she counted ladies with straw hats — fourteen; then men in shirt sleeves — twenty-one. Twisting in her seat to be certain she hadn't miscounted, she caught sight of her mother's disapproving, tight-lipped frown. She stopped and faced forward once again.

One by one, as the men were sworn in, they took their seats in the jury box. They were ordinary looking men, dressed mostly in their Sunday best. Only one was without a jacket. Margaret thought they all looked angry, however. *Why would they be angry with Father? He didn't do anything to them.* She stared intently at each man as he sat down, *willing* him to let her father go.

Once the twelve men were fully assembled, Margaret intended to continue sending the unspoken message *en masse*, but her concentration was snapped by the booming voice of the Prosecutor. He was speaking to the jury in deliberate terms, as if he were instructing slow-witted children.

"...will prove this man, Richard Lawrence Burgher, did embezzle and take for his own use, $2,800 from the Railroad Bank & Trust over which he had control as its president...we will produce evidence to support this charge...." Margaret's attention instantly was riveted to the resonant voice and compelling words. She looked at her mother and sisters, but they were staring at the prosecutor. She looked toward her father. His profile looked chiseled and hard. His jaw muscles alternately clenched and unclenched. Suddenly, Margaret was afraid. *This can't be happening.* A cold wave of dread swept over her. Despite the hot room, she shivered.

The prosecutor resumed his seat and Francis Patrick started to rise; but Judge Calley spoke, interrupting his movements. "Hold up, Mr. Patrick. Owing to the late hour, I'm going to call a recess to these proceedings. And because tomorrow, July 4, is a legal holiday, we will continue this trial on Friday, July 5 at 9 A.M." Mr. Patrick resumed his seat and turned to Lawrence who had started to ask him a question. He laid his hand on Lawrence's arm to quiet him as the Judge continued.

"Deputies Busbee and Mitchell, I'm placing this jury in your custody. You are to keep them together in suitable quarters at the Farr Hotel and bring them back on Friday morning. Sorry gentlemen, no Fourth of July celebration this year. Mr. Patrick, your client is hereby placed in the custody of Sheriff Landers, to be held in the county jail until Friday, when he will return him to answer this indictment."

Lawrence blanched, turned and looked pitifully at his wife. Anna gasped audibly, then covered her mouth. Eileen put her arm protectively around her mother as Mr. Patrick rose to object.

"Your Honor, may I have a word with you? Is that necessary?" He began to approach the judge's bench before actually gaining permission.

In quiet undertones, Patrick pleaded. "Your Honor, this man has been out on his own name for months, worked in Baltimore and came here without any trouble. Don't you think he'll be back on Friday?"

"No doubt you would see to it, Counselor; but the law says otherwise. I'm afraid he's going to have to spend a few nights in our fine jail." He turned to the sheriff and nodded.

As the sheriff approached Lawrence with his handcuffs visible, Margaret began to cry softly. Quickly Sara leaned over and hissed at her. "You stop that right this minute, Margaret Lynn Burgher. Don't you dare cry in public. Do you hear me?" Margaret shook her head silently and snuffled.

Anna, who could not hear the conversation at the bench, sat rigidly watching Lawrence. The only signs of life in her face were the tears spilling from the corners of her eyes. Jenny turned to her and took her hand.

"If they put him in jail, he doesn't have any pajamas, Jenny. Do you think they will give him some?" she asked naively. Anna was so shocked by the judge's order she had been reduced to worrying over Lawrence's basic creature comforts rather than the long-term potential outcome of the trial.

"I'm sure they will," Jenny responded reassuringly.

At the bench, his attorney continued to press his case. "Judge Calley, please. You've known Lawrence Burgher for five years. And you've known me even longer. Don't you think you could make an exception here? I'll guarantee his safe return. Hell, I'll even post a bond, if necessary."

The judge held up his hand to stop the sheriff from putting on the handcuffs as he continued to listen.

"You let him go to Baltimore for a year. He's not going to skip out suddenly at this point. One or two days more won't make him a fugitive. Let him go home until Friday morning," Patrick urged.

"Very well, Francis. You post a $5,000 bond and I'll release him in your custody. Fair enough?"

"Thank you, your Honor. That's very fair," answered Patrick. He turned and smiled at Lawrence as the judge announced his ruling.

"Lawrence Burgher will be placed in the custody of his attorney, Francis Patrick. Sheriff Landers, you can put away your handcuffs."

At the announcement, Margaret let out a yelp of delight. Again, Sara leaned over to chastise her. This time, Margaret glared at her sister defiantly. Lawrence turned and smiled at Anna, as his attorney came to speak to her.

"Anna, we've managed to keep him at home until Friday, but he has to stay at home. I'll bring him along in a little while. We need to talk about the trial. You go on home with the girls and we'll be along shortly." Francis gave Anna a reassuring pat on the arm and turned to go back to his client as the Burgher family filed out of their row. Margaret turned to look once more at her father, as he followed his attorney through the rear courtroom door. The feeling of dread was still there, despite the judge's ruling. She had to look away quickly to keep from crying again. Eileen, who had been waiting for her, saw Margaret's emotional struggle. As Margaret reached the end of the aisle, Eileen slipped one arm through her sister's. Together they pushed open the heavy oak doors and left the courtroom.

Thirty-Eight

Following a restless night and an uneaten breakfast, Lawrence again left his somber household early in the morning with Francis Patrick. Sam had arrived a few minutes before 8 A.M. to stay with Libba and the boys for a second day. Before the trial began he had offered his help and Anna had accepted gratefully. By 8:15 Nate and Jenny were in the driveway, honking the car horn. Anna hugged her small children tightly and ran for the car with her three older daughters.

Despite the early hour, it seemed to Anna the courthouse had lost none of Wednesday's heat. It was as though the massive stones had conserved their warmth over the holiday — not sure how soon it would be needed again. It was not necessary, however; today's temperature was predicted to reach ninety degrees, with no rain in sight. Although the trial would not begin until 9 A.M., the courtroom was almost full when the Burgher family arrived at 8:30 A.M. The first two rows of the gallery were empty, however, as if they had been reserved for Lawrence's family. The five women and one man seated themselves in the same order as before — Nate on the aisle, Jenny beside him, flanked by Anna and her daughters, Eileen, Sara and Margaret. Jenny had brought two church fans; she handed one to Anna.

Anna recognized several of Lawrence's former business acquaintances as she scanned the faces in the audience. *I wonder if they are here in support of Lawrence or...?* Most averted their eyes, unsure of the proper greeting in such circumstances. One man, however, did not. Sitting on the prosecutor's side of the aisle was Edward Keeley. He nodded to her unctuously when she met his eyes. She did not return the greeting. *Dear Lord, he's not on* their *side is he? I wouldn't put it past him.* Looking away from Keeley, Anna saw David Burgher and Lawrence's half-sister Lillian step through the doors. David spotted the family and came toward them, patting Anna's shoulder as he and Lillian slid into the pew directly behind her.

Today, the activity in the courtroom was much more subdued, giving the room a more serious mood. Conversations — the few that were held — were whispered, like in a church. By contrast, Wednesday had seemed like a circus. Today's mood felt to Anna decidedly ominous. She watched Lawrence as he again entered through the small rear door. She thought he looked less confident than before; she hoped it was just her imagination. Shortly, both his table and that of the prosecutor were full. As the jury filed in and the bailiff began his monotone bellowing, Anna smiled down the row at her daughters, feigning reassurance. Today they clutched their own hands, female islands apart. Each returned her mother's look with a weak smile as they stood to honor the judge's appearance.

Judge Calley rapped his gavel at precisely 9 A.M. and the trial resumed.

"Prosecutor Veeley, call your first witness," he instructed.

Jacob Veeley rose and announced, "The State calls W.J. Kerr."

From several rows back, the diminutive man came forward, took his seat in the witness stand and was sworn in. To Anna he looked threatening, despite his size.

"Mr. Kerr, we appreciate your attendance today. Would you please tell us, in your own words, of your connection to this case?"

Kerr explained he had been the Assistant Banking Commissioner from September 1, 1925 until now and in that position had examined the Railroad Bank & Trust on many occasions, lastly in April 1927. He also noted, somewhat proudly, he was put in charge of the bank's affairs after it was closed.

Veeley asked, "And in what condition was the bank over the course of your examinations?"

"Mostly it was in bad condition," Kerr answered.

Francis Patrick objected, but his objection was overruled.

"And during the course of your regular examinations, did you have occasion to examine the accounts of Lawrence Burgher?"

"Yes, from March 25 to April 14, 1927, I examined the personal account of Lawrence Burgher as well."

"And what was the condition of this account?" Veeley queried.

"He was continually overdrawn," Kerr stated flatly.

Anna squirmed at the response while Jacob Veeley lumbered back to the table where his assistants sat. One handed him an oversized piece of paper. He turned and held it in front of his body like a trophy as he walked toward the witness.

"Mr. Kerr, do you recognize this?" he asked, handing it to Kerr.

"Yes, sir. It is a ledger sheet from the books of the Railroad Bank & Trust showing Lawrence Burgher's account."

Veeley asked that it be admitted into evidence. He turned back to Kerr. "Would you read the entries showing Mr. Burgher's overdrafts during that period?"

Kerr did so, reading amounts from $9.52 to $8,045. Reaching the end of the list, he seemed to run out of steam. He drew a deep breath. "Railroad Bank & Trust closed — or rather, failed to open — on April 15, 1927."

As Kerr read the list, Anna had winced, lowered her head and stared into her lap. Jenny put her arm around her sister's shoulders and squeezed her gently.

"Now, will you explain to the jury, in detail, the final entry in the ledger — the one resulting in the final overdraft, before the bank was closed?" asked Veeley

"Very well. Mr. Burgher drew a check on the Bank of Shapely for $2,800.00 and deposited..."

"Take it rather slowly, Mr. Kerr."

Kerr sighed and repeated himself. "He drew a check on the Bank of Shapely, West Virginia for $2,800."

"When was that?"

"On April 14, 1927."

"That is the day the Railroad Bank & Trust was closed?"

"The day *that* bank was closed, yes sir."

"All right. Go ahead."

"Deposited it to his personal account in the Railroad Bank & Trust Company...," Kerr stated, as if there were more to say.

"Go ahead with the whole transaction."

"Well, the check was later returned, protested on April 18. He didn't have the money in the Bank of Shapely to pay it."

Veeley urged him on, careful to cover each detail. "Was this the only check Mr. Burgher wrote in April for that amount?"

"No. Actually there were two more. On April 9, Mr. Burgher had written a check for $2,800 on his personal account at Railroad Bank & Trust payable to the Bank of Shapely and sent it there to be deposited to his account in that bank."

"Was that check paid?"

Francis Patrick stood abruptly. "We object to that testimony as hearsay evidence."

"Objection overruled, Mr. Patrick. Mr. Kerr would have direct knowledge of that because of his position as an examiner. He may answer the question."

"Note my objection to your ruling, your Honor."

"So noted, Mr. Patrick. Mrs. Hash, please read the question again."

While the reporter flipped back through her notes, Anna turned to look at Edward Keeley. She hoped to discern his reaction to the bank examiner's testimony. But Edward sat poker faced, his fat hands laced across his ample belly. The diamond pinkie ring glinted in a shaft of sunlight.

The court reporter read, "Do you know whether that check was paid or not?"

"Yes, it was credited to his account the same day, subsequently cleared through the normal channels and was paid."

"And the second check?"

"He later sent another $2,800 check to the Bank of Shapely, drawn on the Railroad Bank & Trust Company."

"What date was that?"

"The day before the Huntington bank closed, April 13."

"Do you know whether that check was paid or not?"

"No, that check was not paid."

Prosecutor Veeley paused for a moment, pulled a huge handkerchief from his hip pocket, unfurled it and wiped his brow. It was not quite 10 A.M. and the courtroom was already stuffy. He refolded the cloth and continued.

"At the time this second $2,800 check was drawn on the Railroad Bank & Trust and, I think you said, sent and deposited in the Bank of Shapely, what was the balance as shown to the credit of the personal account of Lawrence Burgher at the Railroad Bank & Trust?"

"His account was overdrawn $3,274.77."

"When was that, did you say, with reference to the date the Railroad Bank was closed?"

"It was closed at the end of the business day April 14; in other words, it was closed the morning of the fifteenth — that is, never opened for business the fifteenth."

"And did Mr. Burgher know of the condition of the bank?"

"Oh, yes. Mr. Burgher had full knowledge of the bank's condition. We, the banking commissioner's office, had been down there trying to help them out of their bad situation. He knew the bank would be closed if it wasn't fixed up. He knew this as early as March 10 when he was warned by Mr. McCullough. He was warned again on April 10th. The bank closed on April 15."

Kerr sat quietly waiting for the next question as Jacob Veeley returned to the prosecution table and retrieved another large sheet of paper, similar to the first. Again, he asked Kerr to identify it.

"This is a ledger sheet from the Bank of Shapely, showing Lawrence Burgher's account at that bank. It shows a balance on April 9 of $3,039.69 as a result of the deposit of the first check drawn on the Railroad Bank & Trust for $2,800," Kerr responded.

"Could you tell from this statement, I mean from the statement of Mr. Burgher, whether the defendant had sufficient funds, in the Bank of Shapely to pay the $2,800 check he wrote on April 14 payable to the Railroad Bank & Trust?"

"He did not have."

"Mr. Kerr, at the time of the writing of these checks, what was Mr.

Burgher's position with the Railroad Bank & Trust?"

Before Mr. Kerr could answer, someone in the audience yelled, "Thief, he was a thief."

Heads turned in the direction of the angry voice, as Judge Calley began banging his gavel.

"Order, I say. We will have order in this courtroom. Come to order, now." Nothing more was heard from the unidentified man. Mr. Kerr was asked the question again.

"I'm sorry, Mr. Kerr. What was Mr. Burgher's position with the Railroad Bank & Trust?" Veeley repeated.

"He was the President and Chairman of the Board of Directors, sir."

"And what was his position, if any, with the Bank of Shapely?"

Again the angry voice rang out. "He was a thief!" Near the rear of the courtroom the angry man, dressed in bib overalls and a faded, collarless shirt, stood pointing at Lawrence.

"Remove that man!" ordered Judge Calley. Two deputies rushed toward the man, who continued to rant. "That bastard stole my money in Shapely. Because of him, I lost everything." Seizing him by the arms, they steered him out the courtroom doors.

As Judge Calley hammered the bench with his gavel, the collective murmur of the audience began to subside. Thoroughly embarrassed, Anna had stared at her lap throughout the entire outburst. She continued to do so as the prosecutor asked the question again. "What was his position in Shapely?"

"He was on the Board of Directors, and had been the President at one time."

"Objection. Irrelevant," came Patrick's objection.

"Sustained. Move on, Mr. Veeley."

"Very well, your Honor." Instead of continuing the direct questioning of Mr. Kerr, Veeley again made his way to the table, where he was handed two checks. "Your Honor, the state wishes to admit these two documents into evidence," he announced loudly. He waved them dramatically, one in each hand. Lowering his left hand and continuing to wave one check in his right, he began:

"This check for $2,800, written on April 13, 1927, by Lawrence

Burgher on his account at the Railroad Bank & Trust was made payable to the Bank of Shapely. According to our Mr. Kerr, it was deposited to Burgher's account there, creating a false credit. He lowered his right arm and raised the other, waving the second check like a small semaphore flag. "And this check, also for $2,800, written on April 14, 1927, by Lawrence Burgher on his account at the Bank of Shapely is made payable to the Railroad Bank & Trust. It was returned protested for insufficient funds."

At the defense table, Francis Patrick was beet red and protesting. Jumping to his feet, his voice grew louder and louder as he tried to make his objection heard over the thundering oration of the prosecutor.

"Objection! Objection! The prosecutor is testifying, for God's sake! Judge Calley, *please*!" shouted the defense attorney.

Finally, Judge Calley rapped his gavel. Both men grew silent. "Objection sustained. Mr. Veeley, you know better. Have your witness identify those documents, if you wish; but save *your* remarks for the summation. Mrs. Hash, strike Mr. Veeley's remarks from the record. The jury will disregard them. Continue."

Veeley did as the judge instructed, but smiled smugly as he did so. With Mr. Kerr holding the checks, he began his questioning anew.

"Mr. Kerr, now that you have identified the two checks, do you know whether that check, the one to the Bank of Shapely, was paid or not?"

"The second check was not paid. His account in the Railroad Bank & Trust was overdrawn $3,166.67 on April 9 and continued overdrawn even after the $2,800 deposit on April 14."

"Thank you. For the record, could you explain to the court precisely the meaning of an overdraft?"

"Certainly. An overdraft is a check or draft drawn against an account in which the funds are not sufficient to cover the check or draft."

"Thank you, Mr. Kerr. That will be all, for now." He smiled slightly at Judge Calley and took his seat.

Judge Calley nodded toward Francis Patrick. "Your witness, Mr. Patrick."

Patrick remained seated for a moment, scratching his head as if he were perplexed. Then he rose, deliberately removed his coat and hung it on the back of the chair. He straightened, snapped his suspenders and ambled toward Mr. Kerr. With his coat removed, he looked like a red-headed scarecrow.

"Mr. Kerr, don't overdrafts often occur in banks?" he inquired, as if he were really not sure.

"Yes, they do," Kerr admitted.

"Uh-huh, and were the doors of this bank closed on account of the overdraft Mr. Burgher had in that bank?" Again, he sounded merely curious.

"Well, no that wasn't the cause, but...," he said hesitantly before he was cut off by Mr. Patrick.

"Do you have direct knowledge regarding the accuracy of the two ledger sheets, Mr. Kerr?" The defense attorney snapped his suspenders again for punctuation.

"No, I didn't make the ledger sheets at either bank, if that's what you mean, so I can't know for sure whether they are correct or incorrect."

"Uh-huh. Refresh my memory, what was the amount of Lawrence Burgher's overdraft at the time the bank was closed?"

"I believe it was $474.77. Yes, that is the amount. When the bank opened on April 14, he was overdrawn $3,274.77 and when it closed the same day, the amount was $474.77 by virtue of the credit of the $2,800 drawn on the Bank of Shapely."

"Well, now. That's not such a large sum, is it?"

From the prosecution table, Veeley boomed, "Objection, your honor!"

Suddenly, through an open window came the unmistakable sounds of a vicious dog-fight. It was so loud it seemed as if the animals were in the courtroom. Barking, snarling and yelping drowned out the judge's ruling.

"Sustained," the judge said, but no one heard him. "Bailiff, close that damn window!" As the window slammed, Judge Calley repeated, "I said, 'Sustained.'"

"I'll withdraw the question. Mr. Kerr, was Mr. Burgher the legal custodian of the bank's funds?"

"No, the cashier of state banks is the legal custodian of the funds."

"Not the president?"

"No, it is the cashier," Kerr stated with certainty.

"Thank you Mr. Kerr, that's all. Francis Patrick snapped the suspenders in finality and sat down.

Jacob Veeley again approached his witness. "Mr. Kerr, could you tell the jury, in ordinary terms, the definition of embezzlement?"

Kerr seemed to rise to the occasion. He straightened in the chair to his full height. "Certainly. Embezzlement is the willful misappropriation, by an officer or employee of a banking institution, of the funds of that bank with the intent to injure or defraud the institution or to deceive any agent appointed to examine the affairs of the institution." He sounded as if he had memorized the definition just for the occasion.

"Thank you Mr. Kerr. I believe you've made the meaning of embezzlement perfectly clear. No further questions."

Jacob Veeley turned to face the judge. "Your honor, the state rests its case." An audible murmur ran through the audience, causing Judge Calley to call for order.

Anna leaned across Jenny and whispered to Nate. "That's good, isn't it? They've only got one witness."

Nate replied, "It sure sounds good to me. Now we can hear Lawrence's side of it."

Margaret turned to Sara and said, "Are they through?" Sara shook her head and put her fingers to her lips. "Shh," she hissed.

Judge Calley continued to bang the gavel until the room grew quiet. "Very well, Mr. Veeley. Thank you. Mr. Patrick, you may proceed."

"Your honor, the defense moves the court to strike the evidence of the state and direct the jury to find for the defendant. The evidence presented is insufficient to prove the indictment. If any crime was committed it was merely a misapplication of credits, not embezzlement or larceny."

"Motion denied, Mr. Patrick, call your first witness."

Francis Patrick called a string of character witnesses including several attorneys, the former President of Marshall University, Walter J. Corbly; Sol Hyman, owner of the new Keith-Albee Theater; the State Treasurer and several real estate brokers with whom Lawrence had done business over the past ten years. All testified to his good character and fair dealings. As these men testified, Anna began to feel even better about Lawrence's case. *After all, the only witness the State produced was Mr. Kerr.* Anna knew writing bad checks was wrong, but Lawrence had told her he always made deposits to cover them... maybe they were late, but he always made them. Although she had noticed a juror or two nodding sleepily while President Corbly testified, by the lunch recess she was feeling a bit better. She just wished they had paid closer attention.

Although the Burghers talked of everything but the trial over lunch, it was the only thing on all their minds. They laughed uproariously at one of Eileen's jokes. It was as if ignoring the reason they were eating lunch at the Bon-Ton made it less foreboding. As the afternoon session began, the family nervously returned to their seats. Lawrence was scheduled to testify.

Francis Patrick, following the judge's orders to call his next witness, again carefully removed his coat and hung it on the chair back. He hooked his thumbs in his suspenders and called Lawrence to the stand. Lawrence rose, straightened his coat, took off his glasses and strode to the witness stand. As the bailiff swore him in, Eileen quietly slipped her arm through her mother's and moved imperceptibly closer to her.

In a friendly, inquiring tone attorney Patrick led his client through a recitation of facts about his background: his age, where he grew up, his family status and his career leading up to his position as President of the Railroad Bank & Trust Company. He then asked Lawrence to explain the financial situation at the bank since 1924, which Lawrence did in painstaking detail. The business details of her father's testimony soon bored Margaret. She began to fidget until Sara jabbed her in the ribs with her elbow. Margaret glared at her sister, but she stopped wiggling.

"Mr. Burgher, during this period were you able, at all times, to maintain the legal reserve required by the banking commissioner?"

Lawrence pulled his handkerchief from his hip pocket and wiped his brow. "Not at all times, no. It was often very difficult to maintain."

"And was the banking commissioner aware of this?"

"Absolutely. We had several conversations regarding the problem."

"What was the bank's condition, with respect to the reserve, in early 1927?"

"We were having difficulty maintaining it again. However, in numerous conferences with the banking commissioner, we were led to believe that satisfactory arrangements had been made to keep the legal reserve intact. In April 1927, we were led to believe the bank would not close."

"What sort of arrangements, Mr. Burgher."

"A sizable loan was arranged which would preserve the legal reserve."

"When did you know the bank would be closed?"

"Not until the closing hour of April 14, 1927."

Please tell the court what occurred on that afternoon, Mr. Burgher."

"Very well. I was in my office at the Coal Exchange Building, when I was notified Mr. Kerr was in the bank. This was not unusual. He had been there often, so I went about my business. At the closing hour, Mr. Kerr appeared at my private office to inform me the bank was to be closed. He asked for my keys, allowed me to get my private possessions and escorted me from the bank. As we left, I saw the notice being attached to the doors of the bank."

As Lawrence told the story, Anna remembered her distraught husband on that day. The memory brought sudden tears, but she maintained her composure. Eileen saw the glisten in her mother's eyes however, and squeezed her arm.

"Thank you," Mr. Patrick said. "At the time of the bank's closing, did you have an overdraft?" The attorney scratched his head as if he were puzzled on this point.

Lawrence sighed as if he were sorry it had happened. "Yes, I did happen to have. At that particular time, I had a lot of real estate, for which I had been offered — in the past — fabulous prices. However, at the time I had the offers, I didn't want to sell. As you know, real estate had depreciated substantially by then and I was having a tough time selling anything. Nevertheless, I had one particular piece of real estate and one particular deal pending whereby I was to receive $5,000 cash."

"Was that the only deal you had going at the time the bank closed?"

"No, I was trading off my home. We were planning to move to Pea Ridge. And I had made arrangements with Mr. Edward Keeley to borrow $3,000 which I would have had the next day after the bank closed."

"How did the bank closing affect you, regarding your ability to consummate those deals?"

"Dramatically! Knowing these deals were about to close, I wrote a check on my account in Shapely to cover the overdrafts in Huntington. This would have been covered by a deposit to Shapely with Keeley's money, but that bank was also closed two days later. Therefore, I could not meet the check drawn on Shapely."

"Under what circumstances, Mr. Burgher, were these overdrafts in your Huntington account made?"

"By issuing various checks to pay various indebtedness; interest, curtailment on notes, accounts of one kind and another."

"Made in the usual way? Gave a check, payee would go and have the check cashed?"

"Yes, sir."

"Who was the cashier of the bank at that time?"

"Hershel Tatum."

"Mr. Burgher, did you have any intention, or any purpose to wrongfully deprive this bank of a dollar of its money?"

"Absolutely not! The closing of the bank affected my credit and good name. I was unable to carry through on any deals after that."

"Mr. Burgher, had you overdrafts before this one?"

Lawrence put on his glasses and sat up straighter. He seemed to puff up in size. "Mr. Patrick, over the years I've owned a sizable amount of property — conducted a large real estate business. Overdrafts are common. You do a deal, you know the funds are forthcoming, you write checks to pay your bills and you make deposits. Sometimes the deposits are a little slow and an overdraft occurs. But these amounts are not out of proportion to the business I have done or the funds I'm accustomed to handling. And I've always covered the overdraft — every time!"

"Very well. Each of these was an open transaction, was it? The board of directors knew it, did they? The cashier knew it?"

"Yes sir. It was an open transaction."

"The checks were presented and paid to the cashier by some paying teller, not by you?"

"Yes, sir."

"Just a few more questions, Mr. Burgher." Francis Patrick sounded solicitous of his client's patience. "The ledger sheets Mr. Veeley admitted into evidence — can you say whether they are correct or not?"

"No, I have no knowledge as to their accuracy."

"Fine. And Mr. Burgher, Mr. Tatum, the cashier...does he live here in Huntington?"

"Yes, he does. I believe he was summoned as a witness for the state."

Veeley boomed, "Objection."

"Sustained," came the response from the bench.

Patrick ignored the exchange and continued. "Mr. Burgher, could you look at this document and tell the court what it is?"

Lawrence took a small ledger sheet from his attorney, put his glasses on his nose and read it. Handing it back, he answered confidently. "It is a list of overdrafts in the accounts of some forty different customers of Railroad Bank & Trust."

"Thank you. Please admit this list into evidence," he requested. "Mr. Burgher, one final question. Did you embezzle even one dollar from the Railroad Bank & Trust Company?"

Sara held her breath to be sure she did not miss her father's reply. It seemed to her several minutes passed before he replied. As she waited, she noticed the juror who wore no jacket. He was not watching the witness. Instead, he was staring intently at Sara. Embarrassed, she looked at her lap.

"No sir, I did not," Lawrence answered emphatically.

"Thank you sir; no further questions. Your witness, Mr. Prosecutor."

Although Jacob Veeley, on several occasions, tried to rattle Lawrence with his booming and condescending cross-examination, the only sign of nervousness Anna detected in her husband's manner was the rhythmic sound of his fingers drumming on the chair arm — until the final few questions.

"Mr. Burgher, the fact is you didn't have any money in either account when you wrote those checks, did you?" Prosecutor Veeley sounded downright disgusted at the thought.

Lawrence answered quietly, "No, but...."

Veeley cut him off sharply. "And, as president you knew the condition of the bank and in fact, knew that it was about to close, didn't you?"

"I knew it was in bad condition, but not that it would close."

"In fact, in an effort to cover up your previous offenses, knowing the bank would close, you drew a check on another bank and deposited it to your personal account on the very day the bank closed, didn't you?"

Lawrence spluttered, unsure how to answer. It was like the question, "When did you stop beating your wife?"

Before he could figure out how best to respond, Francis Patrick was on his feet yelling his objection.

"Sustained. Mr. Veeley, restate your question," Judge Calley instructed.

"Never mind. I'll withdraw it. No further questions, your honor." Veeley smiled at the jury as he ambled back to his table.

Lawrence removed his handkerchief and wiped his brow as his attorney approached the stand to make a few final points. Mostly, Patrick reviewed testimony already given; but it was his last chance to leave the jury with a favorable impression of his client. He asked one final series of questions before yielding the floor.

"Mr. Burgher, were you merely an employee of the Railroad Bank & Trust as its president?"

"No sir. I owned $50,000 worth of stock in the bank."

"Then it would be in your own best interest to see that the funds of this bank were protected? To see that no funds were embezzled, correct?"

"Yes, sir. That is correct."

"Thank you, Mr. Burgher. Your honor, the defense rests." Francis Patrick retrieved his coat, put it on and sat back down.

Judge Calley said, "Let's take a fifteen minute recess before we hear the closing arguments." He rapped his gavel and the audience, as if they had been restrained too long, immediately broke into pockets of conversation.

Lawrence seized the moment to come to the rail to speak with his family. After he hugged each of the girls he and Anna spoke quietly to each other until Francis called Lawrence to rejoin him. As Lawrence took his leave, he kissed his wife and held her hand tightly, releasing it only when distance broke his grip.

Judge Calley reappeared, rapped his gavel to reclaim order and called on Prosecutor Veeley to begin final arguments. The imposing looking man rose, gathered a few notes and placed them on the edge of the table. He glowered as he walked toward the jury box. Any juror could have thought the prosecutor was angry with him, personally. But as soon as Veeley began, it was clear that all his anger was directed toward the defendant, Lawrence Burgher.

"Gentlemen of the jury, you have heard several witnesses today, but you need focus only on the testimony of two — Mr. Kerr and Mr. Burgher, who both said essentially the same thing. And that is this — Lawrence Burgher wrote checks when he didn't have any money. That fact is undisputed. You saw the ledgers and Mr. Burgher admits he was overdrawn in both accounts. The question for you to ponder is this: Did he write these checks with the knowledge the bank would close, intending to take money from the Railroad Bank & Trust? The answer is — yes, he did. Lawrence Burgher wasn't a mere depositor of the bank. He was the president — in charge of the bank! He was fully aware, as Mr. Kerr told you, of the bank's condition. Mr. Burgher admits that, too. And yet, he wrote a check for which he had no money, on the very day the bank closed. This was no mere coincidence, gentlemen. He wrote those two checks, timing their deposits to cover up the real condition of his accounts. It's commonly known as kiting.

"Follow this closely, gentlemen. On April 9 he wrote a check on the Huntington bank for $2,800 and deposited it in the Bank of Shapely. This check was paid by the Railroad Bank & Trust and the money was used by Mr. Burgher. He then wrote another check on the same account for the same amount, $2,800, and deposited it in the same way at Shapely. He did this on April 13. However, he had no money in this account, on either date. He was, in fact, overdrawn $3,274.77. Next, to cover up what he had done, he wrote a check on the Bank of Shapely for the very same amount, $2,800, and put it in his account at the Railroad Bank & Trust. Of course, he had no money in that account, either. When did he do this? On the very day he knew the bank would close its doors. And in so doing, he walked away with $2,800 of the bank's money! Clearly, this chain of events shows his intent. Clearly, President Burgher knew precisely what he was doing. Clearly President Burgher is guilty as charged."

Prosecutor Veeley's face was blood red as he returned to his table. His outrage blazed for the twelve men in the jury box. If he wasn't truly angry, it was a damn fine job of acting, Anna thought. She was shocked at his vehemence. She stole an anxious look at Jenny, who managed a tight-lipped smile in return.

Slowly, Francis Patrick approached the box. His manner was altogether different. He affected the very model of reasonableness.

"You know, gentlemen of the jury, Mr. Veeley is right — on one point. You should focus on only the testimony of Mr. Kerr and Mr. Burgher. First of all, Mr. Kerr is the only witness Mr. Veeley had, so you have no choice there. But he clearly testified that he had no personal knowledge as to the accuracy of those ledgers. He merely found them at the bank and read them. Who is to say if they are correct? The state never proved they were correct, did they? No, they did not!

"Both men agreed that Mr. Burgher wrote the two checks in question. Mr. Veeley is right on that point as well. But, do you honestly believe he intended to steal that money? Of course you don't. Witnesses have testified that he is an honest, fair-dealing business man.

After all, he's been out of the city working for over a year...came back here on his own accord to face trial. He had no intention of making off with that $2,800. No, Mr. Burgher intended to make a deposit to cover the $2,800 on Monday, but he could not because Mr. Kerr's office closed that bank as well! Locked it up!

"Mr. Burgher told us of several deals that would have given him the cash to cover all his overdrafts. He'd done the same thing dozens of times in the past. In fact, we probably all have at one time or another. If his story were not true, why didn't the state call Mr. Keeley to refute it? He was right here in the courtroom. Still is, in fact. They didn't call Edward Keeley because Mr. Burgher was telling the truth! If he is guilty of anything, it is merely of writing a check for which he had no funds — a simple misdemeanor. But gentlemen, he is not guilty of the charges of embezzlement or larceny. He was merely caught without sufficient funds when his bank and the Bank of Shapely were closed. Therefore, you must find the defendant, Lawrence Burgher, not guilty!"

Francis Patrick walked the length of the jury box, looking intently at the faces of each man. Their eyes followed him as he went. Satisfied he had made his point, he resumed his seat at the defense table. The silence in the room was palpable. When Judge Calley rapped his gavel, Sara jumped, but it broke the tension. The judge thanked each attorney and turned his attention to the jury, giving them the instructions for their deliberation.

As he dismissed the jury, Eileen let out a long breath. "I think Mr. Patrick gave a very convincing argument, don't you, Mother?" Eileen asked.

"Yes, I do; but Mr. Veeley made your father sound like quite a scoundrel. I suppose we'll just have to pray the jury believes Mr. Patrick. Let's go wait out in the hall. Perhaps it will be cooler there." She wiped her brow with a linen handkerchief and stood to leave.

The family rose and made their way into the narrow hallway, but it was packed with people. As the Burghers walked through the crowd, it seemed to part, giving them room to pass. But, no one spoke to them — in greeting or words of support. In fact, Eileen noticed, conversations stopped and tongues fell silent as her family passed group after group clustered in the corridor. They reached the wrought iron railing circling the four story rotunda in the center of the courthouse and stopped. Margaret first looked up at the decorated dome ceiling, then over the railing at the people below.

"This is making me dizzy," she said. "Mother, can I go outside and watch the squirrels?"

"No, Margaret. I want you to stay right here with us. As soon as the crowd leaves, we'll go sit on the benches outside the courtroom. I imagine your father will join us. I don't want you gone when he does."

"How long do you think the jury will be gone?" asked Sara.

"I'm sure I couldn't begin to guess. Maybe Mr. Patrick will have some idea," Anna replied. It was hard for her to believe she was having a normal conversation about this. It was as if she had developed a life-altering disability with which she would have to cope forever and had grown so accustomed to discussing it, she could do so without crying. Sometimes she thought she was beyond crying ever again; at other times, it was her only response to the burdens she found herself carrying.

Slowly the crowd tired of waiting and descended the marble stairs, their footsteps echoing around the rotunda. When they had gone, Nate marshaled the group back to the hard wooden benches flanking the courtroom doors. As they took their seats, Lawrence and his attorney came toward them from one of the alcoves behind the courtroom. He walked straight to Anna and embraced her, then hugged the girls. Although he was smiling, Anna could see the tension behind his eyes.

Mr. Patrick did not wait for the question he read in their faces. From experience, he knew what they wanted to hear. "Well, I think Lawrence's testimony went very well. And, I think their case is weak. If they had proof, they would have introduced other witnesses — Keeley, for instance. I think we have a good chance. But, I caution you, juries are funny animals. It could go either way. Something Veeley said may have stuck with them. You just never know. However, let me reassure you that in the unlikely case they convict him, we'll appeal. We have that option and we'll take it. So don't worry, all right?"

With a hesitant smile, Anna replied. "All right. It's just so hard to wait knowing your fate is in someone else's hands. How long will they take?"

"Who knows, although, probably not overnight. We should have a verdict before five o'clock," Mr. Patrick replied. "I'm going to let you visit for a while. I'll be back shortly. Don't worry!" With a pat on Lawrence's shoulder, the attorney was gone.

But after he left, there seemed to be nothing to say. They made a few feeble attempts at small talk, but soon lapsed into heavy silence. Anna and Lawrence held hands as they waited. The girls walked the courthouse aimlessly reading signs, legal notices and the names on the glass doors lining the halls. An hour dragged by...then another.

About 4:00 P.M. Mr. Patrick appeared, looking agitated. His red hair looked wind scrambled; his face was flushed. "The jury is back. Lawrence, you need to come with me."

The attorney's demeanor put Anna on edge and she clung to Lawrence. As he kissed her and turned to leave, a cold lump formed in Anna's chest. She swallowed hard and called to Margaret, who was still roaming the rotunda. "Come on, Margaret. The jury is coming back. Let's go in."

Holding hands, the Burghers again took their seats behind Lawrence. Within minutes the courtroom began to fill and the jury returned to the box. Judge Calley entered as the bailiff announced, "All rise."

Anna's hands were clammy as she clutched Jenny's hand on one side and Eileen's on the other. She wanted to smile encouragingly at her girls, but she could not take her eyes off her husband.

Judge Calley wasted no time. He banged the gavel once and addressed the jury.

"Gentlemen of the jury, have you reached a verdict?"

The juror on the far left corner of the box stood. "Yes, sir. We have."

Anna's grip on Jenny and Eileen tightened in anticipation.

"We, the jury, agree and find the defendant guilty as charged in the indictment."

Francis Patrick leapt to his feet as soon as the judge dismissed the jury. The courtroom burst into sound. Chairs scraped as the jurors left the box. The audience buzzed. Brief applause sounded in the rear. Reporters jumped from their seats and ran for the doors.

"Your Honor, move to set aside the verdict and request a new trial...." Patrick began to argue his motion, but his words were partially lost to Anna and her girls.

Margaret cried out, "No! You're wrong! My father is *not* guilty." Sara grabbed her by the shoulders and pulled her close. "Hush, Margaret. Hush." She spoke roughly through her own tears as Margaret began to cry against her.

"...verdict is without sufficient evidence to support it..." came Patrick's voice over the din.

Eileen clutched her mother's arm, fearing she would break down; but Anna was staring at Lawrence through tear-filled eyes. Eileen followed her mother's gaze. She saw her father, still seated at the table. His head was down, his face buried in his arms. The sight of her parents in such terrible pain was too much. Eileen wept openly.

Judge Calley banged the gavel until quiet was restored in his courtroom. "Mr. Patrick, I'll hear your arguments on this motion tomorrow morning at 11 A.M. Court is dismissed." He banged the gavel once more and left the bench.

Thirty-Nine

Saturday, July 6, 1929

lthough it was Saturday, the Burgher family again rose to face the day in court. The routine was the same — Lawrence left early with his attorney; Sam arrived to watch the younger children; Anna and the older girls waited for Nate and Jenny to pick them up. As they waited, Anna reflected on how quickly this morning schedule had become familiar — even oddly comfortable.

But because it was Saturday, the courthouse was much quieter than usual. No clerks bustled up and down the hallways. Today, as the Burghers made their way to the second-floor courtroom, only their footsteps echoed through the marble corridors. Although it was already after 10 A.M., the building seemed cooler, as well. To Sara, it felt like a tomb. She shuddered. Gone, too, was the crowd which had packed the gallery on Wednesday and Friday.

Passing through the double doors, Sara saw only two dozen men, looking more curious than connected to the case, scattered singly or in pairs among the benches. As she spotted a notebook here and there, she wondered if they were all reporters. She whispered to Margaret, "I hope those men don't write a big story about Father for the newspaper. I couldn't stand it if everyone read about us."

Anna saw David near the front and motioned her brood up the aisle to sit with him. They slid into the bench forming a wall of women, flanked protectively on each end by a man — David and Nate.

The open space in front of the rail was also sparsely populated. The jury box was empty. Only a few people, including the court reporter, milled around. Lawrence sat rigidly at the table with Francis Patrick and his assistant. At the prosecutor's table Veeley sat by himself. Like clockwork, at 11 A.M. the bailiff called the meager audience to attention as Judge Calley resumed the bench and banged the court into session.

Francis Patrick rose and came forward to address the judge.

"Your Honor, we wish to enter a motion to set aside the verdict of the jury in this cause and to grant the defendant a new trial on the following grounds. First, we believe the evidence presented by the state's attorney was contrary to the law and insufficient for the verdict. No testimony whatsoever was presented to prove the accuracy of the ledger sheets..." Patrick argued his legal points in such detail, citing decisions in previous cases as precedence, that Anna could tell he had prepared for this possibility in advance. It gave her both a sense of confidence in his acumen and a sense of dread. *He must have thought there was a strong possibility this could happen.*

Patrick continued, further arguing that the instructions given to the jury by Judge Calley — that they should consider Lawrence's intent — were prejudicial to his case. Patrick noted his several objections during the trial to these instructions. He also argued his client was unable to get a fair trial in Cabell County because of the negative sentiment which had formed against him after the bank closed. He requested a new trial be held in another county.

When the defense attorney had finished, Judge Calley spoke only two words. "Motion denied."

"I object and take exception to the ruling, your Honor," Patrick responded. "May it please the court, we further move for an arrest of judgment."

"Motion denied," Judge Calley said once more.

"Again, your Honor, we object and take exception to the ruling."

"So noted. Mr. Patrick, if there was any feeling against Mr. Burgher on the part of the public, it did not develop at this trial. I believe the jury seated in this case was as far removed from the affairs of the bank as any jury that could have been found. I further believe the jury found fairly that the check drawn by the defendant on the Shapely bank was merely a subterfuge to conceal the overdraft in the Railroad Bank & Trust Company. Mr. Burgher himself admitted he had no funds in the Shapely bank.

"Although it is true that Mr. Burgher, as president of the bank, was not the legal custodian of its funds, he stood in the position of a trust officer of the bank and was its manager. As such he controlled its funds. Now, I am frank to say that some of the directors of the bank are not altogether guiltless, if they too, were overdrawn in their accounts. Of course, *they* may not have drawn worthless checks on other banks to cover up overdrafts like Mr. Burgher did.

"The putting in of a fictitious deposit as a subterfuge is a concealment and that act therefore becomes an embezzlement or larceny. The fraudulent intent is shown by his act of drawing a worthless check to cover up his overdraft in the Railroad Bank & Trust Company.

"Therefore, Mr. Patrick, your motions having been presented, argued and denied, do you have anything else to say or offer as to why sentence should not now be pronounced on the defendant?"

"No, your Honor, we do not." For the first time since the trial began, Francis Patrick's voice had lost its tone of utter confidence. He sounded defeated.

Until this moment the five women in the second row had felt sure Francis would prevail and Lawrence would be set free. Now their faces were ashen and drawn. They also looked frightened. Anna's whole body was rigid as if anticipating a severe blow. She held onto Jenny and Eileen with a death grip. Margaret clutched her uncle David's arm. Sara, too, sat bolt upright, looking stoic, but her hands gripped a flowered handkerchief, which she had twisted into knots.

"Will the defendant please rise?"

Lawrence stood with Francis by his side.

"Mr. Burgher, do you have anything further to say or offer as to why sentence should not now be pronounced upon you?" Judge Calley asked.

Lawrence's hand trembled as he reached up to remove his glasses. He shook his head almost imperceptibly, but said nothing.

"Therefore, you are hereby sentenced to confinement in the penitentiary of this state, at Moundsville, West Virginia, for a full period of ten years, as provided by the laws of West Virginia." He banged the gavel once for emphasis.

Lawrence dropped to his seat as though the gavel had struck *him*. He had known from his attorney that the sentence could run from five to ten years. Nevertheless, he was stunned the judge had given him the maximum. Turning toward his family, he saw Sara collapse with a muffled cry and slide, like a lithe sea lion, onto the floor. Anna heard the sound and saw her faint, but could not reach her. She looked helplessly from Sara to Lawrence. Lawrence's face twisted in pain, but he was powerless to help her. She cried out, "David! Sara! She's fainted." But David was already in action. He knelt, wedging his body between the wooden benches and lifted Sara's head onto his knees, slapping her lightly on the cheeks. "Can someone get her a drink of water?" he called.

Judge Calley banged the gavel, trying to restore order as Margaret clamored over her uncle and ran up the aisle, nearly colliding with a deputy sheriff who was approaching with a cup in his hand. Strangers milled around as David took Sara's handkerchief from the floor, dipped it into the cup and wiped her face with the cool cloth. A few moments later she regained consciousness. David helped Sara to her seat while the banging continued. As she became aware of what had happened, Sara began to cry. She cried, not only for her Father, but also for herself. She was mortified she had made such a scene. Before anyone could stop her, Sara suddenly stood, ran up the aisle and fled the courtroom.

Anna, now torn between following Sara and staying with her other daughters, who were equally upset, could not focus on Francis Patrick's next words. She turned to Jenny.

"Could you go see about Sara?" she whispered. With a nod, Jenny deftly slipped past Nate and rushed out. Anna pulled Eileen closer to her right side and motioned for Margaret to take Jenny's place on her left. She wrapped an arm protectively around each crying girl, but Anna's eyes remained dry.

"...of the opinion the said motion is proper, does hereby sustain the motion," Judge Calley was saying.

Anna held her breath, listening for words that would give her back a glimmer of hope.

"Execution of this sentence is stayed for sixty days from today to enable Mr. Burgher and his attorney to prepare an appeal for a Writ of Error and Supersedeas to the judgment of this court, as provided in the Statutes of West Virginia." Judge Calley banged the gavel again.

"Your honor, we request bond be set for Mr. Burgher's appearance before this court at the expiration of the stay," Francis Patrick asked formally.

"Sustained. Bond is set at $10,000.00 conditioned that he make his personal appearance before this court to further answer the judgment. Clerk of Court is hereby authorized to accept said bond. There being no further business to come before the court in this matter, court is adjourned." He banged the gavel with finality, stepped down from the bench and exited the courtroom.

Anna was frozen to her seat. She knew Patrick had planned to appeal, but she hadn't expected Lawrence to have to post another bond. *Dear Lord, where will we get $10,000? We have nothing left. Lawrence is going to jail.* David, however, had risen, walked to the rail and was in deep conversation with Lawrence and his attorney. Anna watched them, perplexed. Shortly, Lawrence came toward his family through the small gate in the rail. Anna released her girls and stood to embrace him. As he reached their pew, all three women moved toward the aisle. Lawrence reached for Anna as Eileen and Margaret reached for him. The quartet clung together.

After a long moment, Lawrence disentangled himself and wiped his eyes. "Anna, David is going to post my bond. We have to go to the clerk's office, but I'll be home shortly. Take the girls home with Nate and Jenny. We'll be there in a little while. It will be all right, my love. Don't lose hope."

Anna managed a weak smile as she wiped her own eyes. "We'll be fine, Lawrence. We'll be fine," she found herself saying.

The following morning the Burgher family went to church. Anna thought about her decision long into the night. She finally concluded it was the right thing to do. Although Lawrence protested, she insisted.

"Lawrence, if we don't go out of this house today — if we stay home from church and hang our heads in shame — we'll never be able to face people."

"Anna, I just can't face them. The story will be in the papers this morning. Everyone will have read it."

"You stay home if you must, but the children and I are going."

Anna wasn't sure how this resolve had formed, but it was there. Now that Lawrence's sentence had been pronounced, she was galvanized into action. Through all the weeks of uncertainty she had been in a state of torpor, unable to think what she would do if he were found guilty. She had always hated not knowing which way things would be decided. On the one hand she had dreaded the outcome of the trial; on the other, waiting was worse than knowing the decision. Now she did know the future. As terrible as it was, she could face it. Instinctively she knew she had to face the music right away, in order for her and her children to go on living in Huntington. People would talk; they always did. But the only way to withstand the talk was to ignore it and go about her business. This much she knew with fierce certainty.

When the children protested, that's exactly what she told them.

"You can heed what they say, but it will begin to make you lose your self-respect. You have no reason to be ashamed. Father's troubles are only money troubles. He didn't do anything wrong, despite the verdict. We'll get through this. You and I are going to church, going to ignore the talk and hold our heads up like always. Remember you are a Burgher. Now go get ready!"

In the end, Lawrence relented. He dressed and drove the family to church. Halfway up the steep steps to the First Presbyterian Church, he stopped short.

"Anna, I can't do this. I don't feel well. You take the children and I'll come back to get you after the service. Please!"

His face was drawn and perspiration beaded across his upper lip.

Anna looked at him, knowing he was not truly ill, merely afraid to face the parishoners; but she did not wish to further embarass her husband.

"Very well," she sighed. We'll meet you out back after church. I hope you feel better." She turned and ushered her family through the arched entrance as Lawrence rushed back down the steps and regained the car.

When Anna and her six children walked down the aisle, it was almost 11 A.M. Heads turned as they slid into their regular pew — seventh from the front, left side — and whispers skittered like brush fires from row to row. A few people nodded and smiled at them with tight lips. Anna met their looks with aplomb. As the organ struck the beginning notes of the processional, she bowed her head in prayer.

Forty

1929–1930

The Monday after the trial, Lawrence returned to his job in Baltimore while Francis Patrick and his partner threw themselves into the frantic preparation of Lawrence's appeal hearing, scheduled for September. In the weeks that followed, life in the Burgher household settled into a lackluster routine. Without Lawrence, Anna's life was hard. She insisted the children pitch in to help with the daily housework, but the worry was hers alone.

Anna knew that the lazy summer days of family picnics by the river, of the children playing "Going to Town" in the gazebo, or the boys banging on garbage can lids behind the plodding burros to make them run faster were gone forever. The burros had been sold. Violin, piano and voice lessons for the girls had been stopped. The piano lay silent. Anna had to insist that chores came first, then the children were allowed to play. She was more protective of them, too. They could ride their bicycles on the sidewalk in front of the house or play games on the porch, but they weren't to go far.

Shortly after the trial, Buddy clashed with the neighborhood bully, Frankie Damron. Buddy had first seen Frankie pushing a skinny kid around at the grocery store and knew he lived in Buddy's block, at the opposite end. He was about fifteen — two years older than Buddy — obese and obnoxious. On the day of their first confrontation, Buddy was riding his bicycle down the sidewalk, unaware that Frankie was watching.

As Buddy reached the end of the block, Frankie yelled from his porch. "Hey, Burglar."

Not realizing he was being called, Buddy ignored him and began to turn his bike around.

Frankie yelled again. "Hey, you! Burglar! Buddy Burglar! Don't you ignore me. I'm calling you."

Buddy stopped in front of Frankie's walk. "My name isn't Burglar, it's Burgher." He thought the bully had just mispronounced his last name.

"Naw. It's Burglar. I heard my daddy talk about your daddy. He stole the bank's money. So, he's a burglar for sure. That makes you a burglar, too. A son-of-a-burglar." He laughed loudly at his own joke and began chanting, "son-of-a-burglar, son-of-a-burglar."

Buddy jumped off his bike and ran toward Frankie's porch, fists raised, ready to fight. "Don't you dare call my father a burglar. You don't know what you're talking about."

Frankie jumped off the porch and met Buddy on the sidewalk. Before the fat boy could assume a fighting stance, Buddy kicked Frankie in the shin then punched him in the stomach. The older boy doubled over, out of breath and in pain. Through his rage, Frankie screamed in a ragged voice. "Just you wait, you son-of-a-bitch. Next time you even come close to my yard, I'm going to run you over with my bike. And then I'm going to beat the crap out of you."

As Frankie struggled to his feet, Buddy jumped on his bike and rode home. He kept the incident to himself. Now, each time Buddy rode his bicycle, the boy lay in wait. It was as if he had radar that signaled whenever Buddy went out of his yard. As soon as Buddy neared Frankie's yard, the boy ran off the porch and rode his bicycle full-speed toward Buddy, threatening to run into him if Buddy continued. Buddy wasn't usually afraid to fight — he'd proven that many times, but this guy was big. Buddy avoided him as much as possible. He either rode his bike in the other direction or stayed home.

With Eileen in summer school at Marshall College, Sara was bored. Now a high school senior, she had little use for her "baby sister" Margaret, who was two years younger and still in junior high school. Sara ignored Margaret most of the time, preferring to read in her room or, more often than not, go out with her friends. She slept overnight with her best friend, Ruth, at least once a week. This infuriated Margaret, but Anna indulged Sara's wishes. After all, Anna understood how hard this whole matter had been on her. Sara had been hoping to go away to college next year, but those plans had been canceled. Anna remembered vividly how disappointed Sara had been at the decision. Her bitter outburst still rang in Anna's ears. "Eileen got everything and now I get nothing. No college, no new clothes. Nothing! It's just not fair." Later of course, Sara had been sorry, but she couldn't take it back.

In late August, one of Lawrence's letters to Anna contained bad news. He spilled it, however, almost as an aside, tucked away to lessen Anna's worry.

Darling,

The heat in Baltimore is stifling with little rain in sight...our appeal was refused by the circuit court. Their order affirmed the conviction and stated there was no error in the lower court's judgment. Of course, I'm disappointed, but Francis and his partner have started on a new appeal to the West Virginia Supreme Court of Appeals. This will be much more detailed and could take months to perfect. Meanwhile, I wish I were with you and the children....

Oh, how she wished the same thing! Each month seemed more difficult than the last. With September approaching, Anna had no idea how to pay for the children's new school clothes. Lawrence's weekly pay check barely covered the essentials. All the smaller children had out-grown their current wardrobe; hand-me-downs would have to do. Buddy, as the oldest boy, had no source of hand-me-downs. He would have to have at least one pair of pants that fit. And, Margaret couldn't fit into Sara's old clothes. She had gained a considerable amount of weight over the summer and was decidedly chubby, while Sara had always been lithe and slim. Anna supposed she would just have to make their clothes; she could afford the fabric if she did without a few personal items. For weeks, she sewed after the children were asleep. Night after night she worked in the stuffy, humid house until she, herself, nearly fell asleep at the sewing machine. Most of the time she was exhausted.

Newspaper accounts of the stock market crash in late October had no immediate effect on Anna. She was more interested in reading about the new Memorial Arch being built at the lower end of Ritter Park. Now and again she heard stories of old friends' husbands who had lost all their investments. Despite the snubbing she had received from many of those same people when Lawrence lost everything, it gave her no pleasure to hear they were now almost as poor as she.

Throughout the long months between the indictment and the trial, Anna gradually had dropped her memberships in various social clubs, remaining active only in the Huntington Women's Club. She was slated to become its president in January. It was an unspoken line of ascension, through four vice presidents' positions to president. She loved this club and looked forward to leading it. On a mid-November day full of the threat of impending winter, the three-member nominating committee came to call. Anna knew this was a mere formality; the nominees were always visited in person before the slate was announced. She opened the door and greeted the chairman warmly.

"Dorothy, what a pleasure to see you, all of you. Do come in. Would you like some tea? If I'd known you were coming today, I'd have made some cookies," Anna said, wiping her hands on her apron. *If I'd known, I would have put on a clean dress.* Dorothy Collier was dressed in a smart black wool coat with a fox collar that nearly covered her face.

"No, thank you, Anna. We can't stay long. We've just come to talk about the club's officers," Dorothy Collier smiled weakly at her companions as if looking for the group's support.

"Yes, I assumed that's why you were here. I'm so excited to think that I will be president of the club next year. Who's to come on as fourth vice president?" Anna asked.

"Anna," Dorothy Collier began hesitantly. "We, that is...the committee, wanted to talk to you about your situation...I mean...whether or not this is a good time...with Lawrence gone and all, won't it be difficult...?" She sighed deeply and looked to the group for help.

"What are you suggesting, Dorothy?" The real purpose of their visit, was beginning to dawn on Anna.

"We think it would be best for you to let Helen Anderson take the president's position this year, pass over you for just one year, until things get sorted out here at home. We know you must have your mind on Lawrence's problems and we think it would be best for everyone if you had fewer outside responsibilities. We hope you understand. We're doing what we think is best — for you, of course," Maime Lewis interjected firmly. She had always been an outspoken woman, not one of Anna's favorites.

Anna's cheeks flamed. She looked at Dorothy incredulously. "Well, of course, I want to do what is best for the club...I hadn't really thought it would be a problem..." Anna trailed off in shock. The women sat for a moment in awkward silence. Finally, Anna spoke again. "Well, I can see that I probably won't have the time to devote to the job, what with having to take care of the children without help. I should have resigned before now, but we've been so busy, I hadn't really thought about it. Please don't give me another thought. I'm sure Helen will be an excellent president."

Now embarrassed, the women dissembled, acted sorry they had mentioned it, tried halfheartedly to take it back; but as Anna rose abruptly, the trio followed suit. She ushered them to the door and said goodbye as quickly as was polite. After the door closed, Anna stood with her back against it. *I can't believe they did that. I thought they were my friends. Now, I embarrass them.* Indignation flooded her body. She ran upstairs to the bathroom, turned on the faucets full-force and cried tears of fury and shame.

By winter Margaret had grown sullen and quarrelsome. She and Buddy fought more than usual; Anna seemed to fuss at her all the time. Just after Thanksgiving, Anna was called to the school to discuss Margaret's deportment. The principal reported incidents of homework not turned in, tardiness to class and name-calling in the halls. Anna was at her wit's end. She decided to confront Margaret, once again. Early Saturday morning, Anna carried a glass of juice to Margaret's bedroom. She sat on the edge of the sleepy girl's bed and kissed her.

"Margaret, I've brought you some juice. Sit up, sweetheart. I want to talk to you." Margaret propped herself up with a pillow and took the juice warily. This wasn't how she usually got her breakfast.

"What is it, Mother? What's wrong?" she asked. A look of panic crossed her face.

"Margaret, I had to go see your principal yesterday. He says you come late to home-room class nearly every day and last week didn't have any of your math assignments. He said when the math teacher, Mrs. Barnett asked why, you just shrugged your shoulders, but wouldn't answer her. I don't like hearing such reports. Just what is going on, Missy?"

Margaret's eyes began to fill, but she didn't answer. Anna continued. "On Friday, did you yell at some boy in the hallway?" Margaret reddened and tried to slide back under the covers, but Anna took her shoulders and looked her straight in the eyes. "Margaret, did you call him a bastard?"

Margaret burst into tears and a torrent of teenage confession. "Mother, you have no idea how awful it is at school. The kids whisper about me whenever I pass by. Some of the girls make fun of me when we undress in gym class. They point at me and giggle. I know they are laughing at my old underwear. I can't stand them. I go to homeroom late so I don't have to talk to them in the halls. I hate school. I can't concentrate on anything, least of all — math. Then, on Friday that awful Frankie Damron, the one that's been threatening Buddy — he called Father a burglar and said Buddy was a son-of-a-burglar. I heard him laughing about it in the hallway and I just couldn't take anymore. I screamed the worst thing I could think of. I screamed, 'You bastard! Don't you dare call my brother names.'" She cried until the bed shook.

Anna held her until she calmed somewhat. "Margaret, I told you not to let what people say bother you, remember? I know it's hard, but you can't scream bad words at them. It doesn't help; you only look as small as they do. Now you are the one in trouble, not him.

Do you understand?"

"I thought you'd be proud of me for standing up for Buddy and Father. But instead, you are angry at me." Margaret began to cry again, but this time it was with the vehemence of indignation, not the pain of ridicule. In fact, Anna was proud of her daughter, but she knew she couldn't admit it. Instead, she had to teach her a better way to handle the ridicule.

"Margaret, I want you to do something. Imagine you have a magic wall. One so thick and tall that mean words or teasing can't get through it or over it. Whenever you hear someone say something to tease you or make fun of your family, you snap your fingers to make the magic wall surround you. Then you can ignore the words, or the pointing, or whatever because the wall will protect you. All the ridicule in the world can't get through. Then you won't have to react. You just hold your head up and go about your business. Can you do that?"

Margaret dried her eyes with the edge of the blankets and sniffed. "I'll try. But if Frankie...."

"No, Margaret, even Frankie can't get through that wall. Understand?"

"All right. But, it hurts so bad when they say things about Father." She looked up at her mother with a tear-stained face. She seemed so pitiful, Anna wanted to cry herself.

"I know it does, sweetheart. But you just have to ignore it. Don't cry. Wash your face and come downstairs. I'll fix cinnamon toast in the oven." As she stood, Anna kissed Margaret on top of the head, retrieved the juice glass from the table and went down to the kitchen.

The Christmas season had brought little joy to the Burghers. Lawrence came home for a few days, bringing bad news and no presents. His job in Baltimore had been reduced to part-time. The stock market crash devastated Bullmoose's real estate development project and Lawrence was no longer needed as a salesman. Bullmoose hadn't laid him off completely because of their friendship, but he only needed him now for clerical help in the office. But as Lawrence told Anna, it was better than nothing; at least he still had a job.

Nevertheless, his downgraded job situation plunged his family deeper into impoverishment. The family was forced to move to a house with cheaper rent. There, the prevailing wind no longer carried the smell of rotting vegetables. Instead, it brought the stench of manure. The two-story brick located a mile farther from town, shared an alley with Huntington's only farrier's shop. Once more, Anna crammed as much of her furniture as possible into the house. The pieces which wouldn't fit, she sold. With one less bedroom, all three older girls were forced to share the one in the finished attic. It was roomy, as their mother cheerfully pointed out; but afforded no privacy, until each girl hung a sheet around her own space and dared the others to enter. As always, Buddy and Stephen gladly shared a room. Libba continued to sleep with her mother.

1930

In February, the State Supreme Court of Appeals denied Lawrence's appeal. They, too, determined that the judgement of the lower court had been properly rendered. Francis Patrick prepared to take the case to the next level — the United States Supreme Court. In his letters, Lawrence still sounded confident, but Anna was beginning to worry more. Not only did she worry about Lawrence's fate, but about how they would survive.

For the first time, Anna worked outside her home. Through Nate, she found a part-time clerk's position at the Zenner-Bradshaw department store, selling handkerchiefs. She worked only two days a week, but it brought in some much-needed income. She did not tell Lawrence. On the days her mother worked, Sara came home immediately after school to watch the smaller children. Usually she didn't mind, but sometimes her patience wore thin. She especially hated being the referee for Buddy and Margaret's increasingly frequent fights. He loved to tease her, especially about her weight and could always make her cry. Libba, on the other hand, was full of laughter. Sara pampered her. At eight, she was still a happy child, relatively oblivious to the hardship the family was suffering. She barely remembered the good times and therefore had no basis for comparison or regret. Often, around Libba, Sara was able to ignore the present for a while and to pretend life had not really changed at all.

As Sara's graduation from Huntington High School neared, one beau began to appear frequently. Sara had always been a popular girl, but fickle. No boy ever lasted more than a few days and she never went with anyone exclusively. But with Charles Landers, dating was different. He came to court Sara every day after school, even on the days she had to watch Libba. And each weekend, they went out. They walked in the park, went to school dances and to an occasional show at Vanity Fair. Chuck's jet black hair and angular jaw gave him an almost aristocratic air. Yet his pleasant manners and easy sense of humor made almost everyone like him instantly. Eileen could see why her younger sister was so smitten.

Forty-One

October 1992

Maggie Malone sat in her car in the parking garage of Sarasota Memorial Hospital staring at the buff block building. She'd been sitting there, with the air conditioning off, long enough for sweat to begin gathering between her breasts, but still she stayed. She dreaded what lay ahead and she could not make herself go inside.

Two weeks ago Maggie's mother, Sara Burgher Landers had broken her hip and had lain on her living room floor for four hours before she was found. Maggie had flown down immediately to be there when her mother had hip replacement surgery. She stayed one week. She was there, but her mother often didn't recognize her — once accusing her of trying to steal her wedding rings. She was there when her mother, in a pain-medication-induced delusion, imagined tiny children playing on the hospital miniblinds. And, mercifully, Maggie was there when Sara finally came to her senses and began to improve.

Now, Sara had been moved to the hospital's rehabilitation unit and Maggie had returned to Sarasota. The most recent daily report from Sara's close friend, Eleanor, had prompted Maggie's hurried flight. Sara was depressed and wouldn't eat. Sara had a long-standing fear of dying in a nursing home, regularly threatening to disown Maggie if she was ever put in one. Now Sara was convinced she had been sent to one. Of course she hadn't, but Maggie was sure her

mother would find a way to blame her for being moved to the rehabilitation unit.

Maggie sighed and took off her linen jacket. It had been a cool
October morning when she left Atlanta. Now it was high noon in
sunny Florida and hot as the hinges of Hades. She got out of the car
and headed toward the building. Maggie hated hospitals. To her, they
were not a place of healing, but of suffering, pain and death. She
often wondered how anyone could work there, day in and day out —
how they could stand all that suffering. Maybe nurses saw it differently. Perhaps they were cheered by the sight of those who regained
health and went home. But for her, a hospital was a place to avoid at
all costs. She would rather take a whipping than be here.

In the hospital corridors, alive with rolling food carts, nurses and
visitors, the familiar medicinal odor hit Maggie's nostrils. To her, it
smelled tinged with blood and urine. Maggie also was struck with
how eerily quiet the corridors were, despite all the activity. It was as
if the volume had been turned down by an unseen remote control.

The sixth floor rehabilitation unit was even more quiet. Maggie
whispered as she asked directions to her mother's room, then felt
silly for doing so. Room 6115 was at the end of the corridor. Maggie
rapped lightly and pushed open the door. Sara lay on her side facing
the window; she did not hear Maggie call to her.

"Mama, are you awake?" Maggie asked softly.

Hearing no response, Maggie rounded the bed to stand in front
of her mother, grateful to see her wearing her own blue silk gown
and robe rather than some hideous hospital fashion. A tray of uneaten food sat near the bed. As Maggie looked down at her mother's
face in repose, something reminded her of one particular youthful
photo she had found in her Aunt Libba's album. In it her mother was
running across the lawn of the yellow brick house by the river. It was
the last smiling photo of the young Sara, Maggie had ever seen. It
must have been taken before her father's troubles were uncovered.
Now, except for the gray hair surrounding the face of the nearly eighty-
year-old woman, Maggie thought her mother looked remarkably
untouched by all she had borne in the intervening years.

Sara's eyes were closed; nevertheless, Maggie laid her hand on her mother's shoulder. At Maggie's touch, Sara started, eyes wide.

"Maggie! You scared me to death!"

"I'm sorry, Mama. Were you sleeping?"

"No, just resting my eyes," she lied. Maggie laughed. It was the standard Landers reply. No one ever admitted they'd been caught napping.

"Did you know your lunch had come?" Maggie asked gently.

"Yes, but I don't want it," Sara said, looking disgusted.

"Mama, you have to eat something. You can't regain your strength if you don't."

As she continued to cajole her mother, Maggie suddenly realized the moment had just passed in which she and her mother had traded roles. In a split second, she had become the parent figure. It nearly brought her to tears, but she continued her good-natured wheedling. Finally, she managed to talk Sara into eating some chocolate pudding. Maggie had to admit the rest of the meal did look pretty unappetizing. *Why on earth do they serve dinner meals at noon? A nice sandwich would be more appealing.* After the tray was removed, the two women visited until an overly cheery nurse came to take Sara for a rehabilitation session. Maggie stood aside while the nurse helped her mother into a wheelchair. She was struck with how frail Sara had become. The woman who had once swum across the Ohio River on a dare now could not lift herself from the bed. It frightened Maggie to think she herself might come to this some day.

She kissed her mother goodbye and left the room with a promise to return at dinnertime. Retracing her steps through the hospital, Maggie suddenly knew the reason she hated coming here. It made her face her mother's mortality, as well as her own. By the time she reached the door to the parking garage, tears blurred her eyes. She welcomed the suffocating blast of heat. She could not wait to feel the sun on her face.

After two more days of the same routine, Maggie sensed she and her mother were about to do battle. Sara continued to pick at her food and Maggie was worn out with arguing about it. After discussing Maggie's work and non-existent love life, they had run out of small talk. She had tried to broach the sensitive subject of a live-in health care provider, but Sara vehemently refused to discuss it. Nursing was not Maggie's strong suit and they were getting on each other's nerves faster than usual. Something, she knew, would have to change.

She arrived the next day with a plan to diffuse the tension. After the half-eaten lunch had been removed, Maggie asked her mother a question. "Mama, tell me the story of how you and daddy got married?"

"Oh, Maggie, I've told you that story a hundred times," her mother said, irritated. "Why do you want to hear it again?"

"I just do. It's a good story and it makes me laugh. I was thinking about you and Daddy today...about your happy marriage...wishing mine could have been like that. Tell me, please?" Maggie asked again.

Sara rose to the bait. She smiled slightly, straightened herself in the bed and began. "Well, you know, we'd only dated for two weeks. But, I knew who Charles Landers was, of course! Everyone in school did. He was president of his class, on the yearbook staff and president of the "Whoo Phlung Dung?" club.

"The what?" Maggie shrieked with glee.

"The 'Who Phlung Dung?' I thought I told you about it. It was one of the social clubs." Sara laughed aloud. "They all had outrageous names that scandalized the teachers, but we thought they were hilarious.

"Anyway, I'd been seeing four or five other boys when he came along. Suddenly, no one else mattered. We dated steady for two weeks right after my graduation. He was home from Millard's school where he had been preparing to go to West Point. He asked me to marry him right away and we eloped before he left at the end of June. Just like that! Of course, we kept it a secret. West Point had two strict rules. Plebes weren't supposed to have a wife or a mustache; so we just had to keep our marriage quiet. Well, I told mother after a month or so, but I swore her to secrecy. Chuck's father would have been so disappointed if he had turned down the appointment." Sara's face had taken on the soft glow of memory. Maggie hadn't seen her mother look this way since her daddy's death three years earlier.

"Where did you go to get married?" Maggie prompted. She knew the answer, but wanted her mother to continue the story.

"To Catlettsburg, Kentucky. It was a beautiful sunny day. Chuck picked me up after classes at Mrs. Wise's Business College. I was wearing a pale yellow linen suit. I remember Mother asking me why I was so dressed up for school.

"We went to the tennis courts in the park, to wait for Helen French and Bill Bradford to finish their match. Of course, they were wearing their tennis outfits, but we didn't care. Your daddy just yelled, 'Get in the car!' and we took off. He had brought a bottle of bathtub gin and we fixed gin-fizzes on the way. Boy, did that stuff burn your throat!

"When we got to the courthouse, we stood in line for our license — the four of us, laughing and cutting up. All of a sudden, we were at the counter and the lady was asking our names. Your daddy got flustered because we couldn't use our real names and hadn't thought ahead to make up fake ones. Maybe the gin-fizz had something to do with it too, because he stammered, then blurted out 'Lancelot... Charles Henry Lancelot.' I had to cover my mouth to keep from laughing out loud. Then it was my turn. I said, 'Mary Sally Allen.' I don't know where that came from, but it's what I said. Maybe I was thinking about getting married, you know? A few years later, when Social Security came along, we realized there was no legal record of our marriage. We had to get married again!" By now, Sara was laughing at her own story, causing Maggie to laugh at her.

"We couldn't have sounded very convincing, but I guess they didn't care. Back then, there wasn't any waiting period or blood tests. We just went to Kentucky to keep it out of the Cabell County records...Chuck's father being sheriff and all. We were married by a Justice of the Peace with Helen and Bill as our witnesses. I'll bet that was a sight they'd never seen...witnesses in tennis garb."

Sara stared dreamily into the distance as if she could still see them standing there. A soft smile settled on her lips. As Maggie smiled along with her mother, she saw the sudden tears which had formed in her eyes. She hadn't meant to cause her Mother pain — quite the contrary. She sprang to her bedside to hug her.

"I'm sorry, Mama. I didn't mean to make you cry," she said soothingly.

"It's OK, Maggs. It's not your fault. I just miss him so. I should have gone first." Sara's face contorted in sorrow.

"No, Mama, you shouldn't have. Don't talk that way. Daddy couldn't have gotten along without you at all. He couldn't even boil water, remember?"

Sara laughed through her tears. "You know, we missed each other so much back then, we wrote each other every single day while he was at West Point."

"Really, Mama? That's so sweet. I didn't know that."

"I numbered the letters and so did he. He brought them home with him. I still have all of them. I reread some of them after he died, but it made me too sad. I had to put them away," Sara said. She settled back into the pillows and closed her eyes. Maggie knew instinctively her mother was through reminiscing, so she left her alone. A few minutes later, Sara was asleep.

It occurred to Maggie as she drove to Longboat Key that the letters her mother had mentioned must have been written at about the time her grandfather had gone to prison. *Surely, Mother would have written to her new husband about her father's departure. If I can't get her to talk about it, maybe I can find out how she felt about it back then. Since those letters are numbered, I can read them, put them back in order and she'll never know.* Maggie grew excited to think, after all these years, she might learn, from her mother's perspective, what had really happened to the family during that time. She had read the facts in the archived records; now she wanted to know how the family had dealt with the tragedy in the hardscrabble day by day.

That evening, after Maggie returned from dinner, she decided to look for the letters. It wasn't prurient interest that drove her from room to room. In fact, she fervently hoped she would not run across a torrid description of her parent's romantic activities. She did not want to think about them actually having sex — she knew they did, of course; she just didn't want to be forced into visualizing it. However, knowing her parents, she doubted either of them would put such intimate details in writing. Instead, Maggie was looking for information about her notorious grandfather — Sara's father.

It was so easy. It took Maggie less than an hour to find the letters. After all, there weren't that many hiding places in the house. However, they weren't hidden in any case. They were stored neatly on the top shelf of a closet in the den in two innocuous boxes — unmarked stationary boxes — that Maggie had seen for years. She'd always assumed they held some of her daddy's treasures, for he was an avid collector of everything — a true pack-rat. When she lifted the lid, she saw the bundles of envelopes, some still tied with a faded ribbon. One large group was held with a new-looking rubber band. *These must be the ones she was reading.* Maggie took the boxes from the shelf and closed the door.

She carried them straight to the dining room table, placed them in the middle and reached for a lid, but hesitated. *If Mother knew I was doing this, she'd kill me.* Quickly, Maggie looked over her shoulder as if expecting to see Sara coming down the hall, then laughed at herself. She stared at the boxes for a long while, until curiosity overcame guilt. She removed one lid and took out the first group of letters. She felt a quick stab of sorrow as she saw her daddy's characteristic scrawl on the address of the first envelope. Numbered **23**, in her mother's hand, it bore the postmark, September 30, 1930. Maggie flipped through the worn envelopes with their red two-cent stamps, until she found the one marked **#1**. It was postmarked New York City, June 30, 1930, 3:30 P.M. The imprinted envelope return address read <u>The New York, New Haven and Hartford Railroad Company</u>, EN ROUTE. *He must have written this one as he left on the train.* Maggie was dying to open it immediately.

Instead, she removed the lid of the second box. It contained more letters than the first. Here she saw her mother's handwriting addressed to *New Cadet Charles Landers, Company D, West Point, NY,* and the numbers neatly penned by her father on the bottom of each envelope. These appeared to be in order, from one to one hundred forty-three. *She* did *write nearly every day during those six months!* Another, vaguely familiar, handwriting appeared on a smaller group of envelopes. Opening one, Maggie saw the letter was signed, "With heaps of love, Mother." *Nana Lander's handwriting...of course. Daddy, you old pack rat, you!* Maggie sat staring at the new found treasure. It was like Stewart Granger's cinematic discovery of King Solomon's mine.

Before she could decide how to begin, the guilt returned. However, she realized it was only the guilt she would feel if she were found out. She knew she must be absolutely certain to put them back in the same order. Her mother's letters would be easy. Before tackling her daddy's and her Nana's, she wrote down the order in which she found the envelopes, by postmark, on a legal pad, then arranged all of them in chronological order. Thus she could replace each group as she had found them — after she had read them all.

The letters were priceless. Maggie couldn't put them down. She read until she was bleary-eyed, took a nap, drank coffee and read some more. The correspondence between her parents consisted, for the most part, of teenage outpourings of love. The letters were deeply tender and agonizingly heartbreaking. The two young lovers wanted nothing more than to be together. Her mother's letters were full of mushy nicknames and lipstick kisses. Their simplicity made Maggie smile. However, tucked among her father's often poetic, lovesick longings for his girlfriend — uh, wife — was a vivid description of the rigorous life of a West Point plebe. He described bracing, "walking the yard" in the stifling heat, having glasses thrown at him during mess while serving as "water steward," hours of shoe polishing and "swimming the Newburg" — a hazing tactic for which upperclassmen could be dismissed if caught administering it to a plebe.

He had drawn sketches of his uniforms and enclosed photos — marked with an X to show his position — of his company in formation. Trips to Army football games, during which the plebes were allowed to remain at ease, he related with great humor. Maggie read with delight her daddy's account of a visit to The Cotton Club, in Harlem, where the cost of dinner was only $2.00.

Sara's letters revealed her daily life was packed, as well. Enrolled in a business course, since college was no longer an option, she nevertheless had time to act like a typical teenager. She attended slumber parties, drove around in cars, hung out at the Bon-Ton listening to the juke box and moping for Chuck. She too, was "so lonesome, she could die," as one song went.

Maggie recalled her mother's stories of her uninterrupted stream of dates, to keep up a facade of single life, while Chuck was gone. Here, in her daily missives, Sara described them in vivid detail. She told her husband of horseback riding and swimming dates; of playing bridge or Russian Rummy; and of all the "Whoo Phlung" and "Hot Feet" club dances. *If I'd been Daddy, I'd have died reading those letters. I'll bet he was jealous as hell.* Of course, Maggie knew her mother had been a very popular girl. *I guess an abrupt halt in her dating habits would have looked very suspicious, but did she have to be so explicit about who she dated and what they did? That seems almost cruel.*

However, under the cheerful reports of daily life, Maggie detected a note of quiet desperation. Clearly Sara wanted Chuck home, but to Maggie it seemed more than that. Little remarks sprinkled throughout the early letters led Maggie to believe her mother's frenetic pace was Sara's way of escaping the harsh reality of life in the Burgher household.

Maggie stared through the picture window into the pitch dark night recalling her cousin Annie's remark that Sara "turned into a Landers," having little to do with her siblings after Chuck returned from West Point. *Maybe this marriage was an escape for Mother. But how could she be certain, in only two weeks of dating, that the marriage would work? Maybe that wasn't important. Folks didn't divorce back then; maybe she just wanted to get out of her house. I must admit, these letters sure sound like someone deeply in love. And, after all, the marriage did last — for over fifty years. And they obviously were deeply in love. Poor Mother. She misses him so badly now!*

As Maggie continued to read, she noticed a change in the letters. In early November, her parents' desire to be together gained a new sense of urgency. Maggie wondered why. After she had read the next few letters, she knew. Word that her father would soon go to prison had apparently been made public and Sara was suffering terribly from both the gossip and the fatalistic air about the Burgher household.

By morning Maggie had read them all — over two hundred letters. Now it was clear to Maggie her daddy had come home from West Point because he couldn't bear to see his beloved Sara suffer without his support. Maggie wept at her discovery. *What irony! He gave up, for Mother, everything he had worked so hard to achieve. At the same time, her father was going to prison because of his blind ambition. It cost him all he ever wanted for his family.* Maggie knew, with certainty, she would never again ask her mother about "Father's troubles."

Forty-Two

November 1930

The November day broke with the morning breath of winter. It was one of those days that makes you want to burrow under the covers, rather than venture outside the warmth of your bed. And that was certainly the case in every bedroom in the Burgher home; no one wanted to face this day. All the appeals had been exhausted; even a plea to the governor for clemency had failed. Three weeks ago, Lawrence had come home from Baltimore to get his affairs in order, in preparation for this day.

Anna and Lawrence had talked until late the night before, gone to bed and tenderly kissed good night, but then had turned away from each other to face their separate nightmares. The distance between them was better measured by the impending separation than by the familiar valley in their double bed. But in the predawn hours, they had come into each other's arms and now they lay together like two spoons. With his left arm over her side, Lawrence held Anna tightly while she gently stroked his forearm. They had lain this way for nearly an hour without speaking. It was the last night they would spend together for ten years and they dreaded dawn. Lawrence stirred about 6 A.M. and Anna clutched his arm almost involuntarily, but he kissed her neck and gently pulled free. "I have to go, love," he whispered into the dark. Anna turned her face to the pillow. She was determined not to let him see her cry. After a moment, when she heard the water running, she blew her nose, pulled herself from the bed, washed her face, and dressed. It was time to wake the children.

On any given Sunday, the Burgher family would have been getting ready for church, but not today. And certainly not this early. Today was different. Today Father was "going away." Anna, still learning the intricacies of doing the cooking herself, was preparing oatmeal, partially because it was easy and partially because everyone liked it. She knew that this family breakfast would be a somber one at best. She wanted to do what she could to lighten the mood. Besides, eggs and bacon were no longer staples on their menu.

"Eileen, would you please see what's keeping the kids?" Anna asked her oldest daughter.

"I just came from upstairs," she said. "The boys are nearly ready. Libba is crying and Margaret won't come out of the bathroom. All she does is yell at me when I tell her breakfast is nearly ready. Sara is trying to make Libba stop crying."

Through clenched teeth, Anna said, "Go back up and tell Margaret that I will not put up with her temper this morning of all mornings. I know it seems like the middle of the night, but see if you can hurry the rest. Sam will be here soon, and they all need to tell their father goodbye."

Within five minutes the entire clan trooped down the stairs like obedient soldiers. Anna didn't question Eileen's enforcement tactics, she was just grateful. After they were seated at the long mahogany table, set with the best linens, pink banded dishes and the good silver, Father spoke.

"I want us to say grace this morning," he said in a low voice. They joined hands as he prayed, "Heavenly Father, bless this food to our use and us to your service. And Father, please watch over my family while I'm away. Amen." Except for the tears which slipped from under some of the tightly closed eyelids, you'd have thought he was leaving on a business trip.

Father's words were more than Margaret could take. "May I be excused?" she blurted out as she rose. Without waiting for an answer, she pounded up the stairs to her room, sobbing loudly as she went.

"Let her go," Father said before Anna could send Eileen after her.

"It's all right. I'll go see her before I leave." Adolescent hunger won out over emotion. The boys ate quickly and were excused. The older girls only picked at their food. Libba had difficulty eating and crying at the same time, though she tried. Consequently, she swallowed and hiccuped, wiping her nose and mouth with one motion. Finally, Anna excused everyone; the older girls cleared the table and went to the kitchen leaving their parents alone to say their private goodbyes before Sam arrived.

Anna moved from the end of the table to sit beside her husband. "Lawrence, I want you to know that despite all that has happened, I believe you are being unjustly punished. I will do everything in my power to continue raising the children to be proud of their father and their family. I love you."

Lawrence did not speak or move for a moment; then he reached out his hand and took hers, saying simply, "Thank you." He folded his napkin, put it in the silver napkin ring and rose from the table. Anna remained seated but her eyes followed his ramrod straight, stoic-looking back as he slowly climbed the stairs to tell his children good-bye.

At 7 A.M. the low pitched doorbell sounded. As Lawrence descended the stairs, his footsteps resonated in the echo like those of a distant New Orleans funeral band. Eileen had already let Sam in by the time her father reached the front hall. Sam stood just inside the door in his gray livery, as he had so many times before. His cap was pulled low on his brow, however, and his remarkable white smile was missing.

"Mistah Burgher, are you ready to go?" Sam asked formally. "I have the car all warmed up."

"Just a moment, Sam. I'll be right there," Lawrence replied. He glanced at his watch.

This exchange had been repeated hundreds of times, but this time, they knew, would be the last.

The private goodbye had been enough for Margaret, but the rest of Lawrence's family gathered in the hall to give him one more fare-well. With choked sobs, Libba had to be pried off her father's neck. He shook hands with the boys and then hugged each one. A kiss on the cheek went to Eileen and Sara, as if he was saving it all for Anna. He took her in his arms, kissed her gently on the lips, then held her at arm's length and looked intently at her face as if to memorize it. He hugged her again. Then he walked out the door without a word. Sam fell in step behind him, opened the black umbrella and held it over Lawrence as they walked down the steps to Sam's secondhand Ford.

The springs in Sam's car needed replacing, so it bounced rhythmically over the brick streets as they drove to the B & O Station. Although the steady rain had slackened to a heavy drizzle, and sun was now backlighting the gray sky, Lawrence didn't notice. He stared at the back of Sam's head, his hands planted on his knees as if trying to keep them from shaking. He had no idea what to expect. *Will they put me in handcuffs? Will anyone be there to see me off?* Absorbed in his own thoughts, he missed the "WELCOME TO HUNTINGTON" sign which had been erected recently in front of the station. In fact, he didn't even realize they had stopped until he heard the squeak of the car door's rusty hinge. Sam stood beside the car with the open umbrella.

Lawrence climbed from the car and stood for a moment watching the city emerge from the fading night sky. Then he turned abruptly and walked into the train station with Sam. Just inside the double wooden doors stood two uniformed West Virginia State Police officers who stepped forward to meet them. As Lawrence put out his hands to accept the handcuffs he feared, he scanned the waiting room to see if he recognized anyone, or more likely if they recognized him.

As the younger of the pair reached for his handcuffs, the older officer shook his head. "That won't be necessary, will it Mr. Burgher?" he said quietly. He looked over his glasses at Lawrence to get his agreement that he would be no flight risk.

"No, sir; it isn't necessary," Lawrence said, chagrined. Six or seven men in heavy overcoats and hats stood talking easily in one corner, their bulging suitcases circling their feet. Lawrence searched each face. He recognized none of them. Several young couples, hands held tightly, knees and shoulders touching, waited on the long slatted benches which stretched down the middle of the station. A mother with three small children stood in the ticket line. She tried vainly to keep the two oldest near her while she jostled her over-bundled crying toddler on one hip.

"I don't recognize anyone," Lawrence murmured, unsure whether he was glad or disappointed. He had thought fleetingly that someone, his lawyer perhaps, would be there to say goodbye. Until the unusual band moved farther into the waiting room, they attracted no notice. But as the police escorted Lawrence across the station, with Sam bringing up the rear, heads were lifted as they passed each group in succession. They stared briefly, then averted their eyes and pretended they hadn't looked at them at all — as if they had been searching the room for someone else. The officers and Lawrence looked straight ahead. Sam tipped his cap in polite deference to each onlooker. The small group strode through the station without stopping. No tickets were necessary; those had been purchased earlier by the officers, and Lawrence had no luggage. Taking a change of clothing to prison was useless.

Out through the matching rear doors and onto the covered platform they moved. Rain dripped from the edge of the metal roof onto the tracks. Lawrence wondered vaguely if he would get wet as he boarded the train. At each end of the block long platform, a tall triple globed lamp threw a watery yellow light on the sidewalk. Single globes of the same pale hue hung evenly spaced under the metal roof, giving an unreal glow to the cold, dreary dawn.

Lawrence couldn't think of anything to say while they waited for the train. He certainly didn't plan to exchange pleasantries with these uniformed men whose job was to escort him to prison. And he was afraid that if he tried to talk to Sam, either he would choke up or Sam would cry. Therefore, he simply stood and watched the rain drip from the platform roof. Periodically, he looked at his watch; not that he was eager for #74 to arrive; rather, it was a career-long habit of punctuality. *7:15 A.M. I guess I don't have to worry about being on time anymore.* In the distance, he heard the train whistle. His stomach churned. Sam heard it as well and came to stand beside Lawrence.

"Mistah Burgher, I know I don't work for you no more, but I'll do what I can to look in on Miss Anna and the children from time to time," he promised.

"I'd appreciate that, Sam," answered Lawrence without looking his way.

The train pulled into the station amid a cloud of steam. Its brakes screeched to a halt, the bell stopped clanging, and the train seemed to settle itself momentarily into the tracks as if to rest before charging ahead. Doors to the Pullman cars opened and uniformed porters deposited step stools while eager passengers formed a line to disembark. Waiting passengers formed a matching line on the platform to take their places. The exchange was made rapidly. The B & O had a good reputation for keeping to its timetable. Lawrence watched as porters pushed great iron-wheeled carts to the train and loaded the mountains of baggage into the belly of each car.

Suddenly, one of the officers said, "Mr. Burgher, it's time to go," as he took Lawrence's elbow. Lawrence paused and turned to face Sam, effectively disengaging the officer's hold.

"Sam, you take care," he said simply. For the first time in their years together, Lawrence put out his hand toward Sam. Sam's smile returned as he shook Lawrence Burgher's hand.

"I'll do that, sir. And you take care of yourself, too," he responded.

Lawrence and the two officers ducked under the curtain of rain and stepped onto the day coach. With watery eyes, Sam watched their progress through the soot-smeared windows of several cars and saw them choose their seats, one officer on the aisle and Lawrence at the station side window. He could not see the other officer. Right on schedule, at 7:35 A.M., the train began to move and Sam raised his hand in case Lawrence could still see him. But through the gray drizzle all Lawrence Burgher could see were the huge white letters — "WELCOME TO HUNTINGTON."

Before going home, Sam returned to the Burgher house "just to check on things." He had composed himself and felt confident that he could face the rest of the family to report on Lawrence's departure. Anna opened the door. Her puffy red eyes told Sam all he needed to know about how she had spent the time since he had been gone.

"Oh Sam, I'm so glad you stopped. Did Lawrence do all right? Was the train on time? Did anyone come to say goodbye?" she asked.

"He did just fine, Miss Anna, just fine. No one at the station even noticed us," he lied, "but none of his friends come down neither."

"Well, it was awfully early and maybe just as well," she rationalized, looking crestfallen. Anna had been making mental excuses for their former friends who had been avoiding Lawrence since his appeals had run out.

"How's the little kids taking it, Miss Anna?" Sam asked kindly. "And is you all right?"

"Eileen and I had a hard time calming them down, but we finally managed. She reminded them that Father had been gone before, when he went to Baltimore, and that we had missed him then, but that he came back. It would be longer this time, she said, but that he would be back. This seemed to satisfy the boys, but Libba is heartbroken. All she knows is that her father is gone, and she really doesn't understand why. I worry most that she'll be nearly grown and won't remember him. He won't allow them to visit, of course. And ten years is a long time for a young child."

"Yes, ma'm. And you, Miss Anna?" he repeated.

"I'll be fine, Sam. Eileen will come over to fix lunch for them while I'm at work, and Sara will come here after school. It's not like we are the only poor people around, so we'll get used to it. We miss you, Sam."

"I give Mistah Burgher my word, I'd do what I can. Might not be much, but I'll stop in, time to time," Sam promised.

"I know you will, Sam. Thank you." Anna took his hand and held it a moment.

This embarrassed Sam. He said, "I'd best be getting on home now." He pulled his hand back and his cap farther over his eyes, opened the door, and left.

Anna went back to the dining room, sat at her place at the table and stared vacantly at the front door. The house was silent, hollow, as if all the life had been sucked out of it. Lawrence's absence was palpable. His things were all still there; even his hair tonic scent lingered. A car door slammed. Anna looked up, eagerly watching for Lawrence to come in the door carrying the Wall Street Journal under his arm. In an instant, reality returned and her face crumpled. He would not return — not for a very long time. She had to figure out how to keep life going for the rest of them. Despite what she had told Sam, she really hadn't thought beyond the daily routines. All she knew was to take one day at a time and pray that things would improve. She put her head on her folded arms and fell into prayer.

Forty-Three

1994

As Maggie's car crawled closer to her destination, over West Virginia roads with more turns than a Slinky, she wondered how long it had taken her grandfather to arrive there by train. She was finally going to see where Lawrence Burgher had spent the last twenty months of his life. Her emotions were as convoluted as the detour she had been forced to take. A lump grew in the pit of her stomach as she visualized herself walking into Moundsville State Penitentiary.

Maggie's curiosity had been piqued a year earlier when she had spoken with Joe Estes, the prison archivist. Yes, he said, he would help Maggie with her research. His manner of speaking told Maggie he took his job seriously. When he said he had worked there for twenty-six years, Maggie imagined him to be in his sixties, tall, graying and with thick glasses. She even had the notion he would wear an eyeshade, like the accountants of the twenties. He had sounded sympathetic and spoke deliberately in response to all her questions. As he talked about the prison, her mind rolled an ugly montage of clips from every prison movie she'd ever seen. *Will Moundsville match my imaginings?* Because the 129-year-old fortress would be closed soon, following federal condemnation, the archivist had suggested that if Maggie planned to visit, she had better do it right away. However, bureaucracy being what it is, a year after the deadline, inmates were still being transferred to the new prison.

The trip had all the earmarks of Murphy's Law in practice. Instead of following an Interstate from the Columbus, Ohio, airport straight to the doors of the Moundsville Penitentiary, Maggie found herself on a two-lane "scenic route." This detour was caused when I-70 broke in several places and collapsed. No one at the car rental desk seemed aware of this startling event, despite the fact that it had swallowed three cars and their passengers; she had been routed straight into the mouth of the asphalt monster. After only three miles on the "official detour," she crested a hill and stared at three more hills, crawling with cars and trucks as far as she could see. *This will never do. The prison will have closed for good before I get there.*

Executing a U-turn Maggie headed south, and found her own "short cut" — a two-lane road reminiscent of her days as a literacy volunteer in rural Appalachia. The woman who suggested it said, "Honey, that road is a little twisty; I know 'cause I drive it ever' day to get to work." That woman should have been crowned the Queen of Understatement. But the view was spectacular, giving Maggie a visual memory book of real mountains for her return to life back in Georgia, where Pine Mountain is regarded as a "big one." *I can certainly see why Congressman Jennings Randolph thought an Interstate through West Virginia was a good idea.*

As she drove, Maggie looked for a phone booth; she needed to let Mr. Estes know she was running late. As she passed a sign that pointed the way to "Cobbler Pat, next left. Boot and shoe repair," she decided that with a sign which pointed back to the previous century, Cobbler Pat might not have too many modern conveniences, so she didn't stop. Just past Barnesville, which looked as if it had been freeze-dried in the 1930s, the long lost interstate reappeared and Maggie stopped at the first rest area to call the prison.

A woman who introduced herself as Pam answered Mr. Estes' extension and much to Maggie's surprise told her that the archivist wasn't coming in today, that he was "out in the field." Maggie's heart went straight to her stomach. *Have I come all the way from Georgia to no avail?* Maggie quickly explained that she had an appointment. Although the secretary thought the appointment was for the following day, she told Maggie to come ahead. Pam offered to meet Maggie if Mr. Estes hadn't returned and agreed to alert the guards to expect her.

Finding the penitentiary was no easier than getting to Moundsville had been. The site was not well marked. As she approached the partially hidden road leading to the prison, Maggie glimpsed massive stone towers behind huge trees. *Oh God, that's it.* The lump in her stomach got larger.

The prison looked just as Maggie had envisioned it; a long, stone building with turrets on each end. It had a parapet roof straight out of the middle ages. As she stared at the walls, she imagined hordes of prisoners throwing rocks or boiling oil over the edge at the guards as they tried to quell a riot. The roughly hewn stones must have been tan at one time, but over time they had blackened. The building exuded a somber tone, despite the sunny spring day. Maggie felt her mood darken. The walls and towers stood in stark contrast to the clear blue sky above and to the cheery white frame houses across the street. She parked the car. *How would it feel to live across the street from the prison? Would you be afraid or would you wonder about the inmates' lives before they became your neighbor?* She could remember as a child going to the courthouse to meet her father and seeing the prisoners in the yard of the county jail. Each time she had wondered what they had done and how they could stand living in just one room day in and day out. Now Maggie faced the stark reality that her own grandfather had done just that. More painfully still, she was about to see exactly where and under what conditions he had spent his last few months of life.

Maggie introduced herself to the guard, and explained that Pam was expecting her. Two uniformed and armed guards opened the gates of the prison without hesitation. Maggie walked in, carrying a camera and tape recorder, for Pam had explained that Maggie was writing an article on the closing of the prison. After signing in at the outside caged area, she was escorted into the family waiting room and met by a female officer. She directed Maggie to the restroom where she was searched for contraband. *Did they do this to my grandfather? I'm sure they must have.*

Following this small humiliation, Maggie was introduced to Pam.

While they waited for Mr. Estes to return, Maggie talked with Pam about the penal system in West Virginia. She discovered that Pam's views on the prison system had changed since she came to work there six month earlier.

"I used to think if a person was in jail here, he got what he deserved, he needed to be here; but I don't feel that way now," she said. "There are too many who are just like you and me, but they've made a mistake. Some of them made big mistakes, but...I also think there are some people here who don't belong here. Some belong in a mental institution and some, I'm convinced, are not guilty. They may not have had a fine lawyer or much money to put up a good defense, so they ended up here." Maggie nodded. She thought of her grandfather proclaiming his innocence to the end.

Mr. Estes arrived. This was no sixty-something Ichabod Crane with gray skin. Instead, he was average height, couch potato chubby and jolly. His plain brown suit could have come from Men's Warehouse or Target. He greeted Maggie with a smile and joked with Pam before escorting his visitor upstairs to his office.

The steel-barred doors to the prison proper opened electronically after Mr. Estes put his hand under a black light. This means of security was relatively new; the word STAFF was visible only under the light. The archivist's office on the second floor had a low ceiling, with standard issue government steel desks, squeaky chairs and rusting, bedraggled file cabinets. For relief, the walls were covered with cheerful murals of West Virginia scenes. Although most of the records had been moved to the new prison, the office still looked chock-full of paperwork. Mr. Estes claimed it was nearly empty, but he had trouble finding the documents he wanted to show Maggie.

As he rummaged through his desk, Maggie spotted a book labeled DEATH BOOK and asked to look at it. Turning the worn pages, which listed every person who died there and the cause, she looked for that familiar name, *Richard Lawrence Burgher*. And there it was, at the top of a page; he was one of the few who hadn't died of tuberculosis in that year. Maggie ran her fingers over the words as if to imprint them on her heart, to make a physical connection with the grandfather she had never known.

Curiously, the DEATH BOOK did not list the cause of his death. So Maggie remarked to Mr. Estes, "One of the newspaper articles chronicling his death, said that the 'unsanitary and deplorable conditions in the penitentiary' had been partially responsible. He was a six foot tall, robust man when he came here and twenty months later he was dead. Sounds like they could have been right." Estes didn't deny, nor did he corroborate, that there could be some truth to her allegation.

As they left Mr. Estes' office to begin a tour of the facility, the pair passed a small group of inmates, trustees who had not been transferred to the new facility yet, on their way to lunch. A more scruffy bunch of men Maggie had never seen in one place. *Is this what one begins to look like after a while in here, despite what you looked like on the outside?* They walked downstairs and out into the prison yard. All she could see was sparse grass, stone walls and the blue sky beckoning from beyond. The prison walls inside the yard were blacker yet than those facing the outside. In answer to her quizzical look, Mr. Estes enlightened her; years of pigeon poop, he said, not a dramatic fire was responsible for darkening the walls.

Now in the yard, facing the administration building in the center of the prison, the North Hall, which would have been the entire prison in the 1920s, was to the right; the newer South Hall to the left. They walked to the right and entered the old cellblock. The metal doors were rusty with peeling white paint. The cellblock contained rows of about eighty cells each; it was four stories high with the same number of cells back to back. Maggie walked into an empty cell which contained one cot and one toilet. There was no furniture and no room for any, if a prisoner had been allowed to bring some. The walls were covered with the remnants of graffiti left by bitter inmates. *A thousand prisoners were housed in each hall. Two thousand restless, bored people.* A long caged area running the length of the cell block reminded Maggie of a dog run except that the top was covered with wire mesh like the sides. The same wire mesh ceiling divided each floor of the cellblock from the one below.

They walked past endless empty cells; about halfway down the row, Mr. Estes pointed to one and said, "Here we are." Maggie walked in and tried to imagine her grandfather living in this dingy space for nearly two years. She could see where the top bunk used to hang from chains in the walls. But she couldn't make herself sit on the remaining lower steel cot or ask Mr. Estes to shut the door. Two men lived in that closet. There was no window, no chair, no table. Nothing but that bunkbed, a toilet and what was now a stainless steel sink, but back then was porcelain. Even with the freedom guaranteed by the open cell door, Maggie felt the despair that her bank president grandfather must have felt as the door closed behind him. She sensed the total desperation he must have known as he faced the next ten years.

Forty-Four

November 30, 1930

The distance between Huntington and Moundsville, West Virginia was approximately 240 miles. That certainly wasn't the farthest Lawrence had been from home, but it might as well have been. The world he entered that night was as different from the one he had left in the morning as civilian life is from the military. The daily routines of life were the same, but he was no longer in charge of when or where he did them.

At the Moundsville station, a smaller, less prosperous looking version of Huntington's, the trio stepped off the train into the same weather they had left in Huntington. It was light, of course, but still cold and rainy. Within minutes of stepping onto the wooden platform, they were met by two men in olive drab overcoats who shook hands with the state policemen, but not with Lawrence.

"I'm Officer Murray," the older of the pair said, by way of introduction, "and this is Deputy Calhoun."

"Pleasure," said the policeman who had sat by Lawrence during the trip, shaking hands. Nodding his head toward Lawrence, he said, "This is prisoner Burgher. I 'spose you knowed that though, didn't you?" He laughed at himself foolishly. Formal introductions between prisoner and guard were unusual, but Lawrence had been allowed to turn himself in, had been given an escort, and had not been required to wear handcuffs, so at least some acknowledgement of Lawrence seemed proper to Murray. However, Lawrence noticed that mostly the prison officials spoke *about* him, rather than *to* him. Suddenly he realized that he had become an object — a prisoner — rather than a person.

In front of the station a black panel truck with "West Virginia State Penitentiary" stenciled grandly in gold on the doors sat at the curb. Lawrence swallowed hard. Deputy Calhoun opened the rear door, motioning him to get in. The drive to the prison was short; through the drizzle, Lawrence could see that the narrow road wound out of town, away from the river and up a hill through a residential area. They made a quick left turn between two rows of neat houses. *Surely the prison isn't in this neighborhood.* He had pictured a great fortress on a hill surrounded by iron fences. He wasn't far wrong.

At the far end of the street, throwing a shadow across the single family houses on the opposite side, stood the brown, stone prison, home to one thousand men and about ninety women. Set apart from its neighbors by a menacing iron fence, its chiseled face looked cold, austere and forbidding to the passenger in the back.

Dear Lord, help me endure this, Lawrence prayed as the car stopped in front of the four-story administration building. It was the stone fortress of his nightmare; huge columns set off the arched front porch. To the left was the actual prison, complete with iron bars at the windows, a medieval looking roof line and a watchtower at the end.

At a signal from Officer Murray, a guard stepped from his iron cage in the fence and unlocked the outer gate. Lawrence was escorted inside the yard and up the short steps to the prison porch. The handsomely carved, arched double doors were nearly hidden by the iron gate which was its Siamese twin. But Lawrence could not focus on their beauty; he saw only the bars. Here, yet another guard stood watch. They all looked alike to Lawrence in their heavy woolen pants, jackets and billed caps. He also noticed that each one carried a long black club.

The second guard unlocked the iron gate and Officer Murray pulled open the massive wooden door. The anteroom into which they stepped was small; at least it seemed small. A massive wheel-like cage in the center took up most of the space. To the right another guard sat behind a small wooden table. Officer Murray halted there and greeted the man.

"Hello Collins, we need to do an intake," he said, handing a folder of paperwork to him.

"Can do," Collins replied as he straightened the single stack of cards on the desk. "Have a seat, there." He motioned to a straight-backed metal chair on the opposite side of his table. Picking up one of the cards, he put it in the typewriter on his left, flipped open the folder and officiously began to type on the intake card. After a few minutes, he stopped and asked Lawrence a question.

"It says here your date of conviction was July 5, 1929. Is that right?"

"That's right," replied Lawrence.

Collins looked up at Lawrence quizzically.

"And you were sentenced the next day?"

"Yes, July 6; that's correct."

"And today is November 9, 19 and 30? Took you a while to git here, didn't it?" he said sarcastically. He laughed at his own joke, but no one else did, especially not Lawrence.

Lawrence started to explain about the appeals, but Murray shook his head and said, "Don't pay him no mind. He thinks he's a comedian."

"And just how long you plannin' on staying?" he continued in his facetious tone.

"My sentence is for ten years," he replied as if this was a conversation between two acquaintances.

"Ever been here before? Or anywheres else?"

"No."

"Nationality?"

"American"

"And where were you born?"

"In West Virginia."

"What was your occupation?"

"I was in real estate," Lawrence replied. "And banking," he added in a lower voice. But the guard was already typing his first response and didn't add "banking."

"You got a religious preference?"

"I'm Presbyterian."

"How about relatives?"

"I have a wife in Huntington and a brother David. He lives in Beckley."

"Are you much of a drinker?"

"Not really, just on social occasions." Collins typed TEMPERATE.

"Smoke?"

"Yes."

"Did you bring any personal belongings?"

"I just have my watch and $20."

Collins stuck out his hand. "Give it to me. We'll log it in and you'll get it back when you leave."

He turned the typewriter wheel and the curled card popped out. Lawrence thought they were finished, and started to stand; but Collins turned the card over and inserted it again.

"Step over there on them scales." Collins continued to talk and type as Lawrence did as he was told.

"How old are you?"

"I'm forty-eight."

Mumbling to himself, Collins said, "Medium complexion, black hair." Then he asked, "Got any scars?"

"None to speak of," replied Lawrence.

"Any medical problems?"

"No, none."

"What color are your eyes?"

"Brown."

"Are your teeth your own?"

"Yes."

"Murray, sing out that height and weight," Collins called across the room.

"5 feet 11 inches and 188 pounds."

"You can step down now," Murray told Lawrence.

He came back toward the wooden chair, but stopped when he saw that Collins was again popping the white card out of the type-writer. He reverse curled it across the edge of the table to flatten it and stood up. "Come with me," said Collins.

He led Lawrence across the room to a painted white square on the algae green walls and handed him a card that read **18764**.

"Hold this at your chest," he said picking up a camera.

Suddenly, the significance of this order struck Lawrence. The busy work of completing the forms had distracted him briefly from the purpose behind it, but this brought him back to reality.

My God, that's my prisoner number. Please, dear Lord, give me the strength to get through this day.

The formalities over, he was handed a small stack of neatly folded clothes and shown to a curtained area. Behind it his legs trembled as he stepped out of his pinstriped pants. He took a deep breath and braced himself against the rear wall to keep from falling. A new guard abruptly drew back the curtains and stepped inside the small cubicle.

"Hold it. We have to search you before you put on those clothes."

He approached Lawrence. "Open your mouth." He peered inside his mouth and then in his ears. "Bend over and spread your legs." Lawrence colored deeply and thought he would faint. When he had completed his strip search, the guard left as abruptly as he arrived — as though this were his only duty.

When Lawrence emerged, he looked smaller than before, as if he had shed part of his stature along with his suit, tie and silk shirt. Standing in the anteroom in the striped prison uniform, he felt greatly diminished. It was as if he no longer mattered at all. *Now I look just like all the rest of them.*

Murray motioned Lawrence toward the huge round steel cage. Dubbed "The Wheel," it was an ingenious contraption because it could not be operated by those who entered it. Instead it operated on a belt system in the floor, much like a streetcar turn-around. It was completely controlled by a guard in another small cubicle.

Lawrence and Murray stepped inside and Collins closed the door. Since it was Sunday evening and he was the only intake guard on duty, he not only performed the clerical tasks; but operated the wheel as well. With a metallic clank and a low grinding sound, the cage turned 180 degrees. A guard inside the prison proper unlocked the opposite steel door and Lawrence stepped into the washed-out green waiting room of the North Hall. It was empty, except for several rows of battered tables with benches drawn up tightly under the edges; but it smelled as if it were full of week-old dirty laundry.

Murray pointed across the room to another barred door. "This is where I leave you," he said. In the next breath he yelled, "Guard."

A guard taller than Lawrence and at least fifty pounds heavier abruptly appeared on the other side of the bars, as if he had been waiting for the call.

"New prisoner," said Murray. "Burgher. Number 18764. Cell Block C. Number 89."

"I'll take him from here," said the new escort. He opened the gate.

Before Lawrence could turn around, Murray had disappeared back into the wheel. As the gears ground again, Lawrence looked back at the new guard, who said, "Follow me."

Into a maze of narrow green concrete corridors, steel girders and thick wire mesh fencing they plunged. Their footsteps echoed loudly with each cadenced stride, until they reached the cellblock itself. Here the cacophony of men's shouts, flushing toilets, banging steel doors and rattling cups drowned out their steps and assaulted Lawrence's ears like the crescendoing roar of an unexpected freight train. He stopped momentarily, frozen to the spot, and looked up. Wire mesh surrounded him. It was above his head and on his left and as far as he could see, cells were on his right. More wire mesh covered these cages, except for the small square openings at about waist height, through which hands protruded periodically. Only the concrete floor was free of the cage material. The area to his left looked like a dog run and he wondered what or who used it.

Is this what a canary feels like? The question flitted through Lawrence's mind, which was refusing to accept his new reality.

Single bulbs dimly lit their way past the endless cells. In some doorways, faces of men anticipated his approach.

Disembodied voices shouted at his passage, "New man on the block. New man on the block."

He shuddered, but looked straight ahead; his jaw set in a strong resolve not to react. He knew that within minutes, he too would be in one of those cages, his freedom gone. And he feared the unknown man with whom he would share that cell. He was filled with loathing at the dirty surroundings and with terror in contemplation of spending the next ten years in this hellhole. His steps slowed. He moved more to the center of the corridor to avoid the cage on one side and the reaching hands on the other.

Finally, the guard stopped in front of a cell, reached into his pocket and pulled out a great wad of keys. He flipped one after another over the ring until he found the key he wanted. He inserted it and unlocked cell 89, addressing its occupant as the door swung open.

"Bledsoe, meet your new roommate, Lawrence Burgher," the escort said from outside the cell. At the same time, he motioned for Lawrence to go in, which he did without a word. Frazier Bledsoe got up from the bunk and slowly walked to one side of the cell, inspecting the man who was going to take up precious space in his small home. Lawrence stood in the middle of the cell, enduring the man's scrutiny, not knowing what to do or what was expected of him. As the cell door banged shut, Lawrence turned around to meet his roommate who was now ignoring Lawrence.

Frazier Bledsoe was a small wiry man of about sixty-five. His pockmarked face looked out through glasses as thick as the base of a Coke bottle. His lank, dishwater blond hair flopped over one eye. As the deputy put his keys away, Bledsoe stepped toward the door.

"Aw, Warner, I just gotten used to having the whole thang to myself," Bledsoe complained. "Cain't you put him in with someone else?"

"Shut up, Bledsoe. He's assigned here and I don't want you bitching about it," the guard barked and walked away, leaving Bledsoe and Lawrence together.

As Bledsoe continued to call to the retreating Officer Warner, Lawrence looked around the cell. Bledsoe had clearly established the lower bunk as his domain. That left Lawrence no choice but to take the top. On the steel wall near the head of Bledsoe's cot were taped a photograph of a woman with several half grown children and a card with hearts covering the front. At the head of Lawrence's bed, small squares of bare steel shone where layers of paint had been pulled away as other pictures went home with their owners. On his bunk, Lawrence could see a small lumpy pillow, a stack of sheets and a thin gray blanket. Although he was nearly as tall as the cell, he was sure he would have to step on Bledsoe's cot to make up his bed. *He isn't going to like this.*

Inspecting the rest of the cell, he saw with revulsion the toilet and sink that occupied the other side of the five foot wide area. The sink hung from the wall between the beds and a toilet that had no lid and no movable seat. The longer he stood in the confining space thinking about his total lack of privacy, the more he noticed the not so faint smell of urine. He thought he would be sick.

Swallowing hard to keep from vomiting, he spoke to Bledsoe. "Excuse me, but if I'm to make up my bed, I'll have to step on the edge of your cot. May I?" he asked, in a manner out of place in his new surroundings.

Bledsoe turned away from the bars and replied sullenly, "I reckon you'll have to, but I don't like it none. Take off your shoes, so's you don't get my blanket dirty." Lawrence obliged and placed them neatly at the end of the stacked metal beds. Standing on the cold concrete floor in his stocking feet, he looked for secure footing on Bledsoe's bed, stepped in the middle and began arranging the sheets and blanket. Because he hadn't made his own bed since he was a boy, he wasn't very good at it. Finally, he gave up and simply smoothed one sheet over the thin mattress and left the rest in a heap at the foot of the bed. As he stepped back onto the floor, he saw Bledsoe leaning against the bars watching him struggle with the chore.

"Burgher, is it? Like hamburger?" Bledsoe chuckled.

"Yes, Lawrence Burgher," he answered as he retied his shoes.

"Well, fresh meat, what'd you do? Or are you innocent like the rest of us?" Bledsoe's upper lip curled in a jeer.

"I was convicted of embezzlement, but I really didn't...."

Bledsoe cut him off. "Oh bullshit, hamburger, they all say that. Ain't a guilty man in this shit hole."

Lawrence didn't want to pursue this conversation. He tried to move away from Bledsoe. With a shock he realized there was no escape — no place to go and nowhere to sit except on the cots. He removed his shoes again and with a questioning look toward Bledsoe, climbed up. Once he was situated on the upper bunk, his legs dangling over the side, Lawrence had to hunch over and lean forward to keep from hitting his head on the steel ceiling. It would be impossible to sit that way for long, he realized. *My back will be killing me.* A picture of his favorite wing-back chair by the fireplace formed in his mind, but he dismissed it before it could grow into a full painful memory. He swung his feet up and lay back on the bed staring at the dirt swirls on the ceiling. The bright single bulb over the sink threw a prostrate silhouette on the wall.

"Does that light stay on all the time?" he asked Bledsoe, although he didn't really want to get him started again.

"No, it goes out when they call for 'lights out'," Bledsoe answered from below.

"When is that?" Lawrence asked.

"Ten o'clock," came the answer.

"Do you know what time it is now?"

"About 9:15, I'd guess."

Lawrence was silent. *Oh my God, I've only been here two hours. And only a little earlier today, I was a free man. How am I going to stand this? I'll go crazy cooped up in here.* His stomach growled loudly and he realized that he hadn't eaten since lunch on the train. Turning his back to the lightbulb, he tried to ignore his sudden hunger and his growing despair. He had no pictures, nothing to remind him of his family. *How long can I hold onto my memories in this godforsaken place?* In his mind's eye he saw Anna's face as he had held it between his hands that morning. *If I can hold onto this, I can hold onto my sanity.* With her face firmly in place, he was able to shut out the light, the acrid smells, the noises, and his hard bed. He fell asleep before "lights out."

Forty-Five

November 10, 1930

At the sudden, rude alarm bell Lawrence was jerked into wakefulness. He sat bolt upright in the dark, completely disoriented. *Where am I? What is that horrible noise? A fire truck? It must be the middle of the night. Why is it dark? I know, Anna forgot to leave the bathroom light on. Where is she?*

Then it hit him. He fell back on his lumpy prison issue pillow on the narrow upper bunk; quick tears stung his sleep matted eyes. As he turned toward the wall, hoping to go back to sleep and find it was a bad dream, the prison was flooded with light. With the flick of a remote switch, his cell went from impenetrable dark to a shadow-throwing half-light that barely illuminated its dingy details. In the distance, he heard a guard approaching from the far end of the cell block, running his wooden "persuasion" stick along the cell bars. "Get up you lazy bastards," the guard repeated over and over. This was his morning greeting.

Lawrence sat up again. He was unsure what to do next. *Do I dress and go to breakfast? Where do we bathe? Do we bathe?* Below him, dressed only in his skivvies, Bledsoe was gathering up his towel and soap and putting on his shoes. As Lawrence had fallen asleep in his clothes, he had only to put on his shoes to be ready for the day. *What do I do in here all day?* He realized, however, that he didn't have a towel or soap of his own. *Should I have brought toiletries from home?*

"Will they give me soap and towels, Bledsoe?" he asked.

"Yeah, I seem to recollect they do when your turn come for the showers," Bledsoe offered.

"When is that?" Lawrence asked.

"Well, you're lucky. Today is our turn. Don't get a shower ever' day. Just twicet a week. Ours is Monday and Thursday."

Lawrence could hardly believe what he was hearing. He hadn't skipped a daily shower or bath since he was a small boy. *No wonder this place stinks. That's disgusting. I can't stand it.*

"Where are the showers?"

"Down at the end of the cellblock. They's a whole row of them."

Before Lawrence could carry this line of questioning any further, the guard returned, unlocking cells along the way.

"All right, you bastards, line up. Put your towel and soap on your heads. You know the routine. It's your turn to clean your filthy bodies."

Since Lawrence *didn't* know the routine, he decided to follow Bledsoe's example, although Bledsoe hadn't actually offered to show him anything. He fell in line behind his cellmate and started toward the open cell door.

"Where you going in those clothes, son?" The guard blocked his way with his night stick.

"To the showers," Lawrence replied logically. *Isn't that where he had just ordered them to go?*

"Then you'd better strip to your skivvies. No place to hang them clothes out there. And you sure want them to stay dry, don't you?"

"Yes sir," Lawrence answered quickly as he turned to take off his prison stripes. "Sir, I don't have soap or a towel. Will there be some in the shower room?"

"Shower room?" he guffawed. "There ain't a shower room, as such, son. But I reckon the guard in charge down there will be able to find you some soap." He jerked his thumb in the direction the line of men were walking.

Lawrence shivered. He stepped into the cold concrete walled corridor and followed the guard to the far end of the cellblock. As he neared the open area he could hear the comingled sounds of splashing water and men's voices. Stepping around the corner, Lawrence saw eight or ten naked men standing in a line to the left and ten or twelve more washing under the shower heads that protruded from the end wall. He tried to avert his eyes, modesty being his nature, but he found himself staring in disbelief. This was not a shower room at all. It was simply the public area of the cellblock. And here were nearly two dozen men openly bathing or waiting to do so with no apparent sense of their exposure to anyone who walked by. Tables and chairs dotted the dry area. If you were so inclined, you could sit there and watch the mass showering or ignore it and play cards as the naked parade passed by. Lawrence was appalled. He hadn't seen another man completely naked since his college days. The thought of exposing himself to such scrutiny was as embarrassing as seeing others do it. At least in college there had been an actual shower room.

"Hang your skivvies on those hooks, son," another guard instructed. "Here's your towel and soap. Don't lose them. Soap's dear."

Lawrence glanced around. But he knew that finding a private spot in which to undress was futile. He quickly stepped out of his shorts and wrapped the skimpy rough towel around his waist. It barely covered him. *If I just stare at the wall, I can get through this.* The line moved quickly. Lawrence stepped into the harsh shower, shut his eyes and let the tepid water cascade over his head. He bathed as quickly as possible, trying to put out of his mind the queue of men awaiting their turn. The soap stung his skin and smelled vaguely like chemicals. He recalled wistfully the round bar of English Yardley soap he was accustomed to using. Mild and faintly scented, its fragrance matched his after-shave. That too, was a luxury of the past. *What about shaving? They certainly won't give us razors. I can't abide a beard.* Calls of "hurry up, we're freezing our asses" snapped him out of his own thoughts. He stepped out of the shower, picked up the towel he'd left on the stool and began to dry off.

"Move to the right, buddy," yelled a man waiting to get to Lawrence's shower head. Now Lawrence could see the pattern: enter from the left; take the next available shower head; shower quickly and step into the open area on the right to dry; return to the left for your skivvies; put them on and go back to your cell. The whole routine took only a few minutes. Lawrence was in the habit of a leisurely and deliberate toilet. It was often the most productive time to contemplate vexing problems. Now he just wanted to get through this nightmare. If he had a problem to solve now, he certainly couldn't do it with two dozen pairs of eyes and an overhead guard with a drawn rifle watching his every move. He reached for a pair of shorts; but quickly realizing they weren't his, drew back his hand as if to avoid being burned. The idea of handling the underwear of other men made him nauseous. He glanced at the other inmates. He hoped none had seen his mistake. Satisfied that he hadn't been seen, he looked more carefully, found his own shorts and quickly put them on his still damp body.

"Enjoy your shower, Hamburger?" sneered Bledsoe as Lawrence reentered the cell.

"It was just fine," Lawrence lied. "How do we shave?"

"You don't. You gets shaved when you gets a haircut. That's usually oncet a month, give or take. Beards sprout like weeds in here."

I'll look just like the rest of these men. It's degrading. These are common criminals. I'm not. Just then his stomach growled. He remembered he hadn't eaten since noon yesterday.

"Bledsoe, do we eat in our cells or is there a dining room?"

"After everyone is all clean and pretty smelling, we'll go to the dining hall. The other cell blocks, the ones who don't shower today — they's eating now."

"Then what?" continued Lawrence.

"Then nothing. Well, nothing for you. Most of us work; but you ain't got a job yet, so you just gonna come back here and sit."

"I'm not used to sitting. Don't think I can do it. I've got to do something. How do we get a job?"

"Oh, they ain't gonna let you have a job till they see if you kin be trusted. All new men stay in their cells, so's they can be watched very carefully. See that guard up there?" Bledsoe jerked his head upward to indicate the portly guard on the upper level of the caged corridor. The guard was walking slowly up and down watching the scene below with feigned lack of interest. This seeming nonchalance was belied by the drawn rifle held loosely at his side.

"Yes," Lawrence replied. "I noticed him when I went to take my shower."

"Well, his only job is to keep an eye on us. Him and his replacements. He's called 'Doggy' 'cause of his huge ears. See 'em? Never seen ears so big on a man."

For the first time since he left home, Lawrence laughed. They were the biggest human ears he'd ever seen as well and the ears did make the man look like a hound dog — a fat hound dog at that.

"Does he keep that rifle drawn all the time?" Lawrence seemed to be asking as many questions as a three-year-old.

"Sure does. They's some crazy folks in here. Fights break out all the time. He can push a button and help just swarms in here. Or he puts that rifle to his shoulder — that calms 'em down too."

"Has he ever shot anyone?"

"Not since I've been here, but I heard tell he did about five years ago. Some guy started a ruckus in the shower line. Just went nuts and was choking another man. Doggy hollered and warned him, but the man didn't pay no mind. Shot him in the leg and busted it. Man turned the other fella loose then."

Twenty minutes later the guard, whose only name for the men seemed to be "bastard," returned. He again unlocked cells as he commanded, "All right, you bastards, let's go have breakfast."

Lawrence joined the line of prisoners in the corridor. Like a sheep following the bellwether, he too, placed his hands on his head and trudged along. Last night he had followed such a maze of corridors that he had no way of knowing where in the prison his cell was located or in what direction he was now headed. This bothered him immensely. He felt he needed, somehow, to have a connection with the rest of the world; even if it was simply to know where he fit into the universally orienting directions — north, south, east or west. He had no sense of time, either, and this was equally disconcerting. The artificial morning light signaled the beginning of his day. But was it dawn — or somewhat earlier? He hadn't seen any windows yet. *If I can just see outside, maybe I can tell where the sun is. And if I can see the sun, I'll know approximately what time it really is.* Although the seasons of the sun had ruled his life as a young boy on his father's farm, his adult life had been attuned more to pocket watches and appointment books.

The noise of the open mess hall assaulted Lawrence as he melted into the existing chow line. Uniformed kitchen staff wearing greasy striped caps banged metal plates of food and tin cups of coffee on trays held out by the prisoners. Crude metal flatware rattled with each action.

Lawrence glanced around the room looking for an empty space at one of the long metal tables. All he could see were identically striped backs, which only varied in girth or height, hunched protectively over trays of food. They looked like striped dogs guarding their bones. The undercurrent of conversation, creating a dull roar, was punctuated periodically with raucous bursts of laughter. The laughter faded quickly. The low roar never stopped.

Now Lawrence held out his tray. He felt like a boy at prep school. The metal plate jumped as the trustee tossed it on the tray. At the next station, a tin cup brimming with coffee appeared and sloshed onto the tray as it joined the plate. Lawrence stared at the plate. It held two pieces of browned bread and a bowl of watery oatmeal. *Is this toast? No butter? No bacon? No jam?* His mind instantly pictured Millie, his former cook, serving thick, steaming oatmeal with a huge dollop of butter in the center and the table at home set with snowy white linens, crystal jam pots and Anna's silver bacon tray full of the crisp, curly strips. *Now that's breakfast — not this gruel. I doubt even Oliver Twist would have asked for more of this.*

Spotting an empty place on the far right bench, Lawrence moved to sit down.

"Thet seat's taken," snarled a rail-thin man left of the seat.

"Pardon me," Lawrence stammered, coloring deeply. He was not used to rejection or rudeness. He felt deeply embarrassed. He moved farther down the table and squeezed into another vacancy without incident. He stared at the sloshing bowl of oatmeal, again. *I don't know if I can eat this.* However, he reasoned that he'd get nothing else until noon, and his hunger proved stronger than his queasiness; so he ate. *At least the coffee is hot and strong.* He washed down each mouthful of food with a swallow from the tin cup.

No lingering over breakfast to read the paper. Lawrence watched others rise and take their trays to the end of the room. He could see that each inmate was responsible for cleaning off his own tray. *Empty food into the trash and put the dishes in an enamel pan. Flatware in one tub; cups in another. Stack the trays.*

A grim-faced guard at the door reminded him to "put your hands on your head, son." *I guess we always walk like this. Hidden hands are dangerous hands.* The prisoners from his cellblock were herded back to their cells. Now Lawrence could see the gray November light seeping into the prison from small barred windows high above the upper catwalk. *It's just now dawn. They sure start the day early. What on earth will I do hour after hour? I wonder if we ever go outside? I sure would like a cigarette.*

Stepping back into his cell, he saw that it was empty. Bledsoe had not yet returned. With a sudden urgency, Lawrence realized that he needed to use the toilet. *Thank God, I'm alone.* He dropped his pants and sat down, hoping no one would walk by his cell. Before he could finish, Bledsoe appeared outside the cell. The accompanying guard unlocked it and Bledsoe entered as if Lawrence weren't even there; as if it was common to walk in on a man seated on the commode. Mortified to be interrupted in the middle of a bowel movement, Lawrence yelled, almost involuntarily, "Do you mind, Bledsoe?"

"Mind what?" he replied, nonplused. "Hamburger, you'd better get used to taking a shit before God and everybody. Ain't no privacy in this hell hole." But he did busy himself with something on his bunk, allowing Lawrence to finish with what little dignity he could muster.

Soon Bledsoe was gone again; this time to go to work. Lawrence was left alone — or as alone as he could be in the noisy cell block. He hadn't been there twenty-four hours, but instinctively he realized that it would always be this loud. He climbed up to his bunk and stared at the wall. *What on earth will I do? I've nothing to read, nothing to write on, no job. Am I meant to just lie here and contemplate my sins? A person could go crazy with only his own thoughts for company.* But with nothing else to do, his mind did reflect on those very issues. It hurt to think of his family left alone to survive both the personal poverty caused by his actions and the overwhelming economic depression that was sweeping the nation. *What have I done? Nothing that Keeley didn't do. Maybe I should have said that. But if I had, he could have brought up all the other things I did. If Keeley had testified, he'd have made me look like a criminal. Then, the jury would never have believed I didn't mean to embezzle the money. No, better I kept Keeley out of it. But, oh God, did my family have to suffer too? If I keep this up, I'll lose my mind.*

Lawrence jumped down from his bunk and began pacing back and forth in the narrow space. It only took three steps to cover the length of his cell. *Maybe I can get some paper to write a letter to Anna.*

"Guard, guard," called Lawrence. "How do I get writing paper?"

"Shut up down there," snarled Doggy.

This is hopeless. Oh Lord, what am I going to do? He climbed back up to his bed and turned his face to the blank wall. He tried to shut out the omnipresent undercurrent of noise.

Christmas Day, 1930

My Darling Lawrence,

How do I write to you today? While I know I should be offering you encouragement, knowing that your Christmas must be just horrible, I cannot find any encouraging words. I know I should fill my letter with funny anecdotes of the children's holiday activities, but nothing seems amusing. My heart breaks for you and for all of us. Christmas without you seemed not worth celebrating. Nevertheless, **_Merry Christmas from all of us!_**

We had a small family dinner last night with Jenny and Nate. Sam came by to bring gifts to the children. Wasn't that thoughtful? How he could afford them I have no idea, although he is working steadily. This morning the children opened the gifts I had made them...mostly clothes. I put an orange in the toe of each stocking, which seemed to please them, too. I bought them with the extra money I made selling Christmas cards. They were especially happy with the letter you sent each one. They promised to write to you in response.

Sara's new beau was here a little while ago. He's home for the holidays from West Point and looked quite handsome in his uniform. I think she's very much in love with this one. Do you remember, his father was recently elected State Senator? Charles seems to think his father will go far in politics. I know he is considered an honorable man, for all that matters in politics.

Take care and write soon,
Your loving wife,

Moundsville, West Va
January 20, 1931

Anna, my love,

So, our little Sara ran off and married her beau! Well, I hope she knows what she is doing! I can't imagine how they ever thought they could keep such a secret for four years. What does his father have to say about Charles leaving West Point? I'm sure he wasn't at all happy about it.

David came to see me yesterday with all sorts of news. The embezzlement charges in Wyoming County against him and Edward Keeley have been dropped because the prosecution failed to act on them in a timely fashion. Since a new prosecutor was elected in the fall, (a man from our party) no one seems eager to try the case. The judge ruled that it had been too long since the indictment to try it. Seems strange doesn't it? Of course, I'm glad for David; but Edward should have had to answer a few questions himself, in my opinion. David also told me Keeley had been named to the list of Who's Who in Coal in America for 1930.

David has a new job now. He's been named bookkeeper of St. Luke's Hospital in Bluefield. He plans to move from Shapely right away. I hope he likes the new position, although it isn't so different from what he had been doing at the bank.

We had a bit of excitement here last week. Two fellows tried to escape. They made dummies from long underwear, stuffed them with old clothes and leaves and covered them with their blankets. They were trying to look as though they were asleep, when all the time they were crawling through an eighty-foot tunnel they had fashioned to the street out front. They had been planning this escape for well over a year. They saved hair from the barber shop to make wigs, which they pasted on the "bodies." The night guard who patrolled that part of the prison said his count was right, but of course it wasn't. They fired him after the escapees were caught trying to catch a train to Parkersburg.

Give all the children a hug and kiss for me and keep an armful for yourself, my love.

Your,

Lawrence

Forty-Six

Spring 1931

Spring arrived with a sweet relief which caught Anna off guard. Just when she thought she would scream if she saw another snowflake, the tender green tree fuzz began to coat the hillsides. Since girlhood, that fresh new color — chartreuse, they called it — had caused Anna a tiny pinprick of pain when it first appeared on the mountains. And yet, at the same time, she found it soft and tender as the back of a baby's neck. She could never express the feeling properly; but to her, it was bittersweet. *Spring is like childbirth —* she had decided, after she became a woman — *both painful and sweet, all mixed together. And you always forget the feeling — until the next time.*

Then the riot of azaleas and dogwood burst forth in a frothy pink and white foam on lawns around the city. There may have been a depression going on, but Mother Nature wasn't having any part of it. It was one of the most beautiful springs Anna could recall.

On an April afternoon redolent with lilac and new-mown grass, Libba, now in the third grade, arrived home from school to find her house dark, the curtains drawn, and her mother prone on the sofa with a cloth over her eyes. Without thinking, she flipped the light switch.

"Turn it off," her mother yelped. Hearing the urgency in Anna's voice, Libba did as she was told, then ran to her mother's side.

"What's wrong, Mother? Why aren't you at work?" Libba asked in a small voice.

"I have a terrible headache. That's all. Do me a favor and bring me a fresh cool cloth, will you? And walk softly, Libba. Don't run." Anna managed a wan smile at her youngest daughter. She did not want to alarm her.

Before Libba could tip-toe into the kitchen, the front door banged open. Stephen bolted through it and headed up the stairs. Foolishly, Libba yelled, "Be quiet, Stephen. Mother is sick." He ignored his little sister and kept going. Libba returned to her mother and placed the cloth on her head.

"Is that better?" she asked anxiously. It frightened her to see her mother so still. Anna was usually a whirling dervish of activity. She had to be. With Sara married and gone from the house, Anna had all she could do to maintain the house for her five children and hold down a part-time job. Eileen helped when she could; but with graduation from Marshall College approaching, she was busy studying for her final examinations and tutoring children part-time, as well.

"Much better, sweetie. Thank you. Before you go out to play, would you do one more thing? Call your aunt Jenny and ask her to come over. You remember the number? 27217." Anna closed her eyes and replaced the cloth, trusting Libba to do as she was asked. Libba looked at her mother for a long time, then with a small lump of fear in her throat, made the call.

Thirty minutes later, from her perch on the front porch ledge, Libba saw Aunt Jenny's car pull to the curb. Jenny rushed up the steps, gave Libba a reassuring hug and went inside.

"Anna, what is it? Libba says you have an awful headache. She says you've been here all day." Jenny spoke as she approached the sofa. She sat on its edge and took her sister's hand.

Anna removed the cloth, raised herself slightly, and tried to look at Jenny. She could not focus on her face. "Jenny, it's the worst headache I've ever had. I can't even see straight. I've been having headaches off and on for about three weeks, but they never last all day. Usually, if I take something, they go away by mid-morning. But today, nothing I did helped. I tried BC headache powders, cold cloths, a dark room, but nothing worked. I feel like my head is in a vise. And it throbs like there's a hammer inside keeping time with each heartbeat. The worst part is, sometimes my eyes won't focus. And if I try really hard, I get so dizzy, I'm afraid I'll faint. That's why I haven't moved..." She stopped talking, clearly dizzy, fell back on the sofa and replaced the cloth on her eyes.

"Anna, if I had to face your life every morning, I'd awaken with a headache, too," Jenny tried to joke. "Seriously, have you eaten anything today? Sometimes if I don't eat enough, I get a headache."

From behind her washcloth mask, Anna replied. "I had some tea and toast this morning."

"Well, they can't be too serious if they usually go away by taking a BC. Come on, I'll help you get up to bed and I'll take Libba and Stephen home with me. You can rest and maybe get some sleep. You'll feel better in the morning, I'm sure."

The next day Anna did feel better. However, over the coming weeks, though she had no other excruciating attacks, the headaches became more frequent. She began keeping a notebook, noting when they occurred and their duration; she also began experimenting with her own treatments. She tried sleeping propped up in bed, hoping the pressure would not build up in her head. She tried taking a BC as soon as she arose, hoping to avert the onset of the throbbing. Nothing worked. Each day she had another bout with the vise-like pressure and the pounding. Gradually she became very concerned, but none of this did she convey in her letters to Lawrence.

To Anna, almost overwhelmed with the daily chores and a job, the headaches were a terrible inconvenience, as well as painful. It made her angry to have to stop to rest. In the evenings, she was trying to make over a dress for Eileen's graduation, since buying or making a new one was out of the question. But because she could only work for a brief period before her eyes blurred and she had to lie down, Anna feared she would be unable to finish the dress on time.

And to top it all, Eileen had become engaged and was talking about a summer wedding soon after graduation. Anna was happy for her and she liked Harold Ellis well enough. But at night she couldn't sleep and worried that she simply didn't have the strength to do it all. *Maybe Jenny is right. Maybe I do worry too much. Maybe that is why I have these headaches.* However, in the cold light of morning, she knew it was something more than just worry. After two months of daily headaches, she finally made an appointment with Dr. Baer, the family physician.

Dr. Baer's examination ruled out high blood pressure and failing eyesight as possible causes of Anna's headaches, but he came to no conclusive diagnosis. He too, suggested she might have too much on her mind, although he didn't actually think that was the primary cause, only a contributing factor. In passing, he mentioned the remote possibility of a tumor; but like everyone else, felt that was unlikely, since BC powders usually lessened the symptoms. Instead, he prescribed a stronger pain medication, if Anna found it necessary. He told her to continue keeping her log of frequency, duration and severity and scheduled another appointment in two weeks.

Before Anna could return to see Dr. Baer, however, she had two more debilitating headache attacks — one right after another. Even the prescription pain killers didn't stop them. She missed work for two days and the department store let her go. There were plenty of people who needed jobs, they said, people who could be there every day. Anna was devastated and nearly at wit's end. "It was just as well," Jenny had told her; "You need your strength to battle those headaches." "But how will we buy groceries," Anna had retorted. To this, Jenny had no answer. She and Nate, and virtually everyone they knew, were struggling to buy their own groceries.

When Anna returned to Dr. Baer's, Eileen went with her. While Anna had not had one of the blinding headache attacks for three days, she admitted to Eileen that the vise-like feeling and its accompanying throb seemed worse. She had found herself resting on the sofa more often, as well. Therefore, Eileen did not want her mother to drive. In truth, Eileen also wanted to be certain her mother asked to see another doctor, if Dr. Baer still had no diagnosis. As the elevator reached the tenth floor of the First Huntington National Bank building, she said as much. "Mother, if Dr. Baer can't find out what's wrong with you, don't you think you should see someone else —

maybe a specialist?"

"Specialist in what? Headaches? Don't be silly. Besides we couldn't afford another doctor. Dr. Baer has been our friend for years. He understands and doesn't mind waiting for his fee, but some specialist will want to be paid right away," Anna replied dismissively.

Eileen did not have to insist on sending her mother to another doctor. Dr. Baer admitted he was stumped and referred Anna to Dr. William Holbrook, Huntington's only neurologist. Although Eileen could see her mother was frightened when they left Dr. Baer's office, Anna insisted there was no money for a specialist, which was true, and refused to make an appointment. Moreover, she emphatically instructed Eileen to tell no one, not even her father, that Dr. Baer was deeply concerned.

Eileen pleaded. "Mother, you just can't *ignore* this. The headaches are getting worse; you have to admit that. *Please* go to see Dr. Holbrook. If you don't agree to go, I won't promise to keep quiet. I'll tell the other children and Father." She was vehement. Over Anna's objections, Eileen made the appointment.

A week after Eileen's graduation, which Anna was too sick to attend, the two of them rode the elevator to the top of the West Virginia Building to the offices of Dr. Holbrook. From its waiting room, his suite of offices offered an unobstructed view of the Ohio River. Eileen immediately was reminded of the same scene, albeit a few miles east, she used to enjoy from her old bedroom in the house on Staunton Road. With a twinge of regret, she pulled her eyes away from the river and surveyed the other people in the waiting room. Surprisingly, no one looked sick. It struck her as odd. Then she looked at her mother, who looked just fine, too. Eileen, of course, realized there were many medical conditions that weren't as obvious as a case of mumps. She chuckled at her own foolishness, then sobered at the seriousness of why they were here.

After they'd waited thirty minutes, a stalwart-looking nurse appeared in the doorway and called to Anna. Eileen escorted her mother toward the examination room as if she were the parent. Dr. Holbrook was as short and round as Dr. Baer was tall and lean. His pudgy hands seemed to Eileen incapable of reconnecting the tiny nerves in a person's body. She wondered idly if he had an assistant, with tiny, delicate fingers, who did his surgery for him. As Anna showed Dr. Holbrook her notebook and told him of the occasional blinding attacks, the daily pressure and pounding in her head and the periodic blurred vision, he listened without interruption.

"Mrs. Burgher, when Dr. Baer told me about your symptoms, he asked if they might indicate what is called a 'migraine headache.' But you aren't nauseated, are you?"

"Not usually. Sometimes, if I get really dizzy while trying to focus, I am slightly nauseated. But I never vomit. I hate to vomit!" Anna winced at the thought.

Dr. Holbrook laughed. "Me, too," he confessed.

"Let me look at you," he said soothingly. The doctor rolled his stool closer to Anna, seated on the tall examining table. He performed all the perfunctory tests — listened to her heart and chest, took her blood pressure, thumped her knees with a rubber hammer, causing a satisfactory jerk in her lower legs, and took her temperature. All tests, he reported, were normal. Then, removing a black scope-like instrument from his coat pocket, he used it to look deeply into Anna's eyes. First he examined the right eye, then the left. He frowned and reexamined the right. Dr. Holbrook rolled back slightly, replaced the scope in his pocket and took Anna's hands in his.

"Mrs. Burgher, do you feel the pressure more on one side than the other?"

"Well, yes, sort of. It seems worse on the right side. Why?"

"Your pupils are unevenly dilated. That suggests something may be pressing on the optic nerve on one side. I believe it may be a tumor...."

Eileen's blood ran cold as Dr. Holbrook continued to talk calmly to her mother. *Oh, my God! No! How can he be so calm? He's telling my mother she has a brain tumor. Oh, God, this can't be happening. Please no!* Eileen tried to shut out the monstrous words as she jumped up from her seat to comfort her mother. However, the doctor was between them and she could not get close enough to touch her. Instead, Eileen tried to steady herself on the metal stand beside the examining table, but it began to roll. So, she pressed her back against the wall while Dr. Holbrook's voice echoed in her ears as if he suddenly was speaking from another room.

"...if that's what it is, the only effective treatment is surgery. Of course, surgery would be out of the question here in Huntington. We've not performed any brain surgeries here...yet. You'd need to go to Johns Hopkins in Baltimore, if surgery became necessary. For now, let's get you some stronger pain medication and watch what happens. If it is a tumor, and it doesn't grow rapidly, you may be able to withstand it with medication. On the other hand, if it does, surgery will be your only option. So, if the symptoms get worse, call me immediately. I'd like to see you again in a month, in any case, okay?"

He patted Anna's hand and flashed a reassuring smile at both of them as he left to see the next patient. However, Eileen had seen the concern in his eyes. She knew he was trying, in his gentle way, to prepare them for the worst. In her heart, Eileen also knew she would not be having a summer wedding...not this year.

Anna was visibly shaken as they left the office. Eileen put her arm around her mother's shoulder as the pair walked numbly toward the elevator. Neither woman said a word. Both were wrapped in their own frightening thoughts.

Finally, Anna broke the silence. "Eileen, don't say a word to the other children. Promise?"

"Mother, how can you keep this a secret? They all knew you were going to the doctor. What do you plan to tell them? What about Father? Aren't you going to write him?" Eileen asked incredulously. But Anna did not answer. Mother and daughter rode home in total silence.

That evening, Anna prepared and served dinner like a robot. Eileen, heeding her mother's warning, said nothing about their visit to the doctor, but she could hardly eat. Mercifully, the other children, absorbed in their own lives, didn't ask. But apparently Jenny had not forgotten the appointment. After dinner, as Anna was watching the sunset from the cool front porch, she appeared and insisted on hearing the doctor's report. When Anna calmly told her what the doctor suspected, Jenny was dumbfounded.

"Anna, how can you be so calm? This could be very serious," she said softly. Jenny was nearly in tears and could not understand her sister's demeanor.

"I don't think it has truly sunken in. I can't make myself believe what he said. With all that has happened, how can one more thing go wrong? Surely, it isn't true!"

"Anna, honey, you can't ignore the possibility. If it is true, you have to decide what you will do. You can't wait until...How would your family survive without you? You have to do all you can to get well, even if it means going to Baltimore for surgery."

"How do you expect this family to pay for me to go anywhere — for treatment or for surgery? I couldn't even pay Dr. Holbrook today. Brain surgery is for rich people — not poor ones. I'm just going to have to tough it out. Besides, maybe he's wrong. Or if he is right, maybe it won't grow. I'm just not going to worry. I have too much to do. I'll take one day at a time; it's all I can do." Anna sounded like she was trying to convince herself as well as her sister.

"And how about Lawrence? Surely you will tell him!" Jenny asked gently.

"Probably not. It would only worry him. After all, what can he do from Moundsville? This is something I've got to handle by myself, Jenny," she said with finality. Jenny had never seen Anna so determined.

But that night, alone in the summer-sticky bed, Anna's resolve melted. She was frightened beyond reason and totally unsure of what to do. *Jenny is right. If I don't seek treatment, I could die. I saw that in Dr. Holbrook's eyes. Then what would become of my children? But where on earth would we get the money? Oh, God, what am I going to do? If I tell Lawrence, he'll only worry himself sick, but I must. Oh God, please have mercy on me and my family. It says in your Holy Word that You never give us more than we can bear, so please give me the strength to bear this, too.*

As Anna prayed, she began to cry. Fear, pain and self-pity joined to wrack her body with huge sobs. She covered her head with a pillow to muffle the sound; but Eileen, in her room down the hall, still could hear the tortured sounds.

June, 13, 1931

My Darling Lawrence,

How on earth do I write this letter? How I wish I were there to talk with you in person, for the news I have to share is not good. Lawrence, my dearest, I have been having severe headaches for the past few months. Dr. Baer was not able to diagnose the cause, so he sent me to Dr. Holbrook, the neurologist here in town. Dr. Holbrook feels fairly certain I have a brain tumor. He thinks the pressure I feel is caused by the tumor pressing my brain against my skull. He has given me some strong pain medication which helps, but he believes I should have surgery to try to remove the tumor.

Oh, Lawrence, I don't want to worry you, but I am so frightened. Whatever shall I do? I know there is no money for such an operation, but Dr. Holbrook indicated that surgery might be my only hope, if the tumor grows. The children don't know, except for Eileen, but I can tell that my headache spells scare them as well.

Eileen has organized them into helping with the housework, so I can rest more often, That has been a big help. Jenny also comes over often to take the little kids to play. Eileen postponed her wedding, even though I objected. In the long run, perhaps it will be best.

Please try not to worry, darling. It will only make you heartsick. I only wish we were together to comfort one another. But it is not possible, so we will have to manage alone. I love you,

Yours always,

Moundsville, West Va
June 26, 1931

David Burgher, Bookkeeper
St. Luke's Hospital
Bluefield, West Virginia

Dear David,

     I certainly enjoyed your visit last week. I know it is a tiresome trip and I appreciate you for making it as often as you do.

     I seem to be asking for your help quite a lot lately and regret finding myself in the position of having to do so yet again. However, this time it is for my family that I write. Anna has written me with terrible news. She has been suffering greatly with severe headaches over the past several months. Finally, they were so painful she went to see our family doctor who, when he could not find the cause, sent her to a neurosurgeon. The specialist, Dr. Holbrook, fears there is a tumor.

     It gives me such grief not to be with Anna at this time, that I find it difficult even to write with a steady hand; but I must ask if you could see your way clear to help my family financially. Because of the headaches, Anna is no longer able to work. Eileen contributes what she can, and Buddy puts in his paper route money, but they don't have enough to eat, I fear. Can you check on Anna and see if there is anything at all you can do in my stead to help? I will be so grateful if you will look after her from time to time. I'm nearly sick myself with worry and in agony that I cannot be there with her.

        Your loving brother,

        Lawr

Moundsville, West Va
July 23, 1931

Samuel L. Vandelind
323 Pratt Street
Baltimore, Maryland

Dear Bullmoose,

How is the real estate business in these hard times? I hope you are still making a go of the development. Your last letter sounded somewhat encouraging. Perhaps the worst is over in the bigger cities.

My dear friend, I am faced with a situation more desperate than I have yet faced, despite all I have been through these last few years. My beloved wife, Anna, has been suffering from a brain tumor these past five months. Recently the neurosurgeon in Huntington said the only chance she has for survival is to have the tumor removed. Unfortunately, such delicate surgery is out of the question there. He has recommended she go to Johns Hopkins, in your fair city, where colleagues of a Dr. Cushing are performing such surgery fairly often. Apparently Dr. Cushing is famous for some of his discoveries and techniques and is highly regarded in the field.

As you, of all people, are fully aware, there is no possibility of our being able to pay for such expensive treatment, but I fear without it, Anna will die. Do you know anyone who could get Anna admitted, either as a charity case, or through private means, so she can be properly treated? I am loathe to ask this of you, but am desperate for the future of my family and the life of my beloved wife.

I remain very truly yours,

Forty-Seven

August 1931

T he pink light of Sunday morning was just beginning to silhouette the night-black trees when the Model-A Ford, reached
the edge of the city and bounced north along the Ohio River
Road. Sam was driving, resplendent in his old gray chauffeur's uniform and cap. Eileen, who had been up for hours fixing the basket of
food now stored in the trunk, rode in the back seat with Margaret,
while Buddy slept up front next to Sam. It was far too early for the
teenager to be fully awake on a summer morning, even if the occasion was a trip to see Father.

Father had been at Moundsville for almost eight months and none
of the family, except his brother David, had been to see him. This
rule, however, had been Father's own. He did not want Anna or his
children to see him in that place. On that score, he had been adamant. Nevertheless, last Monday, Eileen had suddenly announced
she was going to see Father. Margaret, not wanting to be left out, had
begged to go along.

While Eileen's announcement sounded impulsive, her decision
was not. For the past month, she'd noticed a steady decline in her
mother's health. The headaches were more severe, lasted longer, and
put Anna out of commission more often. To Eileen, Mother seemed
thinner, as well. She knew Father had written to Bullmoose for help
in getting Mother into Johns Hopkins, but so far, no trip was scheduled — or was even being discussed.

Although Eileen would never admit it to anyone, she was frightened. Very frightened. Lately, she had felt herself sliding down a
gradual slope into an abyss from which there was no return. She
even had dreamed about it several times and awakened, crying in
terror. Now, she felt a desperate need to see her father, to get his
advice, to be told "everything will be all right."

When Buddy heard of the possible day-trip, he joined Margaret
in cajoling Eileen to be included, claiming his rights as the oldest
son. Eileen, however, suspected Buddy's love of adventure was more
than likely his motivation, rather than his sense of filial devotion.
Even Sara had said she wanted to go, but changed her mind at the
last minute.

Anna thought it was a bad idea altogether. She felt certain that
Lawrence, despite his longing to see the children, would be displeased.
On the other hand, knowing how much she herself wished to see her
husband, it was hard to argue the point convincingly. In the end she
agreed, with one condition — Sam would have to escort them. She
would not have them making the trip alone and she was too sick to
attempt it, even if she had dared disobey her husband.

Now, as the sun rose overhead and the August heat began to shim-
mer in mirages on the road, the trip took on a bit of a festive air. The
siblings organized a contest to count sheep on the roadside farms,
fought off an intruding bee and sang every gospel song Sam had
taught them — until they reached Moundsville. Abruptly, the car
grew silent, as if the disobedient children suddenly realized they stood
a good chance of being reprimanded. The air of adventure had evapo-
rated like the morning fog.

Without stopping to ask directions, Sam drove right to the prison.
Eileen wondered how he had known where to go, but she refrained
from asking. As the sight of the ugly stone fortress loomed through
the windscreen, Margaret's jaw dropped in horror. "Maybe this wasn't
a good idea, after all," she whispered to no one in particular.

As Margaret turned to reach for Eileen's hand, she saw her sister's
face. It was pale as plucked chicken skin. Clearly, Eileen was as frightened as Margaret herself. Sam had admitted early in the trip the idea
of going inside any prison scared him to death. He thought the place

held, along with the inmates, the "haints" of all who had died there. He was going only "because Miss Anna asked him look after her chil'ren," he had said. Now, his eyes looked wild with fear. Only Buddy, fully awake since lunch, looked more excited than afraid. "Wow," he said, again and again, but it was the kind of "wow" that follows the sight of a horrible accident.

Alighting from the car, Buddy, with a "teenage tough guy" swagger, started toward the iron gate nearest a huge pair of arched wooden doors in the center of the building. "Come on," he called. "Don't be such fraidy-cats." Sam took the girls by the arm and cautiously followed.

"How you know where to go?" Sam asked.

"Just looks like the front door to me," Buddy replied. As he approached the gate, a man appeared from out of the guardhouse.

"Can I help you?" he asked loudly. Buddy jumped and nearly fell backwards. He did not answer, so the guard smirked and repeated the question. "I said, can I help you?"

"We're here for visitor's day," Eileen answered timidly.

"Through those doors and to your left," he said flatly, pointing to the arched entrance. As he pulled open the gate, Eileen looked at Buddy. He was hanging back until the others went in; his eagerness and swagger were gone.

Once inside the building they stopped momentarily, waiting for their eyes to get used to the dim lighting. As Margaret's sight adjusted, she gasped. The stark, empty entrance foyer had dingy green walls and a worn concrete floor. Blackened cobwebs hung in the corners of the high ceiling like forgotten dust rags. One yellow light, covered with a wire cage, popped and crackled above an alcove as if it were about to burn out and leave them in darkness. On the far wall, a yellow-painted arrow, head pointing left, contained the word VISITORS stenciled in black. Holding hands, the quartet followed the arrow's silent direction.

The short hallway opened into another open space, this one crammed with people. A mother with a crying baby on her hip paced up and down. In a vain attempt to stop its wailing, she jiggled the slobbering child as she walked. Sullen-faced, slack-haired women in feed-sack dresses stood staring at a thick wall as if they were waiting for the rest of its paint to peel off and fall to the floor. A steady babble of voices rose toward the high ceiling and bounced off the walls, doubling in volume as it rained down on their ears. The room smelled of fetid, unwashed bodies, cheap perfume and the remains of a chicken picnic supper. Margaret, stopping dead in her tracks, nearly retched.

"Oh my gosh, look at all those people, Eileen. Do you suppose they all have a father inside?"

"Or a brother or a husband. Yes, I do. Why else would they be here?" Eileen answered rhetorically.

To one side of the crowd, Eileen spotted a guard seated at a small table. In a tight bunch, the family approached him.

"Excuse me. We've come for visitor's day, but we don't know what to do next. Do we wait here or..." Eileen asked.

"Name?" the guard said in a bored tone.

"Eileen Burgher," she replied, "and these are...."

"Not yours," he snapped. "The prisoner's."

"Oh," she said, startled by his rudeness. "Lawrence Burgher," she said, almost whispering. "Richard Lawrence Burgher."

The guard consulted a huge book on the table, scanning down several pages with his finger until he found the name, made a check mark beside it and wrote "Burgher 18764" on a piece of paper.

"Wait here 'til they call the name. Then take a seat before one of them four windows. He'll be there directly." As he spoke, he nodded toward the wall with the peeling paint. Following his nod, Eileen saw the four windows, which were about the size of large picture frames. They were covered with bars and wire mesh.

Inside, the prison was a beehive of activity. Cell doors slammed, footsteps echoed along the concrete corridors, guards called to prisoners to announce their families' arrival. But in his cell, Lawrence Burgher rested quietly, reading a well-worn book from the prison library, for he expected no one. Suddenly, a guard rapped his wooden baton against the cell door bars. Lawrence sat bolt upright.

"Burgher, someone here to see you," he hollered unceremoniously. "On your feet."

"To see me? That can't be. David isn't coming back until next week," Lawrence replied incredulously.

"Suit yerself. But they's a bunch a folks here to see you. One's a colored fella in a uniform," the guard offered as he unlocked the cell.

"Sam!" Lawrence yelled. He jumped off the top bunk and rushed toward the door. "Sam's come to see me!" he said excitedly.

Once outside his cell, Lawrence regretted not taking the time to comb his hair. As they walked toward the visitor's room, he smoothed it back from his temples with both hands, then tucked in his shirt more neatly. Although he needed a haircut and a shave, he was trying to look as presentable as possible for his former chauffeur. He realized, however, his striped prison garb was a far cry from the hand-tailored three-piece suits Sam had been accustomed to seeing on him. He hoped Sam would not be shocked.

The Burgher family waited nervously in a corner, as far from the crowd as possible, listening to a burly guard with a shaved head bellow out other people's names. They said very little as they watched the changing tableaux at the four windows. Buddy was unusually quiet, especially given his earlier posturing. To Eileen, he seemed particularly withdrawn, as if he were sorry he had come. She would have comforted him, but she knew that her almost sixteen-year-old brother would be embarrassed by that gesture. After an hour or more, the guard yelled, "Burgher." They rushed toward one window and Eileen took the only chair. The rest gathered expectantly behind her.

On his side of the thick wall Lawrence entered the visitor's room and waited for a stool. Finally, his turn came and he took a seat, peering through the window expecting to see the familiar black face of his driver. A flood of emotions swirled through Lawrence. Initially, shock and outrage flared in his face as he realized his children were clustered on the other side of the wall with Sam standing proudly and protectively behind them. He wanted to leave, to run back to his cell, to hide from his family — rather than have them see him here, but he sat rooted to the spot drinking in the familiar loving faces.

"Eileen, Margaret, Buddy! What are you doing here? I thought I told you never to come!" he suddenly exploded. At his thoughtless tone, all three burst into tears.

"We thought you'd be glad to see us, Father," Margaret wailed. "We missed you so much, we just had to come."

Immediately his initial anger at their disobedience melted into overwhelming sadness at the look on their faces. He nearly wailed in agony. "Oh Margaret, sweetheart, I *am* glad to see you. I've missed you, too. I've missed you all so much! I'm sorry I shouted at you." He began to cry, his head resting on the narrow concrete ledge below the window. Relief mixed with joy and the children cried along with their father, only harder. Sam was overcome at their tearful reunion and wept as well, but he was the first to regain his composure.

"Here now. Buck you-selves up. You didn't come all this way to spend a hour crying," he fussed at the children and by inference, Lawrence. Lawrence laughed self-consciously and dried his eyes with his sleeve.

Soon tears turned into jumbled conversation as the children jockeyed to tell Father their latest news. As he listened to them talk, Lawrence beamed in his old, familiar way, but Eileen could see the change eight months of prison life had wrought. She was shaken by the visible difference. Perhaps it was merely the ill-fitting prison uniform, but she thought he looked thinner, more finely boned. His hair, which needed cutting, had begun to gray at the temples and his bony nose looked more hawklike than ever. In contrast to Margaret's deeply tanned skin, a look she had carefully cultivated over the summer, Father looked as pale as if they were of two different races. An uncharacteristic stubble lined his jaw. Eileen had never before seen her father when he wasn't clean shaven. Dark circles accented his deeply set brown eyes. Furthermore, they had lost their familiar sparkle. Eileen had come seeking strength from her father, but now she wasn't sure he had any to give. Now, she heard herself trying to make him feel better.

"Oh Father, graduation was grand. Mother made over a dress for me. All the students marched into the Old Main auditorium wearing their caps and gowns. The speeches were boring, but it was thrilling to receive my diploma all the same," Eileen exclaimed. "Now I need to find a job."

"Your mother must have been so proud of you. I know I am," Father said.

Because Buddy interrupted, Eileen was spared from admitting that Mother was unable to attend.

"Margaret has a new boyfriend. I saw them kissing on the front porch," Buddy teased.

"Buddy!" Margaret was indignant, but Lawrence only laughed.

"I was not, Father," she protested. "That was Eileen kissing Harold. Besides, Buddy should mind his own business."

"Eileen, tell me about your fiance'. Mother says he's a very nice boy," Lawrence said.

Before she could respond, a man suddenly screamed, "You *bitch*. You *stupid* bitch. I ought to *wring* your damn neck." Buddy cowered. As the prisoner jumped up, knocking over the stool, his visitor, a slatternly looking woman wearing bright red lipstick, burst into tears.

Sam leaned over Eileen's shoulder and whispered. "Pay no attention," he said. "They's just white trash. Go on; tell your father about Mr. Harold."

Eileen blushed as she talked about Harold Ellis and their plans for the future, but she neglected to say those plans had been delayed because of Mother's illness. On the way, they had agreed to avoid talking about sad or unpleasant topics. Now each reply was ripe with what was not being said. Throughout the better part of thirty minutes they visited; but it was difficult to hear over the conversations of the other families and comments often had to be repeated. As the small talk began to wane, Buddy had the temerity to ask a question they had all voiced to each other.

"Father, what do you do all day?" he asked. Eileen thought she would sink into the floor but her father answered with equanimity.

"Well, Buddy, I work. We all do. Some make brooms or work in the print shop. Some farm and some work in the greenhouse. I'm

learning to sew, believe it or not. We make all of our own clothes."
Buddy laughed at the thought of his father leaning over a sewing
machine. "On my day off, I read or write letters. It's pretty boring, to
tell the truth. How's the paper route?"

"It's fine, Father. I found a puppy one morning while I was passing papers and it followed me home. Mother let me keep it and I
named him Sparky. He was really cute, but after Mother got real sick,
we had to give him away."

Eileen shot him a warning look. Buddy had broken their pact.
Father saw Eileen's frown and sensed Buddy's consternation.

"It's all right, Buddy. I know what you've been trying to do all
afternoon, but we can't ignore the fact that your mother is seriously
ill. I need to know how she is doing, really. Her letters shield me
from the truth, I'm sure."

Margaret looked as if she would cry again. "She's so sick, Father. I
hear her throwing up in the bathroom sometimes. She closes the
door, but I still can hear her. She seems to be tired all the time, too.
We have to clean the house and everything."

"Hush, Margaret," Eileen warned. "Father doesn't want to hear
how hard you have to work. We all have to do our part, even Stephen
and Libba." She turned back to the window, leaning closer to make
herself heard over the confusing din.

"Father, I'm really worried. Margaret's right. Mother tries to hide
it, but we can all hear her crying in pain and throwing up in the
toilet. Nothing seems to help any longer," Eileen admitted.

Father looked so pained, Eileen was sorry she had burdened him
with the truth.

"I've written to Bullmoose to see if he can find a way to get her
admitted to Johns Hopkins for the surgery. He's working on it, but in
the meantime, Eileen's right. You all have to stick together and help
out. I can't be there, so you have to be there for me. Promise you'll
stop bickering and help each other. For now, all you have is each
other. Promise?" Lawrence looked sternly into the faces of each of
his children.

"We promise," they chorused. Lawrence's demanding look crumbled
at the brave air in their voices, but he avoided breaking down.

As an intrusive bell rang, a guard moved toward the Burgher family. "Visiting hours is over, folks."

The children rose at Sam's urging and stood awkwardly looking through the mesh covered window at their father. Their desire to be able to hold each other was so strong it was obvious on every face. Sam could not bear to watch as the Burgher children — not really children any longer — said goodbye to Lawrence. As Sam began to shepherd his charges out of the visitors' room, he looked back at his former boss. Lawrence now stood in the window, unashamedly crying. His shoulders shook with the sobs while the guard urged him back to his cell.

Sam could hold back his own tears no longer. He put his arms around Eileen and Margaret and the sobbing trio walked out the door. Buddy marched behind, his face glistening, his head bowed.

Moundsville, West Va
September 4, 1931

Senator Lucas Landers
West Virginia State Capital
Charleston, West Virginia

Dear Lucas,

It seems odd after all these years and in this circumstance to be addressing you by your Christian name, but I suppose since we are now "related" by the marriage of our children, it is only proper to do so. I trust the young couple is making their way well enough in these tough times. While I don't know your son, if he is as fine a gentleman as his father, I'm sure he will be an excellent husband for my beloved Sara. I know, as a father myself, you must have been disappointed young Charles was not able to complete his education, but I trust you will not hold that against Sara. Young folks in love can be very impetuous. Until I am able to return to Huntington, I pray you will act in my stead to be a father to Sara.

Your kindnesses to me and my family have not gone unappreciated over the years. Your past willingness to help a fellow man leads me to request your most urgent help at this time. I'm sure you are not unaware of the delicate health of my wife Anna. She has been suffering these past months with a serious brain tumor and is scheduled for surgery at Johns Hopkins Hospital in Baltimore on October 1.

I have spoken with the Warden here about the possibility of attending my wife at the time of her surgery but he tells me only an order from the Governor can make it possible. In your position as Senator, could you have any influence in this matter? And would you be willing to put in a good word on my behalf? Anna will have to travel alone to Baltimore by train, which is bad enough, but for her to endure the surgery alone, is more than I can stand. I would be in your debt forever, if you could secure my temporary release so I may be at her bedside.

      I remain

                Very truly yours,

Forty-Eight

October 1931

The morning of Anna's surgery dawned crisp and clear; a beautiful fall day was ahead. But to Lawrence, it felt like winter. He was numb inside; yet, on the outside he felt jumpy and jittery, as if he needed to move to stay warm. His mind flitted too, as if it couldn't stick to one subject long enough to truly grasp its meaning. His thoughts veered wildly from serious concerns for the future to the most trivial, irrelevant topics. Now, as he stared out the window of the Johns Hopkins Hospital surgery waiting room, Lawrence prayed God would be willing to work one more miracle for him and his family. *God, you let Bullmoose find a way to pay for Anna's surgery, then you softened the Governor's heart to let me come here with her. Now God, please have mercy on us once more. Let her come through this operation, please!* Again and again, he prayed the same thing.

Anna had been in the operating room since 9 A.M. that morning. It was not quite 11 A.M. Outside the window stood a huge maple tree, its frost-nipped leaves heralding the splendor of an early fall. Lawrence had stared at the tree, unseeing, while he prayed. Suddenly, its gloriously mingled shades of orange and red captured his attention. He turned away from the window and addressed the only other person in the waiting room, his brother David.

"You know, its funny. After nearly a year inside that prison, you'd think one of the first things I'd notice would be the fall colors," he remarked idly.

"Well, you must admit, you've been a bit too preoccupied to be marveling over Mother Nature's latest get-up," David chuckled.

"What I *did* notice was the color of these hospital walls. It's the same dismal green as the walls in the prison. Do they make this paint exclusively for institutions? No one in their right mind would use it in their home — it's far too ugly." Lawrence glanced around the room at the groupings of a table, two chairs and a floor lamp, as if he had just noticed them. Scattered among them, sat a few hard looking two-seater benches. None looked inviting. He had tested several chairs and found they were all uncomfortable, so he stood — and paced.

Worry etched his face. Despite the lighthearted conversation, he was scared. However, talking about trivial subjects seemed, to Lawrence, a way to avoid thinking about what was happening to Anna. It was like trying to keep the pain of death away by telling funny anecdotes about the deceased at their wake.

That morning Anna's surgeon, Dr. Floyd S. Robertson, had told Lawrence the operation would be very risky. Even at Johns Hopkins, brain surgery was by no means routine. In only a small percentage of the cases were doctors able to completely remove a tumor. Nevertheless, it was the only course of treatment remaining which could relieve Anna's excruciating pain, and they all hoped, save her life.

David, seated in one of the chairs, watched Lawrence pace. "Maybe you just think it's ugly because of where you are used to seeing it." He paused for a moment, then whistled. "I'll tell you, you are one slick devil, getting yourself released like that. Weren't you surprised they let you out?" David queried.

"Are you kidding? Of course, I was. Although, I had written to Lucas Landers, Sara's father-in-law, asking for his help. He had said he'd see what he could do, being a state senator and all. But I wasn't at all sure even his help would be enough. So, when Governor Conley himself called the warden, I *was* surprised. It sure impressed the cell block, I'll tell you — and the warden. He called me into his office. Wanted to know 'just who I knew that could get the governor to release me just like that.'" Lawrence snapped his fingers. "And Bledsoe, my cellmate, started calling me 'Top-Grade.' He had been calling me 'Hamburger' — they give everyone a nickname, it seems — but now it's 'Top-Grade.' He said I must be top-grade meat to get a direct call from the governor." Lawrence laughed sardonically, then sobered. "I'll never be able to repay Lucas. No matter what happens, I owe him a great debt of gratitude." Then his face crumbled as he recalled his earlier conversation with Anna's surgeon.

"David, if something happens to her, I don't know what I'll do. How could I go back there and leave my children to fend for themselves? I swear, I don't think I could stand it. The hope of being with Anna again is all I live for." Lawrence's legs suddenly felt weak, as if he'd walked for miles. He dropped onto one of the hard benches and sat with his head in his hands.

David rose and took up the pacing, looking like a younger, more robust, version of the man who sat down. The two had often been mistaken for twins. But now their relationship almost could be misinterpreted as father and son. It was obvious Lawrence had aged in the past year. His clothes, held at the prison since his intake, no longer fit properly. When he had ordered them from the George H. Wright Men's Fine Clothing Store, they were tailored perfectly. Now his belt bunched the trousers into a wad at the waist and the vest and jacket hung limply from his shoulders.

David stopped pacing. "With Anna's surgery being so risky, I can't comfort you and tell you everything is going to be just fine, Lawrence. I pray that she will recover, but you had better be prepared for the worst. I hate to say that to you, but you are in a tight spot. You have no choice. You will have to go back, regardless of what happens."

"David, for God's sake. I can't think like that. She's got to get well. I've got to have a chance to make everything up to her afterward. Maybe I'll get out early for good behavior, who knows. But she's got to be there whenever I get out. I've made such a mess of her life, I've got to have a chance to make it better." As he spoke, Lawrence's face contorted in such pain, David instantly regretted being so forthright.

"I'm sorry, Lawrence. You're right. We just have to hope for the best." David tried steering the conversation onto less painful ground. "Where do you suppose Jenny is? Didn't you say she had gone for a cup of tea? Shouldn't she be back by now?"

"Well, she said that's where she was going. Maybe she decided to eat a bite as well. She probably didn't have time for any breakfast since they took Anna to get her ready for surgery so early this morning. Jenny was here all night with Anna, you know. Since our train didn't get in until so late, she had said she would stay. Poor Jenny, this has been hard on her, too. She said Anna had a very rough trip; she got sick on the train. Lying back in the seat didn't help; in fact, it made the pain worse. Jenny said she threw up as well. That must have embarrassed Anna terribly."

Lawrence looked up at David, a rueful smile crossing his lips. He shook his head slowly, then lowered his face into his hands again, and resumed staring at the floor. As the minutes crawled by, the brothers remained silent, each absorbed in his own thoughts. Periodically, they exchanged places, as if signaled by a whistle frequency only they could hear. One sat and stared at the blank walls; the other paced, jingling the coins in his pocket, always on alert for the doctor's emergence from surgery.

When Jenny appeared around 11:30 A.M., it was a welcome change. The two men were out of things to say to one another, but Jenny brought new stories from home, which Lawrence was eager to hear. For the better part of the next hour, he pressed her for news of the children, friendly gossip and the economic situation back home. Jenny animatedly told him of his children's progress in school, Eileen's courtship, Sara's adjustment to married life and all the tidbits of local gossip she could think of. But she hesitated to tell Lawrence just how bad things were financially, at least for his family. She didn't want to add to his worries.

"You know, Eileen is lucky to have her degree. It got her that teaching job. If she hadn't, she and Harold probably couldn't get married because he doesn't have a job right now. David, you're lucky, too. There are lots of folks out of work," Jenny said simply.

What she didn't say — that Eileen's meager salary and the money David sent them were supporting Lawrence's family — hung in the air like a bad odor. Lawrence detected the smell, however. He knew Jenny felt her sister's troubles were all his fault.

"Jenny, I know Eileen and David are responsible for the food on my family's table and the roof over their heads, and I'm grateful to them. And, to you and Nate, for all you've done, too. Someday, I hope I can make it up to you — to all of you." Tears formed in Lawrence's eyes, but he hastily wiped them away with his sleeve. "But right now, all I can think about is Anna. She looked so small and frail in that bed this morning. I was so glad to see her, though. She's thin isn't she? She said I looked just the same. I know she was lying to make me feel better, but it does feel good to be back in my own clothes, even if they don't fit." He laughed slightly.

Jenny said, "You are thin. Why don't you go eat some lunch? David, you go too. I'll stay here and wait for the doctor."

Lawrence blanched at the thought. "I couldn't eat a bite. I'd be sick as a dog. Besides I want to be here when Dr. Robertson comes out."

David agreed, "I'll get something later, after the doctor..." He let the sentence trail off.

They waited through the lunch hour and into the afternoon, as others began to fill the waiting room. A well-dressed matron, wearing a black veiled hat, entered alone, took a seat in the corner and cried softly into her handkerchief. A young couple sat, silently holding hands. An elderly man on two canes was helped onto one of the hard benches by a thin younger woman, obviously his daughter, and began asking her questions in the overly loud voice that often indicates deafness on the part of the speaker rather than the listener. Now, Lawrence, David and Jenny remained in their seats as well, huddled together as if to isolate their unique pain from the growing accumulation of other people's misery.

Finally, after six long hours, Dr. Robertson came through the double doors. He was a square-set man of ordinary height who would have passed unnoticed in a crowd except for his thick shock of silver hair. As he walked, it flew loosely around his head, shimmering like the halo of an elderly angel. This combination of hair and the unlined face and thick black eyebrows beneath always confused those he met as to his real age, which was only forty-five. As he approached Lawrence, his deeply set dark blue eyes looked tired.

"Mr. Burgher, I'm happy to report your wife came through the surgery just fine."

Lawrence's shoulders relaxed at Dr. Robertson's words. *Thank God! She's alive.*

The doctor continued, "The tumor did involve the optic nerves, as we suspected, but it was larger than we thought it would be. It was a complicated procedure and we don't know how successful it will prove to be."

Lawrence's earlier joy drained from his face. "What do you mean? I thought you just said you removed it."

"Yes, we did remove all we could. But we may not have gotten it all. As I said, it was very complicated. We'll just have to wait to see how she does. Of course, she's still asleep and will be for some time. In fact, you won't be able to see her until morning. Once she comes out from under the ether, we'll have to give her something for pain which will allow her to sleep through the night. If I were you, I'd go get some supper and a good night's rest. Come back tomorrow. You can see her then." Dr. Robertson patted Lawrence on the arm, turned and disappeared through the double doors, leaving Lawrence and his family to absorb what he had said.

Early the following morning when they arrived, Anna was still heavily sedated. While Jenny and David waited, Lawrence crept quietly into the semi-dark room. Four white curtained cubicles, presumably with their own occupants, made up the ward. He pulled back the first white curtain and slipped inside. Anna lay flat on her back on the narrow iron bed, her head encased, like a mummy's, in white bandages. Except for the slow, rhythmic rise and fall of her chest, she looked dead. Lawrence gasped, rushed to the bedside and took her hand. The warmth of her skin brought a flood of relief, and with it a torrent of tears. He dropped to the chair beside her, put his head on the edge of the bed and cried profusely.

Throughout the day he sat beside her, waiting for a sign of consciousness, and he could not be pried away. David and Jenny came to spell him, but Lawrence would not leave. Finally, toward evening, the nurses convinced him it would be another day before he could expect Anna to come around. Reluctantly, he went back to his rooming house.

They arrived the following morning to a very different scene. As Lawrence approached Anna's room, he could hear her crying; but it was not a cry of pain. It was an agonizing wail that froze him momentarily in his tracks. *Dear God, what are they doing to her?* Behind him, David put his arm protectively around Jenny as Lawrence rushed into the room.

The curtain around Anna's bed was open. Lawrence could see Anna propped up slightly on the pillows. Beside her a nurse stood holding her hand and patting it. Another nurse was preparing a syringe. Anna was staring straight ahead, eyes wide open, sobbing and crying out, "No! No! No!"

Lawrence rushed toward the bed in a panic. "What is it Anna? What's wrong?"

"Lawrence, is that you? Oh, my God, Lawrence, I can't see! I can't see! I'm blind!" she screamed as she jerked away from the nurse and flailed the air wildly, hoping to find her husband.

Brushing past the nurse, he reached her side in two steps, wrapped his arms around her and held her as tightly as he dared. "Shh, Anna, my love. Shh, calm down. It will be all right. It's only temporary. Shh, don't cry," he said over and over as he rocked her like a hurt child while his own tears blurred his vision. The nurse who had readied the syringe looked down at Lawrence as if for permission; he nodded and she administered the sedative.

A few moments later, Anna was asleep — a sort of half-sleep, really — for tears continued to ooze from under her closed lids, but no sound accompanied them. Only then did Lawrence lay her back against the pillows. Wiping his own eyes, he turned to look at Jenny and David. Standing at the edge of Anna's cubicle, they both looked horror-stricken.

"Dear God," Lawrence cried. "It can't be true. Nurse, is this possible? Is this normal? Could she really be blind? Where is Dr. Robertson? I've got to talk to him."

The nurse looked sympathetically at Lawrence. "Mr. Burgher, I'm not sure, but when she woke up this morning, she couldn't see. It scared her and she commenced screaming and crying. That's when you came in. As for Dr. Robertson, he's making his rounds now and should be here shortly. Why don't you wait here for him. Then he can tell you what to expect."

Lawrence nodded, suddenly afraid to speak for fear he, too, would begin to wail like Anna. He resumed his bedside vigil. David came toward him and put his hand on his brother's shoulder. "We'll wait outside, Lawrence." Again, Lawrence only nodded.

Fifteen agonizing minutes later, Dr. Robertson appeared, his hair untamed as ever. He came to the bedside and spoke to Lawrence.

"Good morning, Mr. Burgher. How are you today?"

"The question is not how I am, Dr. Robertson, but how is my wife? When I arrived this morning she was screaming that she was blind. She had to be sedated, again. You didn't mention this. It *is* a temporary condition, right?" Lawrence was visibly upset. His voice trembled.

"Mr. Burgher, why don't you step out into the hall so I can examine your wife. Then we'll talk." Dr. Robertson reached for Lawrence's elbow, urging him to stand. Lawrence stood slowly and woodenly did as the doctor suggested.

A few moments later, Dr. Robertson stepped into the hall. "Mr. Burgher, while the operation successfully removed most of the tumor it apparently also affected her sight. I'm so sorry, but in cases like this, with such delicate surgery, these things can happen — not always, but sometimes. Of course, I didn't mention it beforehand; I didn't want to frighten you. And we really had no other choice but to operate. I wanted to wait until she was fully awake, and I'm sorry you had to find out like that."

Lawrence reeled, staggered and caught himself with one hand on the corridor wall. "It's not temporary? She's permanently blind?"

Dr. Robertson nodded.

"Oh my God! Oh my God!" Lawrence cried over and over.

Dr. Robertson put his hand on Lawrence's arm. "She will need to recover here for at least two weeks, but after that she could be transferred to a hospital closer to home."

Lawrence could hardly believe he was having this conversation. It was his worst nightmare. He was scheduled to go back to prison in a week. "You mean she won't be able to go home?" he asked, fearing the answer.

"Perhaps, but not for some time. She needs to be watched carefully, to see if the tumor reasserts itself."

"And if it does?" Lawrence asked, again dreading the reply.

"I'm afraid there would be nothing more we could do for her. We could control the pain, but..." Dr. Robertson trailed off.

Lawrence, now numbed by the horrible possibilities outlined by the doctor, simply mumbled, "Thank you, Dr. Robertson." In a daze, he walked toward the waiting room to repeat the news to his family.

POSTAL TELEGRAPH

NA23 23 NL   1931 OCT 10 AM 531

CHARLESTON WEST VIR 9

R L BURGHER
CARE DR F S ROBERTSON 719 MEDICAL ARTS BLDG
BALTIMORE MD

HAVE GRANTED THIRTY DAY LEAVE FROM DATE OF YOUR
RECOGNIZANCE AND REQUESTED SCROGGINS TO COMMUNI-
CATE WITH YOU. STOP. SEE LETTER WRITTEN GOVERNOR
CORNWELL

WM G CONLEY GOVERNOR OF WEST VIRGINIA.

PHONE: VERNON 8121

F.S. ROBERTSON. M. D.
719 MEDICAL ARTS BUILDING
BALTIMORE, MD.

OFFICE HOURS 11 TO 1PM
AND BY APPOINTMENT

KNOWN ALL MEN BY THESE PRESENTS:

That I, R. Lawrence Burgher, Serial No.18764 a
prisoner in the West Virgina Penitentiary at
Moundsville, West Virginia, do acknowledge myself held and firmly bound unto the State of
West Virginia to present myself again at said
Penitentiary at the expiration of thirty days
dating from October the 3rd,1931 being an additional extension of 20 Days from my original ten
days leave, same having been granted by Governor
Conley, Agreeing to return to the Penitentary on
the 1st day of November to serve out the remain-
der of my sentence or until otherwise released
by the proper authorities,it being understood
that I am released for said period of thirty
days from October the 3rd for the purpose of
being with my sick wife now an invalid in the
Johns Hopkins Hospital at Baltimore Md. and that
I am to present myself as aforesaid unless a
further respite be granted by the Governor of
the State of West Virginia.

Dated and Signed this the 12th day of
October,1931

Lawrence Burgher

Witness   F. B. Robertson

Forty-Nine

1931–1932

S t. Luke's Hospital in Bluefield, West Virginia, founded in 1905
by Dr. Charles M. Scott, was, according to the information
Lawrence received, "a thoroughly modern facility;" it boasted
an "excellent laboratory, operating room, x-ray department, and an
able staff of eight full-time doctors" and one who rendered his services part-time. David Burgher was its bookkeeper. David had convinced Dr. Scott, a kind and sympathetic Catholic, to accept Anna as
a charity patient. David had also agreed to pay any unusual charges
the good doctor felt he had to levy, although David prayed these
would be few.

It was this financial arrangement, rather than the glowing bro-
chure, that convinced Lawrence to move Anna to St. Luke's. Although
Lawrence was completely mortified at being the recipient of other
people's charity, he simply had no choice. He couldn't send his wife
home; there was no one to care for her. Besides, she needed hospital-
ization and skilled nursing care if she was to have any hope of recovery at all. That hope was all Lawrence clung to as he transported
Anna, by train, from Baltimore to Bluefield.

The trip was horrible for both of them. Anna, unable to walk,
was jostled and bounced from the ambulance to the train on a cot.
Unable to ride sitting up in coach, she was forced to travel on the cot
in the baggage car. The cost of a sleeper was beyond their means.
Lawrence sat on a steamer trunk in the dark, next to Anna's cot

throughout the long trip. He never relinquished her hand. At the station they were met by the hospital ambulance and Anna, in pain and thoroughly disoriented, was moved to St. Luke's Hospital. By the time the ordeal was over, Anna had to be sedated and Lawrence was exhausted, physically and emotionally.

For the next week, Lawrence spent every waking moment at Anna's bedside. Some days were better than others. Sometimes, she was without pain for an entire day; but being unable to see, she required total nursing care, nevertheless. She could not feed herself, could not get out of bed to use the bathroom, could not bathe without assistance. In short, Anna was an invalid. It broke Lawrence's heart to see her. Each day he left the hospital crying. His nights were filled with nightmares. In them, he was trapped under a huge boulder, unable to free himself. Anna called to him from far away, crying for help but he was unable to reach her. The dreams ended only when he awoke in a terrified cold sweat.

As agreed, Lawrence was scheduled to return to Moundsville by November 1. On Halloween night, the regular evening nurse asked Lawrence if he would like to feed Anna her supper, so the couple could have a little privacy. He readily agreed. Afterward, despite the activity in the four person ward, inside Anna's cubicle, Lawrence felt totally alone and afraid. He tried to put on a facade of optimism, but failed miserably.

"Well, love," he began. "I don't know when I'll see you again, but I'll do everything in my power to get out early. Perhaps Sara's father-in-law can help again. Meanwhile, please take care of yourself. Do what they tell you, so you can get well, darling. *Please.* I don't know what...I couldn't stand it..." he began to stammer with the weight of emotion.

"Lawrence, shh. Just hold me. I'm scared, too. Let's don't talk. Just hold me until I fall asleep. Then you can go. We'll pretend it's just good-night," Anna said through her own tears.

Lawrence quickly moved to sit on the edge of her narrow bed, scooped her into his arms and held her against him as they both sobbed uncontrollably. After a few minutes, recovering somewhat, Lawrence laid her back against the pillows.

"Here, love, turn on your side and I'll spoon with you. I'll stay until you fall asleep, I promise," he said thickly.

With Lawrence's help, Anna turned to her side. Lawrence snuggled against her back as he had done almost every night of their marriage. With his arm across her waist, he gently cupped her breast. At his touch, Anna reached up to stroke his arm. Lawrence kissed the back of her neck as he whispered to her. "Sleep warm, my love. I'm right here. I love you."

She answered, "I will. I love you, too, darling. Good night." Lawrence's tears fell onto Anna's shoulder as her crying slowly subsided. Soon he felt her rhythmic breathing and he relaxed.

An hour later, the night nurse gently shook Lawrence. "Mr. Burgher, I'm sorry. It's time to go. We'll take good care of Mrs. Burgher. We promise."

Lawrence sleepily disentangled himself from Anna's side, rose and kissed her on the cheek. Mumbling his thanks, he stumbled out of the room, afraid to look back. Out in the corridor, he knew if he didn't go now, he'd never be able to. He rushed down the hall and out of the hospital to the sidewalk. David was waiting to take him to the train station.

Lawrence returned to the cellblock the next morning as everyone else was lining up either for breakfast or the showers. He wanted neither. As the guard escorted him back to his cell, loud jeers came at him from all quarters.

"Hey, boys, look who's back. Welcome home, Top-Grade. Threw you back, did they?" laughed a prisoner on his cellblock. "Found out you was just hamburger meat after all," called a second inmate. "Found out he was spoiled meat," yelled another. They laughed raucously, but Lawrence was in no mood for their jokes. He did not look up and entered his cell without a word. Relieved to find Bledsoe gone, Lawrence climbed onto his bunk and turned to face the wall. Miserable and worried sick, he just wanted a moment to himself before he had to go back to work.

After his return everything Lawrence did, everything he looked at, either reminded him of his last night with Anna or underscored his utter inability to be of the slightest help to her or to his children. If he slept on his side, he thought of holding her in the hospital bed. When he put on his drab prison uniform each morning, he remembered the feeling of the familiar three-piece suit he'd worn again just a short time ago. At his sewing job, he thought of his family's poverty and their lack of clothes. His cell seemed to have shrunk during the time he was away, and everything Bledsoe did annoyed him.

He was far more depressed than he had been after his initial intake. Back then, he'd been scared and lonely, but able to hold onto the dream of being with Anna again. Only a year later, that dream was gone; now he feared she would die before he was released. In any case, their life would never be the same. He would trade his current feelings for that old dream any day. Bitterness crept into his daytime depression and a morose feeling of doom pervaded his sleep. He felt horribly wronged by the justice system — and helpless to do anything about it. He could see why men tried to escape.

As Thanksgiving approached, Eileen sometimes wondered what the Burgher family had to be thankful for this year. She worried continually about what they would eat, not just for the holiday, but all the time. Aunt Jenny invited them for Thanksgiving dinner, but Eileen declined; she knew Jenny and Nate could not afford to feed five extra mouths. On Wednesday, the owner of the grocery store where Stephen was a part-time bag boy, gave her a skinny chicken, which she stewed. She fixed mashed potatoes and green beans. Margaret baked oatmeal cookies. It was more like an ordinary dinner from the old days; to make it as festive as she could, Eileen used the damask table linens, the Haviland china and all the silver, which Margaret grudgingly polished. As Eileen bowed her head to say the blessing, all she could think of was that the children were together. Then she remembered the grocer and thanked God also for his kindness.

A month later, they spent Christmas amid the packing barrels and detritus of another move. No longer could Eileen afford the rent on the yellow brick. Her salary barely covered the other living expenses for the growing family. Now that most of Uncle David's extra money was paying Anna's hospital bills, he could send only a reduced amount to help the rest of Lawrence's family. Eileen had found an older frame home on Eighth Avenue — not the most desirable neighborhood, she admitted — which rented for only $50 per month. Uncle David had agreed to pay the rent directly to the landlord.

While the house was large enough for the five Burghers, it was drafty. Gas stoves heated the rooms on the first floor, but upstairs it was cold. As she stood surveying the empty house, before she signed the lease, Eileen wondered if they would ever get used to the window-rattling noise caused by the trains that periodically thundered past, almost in their backyard. Nevertheless, she had agreed to take it. There was nothing else they could afford.

With the help of Harold and his friends, they moved during the Christmas holidays, while Eileen was out of school to supervise. If they could have bought a Christmas tree, which they couldn't, in all the mess, she'd have been hard pressed to find the fragile glass balls and candle-lights with which to decorate it. She had packed them weeks ago along with the Christmas stockings. It was just as well; she couldn't afford to fill them, either. Gifts, except for those the younger children made in school, were out of the question. All in all, it was a dismal Christmas, marked only by the two red numerals on the kitchen wall calendar.

February 1932

Within two months after her surgery, Anna's brain tumor was growing again. Her headaches were now controlled only by heavy medication. In January, during one of Jenny's visits, Dr. Scott sadly suggested that before Anna's condition worsened, the children should come see her. Jenny relayed this tragic news to Eileen, and together they decided to keep the news from the other children. Eileen was devastated. She was racked with worry — about her mother's impending death, her father's well-being in that wretched prison, the constant lack of money and the daily struggle to keep her family together.

She prayed nightly for the legendary strength of her Grandma Miller and for the strength she had seen first-hand in her mother. She would not let them down. Despite her daily worries, she organized a family trip to Bluefield to see her mother. It would have been easier to stay away, to shield the younger children, to remember her mother as she was. Nevertheless, Eileen knew it was important and the trip was set for February 13. Sam wanted to take them, but Eileen demurred. With Sara and Stephen, there would not be room for him. Eileen herself would drive.

Sara awoke that morning in a swirl of confusion and dread. As she pulled the covers over her head against the morning cold in the Lander's tiny, third-floor apartment, she tried to pinpoint the source of her feelings. Then it struck her. She was going to Bluefield to see her mother. Of course, she was eager to see her — it had been five months since her mother had left for Baltimore to have surgery, and she missed her terribly. None of the children had been allowed to visit Anna in the Bluefield hospital, until now. At the same time, however, Sara was very apprehensive about the visit. She envisioned huge red scars on her mother's shaved head. The mere thought of Anna blindly groping to hug her children frightened Sara beyond words. *Being blind!!!* Sara could think of nothing worse.

Across town, Eileen awoke to the bed-rattling roar of the 5:40 A.M. train. She did not have time to give in to her thoughts or fears. Even though it was Saturday, she awoke the other children, fixed breakfast and had Libba ready to go to Jenny's by 7 A.M. Eileen had decided it would be too upsetting for Libba to see her mother; so despite the little girl's protests, she was left behind.

A raw wind buffeted the Model-A Ford, causing the Burgher clan to huddle together under blankets. As an occasional spit of snow splattered on the windscreen, Eileen prayed it would not intensify. Simply driving in snow around town made her nervous; she hated to think of climbing a West Virginia mountain in a full storm. Her prayers were answered when the snow stopped and the day turned merely gray and dismal. Second thoughts about the wisdom of this trip had bothered Eileen, as well. She was worried about her siblings' reaction to their mother's appearance. But they seemed absorbed in their own thoughts, so for the moment, she dismissed her concerns. Eileen decided to take the change in the weather as a good omen.

Aunt Jenny's directions to St. Luke's were easy to follow; Eileen drove directly to the corner of Bland and South Streets, wondering idly why the town was called "Bluefield." As far as she could see, "Blackfield" described it better. Coal dust hung in the damp air and sooty piles of snow, left over from the last storm, dotted the street corners, looking like miniature slag piles.

St. Luke's Hospital, originally a rambling two-story residence, now occupied the entire block. Over time, the hospital had acquired other nearby houses and these were now connected by long, white frame passageways. The entire structure looked like a builder's patchwork quilt. Spanning the front of the original house were two iron-railed porches — one on each floor — where the patients could be wheeled in good weather. Today both porches sat empty.

As the Burghers stepped into the hospital foyer, the stuffy, over-heated air of steam heat hit them. The square foyer was lined with leather couches. Huge pictures of Christ on the cross hung protectively over each; wooden magazine racks flanked each arm. In the middle of the room a plump woman sat behind an ornate wooden desk. Buddy and Stephen removed their coats while Eileen asked the lady for directions to Anna Burgher's room.

Following her directions, the Burghers took the stairs to the second floor, then turned right down a hallway. They tried to walk quietly, but the sound of their footsteps on the linoleum sounded like a platoon marching in cadence had invaded the wards. The stuffy, humid air was rank with noxious, medicinal smells. Stephen dramatically held his nose. As they rounded one corner of the passageway maze, they nearly ran over an elderly woman who had been left in the hallway in her wheel-chair. Slumped in the seat, the woman looked dead, though she was merely asleep. A puddle of urine had collected below her chair. The stench was overpowering and Buddy gagged.

Before they found Anna's room, they made one wrong turn. Opening what they thought was yet another corridor door, they found themselves in what appeared to be a ward for crippled children. The large room was filled with adult-sized iron baby beds, occupied with grotesquely misshapen children of all ages. Babies with huge heads lay flat on their backs, their tiny bodies looking pitifully out of proportion, rather than the reverse. Some toddlers were in casts and traction; black iron pulleys tethered them to their beds. Other children with twisted spines or shrunken limbs sat staring at the Burgher children as if imploring them to provide a release from their suffering.

Sara, who had opened the door, shut it as quickly as possible, but the image of the children did not disappear. She gasped, "Oh, my God, Eileen, I don't know if I can stand this place."

"Come on, Sara. Let's go find Mother," Eileen said angrily. She was in no mood for Sara's sudden panic. She'd been irritated with Sara since she backed out of the trip to see Father and her sister's current reticence only exacerbated her feelings.

A few turns later, they reached room 214, a four bed ward. Anna, they had been told, was in the far left bed, by the window. The children crept through the door, past the first pair of curtained cubicles and stood apprehensively to one side as Eileen pulled back the curtain.

Anna lay slightly propped up, staring straight ahead, seeing nothing. Aside from being thin, she looked, to Eileen, just the same. Relief flooded over her.

"Mama?" she called softly. "Mama, are you awake?'

Anna turned toward the sound. "Jenny, is that you? I thought...," she said, confused.

"No, Mama, it's Eileen. Your daughter, Eileen," she said, her voice catching. When she realized her mother had mistaken her for Aunt Jenny, Eileen's heart sank.

"Eileen, oh my goodness. I didn't expect you." Anna instinctively reached up to smooth her hair into place as Eileen rushed to the bedside to hug her mother. "I'm so glad to see you," Anna cried. Her simple greeting caused all of the children to burst into silent tears. What she could *see*, they knew, was...*nothing*.

Eileen sobbed, "We're all here, Mother. All but Libba. She's at Aunt Jenny's."

One by one, Eileen prodded her siblings to their mother's bedside, like a proud mother forcing her children to greet the new preacher. Stiffly at first, then warmly, they each hugged their mother, as they said their names. At the familiar touch and scent of their beloved mother, each child, in turn, dissolved into tears. Suddenly, all their apprehension disappeared. They were just glad to see her again. Sara was last and had to be pulled away, crying audibly.

For thirty minutes the children interrupted each other with news they wanted to share. Then, unsure of what they should ask her, they all began to grow silent. Although it obviously had tired Anna to discern which child was talking, she had kept up the conversation as long as she could.

Finally, she said, "Children, I'm a little bit tired. Do you think you could come back later? Maybe when I'm stronger? I'm sorry, but I'd really like to take a nap now." She lapsed into silence and began to breathe more deeply.

The children looked incredulously at each other. It was as if their mother did not realize they had driven half a day to come to Bluefield. In that instant, Eileen suspected her mother did not know the seriousness of her condition. She also guessed the pain medication was partially responsible for her confusion. Quickly she tried to cover her mother's sudden dismissal of her own flesh and blood.

"Mother's just tired. I think what they give her for her headaches makes her forget, too. Why don't you tell her goodbye and go wait in the hall. I'll be out in a minute," Eileen said lightly.

Anna roused as the children kissed her goodbye, but she looked tired and relieved to be allowed to rest. It broke Eileen's heart to watch her brothers and sisters tell their mother goodbye, seemingly unaware it was probably the last time. She wondered if it would have been better or worse if they had known. She dismissed the morbid thought as they left the room and she sat on the edge of the bed to tell her mother goodbye.

"Mother, we're going now. I want you to know that I'll do whatever it takes to keep our family together, until you come home.

I love you and Father and I will always be proud to be a Burgher. I won't let you down," Eileen promised through her tears.

Anna held her daughter tightly. To Eileen's surprise, she spoke quite lucidly. "I know, Eileen. You've always been my strong girl. I know I won't be coming home, but I want you to take care of the little ones until your father comes home. Marry your Harold; he's a good man. I won't be there for the wedding, but I'll be with you in spirit. I love you very much," Anna cried.

The two women clung to each other. They both knew it was probably the last time they would touch. Finally, Eileen laid her mother back on the pillows and dabbed at her own swollen eyes. In a few minutes, somewhat regaining her composure, she looked again at her mother. Anna was asleep, her eyes closed. Tears streaked her face, but she wore a faint smile. Eileen rose from the bed, sobbing. She stumbled to the door and leaned against it for strength, fighting to pull herself together before she rejoined her siblings. Eventually, she wiped her eyes and with two deep breaths, stepped into the corridor.

"Let's go," she announced. "We've got a long drive ahead of us."

Fifty

March 11–13, 1932

Friday, March 11

Daylight was at least an hour away when a guard awakened Lawrence shaking his shoulder. "Burgher, Burgher. The warden wants to see you," he said in a loud whisper. Lawrence jumped from his bunk in a sudden cold sweat. He could think of only one reason for such a startling intrusion. *Oh, my God! Something has happened to Anna.* Pulling on his uniform and shoes, he followed the guard without question, but with every step he prayed he was wrong.

As Lawrence entered the office, the warden stood up. One look at his pillow-creased face and rumpled hair was all Lawrence needed to confirm his fears. His knees began to quiver. Warden Jenkins rounded the desk and placed his hand on Lawrence's shoulder.

"Mr. Burgher, I'm afraid I have bad news for you. Your wife died about an hour ago. We got a call from the hospital in Bluefield. They asked us to convey the message to you. Please accept my condolences."

Lawrence heard no more than the first two sentences before he collapsed into a chair in front of the desk. He wailed in agony, covering his ears against the warden's words. "Noooooo! Please God! No!" he screamed.

His head fell into his hands suddenly, as if his neck had snapped. He rocked back and forth, sobbing uncontrollably. The warden stood above him, accustomed to displays of grief, patiently waiting for the initial shock to subside. When Lawrence's crying kept up, the warden placed his hand on the inmate's shoulder.

"Mr. Burgher, if you need to make some arrangements, you may use my telephone," he said quietly.

Lawrence seemed to gather a measure of strength from the warden's touch. His crying slowed, then stopped. He wiped his face on his sleeve and looked beseechingly at Warden Jenkins.

"Would it be possible for me to go to Bluefield, so I can take her home? I probably could petition Governor Conley again, through Senator Landers," he said tentatively.

The warden shook his head. "That could take several days. This is Friday. You couldn't get permission until Monday at the earliest. But here's what I'll do. I'll release you, with a guard, today. I can do that without any higher authority. I'll give you time to get her body, take it to Huntington and hold the funeral. But that's all. And a guard must go with you. I can't let you go alone without the governor's say-so. You make the choice. Which will it be? Today with a guard or...."

"Now. Today. I have to go today," Lawrence replied anxiously. "Thank you, sir. May I use your telephone now?"

The warden responded with a nod toward the telephone on the corner of the desk. Lawrence picked it up and dialed David's home number. Respecting Lawrence's privacy, the warden moved to the other side of the room, but he could still hear Lawrence's sobbing, broken words.

As he replaced the receiver, Lawrence relayed his conversation to the warden as if the man had a personal interest in the funeral arrangements. "My brother is contacting the funeral home and will meet me at the train station in Bluefield. May I make one more call? I need to get someone to tell my children." At this, Lawrence began to cry again.

The warden nodded again. "Of course," he said shortly. This time, Lawrence called Anna's sister, Jenny.

He began valiantly, "Jenny, it's Lawrence. I'm sorry if I woke you. I know it's very early but...." He trailed off as he began to cry. "Oh,

Jenny, she's gone. Anna's gone," he finally blurted out. "I'm sorry to tell you like this, but I didn't want...I didn't know...will you please go tell the children? I just couldn't call them...Oh Lord, Jenny, what are we going to do? God! I can't live without her, Jenny!" He sobbed heavily and could not continue. Finally he stammered, "They're letting me out to bring her home. I'm going to Bluefield today. I'll call you from there to let you know when we'll be home. I'm sorry, Jenny, so sorry." Crying like a baby, he hung up without saying good-bye or thank you. A few moments later, regaining his composure, he drew in a deep ragged breath, wiped his face and addressed the warden again.

"Warden Jenkins? Thank you, sir. You've been very kind. When will I be allowed to leave?"

"I made all the necessary arrangements for your escort while you were on the telephone. You may leave as soon as you gather your personal items. There's a train to Bluefield before noon."

"Thank you, sir. I'll never be able to repay you for your kindness," Lawrence said humbly.

"We'll see you on Monday morning, Mr. Burgher," the warden responded simply.

Lawrence returned to the cell block, dreading the shouts and catcalls which always accompanied the passage of a single prisoner. However as he approached, the area grew uncharacteristically quiet. Word of his wife's passing had spread quickly throughout the prison. As Lawrence passed, he saw each man standing at the front of his cell in a gesture of silent respect. Entering his own cell, he climbed onto his bunk. Then he buried his face in the lumpy pillow and cried.

Jenny sat with the dead receiver in her lap, staring straight ahead. Tears rolled down her cheeks, as she wrestled with the reality of Lawrence's words. Her mind darted as if charged with electricity. The loss of her only sister and the sadness of Anna's all too short life were nearly overpowering. Then Jenny realized Anna was no longer suffering and she thanked God for that small favor. Her mind next darted to how on earth to tell the children, who now might as well be orphans. She cried tears of pity for them and uttered a prayer for them, as well. In the next instant she raged with anger at Lawrence, until another wave of pity hit her and she cried for him, too. Finally, she dried her eyes, went to look at her own children who were sound asleep in their beds, and thanked God that her family was intact. She woke Nate to give him the sad news then dressed to go tell Anna's children their mother had died.

Saturday, March 12

A cold, mean wind whipped across the bleak train platform. Only a few hardy souls dared brave the elements by waiting outside for the noon train from Bluefield. Eileen and Libba were among them, looking more like mother and daughter than sisters. Libba clung to Eileen's hips while Eileen wrapped her coat hem protectively around the child.

With a ground-shaking rumble and a squeal of brakes, the train pulled in only slightly behind schedule. Libba abandoned the warmth of Eileen's coat cocoon to cover her ears. The two girls peered through the billowing steam, hoping to spot Father before he saw them. Libba saw him first and darted away from Eileen to run down the platform toward Lawrence.

"Father," she yelled. "Father, we're over here!"

Eileen watched as her father and little sister met and exploded into an embrace. Libba fairly jumped into his arms and, despite her gangly legs, he picked her up easily. They held each other for a moment, then he put her down, took her hand in his and walked with her toward Eileen. As the pair drew closer, she could see the tears in their eyes.

When Lawrence reached Eileen, he dropped Libba's hand to hug his oldest child. The two stood silently crying in an embrace of mutual comfort. Finally, they pulled apart, although Lawrence kept one arm firmly around Eileen's shoulder. Without a word, he again took

Libba's hand as they walked toward the car. Behind them strode a tall, red-headed guard in full prison uniform.

Libba tugged on her father's hand. "Father, why is that policeman following us?" she asked innocently.

"That is Officer Sullivan. He's come with me to make sure I'm safe." Lawrence looked over his shoulder at the guard and winked. The officer nodded formally.

"Father," said Libba. "You're always safe with us." Lawrence laughed shortly but gave no further explanation of Officer Sullivan's stolid presence.

As they reached Eileen's car, Lawrence looked back at the train. A casket was being removed from one of the baggage cars. As Lawrence watched through his tears and the swirls of dirt and debris, four men loaded it into a hearse marked Steele Funeral Home. Lawrence turned to Eileen, who was also watching. "Your mother's safe, too, now," he said quietly.

As Eileen embraced her father again, he wept into her shoulder. "Come on, Father, let's go get something to eat," she said. "There's lots of food at home. Everyone has been so nice; we'll never eat it all."

Sunday, March 13

A cold rain had begun to fall as the funeral car pulled under the porte cochere of Steele's Funeral Home just after 1:30 P.M. This elegant entrance was a relic of the days when the building was one of the city's most distinguished homes. Over the years, however, the business district had swallowed up the neighborhood and the big red brick was converted to commercial property.

The somber occupants of the first car climbed out and waited on the covered porch for those riding in the second car. Lawrence stood slightly apart, looking forlornly down the street as Eileen enfolded her brothers with an arm around the shoulders of each. As the boys each wrapped an arm around her waist, it was unclear who was comforting whom. Margaret held fast to Libba who had tried several times to break free to join her father. At a respectful distance from the rest stood Officer Sullivan. Soon the second car, carrying Sara and Chuck Landers, Nate, Jenny and David arrived and the entire family went inside to pay their last respects to Anna before the other mourners appeared.

At first, the warmth of the tastefully ornate interior felt cozy. The rich paneling and Tiffany chandelier reminded Sara of their former home on the river. She shuddered as she thought of all that had happened to her family in three short years. Suddenly, the extravagant decor seemed oppressively stuffy to her. Feeling slightly nauseated, she slipped off her coat as they crossed the wide, carpeted foyer to the parlor where her mother lay in an open casket. As they stepped inside, one of the funeral directors, who walked so lightly he could not have left foot prints, closed the pocket-door behind them.

Anna's simple casket lay at the far end of the room. The Tiffany floor lamps flanking its head and foot cast circles of yellow light on the ceiling above and threw gold shadows on the pale face below, giving it a darkly jaundiced look. Sara started and drew back, clearly reluctant to go closer. Tears sprang to her eyes as she willed herself to keep walking. Without a word, the family moved en masse to Anna's side. Lawrence picked up Libba, who after a quick glance, buried her head in his shoulder, sobbing. At first, the boys stared mutely, then they too began to cry. Buddy covered his face, turned away and retreated to a far corner. Soon, the parlor resonated with the family's chorus of pitiful, strangled crying underscored by the faint strains of an organ from another part of the building. One by one, as the scene became more than they could bear, family members slipped from the room, until only Eileen and her father stood side by side, holding each other, staring at — but not really seeing — Anna.

"She was my life, Eileen," Lawrence sobbed. "I don't know what to do without her." Eileen wanted to say "What about us? Aren't we your life, too?" Her father's shoulders shook; he needed comforting, not chastising. Eileen put her arm around his thin shoulders. "I know, Father; I know," she said softly.

Out in the foyer, Margaret sat on the heavily carved teakwood bench, dabbing at her swollen eyes. Sara sat down beside her and placed one arm protectively around her shoulders. Margaret said, "She looks peaceful, doesn't she?" to which Sara replied numbly, "No, she looks dead."

When the mourners began to arrive, the family was already seated on the front two rows staring straight ahead at the now closed casket nestled amid a profusion of flowers. Libba sat on Lawrence's lap, her face still buried in his neck. Eileen sat beside them, flanked in order on her right by Margaret, Buddy and Stephen. Completing the row at the other end was David. Officer Sullivan had taken an unobtrusive seat in the rear, although his uniform signaled to all his reason for being there.

Sara hated funerals. She thought parading a family's private grief before the public was a barbaric custom. Now, seated with her husband in the row behind her father and siblings, she had begun to tremble inside with a roiling of grief, anger and a strong desire to be anywhere but here. She clutched Chuck's arm, determined not to break down in front of all those who had gathered to pay their last respects to her mother. *Where were all these nice people when Father went to prison? Where were they when Mother needed them?* It made Sara half sick to recognize among the mourners some of those she had seen at church talking behind their hands after her father was convicted. She dragged her attention back to Dr. Belk's service.

As his booming voice rang out the words of Psalm 23, "...Yea, though I walk through the valley of the shadow of death, I will fear no evil...," Sara began to cry. Reality finally struck her full in the face. *My mother is dead. The* one *person who loved me unconditionally is gone. Oh, God, I miss her so much already. How can I stand this?* She struggled to maintain her composure, but when she saw the trembling of her father's shoulders, she could no longer contain her emotions. Turning to Chuck, Sara buried her face in her husband's comforting embrace, crying audibly; she was past caring what others thought.

A much smaller group of mourners climbed from their cars at

Woodmere Cemetery to witness the burial rites. The Burgher children clung to each other for mutual support as they walked the short
distance to the grave site. They barely noticed the cold wind that
whipped around their legs and blew remnants of the earlier rain off
the trees. Lawrence leaned heavily against Eileen. He looked beaten
and lost as the funeral director guided him toward one of the wooden
chairs under the sheltering canopy. As Lawrence looked up at the
casket directly in front of him, he broke into a new round of shud-
dering sobs. Rather than sit with their Father, Margaret and Eileen
stood protectively behind him and placed a hand on one of his shoulders. Chuck ushered Sara to a seat beside Lawrence where she was
joined by Stephen and Buddy. Off to one side of the small group
Jenny held Libba close to her. The child had buried her face in Jenny's
coat and refused to look at the casket.

The service began with a prayer during which Dr. Belk intoned,
"...Grant to all who mourn a sure confidence in thy fatherly care,
that casting all their grief on thee, they may know the consolation of
thy love..." As the service continued, the gathered mourners stilled
and only a few isolated sniffs were heard. Lawrence seemed to draw
comfort from the pastor's words, for he had stopped crying.

Within minutes it was over. As Dr. Belk spoke the final invoca-
tion, "Into thy hands, O Lord, we commend thy servant Anna...,"
the funeral directors began to turn the mechanical crank which lowered the casket. At the grinding sound, Buddy rose abruptly, stumbled
from the tent and ran across the adjacent graves toward a huge oak
tree. Sobbing loudly, he fell on the wet ground near its base. His
wails drowned out the final words of the minister as Anna's casket
sank into the waiting grave.

Fifty-One

March–May 1932

T he familiar cramped cell to which Lawrence returned was no
more confining than the prison in which his mind now felt
trapped. When he had first arrived at the Moundsville Penitentiary, less than two years before, he had tried desperately to hold
Anna's dear face in his memory. It had been his talisman, his symbol
of eventual release. Now her face reflected all his failures and try as
he might, he could not escape her. She was gone and he had not
been there to help her. She haunted him, day and night. It was not
Anna's sweet, smiling face he saw; it was her waxy, lifeless image
nestled on the satin lining of her casket.

As he wandered through each day like a zombie, her pale, yellow
face flitted before him wherever he looked. He tried mightily to recall her warm smile, but at this he failed. Instead, all he could remember was the way she looked in the casket — stiff, yellow and, as
Sara had exclaimed — dead. He wished he had never looked at her
still, wan face at the funeral home.

Lawrence both craved sleep and dreaded it. Each night he dragged
himself into his bunk hoping to shut out his final memory of Anna.
He prayed fervently for release from that sight, but his plaintive words
seemed unable to penetrate the steel ceiling of his cell. Although
Lawrence previously had grown accustomed to the constant undercurrent of noise in the prison and was able to sleep in spite of it, after
his return to prison, every clang of metal on metal, every toilet flush,

every cough disturbed him. He covered his head with the pillow, but the constant coughing particularly grated on his ears, reminding him of Anna's hospital ward, of desperately sick people, of Anna, of death. Once asleep, he dreamt horrible dreams. In them, Anna screamed and cried, groping for him with wild, vacant eyes, and accused him of causing her death. When she was alive, Anna had never blamed Lawrence for the family's troubles; but in death she berated him nightly. He tossed and turned each night. Early mornings found him exhausted, spent.

The coughing was a matter of grave concern for the prison officials. Tuberculosis had become increasingly virulent in the damp, cold prison despite the doctors' valiant attempts to prevent its spread among the two thousand inmates. Horrible stories of men coughing up pools of blood and dying curled into the fetal position on their beds spread like the plague up and down the cellblocks. The truth of these stories was never corroborated, but the fear they engendered was enough to keep all the men on edge.

One morning in early April, a fight broke out in the shower line simply because one man coughed in the direction of another. Lawrence watched as the men, one much larger and more muscular than the other, went at each other, splashing water everywhere. Cheers echoed from the gathered crowd urging the smaller man—the one who had been coughed upon— to "Whip his ass!" Only Doggy's rifle aimed squarely at the two half naked men from the catwalk above stopped the melee. As the guard on the floor stepped in to separate the fighters, Lawrence pulled the thin towel more tightly around his skinny hips and moved one step closer to the showers, as if he had not even noticed the ruckus.

As the days dragged by, Lawrence found it impossible to climb out of his emotional morass. He stumbled through each day alone, avoiding contact with the other prisoners. Although he had never spent a great deal of time in their company, he had fallen into the habit of visiting with one or two men at meal time. Now he ate alone, or rather he picked at his food alone. The smell of the over-cooked food often took away what little appetite he brought to the dining hall. By the time he had moved through the long mess line, he could scarcely bear to look at his plate, let alone eat from it.

The redbud trees that dot the West Virginia hills each spring bloomed late in 1932, but when they did, the weather turned unseasonably warm overnight. In early May the prison guards switched abruptly to short sleeves for the eighty-degree days, while the inmates in the tailor shop sweated over their machines to produce new summer uniforms for themselves. Therefore, one afternoon as he returned from the dining hall to his sewing station, Lawrence was shocked to see another inmate, wearing a heavy coat, asleep on the floor of the shop beside his own station.

A waif-thin colored man, who had reminded Lawrence of Sam when they first met, was curled up like a napping child. His knees were drawn up close to his chest; his arms were wrapped tightly around his shoulders, as if he were hugging himself. At first Lawrence ignored the sight, but the man's resemblance to Sam was so unnerving, Lawrence finally felt compelled to check on him. He knelt beside the young man and shook his shoulder. The prisoner slowly raised his head, opening one eye with what seemed to be great effort. Lawrence noticed the eye was glazed; he wondered if Truman had a fever or was merely still asleep.

"Truman, what are you doing here? Come on, Truman. Wake up!" Lawrence said. He shook him again. As Truman struggled to sit upright, he began coughing.

When it subsided, he thanked Lawrence. "I 'preciate you wakin' me. I jist cain't seem to keep my eyes open. I'm freezing my ass off, too. Reckon I have a cold."

Lawrence dismissed his act of kindness. "You ought to get to the infirmary; you look like you might have a fever. This is no place to be sick. I hear there's all kinds of terrible diseases in here. Take care and get yourself looked at," he cautioned. He rose and went back to his sewing machine as Truman pulled himself off the floor and stumbled out of the tailor shop.

On May 19, as Lawrence and the other Thursday bathers lined up

for their twice-weekly showers, news of the most recent escape attempt passed down the queue. A fellow from Wayne county was telling the tale when Lawrence heard it.

"You know they's a bunch worked over to the greenhouse. Well,
two of them cooked up this here plan to escape. I reckon more was
gonna go, if'n it'd worked, which it didn't, but it was purty clever.
When they started bringing all them spring plants into the warden's
office, what nobody knowed was that the dirt in them plants was
a'comin' out'n this tunnel they had dug under the greenhouse and
under the wall behind it. Plants was appearin' everwhere. All the big
bosses had 'em in their offices. The boys what planned it was gittin'
a big laugh, 'til they was caught. Then the laugh was on them. I hope
they don't shut down the greenhouse. Them plants they was fixin'
to put in the yard was real purty," he said.

The other men, some standing completely nude, laughed appre-
ciatively at his story. It still amazed Lawrence to see the openness
with which others displayed their bodies. His modesty had not lessened in the months at Moundsville; in fact, it had increased. Keeping himself covered among the other inmates was a way to distance
himself from them. It helped him feel he was not like them, no, not
like them at all.

Lawrence left the line to take his place in the showers. Placing his
towel on the already damp stool, he stepped under the water and
faced the wall. He held his sliver of soap under the shower for a moment, then stepped back and began to lather his body. As he moved
back under the hesitant spray, which suddenly had grown lukewarm,
a knife-sharp, hot pain coursed through his chest and arm. Lawrence
pitched forward and grabbed at the cold wall. The bar of soap dropped
to the floor. His body followed.

As he hit the wet concrete, Lawrence could hear muffled laughter
and hoots in the distance. "Don't bend over, Burgher. You's choice
meat, remember." "Grab that soap!" "Shit, man, get out of my way.
Can't you stand up?"

Lawrence lay face down, as the soapy water swirled toward the
drain beneath him. Suddenly, Frazier Bledsoe yelled, "Hey man,
Burgher's not moving." He dashed from the line toward his cellmate.

"Someone help me," he called. Truman, the colored man from the tailor shop, was at the far end of the shower heads. He splashed through the other bathers to Burgher's side.

Together, he and Bledsoe pulled Lawrence to the dry area and turned him on his back. Truman yelled, "Someone get the Doc! Doggy, get the Doc!"

Lawrence lay unconscious and nude on the floor as Bledsoe slapped at his chalky white face. The ignominy of Lawrence's exposure was not lost on one obnoxious man. His low remark could be heard by all the men in the shower room, wet or dry, who had gathered around and were staring with macabre fascination at the prostrate form. "He's not choice meat now. He looks like *dead meat* to me."

May 21, 1932

Dearest Father,

Today I took the children to church for the first time since Mother's funeral. You will be pleased to know that many people came over and offered their sympathies. I almost wish they hadn't, however; it's easier to bear when you are not constantly reminded. I think it was also very difficult for Margaret as she turned away as if to escape each greeting.

But enough of sad news. How are you faring? I hope you are keeping up your strength. You looked very thin, Father. You must take care of yourself. We can't have you becoming ill.

My big news is this....Harold Ellis and I are planning to be married on June 18. Dr. Belk has agreed to perform the ceremony in the church chapel with just our immediate families in attendance. How I wish you could be there. Mother wanted us to go ahead months ago, but I just couldn't with her so ill. Now we've decided that having Harold here will be good for the little kids. Of course, he could never take your place, but he can help with the discipline.

On Wednesday Stephen brought home a puppy and wanted to keep it. He claimed it followed him home, but Margaret saw him drag it home on a rope. I hated to tell him he could not keep it, but I explained money to feed a dog was too dear. He finally convinced me it could live on his scraps, so I said it could stay. I hope it stays a small dog and doesn't eat us out of house and home.

The weather here is beautiful — warm days and no humidity. The kids are managing in school, but Buddy's grades could be better. They are all counting the days until summer vacation, especially Buddy!!

Write and let me know how you are. We all miss you.

Your loving daughter,

Eileen

Fifty-Two

June–July 1932

The prison infirmary was a basement dungeon of a room; it looked as if it had once been a wine cellar. Whatever its former use, with no windows and poor ventilation, now it smelled of tincture of green soap, iodine, camphor and alcohol. Suspended on fraying cords from the high ceiling, two dirty lights dimly burned day and night, more for the convenience of the nursing staff than for the comfort of the patients. The three narrow iron beds that lined each side of the ward were full.

Lawrence, whose bed had been shoved as far as possible from the others into the far right corner, was the only quiet patient. Four men hacked intermittently. The fifth man, whose head and forearm were swaddled in bandages, swore vehemently that he was "going to kill" whoever had inflicted his injuries. The nurse on duty, a stout, square matron who called everyone "honey," yelled back at the angry patient. "Honey, you'd better be quiet, or you'll be back in here with worse than you got right now."

Initially, Lawrence was quieted by the heavy sedation that followed the doctor's diagnosis of a heart seizure. The prescribed treatment was complete bed rest until Lawrence and his heart had regained their strength. Now, two weeks later, although the dosage had been reduced, he was still a docile patient who caused Nurse Bumpers only one problem — he wouldn't eat.

Today, as he lay with eyes closed, tears oozed from under his lids.

Oh Lord, why didn't you let me die? My life is over anyway. Why couldn't you have taken me right there in the shower? It should have been me—not Anna. A slight cry escaped his lips, then turned into a low keening. Nurse Bumpers, who had just retrieved a full bed pan from across the aisle, heard him and stopped.

"Honey, are you in pain?" she asked from the foot of his bed. Lawrence shook his head and turned on his side toward the wall, quiet once again.

Several hours later, Nurse Bumpers returned. She placed her hand gently on Lawrence's shoulder. "Honey, are you awake? You have a visitor. Would you like to see your brother?"

Lawrence stirred slightly and nodded. Rolling onto his back, he said, "David? David is here?"

"Sure, honey," she replied as if speaking to a small child. "He's come to see how you are." She helped Lawrence sit up, fluffing the worn pillows as best she could, then moved away to attend to one of the men who had begun to moan. As she left, David took her place.

"Hello, Lawrence," he said. "I'm glad to see you sitting up. How are you feeling?"

"Tired, David. Very tired. And my chest hurts when I breathe. How did you know I was here?" Lawrence said. He spoke softly and deliberately as if his voice might give out before his thoughts did.

"The warden called me when you collapsed. I've kept in touch for the past two weeks and came as soon as they would allow you to have visitors. The doctor said you had a heart seizure. The nurse also told me you don't eat much. That's no way to regain your strength, Lawrence. Look how thin you are."

With a weak wave of his hand, Lawrence dismissed David's rebuke. "I'm not hungry, David. I can't eat. Since I came back...food makes me sick."

"They said you also have an infection in your heart, endocarditis, they called it. The doctor said sulfa drugs alone can't fight that; you have to eat. How do you expect to get well if you don't?" David sounded like a scolding parent, but he was clearly worried about his older brother.

"I don't care whether or not I do get well. What have I got to live for now that Anna's gone? Eight more years in this place? By the time..." Lawrence had spoken with more strength than before, but he ran out of energy before completing his thought.

Now David exploded indignantly. "What do you have to live for? Six children, that's what. They miss you! They need you! You can't do them any good by dying, Lawrence!"

"I can't do them any good in prison either. By the time I get out, they'll all be grown, even Libba." He began to cry. "David, I ruined Anna's life and I ruined theirs. Now she's dead and they'd be better off without me, too." Despite his tears, his voice had regained its usual force. He wiped his eyes with the sheet as David pulled a chair close to the bed and sat down near Lawrence's shoulder.

"Listen, Lawrence. We still have some land left in Shapely that the courts didn't take. It's in my name. I'll sell it and get you a good doctor, one who specializes in hearts, not this prison saw-bones. We'll find someone who can treat endocarditis and..."

Lawrence interrupted him. "David, it's too late. Sell the land if you can, but give the money to Eileen to use for the children. If you can do that, maybe it will make up for all I did. I've had plenty of time to think about what happened. I realize I took too many risks, did some things I shouldn't have. I should have done things differently. Maybe if I had, Anna would...she'd be..." He began to cry again. "I can't change the past, David, but maybe..." Now he was exhausted. His breathing was labored; his previously gray face was flushed.

"All right, Lawrence, all right. Just rest now," David said anxiously. It was obvious this conversation had been too taxing for his brother. David tried to change the subject, but Lawrence had more to say.

"David, tell the children I'm sorry. I never meant for it to turn out this way. I just wanted them to have a good life. Ask them to forgive me. Don't let them come visit me here. Tell them I love them," he finished almost in a whisper.

David watched his brother's shallow breathing through tear-filled eyes, unable to think of anything to say that would comfort this tortured man. Lawrence was sleeping when David finally rose to leave.

Lawrence remained confined to the infirmary four more weeks, but he regained little strength. Finally, after the admission of a man with meningitis, the doctor sent Lawrence back to his cell to continue recuperating. According to the doctor, bedrest was bedrest; the location didn't much matter. Lawrence's hospital bed was needed for the new patient.

It was mid-morning when Lawrence was wheeled back to the cell-block. Most of the prisoners were at work, therefore only a few good-natured shouts echoed in the wake of the wheelchair's squeak.

"Hey Burgher, good to have you back home."

"Hey man, you back in Top-Grade condition again?"

Lawrence smiled wanly and waved a weak hand at the men, wondering vaguely if they had been in the shower room when he collapsed. He flushed as he recalled being told of the embarrassing scene. At Cell 89, the guard stopped, unlocked the barred door and began to help Lawrence from the chair.

"Which one is yours?" the guard asked, gesturing toward the bunk beds.

"The top one," replied Lawrence.

"Whoa, that ain't good. You'll never make it up and down with that ticker of yours. We're gonna hafta' change that. Hold up a minute," he said. Lawrence eased back into the wheel-chair.

As Lawrence waited, the guard switched Bledsoe's bedding with Lawrence's, moved Bledsoe's pictures to the wall above the top bunk and then patted the lower bunk.

"Now, this'n's yours. Come on, let's get you into bed."

Lawrence said in a warning tone, "Bledsoe's not going to like this one bit. He's very protective of his bunk."

As the guard helped Lawrence from the chair and into the bed, he tried to reassure Lawrence. "If ol' Bledsoe gives you any trouble, just let me know. I'll tell him it's strictly on doctor's orders." Lawrence was too tired to argue further, but he guessed Bledsoe wouldn't take it lying down.

Just as Lawrence predicted, when Bledsoe spotted Lawrence

ensconced in the lower bunk as he approached the cell after work he began to shout. "What the hell are you..." But when he saw how thin and frail his cellmate had become, he stopped short. After Lawrence explained the problem, Bledsoe's ranting changed into a grumbled acquiescence. "Well, you'd better get well quick. I ain't sleeping up there forever," he groused.

Over the next few days, as if his efforts could hasten a return to their original living arrangement, Bledsoe became Lawrence's self-appointed nursemaid. He good-naturedly badgered Lawrence into eating at least a portion of each meal and reminded him to take his medications; but despite Bledsoe's best efforts, Lawrence made scant progress toward recovery.

The entire month of July was sleep-in-the-nude hot. The air in the cramped cell was as damp as a wet basement and more fetid than usual. Lawrence, still confined to his bed, was miserable. His body stuck to the hot sheets, which were changed only once a week, and he stank of fever and perspiration. During his stay in the infirmary Lawrence had grown unaccustomed to the cell-block noises again and now found it impossible to readjust. He tossed and turned nightly, disturbing Bledsoe above him. Both slept badly. They never got a full night's rest.

After two months, Lawrence could sit up only long enough to eat or use the toilet. Showering in the common area was out of the question, so he was forced to bathe from the sink, which he did only when he could stand himself no longer. The effort exhausted him. He was still as weak as a premature baby; his chest hurt when he inhaled and still he had little appetite. Each week, however, the doctor who visited him insisted he was making progress, however slight.

On July 24 Bledsoe was in the dining hall when Lawrence's noon tray arrived. The guard entered the cell, placed the tray at the end of the bed and offered to help Lawrence sit up. Feeling somewhat stronger, he refused and managed to sit up on his own. Dangling his feet over the side of the bunk, he placed the tray on his lap as the guard left the cell.

"Put it on the floor. I'll pick it up when I bring your supper. Enjoy your meal," the man called out as he did every day.

As Lawrence picked at his meal, the only item that looked appealing was the oatmeal cookie. He decided to eat it first, then work his way through the rest. As he bit into the cookie, a wave of nausea swept over him. Suddenly, the cookie fell to the tray as a crushing fist of pain grabbed his chest. Lawrence clutched at his shirt front; his body stiffened, flinging him backwards. The tray clattered onto the concrete floor, breaking all the dishes. Lawrence's body flopped back against the rumpled sheets. He lay still, his hand twisted in his shirt front, oatmeal cookie crumbs on his lips.

When Bledsoe returned from his work shift at 4 P.M., congealed food and broken dishes littered the floor; the smell of feces and urine filled the cell. As the shift guard unlocked the cell door, Bledsoe saw Lawrence splayed awkwardly across the bunk. Bledsoe covered his mouth and nose against the smell as he rushed toward the bed, seemingly unaware of the mess on the floor.

"Burgher," he said, reaching to shake his shoulder. When he saw Lawrence's face, Bledsoe drew back. The open eyes seemed to be staring at the picture of Anna wedged into the upper bed's springs, but they saw nothing.

"Guard," Bledsoe yelled hysterically. "He's dead! Burgher's dead! Call someone! Get him out of here! Oh, God! Get him out of here!" As his words echoed throughout the cellblock, Bledsoe turned toward the toilet and vomited.

Fifty-Three

July 24–26, 1932

July 24

As Eileen washed and Margaret dried the supper dishes, they sang. The soprano voices, the heat from the sink and the humid evening air pouring through the back door and open windows made the kitchen feel like girl's locker room at school. Eileen lifted her arm to wipe her face with her sleeve just as the telephone rang.

She called out to no one in particular, "Get the phone." It rang again, and again.

"Someone get the telephone! My hands are wet."

The instrument continued to ring. Finally, Eileen heard Stephen's voice and the ringing stopped. Soon he appeared in the kitchen.

"It's Uncle David," he said. "He wants to talk to you."

"Can't you talk to him? I'm doing the dishes."

"No, he wants you, Eileen." With a bang of the screen door, Stephen tumbled outside.

Eileen sighed, dried her hands and went into the living room to take the call.

"Hello, Uncle David. It's good to hear from you. How are you?" she began cheerfully. A long silence followed. Eileen dropped to the sofa in obvious shock as David told her of her father's death. She listened, stunned, as he explained that the warden had called him, that Lawrence apparently had suffered a massive heart attack, and that the doctor thought the endocarditis had probably weakened his heart. David ended the call by saying he would make arrangements himself to bring the body to Huntington.

Numbly, Eileen mumbled, "Thank you," and replaced the receiver on its cradle. No tears came. Wiping perspiration from her face with the tea towel, she rose and walked back into the kitchen.

"Margaret, find Libba and Buddy. Tell them to come here. I have to talk to you, all of you." Then she turned and called out the back door, "Stephen, come here, please."

Margaret did as she was asked. It was clear from the look on her sister's pasty-white face she should not question the demand.

By the time they had gathered in the kitchen, Eileen had begun to tremble. As she spoke, she fought for emotional control.

"Uncle David just called with bad news. Father has died," she said simply. Her voice wavered.

At her words, bedlam broke loose. Buddy screamed, "God damn it," and ran from the room. Stephen buried his face in his crossed arms and began to sob. Libba flung herself into Eileen's open arms and wailed, "No! No! Father can't die! He *promised* he'd come home." Margaret stood in stony silence by the sink, a towel in her hands, as the tears flowed.

Smothered by the weight of this collective grief, Eileen broke down. She nestled her face in Libba's hair and cried, her shoulders heaving. Finally, she dried her eyes with the damp towel and took a deep breath before speaking again. "Uncle David is bringing him home. I've got to go call Sara." But Libba would not release her sister; she clung to her, crying as if her heart could never be mended.

Eileen tried to calm her, talking in soothing tones. "Sweetie, come on. It's going to be all right. I'll take care of you just like I've been doing. Nothing is going to change. We're still a family, even if Mother and Father are gone." Her voice broke, but she continued.

"Listen to me — all of you. Father is in a better place now. In prison he was sick, cooped up in one room and alone. Now he's in heaven with Mother. And he isn't sick anymore. Now he can roam all over heaven — with her. Father's troubles are over." She had begun to cry again, but did not stop talking. "And we'll be just fine. We'll stick together and take care of each other, no matter what! Okay? Okay!"

She pried Libba's arms from around her neck, kissed her on the cheek and rose to call Sara. As she left the kitchen, Eileen said, "I'll be right back, sweetie."

With trembling hands, Eileen dialed Sara's number. As she waited, she took several deep breaths to keep from crying again.

"Chuck, it's Eileen. Is Sara there?" Eileen said without any friendly chatter. She took two more breaths while she waited.

"Sara...," Eileen began, then hesitated. "Sara, I don't know any easy way to say this — Father died today."

Sara's piercing scream ripped through the receiver.

"Sara, honey. I'm so sorry I had to tell you this way, but I didn't want to leave the others." Eileen tried to soften the blow by apologizing, but Sara heard none of it. Eileen could only listen mutely to Sara's agonized cries. Finally, she heard Chuck comforting his wife.

Sara blew her nose, then struggled to ask, "What happened? I thought he was getting better?"

"Uncle David said he had another seizure. They found him on his bed," she explained. "He's making arrangements to bring Father back here. I suppose the funeral will be on Tuesday."

Sara then asked in a strangled voice, "Are you okay? What about the others? Are they okay?"

"We'll be fine," Eileen replied. "We'll be just fine."

July 25

On Monday, the newspapers trumpeted the news that Lawrence Burgher, fifty years old, was dead. Under bold headlines reminding everyone about his banking troubles, the lengthy article briefly chronicled Lawrence's rise to bank president and repeated in excruciating detail his fall from grace. A vivid description of the overcrowded and aging condition of the Moundsville penitentiary followed, complete with the warden's conclusion that "the noise of the men...troubled him and impeded his recovery." The article also reported that "the death of his wife in March, was believed to have contributed to the downfall of his own health and to have hastened his passing." In the final paragraph, the surviving children were listed.

When she saw the morning paper, Sara threw it on the floor in obvious disgust, then broke into sobs. "There it is again — Father's troubles — all over the front page. Why do they have to do that? Can't they leave us alone? It's just too much," she cried. Although she railed at Chuck as if it were somehow his fault, he did not respond. It was clear she just needed to lash out at someone...anyone.

July 26

On Tuesday, the Burgher children gathered once more at the Steele Funeral Home. Despite the newspaper publicity, it was a small funeral attended mostly by family and very close friends. It seemed as if, during Lawrence's months in prison, the business community had removed him from their little black books. To see the small number of mourners, one would not have guessed the deceased was once an influential force in the city's life. Only two of his pallbearers were non-family members — Francis Patrick, his steadfast attorney, and Sam, his faithful driver, who had always told people he *was* family.

Throughout the service, which was nearly a carbon copy of their mother's four months earlier, the older Burgher children sat in stoic silence on the front row, staring at the closed casket. Only Libba cried, wiping away her quiet tears with her mother's lavender handkerchief. As the family stood to leave, Eileen tried to put her arm around Buddy's shoulder, but he shook it off and glared at her.

Buddy had been sullen and moody ever since Uncle David's phone call. Eileen had accused him of acting like his father had died on purpose, just to upset Buddy; but the remark didn't change his behavior. He had spent hours locked in his room, refusing to share his feelings with anyone — not even his brother, Stephen.

When the funeral car stopped at the grave site in Woodmere Cemetery, Buddy bolted from the car, ignoring Eileen's stage-whispered call to stay with the rest. He stalked toward the oak tree where he had laid during his mother's burial service. Eileen gave up and took her seat in front of the open grave, with Libba tight beside her. Surreptitiously she glanced around looking for her mother's grave, but it had been covered with the funeral home's ground cloth.

Eileen watched through her gathering tears as the pallbearers — her husband Harold, Chuck Landers and his father, Senator Lucas Landers, Francis Patrick, Uncle Nate and Sam — carried her father's coffin to the grave. Eileen broke down when she saw Sam. Dear Sam — Sam, whom she had tried to kiss when she was a little girl; Sam, who loved her father as his own; Sam, who joked that his last name was Burgher — Sam was crying like a small child.

The pall-bearers gently positioned the coffin and solemnly retreated. As they moved away, Eileen followed Sam with her eyes. He continued to walk away from the tented area toward the oak tree. Approaching Buddy, whose head was bowed, he turned and placed his arm around the young man's shoulders. Buddy looked up, gave Sam a wan smile, and together they watched the burial service, heads erect, tears flowing freely.

October 4, 1932

Dear Uncle David,

I wanted to let you know that the markers have been placed on Father's and Mother's graves. Sunday, I took Libba and Stephen to see them and was very pleased to see how dignified they are. I know how tight money is for everyone now, so I can never thank you enough for providing the markers. It is so comforting to see them together once again, even if they are gone from us.

Now that school has begun again, everyone seems to be adjusting to our new "family." It is still difficult to discipline the boys, but Libba minds me as if I had always been her mother. I think she's just grateful to have less turmoil in her daily life. Of course, she dotes on the baby and is willing to watch him whenever I ask. He's growing like a weed and looks just like Harold.

My biggest worry is having enough to feed this brood; but with both boys working after school, we scrape by. After Sonny gets older, I'll go back to teaching. That will certainly help. And if Margaret can find a job after graduation, she will help out as well. Jobs are dear, though; we're just thankful that Harold has one. Thank you again for all your help. Without that rent check each month, I don't know what we'd do!

Sometimes I find it hard to believe Mother and Father are both gone. It happened so suddenly, and at the same time it seems like it took an entire life-time to get through the past year. As I tell Libba, when she gets to crying about what happened, "Just remember it this way—Mother got sick and died. Because he loved her so much, Father died of a broken heart. Now they are together. We'll always love them and remember them. But now we have to stick together and get through our lives, one day at a time. We'll be fine. We'll be just fine." It comforts her, but I often think I'm saying it for myself as well. And it is true — we will be just fine!

Your loving niece,

Eileen

Fifty-Four

November 26, 1942

now lay thick as a feather mattress. The gathering four o'clock shadows made Eileen's house look as if it were snuggling deeper by the minute into a downy bed. The front hallway was a jumble of baby paraphernalia and discarded clothing. Two baby buggies stood against the wall next to a highchair, assorted toys and four overflowing diaper bags. Scarves, hats and overcoats obscured the coat stand so completely that it looked like a pillar of clothing. The smell of turkey and pumpkin pie lingered, even though the Thanksgiving dishes had been cleared away hours ago. Eileen's kitchen sparkled like a freshly scrubbed child, but the living room and dining room still lay in chaos. The extra table, where the older children had been fed, remained halfway between the living room and the dining room. A wooden playpen, which sat in front of the sofa where the coffee table would return tomorrow, held three chubby babies. Each looked surprised to find someone else plopped down in their space.

In the dining room, the table had been expanded to its maximum size; odd chairs from the kitchen, mismatched in style and wood, had been added to the original six. Around the table sat five women and two men, their elbows resting in several places on leftover crumbs. Drink glasses on paper napkins and playing cards dotted the white cloth. Sharing ashtrays and gossip, the Burghers were playing penny-ante poker and drinking beer chintzles, a family concoction of beer, gin and lemonade. In on the game were Eileen, still in her apron, and her second husband, Jack Ross, Sara, Margaret and her husband, Stewart Hudson, Libba and Buddy's wife, Jean. As usual, Chuck Landers napped in the overstuffed chair closest to the fire. Stephen's pregnant wife, Hannah, sat nearby quietly rocking Buddy and Jean's new baby, Johnny. Neither Buddy nor Stephen were with the family; both were overseas. Buddy was stationed in Germany while Stephen recently had written that he was "bombing the hell out of the Japs" somewhere in the Pacific.

Suddenly, as if on a signal, a trio of indignant squalls rose from the playpen. At this universally accepted maternal cue, Eileen, Margaret and Sara pushed back from the table in unison and went to retrieve their babies, each apparently wondering which of the others had started the uproar. Eileen's two oldest boys, Sonny and David, clattered down the steps begging to go out to play in the snow. Since their card game had been interrupted, Jack and Stewart offered to teach the boys to build a snow fort. Now the house was left to the women and the sleeping Chuck Landers.

Although Hannah occupied the only rocking chair in the house, the mothers soon were rocking in their straight chairs. Eileen, Margaret and Sara had been pregnant at the same time; their babies were born about two months apart — Eileen's son in September, Margaret's daughter in November and Sara's girl, Maggie, in January. The room looked like a Sunday school nursery.

"I feel left out," said Libba with a mock pout. "Everyone has a baby but me — or will have one soon." Libba pointed to Hannah's seven-months-pregnant belly.

Hannah was the newest member of the Burgher family, having married Stephen last March. They had met while Stephen was a traveling salesman in southern West Virginia, had run away after dating for only a short time and married. She was fair, blond and beautiful — if a little immature. When Stephen left for the war two months after they were married, Hannah was pregnant. She had said her biggest fear was that the baby would be born before her husband returned; it never occurred to her that he might not return at all.

"You're too young," chided Hannah. "You've got plenty of time for babies. Don't rush it, Libba." As she spoke, it seemed clear she was thinking about her own situation.

"I am not too young; I'm twenty. That's plenty old enough to be married and have a baby. Sara ran off and got married at seventeen. No one fussed at her, did they?"

"That was different, Libba. Things were different back then," Sara said. Her solemn face rested lightly on the back of her baby's silken head. Maggie nestled into her mother's shoulder, sucking her thumb as Sara kissed her sweet-smelling neck.

Eileen spoke quietly. Jackie had just fallen asleep on her shoulder. Through the distance of memory and the beer chintzles she said, "I'll say things were different. Now that we've lived through it, it's hard to believe how hard life was ten years ago. It seems like another lifetime. There were days back then I wondered how we would survive. I knew we would, but I sure wondered how. If it hadn't been for Uncle David, Harold and I wouldn't have been able to keep a roof over our heads.

"I always felt bad about leaving you to do it all, Eileen," confessed Sara. "Of course, Chuck and I were poor as church mice ourselves, but I wish I'd been able to help."

"Oh pooh, Sara. You were so blind in love with Chuck Landers and your new life, you didn't even see us go hungry. Not that I blame you, but you don't know the half of it. You left. We had to take cold showers when Eileen couldn't pay the gas bill. We never had new clothes like you did, and we had to walk to school when there wasn't gas for the car," said Margaret. Her chubby baby, Drew, squirmed on her lap, refusing to settle down. "Did you know that Eileen would never let me invite friends to spend the night because we didn't have enough food for breakfast for ourselves, let alone for anyone extra?" Margaret obviously was still bitter about her lot in life; the alcohol apparently had unleashed her true feelings.

But Eileen stopped her before her remarks got too caustic. "Margaret, if you are going to fuss at Sara, we'll change the subject. That's all past, now. It wasn't Sara's fault we were poor. It wasn't anyone's fault. Not even Father's. When he had his troubles, it was the Depression. Everyone was poor, not just us."

Jean, who was the kind of a woman who would surreptitiously

run her finger over your doorjamb to check for dirt and sneer satis-
factorily if she found it, interrupted, "Yes, but Buddy always says, 'we
were poor, poor.' Worse off than a lot of folks. Didn't the boys have
to put cardboard in their shoes? Buddy said so. Is it true?"

Before Eileen could answer, Libba said, "I remember being so poor
that when I first started having my periods I had to use toilet paper
since we didn't have money for sanitary napkins. One time, when I
was cleaning Margaret's room — she paid me fifty cents a week to
clean it for her — I stole some Kotex from her. She caught me and
fired me." Libba laughed, "Do you remember how angry you were,
Margaret?"

"I sure do. I'd spent my last bit of money on them and wasn't
going to get paid again for two weeks. I was afraid I'd need them
myself before then. And I wouldn't ask Eileen for money. She had
enough to worry about just buying food. Remember how she'd set
the table with Mother's damask tablecloth and napkins, use the good
silver and china and serve fried bologna? She always made us eat it
like it was a proper meal, however." Margaret smiled at Eileen, clearly
over her earlier fit of pique.

Suddenly, out of the clear blue sky Hannah said, "We were poor
back then, too. But, my parents didn't want me to marry Stephen,
because of what happened. That's why we ran away."

Eileen looked as shocked as if she'd just been shot by Hannah.
The color drained from Eileen's face as all the laughter went out of
the room.

Eileen said sternly, "Hannah, I'll tell you, so you'll know from
now on. Father's troubles are a subject that we don't *ever* discuss,
inside or outside of the family. Stephen should have told you that.
Maybe he would have when he came back. Father's bank had some
financial trouble and it was closed just before the depression. Then
Mother died of a brain tumor. After she died, he just gave up and
died of a broken heart. Beyond that, some things are better left unsaid."

Hannah winced at the pain etched on Eileen's face as she sto-
ically repeated what had been adopted over time as the Burgher man-
tra. "How awful, Eileen. I am so sorry. I didn't know. Please forgive

me." As she looked around the room, she could see Eileen's pain mirrored in every face but Jean's.

"It's all right, Hannah," Eileen replied shortly. "We survived."

Libba brushed away a quick tear as she tried to lighten the tension. "No one could have been a better mother. I don't know how you did it, Eileen. All of us kids and your own two...it's a wonder we did survive. Especially after Harold died."

Eileen said, "I just did what Mother would have done, or her mother before that. I got up each day, did what I had to do to keep us all fed and together, went to bed and did it again the next day. And in between, I prayed — lots. In the early days, right after Mother and Father died, someone in town wanted to adopt you, Libba. Did you know that?" Libba shook her head. "I don't guess I ever told you. Anyway, I said, 'no, thanks — we'll manage on our own.' And we did. I guess when you have something like that happen to your family, you just do what you have to do. You don't really think about it; you just do it. I don't really remember thinking there was any choice. I guess that's the way Mother raised us."

"And here we all are — well, almost all of us — together with our own babies. Like I said before, I want one of my own." Libba laughed.

"Here, you can have one of mine," Eileen said, handing Jackie to her. She laughed as she stood up. "I've got to go to the bathroom. Anyone want another beer chintzle while I'm up?"

"No, thank you, Mother," Eileen's sisters chorused, breaking into laughter at their simultaneous response.

"Sounds to me like we've all had plenty," said Sara as Chuck stirred in his chair.

"What's so funny?" he asked.

"Nothing, dear. Come on, I'm ready to go home. Would you help me gather up Maggie's things?"

Soon they all had left amid a flurry of pulling on boots, coats and gloves, juggling snow-suited babies and leftovers. The house was quiet. Eileen sat in the overstuffed chair where Chuck had slept away the afternoon. Staring into the fire, she thought about the afternoon conversation. Over the intervening years, talking about the "old days" had become acceptable — as long as the stories began with what happened after Father and Mother died. However, as she had told Hannah, no one ever discussed Father's "troubles." Eileen rarely even thought about it now, pushing the terrible memories to the back of her mind. But today, Hannah's unthinking remark brought it all forward again.

Yes, they were right — the poverty was hard; but the hardest part was the way people acted. I remember one particular time when the little kids came home from school after being teased. Buddy, Stephen and Libba marched up on the porch like little soldiers. I held the door as they filed in without stopping to say a word. Buddy went to the kitchen and opened the ice-box door. When he couldn't find anything to eat, he slammed the door and headed for his room. Stephen had followed him into the kitchen and plopped down at the table. He grabbed a banana and ate it while I helped Libba with her coat. As I leaned close to her, I could see she had been crying. Her little eyes were red and puffy; her mittens were damp. When I hugged her, she began to cry again. Between her sobs she said the kids had teased her, calling her father a jail-bird. They told her he had died like a bird in a cage. That was one of the few times I was ever angry at Father. I thought, "How could you have done this to such an innocent little girl?" I remember Buddy had almost gotten into a fight the same day because some boy on the playground teased Stephen, too. Buddy had shoved the boy, but the teacher saw it and stopped the teasing. Buddy said that what upset him most wasn't the teasing, but the way the teacher looked at him with these big sad eyes. She patted him on the shoulder like she felt sorry for him instead of punishing him for shoving the boy. He said he didn't understand why she should feel sorry for him, but it made him furious to be the object of such pity. I had to explain that adults feel sad for children who don't have parents. I told him to forget about Father's troubles, to hold up his head and be proud of who he was. I told him that if he fought, he was as bad as his persecutors. I remember thinking that I sounded like Mother. I remember that it wasn't just the little kids who were tormented. Margaret took a lot of abuse, too. She didn't make friends easily and many of those she thought were her friends, dropped her when she couldn't afford new clothes. Seeing the sad faces of my brothers and sisters day after day made me determined to erase what Father had done to all of them. Over and over, I told them always to hold up their heads and ignore it all. And we never talked about it again. It was hard, but I think I was right. Some things are better left unsaid.

Unaware that she had been crying, Eileen dabbed her eyes with the hem of her apron. Suddenly, she saw the faces of her parents in the flames. They were both smiling at her as if they approved of the job she had done raising their children. Eileen smiled back at them and the flames flickered. She blinked her eyes and they were gone. From upstairs Jackie was crying. Eileen wiped her eyes and rose to go tend her baby.

Fifty-Five

October 1995

The sun burned low in the western sky as Maggie crossed the causeway onto Anna Maria Island. Once again she had arrived at sunset, but this time she barely noticed the orange streaks that stabbed the hovering gray clouds. Two weeks earlier Maggie had buried her mother. Since then she had dreaded this trip to clean out the Florida house and put it on the market. *How do you obliterate the traces of someone's life in a few short days? Shouldn't it take longer than that?*

The finality of her mother's death had not yet hit Maggie. Until now, facing this last act, she had simply mourned. At the same time, however, she was glad her mother's travail was over. It had been a terrible year for both of them. Sara Burgher Landers had suffered from kidney disease, daily dialysis treatments and periodic episodes of congestive heart failure, which ultimately killed her. Maggie had gone to Longboat Key as often as possible, but most of her mother's care had been administered by strangers — many of whom Sara detested and often fired. Maggie's job made staying in Florida impossible, but she had felt guilty for not taking care of her own mother. In her heart, Maggie also knew she couldn't have watched her mother die.

Each time Sara was rushed to the hospital, Maggie had prayed it would be the last, for there was no recovery expected for Sara— only more dialysis, pain and suffering. Finally, Maggie convinced the doctors to institute a DO NOT RESUSCITATE order, then felt guilty about it. And Sara had died, in the hospital — alone. When the call came to Maggie in the middle of the night, she wept for both of them, thanked God and slept soundly for the first time in months.

Now, Maggie dreaded the moment her mother's death would become real to her. She was afraid closing down the house where her parents had lived for thirty years would bring on the full-blown crying jag she feared would accompany the realization that she was now an orphan. The last person in the world who loved her unconditionally was gone. The trouble was, Maggie had never been sure her mother felt that way; she mourned that fact as much as she mourned her mother's passing.

Maggie turned the car onto the long crushed-shell driveway and pulled to a stop in front of the garage. The house was quiet as a tomb. Although it was still light, the porch light burned brightly. She sat staring at the house, half expecting the front door to burst open as it always had upon her arrival. Tears sprang to her eyes with the memory; hastily she brushed them away. She knew if she continued to think about it, she would not be able to go inside. She threw open the car door, got out and dashed onto the porch.

She opened the wide front door; the air inside smelled like antiseptic. Or was it her imagination? Maggie left the door standing open as she crossed the great room to slide back the draperies and throw open the window walls. As the draperies slid away, the after-glow of the sunset flooded through the screens along with the sea air, giving the room a warmth Maggie did not feel. With both of her parents gone, the house exuded an empty chill even the warm October evening could not dispel. After her daddy died, Maggie had felt a void in the house, but now.... She knew instinctively this would be her last visit to the house on the bay. She planned to sell it; without her parents it held no charm for her.

Slowly she walked through the house noticing, as if for the first time, all their prize possessions — furniture, paintings, photographs, books. It was like a trip down memory lane, yet since they were no longer attached to her parents, the objects seemed to have taken on a life of their own. Now they belonged to Maggie. *What on earth will*

I do with all this stuff?

In the den, she opened her daddy's desk drawer. Inside were bits of scrap paper filled with his distinctive scrawl — the plumber's phone number, a reminder to check the oil in the car, a service date for the boat. Maggie laughed at his familiar habit of writing these notes, then forgetting where he put them, but she sobered as she realized nothing had been disturbed since he died. *Poor Mother, she just couldn't bear to throw any of this away. Now it's up to me.*

In the bedroom, where the smell of medicine seemed stronger, Maggie opened her mother's closet. The scent of Sara's perfume wafted out, dispelling some of the stale air. Maggie breathed in the familiar scent, then shut the door against the grief it unleashed. Yes, her parents had departed for good, but Maggie's memories were strong.

Returning to the great room, Maggie fixed a drink and sat staring at the mangrove island aglow in the moonlight beyond the sea wall. She was filled with nostalgia and grief. *Oh, Mother, why didn't we have time to get it right? Now that I know all about your father, why aren't you here to explain what that had to do with me, if anything? I know how badly you wanted me. I know you stayed in bed for six months to save the pregnancy, to protect me. I know you loved me. But why did you always seem to be mad at me? Why couldn't we connect?* Maggie heard no answer in the still West Florida breeze. Exhausted, she rose and went to bed. But she slept badly. Her dreams were filled with memories of her mother. Snatches of arguments from Maggie's childhood mixed with scenes of her mother's hospital hallucinations.

She woke the following morning with a headache, dreading the task ahead. After several cups of coffee and a stale bagel found in the refrigerator, she began. She took one room at a time, assessing what she could use, what she wanted and what she had room for that she didn't really want but couldn't bring herself to toss out. She tagged the items she intended to keep with a little sticky red dot; on those her children could use or would cherish, she put a blue one. The rest was going to Goodwill.

The task felt overwhelming. In the kitchen she found spices so old the cans were rusted shut. Pots and pans she remembered from childhood, Maggie boxed for Goodwill. Garbage cans overflowed with stale food items from the pantry. In the den, she tenderly packed all her father's photograph albums, wishing she had time to look at them. The love letters she previously had read were packed as well. Some day she would reread them and share them with her children.

On the second day, she worked on the clothes closets. First she counted and stuffed in black garbage bags all her daddy's clothing. Not surprisingly, her mother had kept it all after he died. While he had one closet, her mother had three. They were chock-full of clothes Sara hadn't worn in at least twenty years. Maggie found blouses with Peter Pan collars she knew her mother had bought when Maggie was in the seventh grade. She had always known her mother rarely threw away anything; now she was convinced she never had. The pile of donation bags grew into a shiny, black mountain.

By late afternoon, Maggie had started on her parents' dresser drawers. Somehow, going through their underwear was just too personal, so she had put it off, saved it until last. She began by throwing away bathing suits with worn-out elastic, shorts neither of them had worn since the grandchildren were young and a pile of hosiery Sara hadn't touched in years. When she found her mother's blue silk nightgown, she nearly cried. It was Sara's favorite and Maggie couldn't bring herself to throw or give it away. Although she doubted she would ever wear it herself, Maggie put it aside to take home.

As she reached for a stack of her mother's panties, Maggie's fingers scraped against a piece of paper. Placing the underwear on top of the dresser, she pulled forth a yellowed newspaper clipping from the bottom of the drawer. Maggie's hands trembled when she saw the familiar newspaper headline: **FORMER BANKER DIES IN PRISON.**

Oh, my God! Mother kept this hidden in her underwear drawer for over sixty years. Hidden so well that no one, not even Daddy, would see it. The realization brought Maggie to her knees in shock. Sinking to the floor, Maggie read the article as if she'd never seen it before. A corner of the tattered obituary broke off and fell to her lap. *She has carried this from house to house, unprotected...never put it in an album or anything. She couldn't bring herself to throw it away, but she couldn't bring it out in the open, either. Poor Mama!*

Maggie sat staring at the picture of her grandfather, remembering the first time she had seen it on microfilm at the archives ten years ago. *I wonder how often she looked at this. Had she kept it as a reminder or hidden it out of shame?* Finally she rose from the floor, her task forgotten, and carried the newspaper clipping to the living room.

As she sat by the window, holding the evidence of her mother's simple act of stealth, it slowly dawned on Maggie what "Father's troubles" had cost her mother and her siblings. *It was necessary for their survival to look forward, not backward; necessary to deny, by avoiding any mention of it, that such horrible things had happened to them; necessary to build defense mechanisms as impenetrable as a castle wall. Whether the myth I knew about Father was fabricated out of tacit agreement, deceit, denial, resentment, guilt, shock, shame or sorrow, or was simply perpetuated out of habit, I'll never know. But what I feel sure of is this — Father's troubles also created the wedge between me and my mother. Maybe Mother was always checking my behavior against that of her father, afraid of more disappointment. Whenever I did anything wrong, however small or large, perhaps she was reminded of what he did. Or maybe it hit her broadside when I was a teenager, I don't know.* Then it came to her. Tears sprang to Maggie's eyes as she realized it was her mother who was damaged, not herself. Now she understood.

Suddenly Maggie found herself talking to her mother, pleading with her to understand. *"It wasn't me at all, it was the reminder of your father's troubles. But, because you couldn't talk about it, you made me feel it wasn't what I did that angered you, it was me. Not the deed, but the doer. And all my life, I've felt that I was inferior, could never measure up, was unworthy of love — yours, Daddy's or anyone else's. But now I know I was wrong. Mama, I am sorry for the pain I caused you. And I'm sorry for what your father did to both of us. Yes, what I did — getting pregnant at fifteen — was bad. No wonder you were angry with me — I did bring more shame to our family. It wasn't my daddy's heart I broke, but yours. But I made a mistake, just like your father. He wasn't a bad person, Mama. And neither am I."*

After midnight Maggie still sat facing the bay-side windows, mulling over the impact her grandfather had on her mother's life and ultimately on hers. It occurred to her that several of her cousins had a rocky relationship with their Burgher parent, as well. *Maybe if our parents had talked about it, or had counseling....* Maggie laughed at herself. *No one went for counseling in those days. Because they hid such a crucial fact from us, we didn't know our parents at all! Good grief; it was central to who they all were. If we'd known the real story, maybe we all would have understood them better. Instead, we grew up not understanding them at all. Why did they have to keep it buried inside? Well, I've learned a valuable lesson. I will not do the same thing to my children.*

Over the next two days, in the quiet hours, Maggie thought often of her Burgher aunts and uncles. The heroic story of Aunt Eileen was well known — the difficulty of raising her siblings and two children of her own on a teacher's salary right in the midst of the Depression, the tragic death of her young husband, and through it all her remarkable sense of humor. Aunt Margaret married and divorced two alcoholic husbands then, as a single working mother, raised her only daughter. Aunt Libba became a career woman without benefit of a college education and through the years had laughed her way through several life threatening illnesses. Looking back, Maggie could see that they all did what they had to do, with humor and dignity in the face of great adversity. Even Uncle Buddy was a survivor — of a German prison camp. Truly, they had all survived Father's troubles. Perhaps they were emotionally scarred, but they did the best they could with what they had, and made it through.

In her reverie, Maggie saw her younger self, dressed in the formal gown Sara had remade again and again. As she stared out the window, the young girl seemed to dance on the shimmering moonlit water. *Poor Mother, she was doing the best she could — wishing it were more — and I resented the fact that she made my clothes. Oh Mother, I'm so sorry.*

Then Maggie thought about her own life — married at fifteen, divorced with a child by seventeen, married again to an alcoholic husband, two more children, completed a college degree after twenty years, moved to Atlanta to begin a new career at forty — she too had persevered in the face of adversity. *You may not have been able to talk about your past, Mother, but by your example you taught me so much. When you forced me to play the Virgin Mary, it wasn't a punishment. It was to make me uphold my commitment. Over the years, you showed me how to be tough, independent, resourceful and strong. My God, you were strong! I never realized how strong, until Daddy got sick. And you never complained about your arthritis or your failing sight, either.* Maggie blinked and began to cry. It wasn't the gut wrenching crying jag she had expected; it was the pitiful crying of a child who wants her mother. *Oh, Mama! Thank you! I love you! I forgive you!* Soon her crying slowed. With dryer eyes, she finished, *Mama, I miss you.*

Maggie rose from her chair and walked into her mother's bedroom. She put on her mother's blue silk nightgown and climbed into her mother's bed. The smell of Sara's perfume permeated the pillows and Maggie, as if reassured by her mother's presence, slept peacefully.

Some Words After. . .

June 30, 2003

F*ather's Troubles* is neither classical memoir nor pure fiction. The story is based on actual family history, although many events and characters have been either compressed or invented for the sake of the story. The central facts, however, are true. My maternal grandfather did go to prison and die while serving his sentence. His wife did die of a brain tumor while he was in prison, leaving seven children to fend for themselves during the depression. And, while I always knew they died long before I was born, I did not know the rest of the story until I was nearly forty.

It took more than twenty years to write this story. During that time, I struggled with whether or not to write it and if so, how to present it. Would the disclosure of the family secret damage my relationship with my family? Could I portray my grandfather in such a negative light? If I had known these grandparents, no doubt I could not have done so, but I never met them. They both died almost ten years before I was born. Still, I wrestled with the truth I had discovered, trying to come to grips with how it had affected our family. And as I dealt with it, my struggle passed through stages similar to those in the grieving process — denial, anger, bargaining, depression and acceptance — as described by Elizabeth Kubler-Ross in her seminal book *On Death and Dying*.

At first I denied the harsh reality of my grandfather's errant life and told no one. I clung to the fairy-tale ending I had learned as a child: *Mother died at forty-six of a brain tumor and Father died very soon afterward of a broken heart.* That version was so much more romantic.

But as I read the gathered material, the myth faded. It became painfully evident that Father was guilty. Anger set in. *How could he have done this to his family?* I railed. *What does this say about my heritage, about me — to have a grandfather who would do this? Look at the devastation he caused! His wife and children were pariahs in the community because he went to prison. Even as adults, his children lived under a shadow of shame.*

Sometimes, I have wondered if this situation would be different in the 21st century. Would the family feel the same isolation? I think they would. When a family or person suffers a personal tragedy, it often occasions a feeding frenzy of gossip. Otherwise polite, church-going members of the community discuss the terrible details as if retelling the latest episode of a soap opera. It is not that they mean to be hurtful. People are drawn to do so because giving voice to the story allows them to reassure themselves, and others, that it did not happen to them. It is similar to watching a distant tragedy on CNN. It allows us to suffer — vicariously, safely.

Later, I felt if I could find some redeeming quality, some shred of evidence to show why Father did what he did, I could somehow restore the family's honor. I reread the material, interviewed people who might have remembered, pondered the cloak of silence his children had donned. Nothing seemed to absolve him.

At some point, my anger dissolved into heartbreaking sadness. What a tragedy! I wept for my aunts and uncles, whom I knew well, and for my grandmother whom I did not. Imagine keeping this a secret all your life! And I wept for my mother and me. No wonder she and I had a strained relationship, I reasoned. I never really knew her. Maybe if I had known the true story, I would have understood her, made allowances for her faults, as I saw them.

Finally, I understood. I knew that I had to write this book from the perspective of the next generation. Yes, the true story was tragic; but classic tragedy requires that some affirmation come from it. This story is no different. It is not solely about Father and his troubles. It is also, and more importantly, about the incredible strength of the

..n who endured them. This determination to survive must have ...anated from my great-grandmother who left England with two children to join her husband in America, after suffering a miscarriage and the sudden death of her firstborn child.

She, no doubt, instilled this strength in her daughter, my grandmother. Following her husband's conviction, my grandmother did what was necessary to survive and raise her children while enduring the shame and humiliation her beloved husband's actions had caused. After he went to prison, she lost her fine home, her friends, her social status. She felt the sting of gossip and the pain of pity. Destitute, she did whatever she had to do, day after day, to keep her family together until she became ill and died.

And in the process, she passed that sense of duty, that spirit of fortitude on to her five daughters. Today, it is likely that their children would have become wards of the state.

When I reached the age to understand such things, I knew that my mother's sisters had not had easy lives as adults, either. But through it all, they were always jolly and fun-loving. They had all learned the hard way — what doesn't destroy you, makes you stronger. They faced all adversity with humor, faith and each other. They took each day as it came, did the best they could, and survived.

When my father had surgery for a benign brain tumor, my mother's strength is what I remember most. At the time, she herself had rheumatoid arthritis and retinitis pigmentosa and was legally blind. At the end of her life, she was on kidney dialysis but rarely complained about her lot in life.

This strength, this ability to endure by simply doing what you have to do, one day at a time — is the legacy I was given. It was the only inheritance from my maternal grandmother. And, even if that ability is all I pass on to my children and grandchildren, I will have given them a priceless treasure.

Carter Taylor Seaton